THE WHITE HOUSE SYNDROME

SYNDROME

Dennis J. Cleri

ISBN-13: 9781234567890
ISBN-10: 1477123456

Cover design by: Art Painter
Library of Congress Control Number: 2018675309
Printed in the United States of America

LOVINGLY DEDICATED TO

MY PARENTS
DOMINICK AND
EMMA CLERI,

AND MY LOVING WIFE
LINDA MARIE,

And My Mother-In-Law
Frances 'Frannie' Ciuppa.

Emollients to the left of them
Emollients to the right of them
Emollients in front of them
Though tempted they plundered
Stormed at by press from hell
Boldly they hid as well
Into the jaws of court, they swelled
Into the mouth of their own hell
Bravely marched the Special
Prosecutor's henchmen
All six hundred

*[From an Anonymous Informant in the Special
Prosecutor's Office, March 14th, 2020]*

U.S Department of Justice
Attorney Work Product // May Contain Material
Protected Under Fed. R. Crim. P. 6(e)
[Office of the Special Prosecutor - 'Ostende
mihi homo ego ostenam tibi crimen']
Second Interim Report – Volume One of One Volume of the
First Encyclopedic

Report On The Investigation Into Communication Intercepts to and from Foreign and Deep State Actors: Interference, Specifically The Russian Federation, The Peoples' Republic of China, The Islamic Republic of Iran and The Democratic People's Republic of Korea (DPRK), into the office of President of the United States from, to and at the White House: Provisional Report One

[Subject the Special Counsel's amendment, alteration, editorial prerogatives as necessary and/or dictated by the Special Council Act or future legislative amendments, additions, or alterations under all applicable sections of Federal Law or regulation]

Special Counsel
Rex P. Seplechre, IV, JD

Submitted Pursuant to
28 C.F.R. $600.8 (c)

Orlando, Florida
November 2020

> **The great masses of the people...will more easily fall victims to a big lie than to a small one. Make the lie big, make it simple, keep saying it, and eventually, they'll believe.**
> [Adolf Hitler, 1889-1945]

Introduction

This interim report of the provisional report is submitted to the Attorney General pursuant to 28 C.F.R. $ 600.8(c) which states that, "[a]t the conclusion of the Special Counsel's work, he...shale provide the Attorney General a confidential report explaining the prosecution or declination decisions [the Special Counsel] reached. As the conclusion is not forthcoming nor within the foreseeable future (ever – as long as I remain gainfully employed, handsomely compensated, and for as little effort as possible – and that's just between you and me), I am now and will be submitting future regularly and irregularly timed intermittent interim provisional reports, subject to change, alteration of any truthful content, proposed actions or reasons for inaction and hypothetical and real conclusions at any time. All hypothetical conclusions will be listed in the provisional appendix one marked, 'Appendix One - Hypothetical Conclusions - Provisional' as will any hypothetical facts be listed in the provisional appendix two marked, 'Appendix Two - Hypothetical Facts - Provisional'. Final interim reports will always be subject to change [in true and hypothetical facts and/ or conclusions presented] and subject to editorial stylistic alterations. [Alterations of past and future interim reports will be forwarded separately with copies of all prior renditions of the interim reports, so as not to create any confusion. The corrected interim report will be clearly marked with the date of the original interim report, the date of the interim report it is correcting, the correction that the corrected interim report corrected was issued for, the publication date of the referred correction, and lastly the distribution date, all of which will appear in the title and be indexed as such, for the sake of clarity, in the order above. Any and all alterations will be *italicized.*] This should assure the Congress, the administration and, most importantly, the American people that we are working diligently at our mission to clearly communicate any and all of our interim real and hypothetical findings. We know this will unambiguously and without contention guarantee continued full funding of our essential investigations far into the future. Congress and most importantly, the American people must realize that this is all integral, vital, and necessary to the national interest, our individual and collective wellbeing, economy, security, and defense. [All forms or any reports will be transmitted to the designated parties in certified, verified, and duplicate print form only. No electronic transmittal of reports will be made available as these may be too easily altered.]

The funding level must allow for inflation, contingency, ongoing expected expenses both budgeted and not budgeted, unexpected expenses both budgeted and not budgeted, and performance incentive increases in direct, and indirect, occasional appreciation and discretionary cash nontaxable untraceable bonuses for unofficial incentives to unnamed staff, named and anonymous informants, artisans, technicians, consultants, and assistants and other always anonymous government officials to incentivize their efficient cooperation. Heretofore unenumerated nonmonetary, real property, leases, contractual arrangement emoluments for the Special Prosecutor, his designated assistants and other key personnel designated by the Special Prosecutor are to be the responsibility of and administrated only by the Special Prosecutor or his designee. If funds remain after all disbursements, we request that Congress enact legislation to appropriate funds and appoint a bipartisan commission to allocate the aforementioned funds, real properties, and other miscellaneous equipment deemed redundant to a new sub- department for 'Overflow Funds, Redundant Equipment, Excess Real Estate and Miscellaneous Assets' to be administered directly and solely by the Special Prosecutor, his designee or his appointed subcommittee. If needed to complete our mission, Congress may need to appropriate funding for an exploratory subcommittee to see if the aforementioned new subdepartment is necessary, should be elevated to a Cabinet level ministry or be assigned to an existing Cabinet level agency, or subagency of the Cabinet level department it is assigned, provisionally.

This second of the interim reports on our investigation consists of this one volume – titled 'Second Interim Report - Volume One'. To avoid any contention that occurred with previous Special Counsel's investigation of President Trump, I insisted upon, and was granted the following conditions, concessions, and stipulations from the House and Senate judiciary committees and subsequently from the entire Congress of the United States. These conditions, concessions and stipulations are: (1) I [personally] meet individually with each of the members' wives of the Senate and the House of Representatives, promising to hire at least one of their unemployable relatives (priority given to presently unemployed, then unemployed the longest, and finally most recently unemployed – in that eternal order), in most cases in-laws. I will meet personally with the few female members of the Senate and House of Representatives with the same proposal. Committee chairmen's or ranking members' wives or, where rarely applicable, the chairwomen and female ranking members will be allowed to send two unemployed relatives by blood or in-laws (with the same priority rules), and the Speaker of the House, House Minority Leader, Senate Majority and Minority Leaders' wives, or if female, those said individuals, and the majority whips' wives or female members of both houses, will be allowed to send three unemployed relatives by blood or in-laws, observing the previously stated priority scheme; (2) At the Special Council's discretion, identity of all members of the Special Counsel's staff will be kept confidential from the public, the press and each other where possible unless deemed in the interest of the Special Council; (3) Unlimited scope, budget and time to complete the investigation; (4) automatic extensions (with full funding including the additional administrative costs for the restart) if prematurely terminated by Congress, the President or the Supreme Court, security agencies, other regulatory agencies, the courts, or by the Special Council himself; (5) Move all the relatives and/or in-laws far from the legislators and spouses in Washington, DC [to Orlando, Florida] giving them free passes to all area amusement parks, theme parks, water parks, zoos, aquariums, movie theaters, museums, concert halls, golf courses, miniature golf courses, and other [unnamed and unenumerated] entertainment venues; (6) reimbursement and free minibar, in room movie privileges, valet and self-parking, and room service if hotel or motel accommodations are necessary during the transition to our Orlando headquarters (all receipts required); (7) Establish two special sections in the Special Counsel's Office for media leaks – one for the Democrats and one for the Republicans, and; (8) Wherefor and whereof expand or extend the investigation as needed to investigate all leads and evidence of possible, probable, likely and unlikely crimes, technical infractions or bad faith or [forbidden] evil thoughts including 'rootless cosmopolitanism', that may be suspected, overheard, or may or may not have occurred; (9) At all times, ongoing investigations will be carried out only on targets whose names were deposited in the locked and video monitored suggestion boxes outside the Senate and House of Representative chambers in the United States Capital Building. The targets' families, friends, business, and other associates (including golf foursomes, bridge partners, domestic help and spouses and offspring's friends and/or acquaintances) will automatically be included and added to the target investigation list. Unnamed individuals may be also investigated (meaning added to the target list) depending on where the investigation leads. All individuals will be continuously surveilled for the duration of the Special Counsel's investigation by the FBI, the IRS, US Marshalls, Postal Investigation Service, railroad police, all military law enforcement branches, and specially deputized and incentivized local and state law enforcement agencies. If on foreign soil, targets of this investigation will be surveilled by the CIA Clandestine Section. This activity will be supervised by Homeland Security's special section for the Special Council's activities – under the direction of the Secretary of Homeland Security who will be supervised by the Special Council; and (10) Make Presidential pardons or commutations of any of the targets, before indictment, during or after trial, incarceration or execution, a crime resulting in mandatory impeachment proceedings against the President of the United States and all members of his administration, participating judiciary and law enforcement who facilitate or participate in these pardons or commutations; (11) An order of succession for the Office of the Special Council be established by the Special Council in case of his inability to perform his duties, temporary illness or death. That order of succession will be effective until all members of the Special Council's section are exhausted, and a new order of succession is established by the last Special Council.

*   *   *   *   *

What luck for rulers that men do not think.
[Adolf Hitler, 1889-1945]

Legislative Authorization

Mr. Attorney General, I am pleased to report that the House of Representatives and the Senate (after guaranteeing not to investigate any of the seated members of Congress or their families, business partners or friends) have unanimously approved of this bill except for three abstentions, making it not only bipartisan but absolutely veto-proof. [We have begun investigating the three abstentions as being part of a conspiracy. We can and will investigate any and all spouses, mistresses, friends, or associates of the members of Congress, and their legislative aids as needed to maintain persuasive influence over both legislative branches.]

At regular intervals or intervals to be determined in the future, audio and video recordings, and written transcripts, any physical or virtual evidence or other related objects will be deposited in the National Archives, Washington, DC, catalogued by the Archivist every fiscal quarter with copies available to the appropriate presidential libraries [at cost] fifty years from date of deposit in the National Archives. Copies will be available to the press and public on-line [at cost plus a modest processing fee payable to the offices of future special prosecutors fifty years from date of deposit in the National Archives.]. Fees, special handling and delivery costs and appropriate surcharges for any leaked copies will be levied against any press credit cards on file with the Special Prosecutors billing office – Official Leaks Directorate (the 'OLD'). Cash payments (in small denomination unmarked wrinkled and used US Federal Reserve notes with nonconsecutive serial numbers) will result in a ten percent discount. Use of PayPal is acceptable, although there will be an additional handling charge. On-line payments will be accepted for those members of the press or their credentialed organizations with accounts with the OLD. Bank and certified checks must clear prior to any transaction. No personal checks will be accepted at any time except when accompanied by a cash incentive to the supervisor at OLD. Fees for nonpayment, delayed payment or returned checks will result in a levy to be determined by the new supervisor at OLD (the replacement for the old OLD supervisor who accepted the bad check).

*　*　*　*　*

Materials and Methods

"Fures privatorum in nervo atque in compedibus aetatem agunt; fures publici in auro atique in purpura."
[Thieves who steal from private citizens spend their lives in bonds and chains; thieves who steal from public funds spend theirs in gold and purple.
Marcus Porcius Cato, Cato the Elder, 234-139 or 149 B.C., Praeda Militibus Dividenda, XI, 3]

Again, trying to avoid the errors of the last Special Counsel, this interim report will be a narrative from both the most important and least consequential parties implicated and/or their personal recordings of conversations. Other attributed and anonymous documents, interviews, information from the public record and confidential or classified legally and possibly illegally obtained documents, electronic communications, recordings, conversations, and verbal recollections are included for background. Personal recordings and other surveillance recordings have been integrated into the narrative for the sake of continuity. Recordings will be made both with and without the consent or knowledge of the subjects or our investigators. And frankly, the last Special Counsel's report was mind-numbingly boring, and we will go to great lengths to be interesting and complete. Be assured, all cooperating or coerced witnesses will be subject to prosecution by the Special Prosecutor, the IRS, US attorneys in any and all jurisdictions, and state and local district attorneys as time and resources permit. Prosecution, court costs and miscellaneous handling fees for state and local prosecutions will be paid directly to the district attorneys of that jurisdiction.

This document may be used as you wish, but would make an excellent basis for political advertisements, fund raising, movie script, Broadway musical, and/or made for TV movie, limited series, or a potentially long-running sitcom.

Any and all residuals will, by Congressional decree as part of the original Special Council enabling bill, will revert to the Special Council. (And if produced, it will no doubt become a big hit no matter the format or who is President of the United States and by whatever means he [or she] got there. This will be especially true if President Donald J. Trump runs and is reelected in 2024.) The General Accounting Office projects that before the end of the next administration's first year, the government can recoup at least the first one hundred twenty-five million dollars over and above this investigation's estimated initial and ongoing operating costs by selling advertisements for our press conferences, if not make a greater profit if the press conferences are syndicated in reruns on broadcast television and/or the subscription cable services. Excess revenues can be allocated for the next Special Counsel's production costs, investigation, foreign aid, the domestic debt, and the cost of the next Presidential impeachment. (I am formerly requesting we sign Michael Avenatti as our press spokesmen with a work/release agreement. He'll work cheap especially if we offer him a full pardon. We will tie his entire compensation package to the press conferences' Neilson ratings.) Press conferences will be daily, between eleven AM and noon eastern standard time (opposite The View).

Let us proceed to the pertinent testimony. Before being sworn in, and off the record (but they won't be told this is off the record) all witnesses will be informed that they will be given complete immunity, including for any crimes, felonies, misdemeanors, traffic, parking violations, and nonpayment of alimony, child support, overdue student loans, library books, mortgage and time share payments, car and boat payments and credit card debt, and/or financial fraud they have committed, are presently engaged in, or may plan or commit in the future in order that they may testify and provide recordings without fear of prosecution or reprisals. Henceforth, we will refer to this immunity as the Hillary Clinton Immunity. [As you already know, President Biden has preemptively sent his defense pleas to both the House and Senate judiciary committees – 'diminished capacity.' No one either in Congress or the Justice Department plans any Biden investigations. He will never and can never be implicated in any skullduggery or impeached, even under the Special Prosecutor's legislation. He doesn't need immunity. He is bullet proof. That's because everyone is more afraid of his Vice-President.]

Inclusion in the witness protection program for all those testifying on the record will be by request only, will not be automatically granted, and be considered by the Special Council on an ongoing basis. All witness protection subjects will be situated in the homeless camps of the police-free zones of Oregon, Washington, California, and other designated states. Henceforth, the witness protection program will be known as the Hunter Biden program.

I am sending this communication from our secret, triple encrypted and secure server at our Orlando headquarters to your secret, triple encrypted and secure server in the Justice Department with a copy to they who cannot be mentioned. Please acknowledge receipt.

*   *   *   *   *

CHAPTER ONE

**"In this country [America] a man is
presoomed to be guilty ontil he's proved guilty an'
afther that he's presoomed to be innocent.**
[Finley Peter Dunne, "On Criminal Trials,"
Mr. Dooley on Making a Will, 1919]

**"When one door closes, anther door
opens, including to your jail cell."**
[*Uncle Jimmy Buonarratti, Corner of Tenth Avenue
and Twenty-Third Street, Manhattan – Date, Unknown*]

"Thank you for coming in, Colonel." The last time I interviewed Buonarotti was during my previous Presidential Special Council investigation. I wasn't as well organized or well-funded as I am now. The new enabling legislation has given me and my staff a lot of flexibility – 'flexibility' is Federal parlance for unlimited funds, authority, power, permission to use lethal force at our own discretion, and unnamed and unenumerated resources you can't buy for your investigation, prosecution, and eventual imprisonments. Pursuing the death penalty, even for the guilty always takes too much time and resources, even for us. And after endless appeals, then they complain about the manner of execution – are the drugs for lethal injection expired? Who ever heard of such a thing? Great grand PaPa (PaPa) must be laughing from yonder high or wherever he is.

On the plus side of the equation, I have my own dedicated armed enforcement contingent. (Great grand PaPa would be proud of me.) Technically, their part of Homeland Security – and so am I, but I answer to no one. The SPAF – Special Prosecutors Armed Forces have their own amphibious land-

1

ing crafts, small aircraft and transportation section and their own uniforms – a striking deep blue with black insignia and black and blue tartan tam o'shanter cap, and of course, black leather holsters for their .45 caliber Glocks worn outside their uniform jackets. They train at Quantico with the FBI, Camp Perry (the Armed Forces Experimental Training Activity – 'The Farm') with the CIA, and the Warrington Training Center for communications training. I insisted that all the agents train at Warrington if we someday need to go after big tech. I have plans for our own academy in Orlando modeled after the Communist Chinese Ministry of State Security – The MSS or Guongu. which combines intelligence, security, espionage, and all secret police activities. They're quite lethal, but not as thorough as the NKVD/KGB/FSB, and nobody approached attention to detail the way the Stasi did. The Guongu is the ultimate one stop shopping in state control anywhere in the world. Their own agents complain (those who escaped) may be spread too thin for their multiple missions over such a large population and land mass.

Our SPAF Academy will be officially inaugurated during the next fiscal year, and will no doubt take several years to get completely up and running. Many of the faculty we are seeking are still in hiding. They're wanted for war crimes, but we put out the word. And you know as well as I, the best way to recruit war criminals is to put up those little notices with the tear away telephone numbers at the bottom on the bulletin boards in the United Nations Secretariat Building in New York City. It'll take time to find the right faculty. It will take more time to graduate our first fully trained class of SPAF agents.

We have to remember that the Chinese had more than a half century to develop the Guongu and the Russians a little more than a century for the evolution of the FSB the KGB and the FSU. The Stasi started from the ashes of the SS, and by 1950 was fully operational and had files on everyone in East Germany. Amazing! Simply amazing! They were the most dedicated secret police the world has ever seen.

We just got started recruiting. Now, there are only seventy-two officers, two pilots, two ship captains, three frog men, and three people trained to crew the Abram's tank. (We haven't been funded for the tank – but it is part of our next budget request.) We're still waiting for delivery of the fully automatic AR-15's, body armor and a backup supply of pistol and armor-piercing ammunition and other ordinance.

The legal term for ruthless exercise of that power is what we call 'democratic constitutional and even-handed prosecutorial discretion'. I have use, although not exclusive use of a small cadre of FBI agent-investigators who are generally clueless for whom they are working. The advantage of using the FBI for the investigation, is if anyone lies to them, or is even mistaken in their recollections, it's a felony we can have one of the US attorney's offices prosecute for us. My SPAF officers are not trained as investigators, but they are capable of conducting complete and aggressive interrogations not hampered by the FBI or the Army interrogation manual.

The FBI agents are not stupid, though. This is not their first shady operation. I understand that some have even taken out private liability insurance. I made sure my insurance and my staff's private liability insurance is paid for from government funds – under the legislative title of 'civil service health, welfare, and retirement benefits'. The fact is all the prosecutors' offices I know of have shady operations – and they're all insured by the same company. We all buy our insurance from the 'The National Shady Insurance Company, LLC', the NSIC. They're the biggest insurers for lawyers against legal malpractice. They were established when the Pilgrims brought the first lawyer on the Mayflower and he set foot on Plymouth Rock. When he slipped on the wet rock, he immediately sued Plymouth Rock, and the Pilgrims. And to this day, they haven't settled the case.

You need NSIC to deal with all the lawyers, shady criminals, and even shady non-criminals. Lawyers especially need the insurance to deal with other lawyers. (It's redundant to add the adjective 'shady' in front of anyone in the legal profession, whether or not they are members of the bar.)

During our original investigation, Buonarotti was a major. (A major idiot to stay married to Rose, to begin with. A major idiot for staying in the Army. He could be raking in the dough doing little or nothing, just programming for any of the left-wing, nearly, or actually criminal big tech companies. He would have to be a little less particular about his moral compass. Put a small magnet (lots of money) by its side just to set it off course a little bit – just a little bit. My fear is, even if he's tempted by the money, Rose is the moral compass of that pair – she's a gyroscopic compass not affected by any money or power magnetic fields. She's the kind of woman who wants power for her husband, achieved without sin or disgrace. She wants power and be able to sleep soundly every night. And she knows she's the one that can pull that off. She's the kind of woman who dreams about being First Lady, not President of the United States. She knows like everybody knows, that's being President is not a woman's job, not like being prime minister of Great Britain or Germany. Smaller countries women can run.

Besides, Lt. Col. Buonarroti would make an awkward First Gentleman. He'd be better at being President, where he's watched around the clock and she can completely manage what he says and all his activities. I know Rose would never let me get away with what I'm doing as Special Prosecutor. At least not to her husband.

If I ever run out of guilty and innocent targets in the Federal Government, big tech companies will be my next ones in my prosecutorial sights. The big tech oligarchs believe in their heart of hearts they are right about their views, and that's why God gave them all the power and money they have. They are the new Holy Prophets. They know that for sure and try to be humble explaining that to their employee-devoted followers. And they only employ the devoted faithful. All heretics and apostates are driven out, even though the tech oligarchs and their fanatical followers would prefer stoning them to death or having them burned at the stake.

And these leaders of big tech are never worried about public opinion. To paraphrase Winston Churchill, they have the arc of history on their side, because they will write history. And they have the power – which means the money to impose their will on the rest of the nation without having to deal with the consequences themselves.

This is their justification in dealing with everyone in a heavy-handed way. No one dares gets out of line and interferes with their plans for 'the greater good'. And they have so much money, that their 'greater good' will never affect them, their families, friends, or social circles. And most don't even know that. But there's always a disgruntled employee. I am keeping a list of them I can roll out at a moment's notice, or whenever our present prosecutions are paused long enough for the on-going appeals of some innocent convicted defendants.

And no matter how much money the tech giants have to fight in court or for appeals, the Federal Government has more, and can print its own money. The Federal Government by ob-scure rules read into the Congressional record, legislation not necessary, can regulate the tech giants to the 'death by a thou-sand cuts' technique, to near oblivion but never completely out of business. Just revoking section 230 removing their liability protection would be a big blow. Too big a blow for it to have long term effects. They would adapt easily to a single change on the playing field. But changing the rule every few weeks, that would be almost an artistic corporate torture.

They won't even know we're behind it all. Just create enough different and unconnected Federal agencies, subcommittees, or commissions to attack them from multiple angles. It can go on for years or until they give up or they die off. And it will be popular with the public. It may become so popular that they will plea bargain just to get it over with. But I'll see to it, it never, not ever ends once it is starts.

And big tech is the reason I formed SPAF. Each one of these companies have their own contingent of armed 'security' men working out of dummy corporations. In the near future I will need to execute search warrants, arrest these big tech people – the heads of the companies, not the underlings who were pre-setup to take the fall, and shut down the companies who openly oppose me on their media platforms. I can always keep the prosecution of big tech in my back pocket. I can turn to them when either what I'm doing becomes so unpopular or state governors and the President start issuing pre-emptive pardons.

There's so much corruption at most state-level politics and all city-level politics, you must ask yourself why don't I direct my efforts there? Investigating any of those local corrupt politicians, even for a major federal crime would barely make page three of the newspaper. And what I mean is the local newspapers and local TV broadcast news after the sports news and inevitable lost dog story. These investigations never make it to cable, except after they play the National Anthem opening their broadcast day. And then, at the end of the first morning news broadcast, after the lost dog story. If you're successful, and you will be because it's like 'shooting fish in a barrel', even though I've never heard of anybody doing that, these corrupt politicians are just replaced by not as smart corrupt politicians from the opposite party who couldn't get elected in the first place.

Buonarotti looks exactly the same – harried and sweating - worried about saying the wrong thing that might get back to his wife. I know guys like him. Everything gets back to their wives because they tell them everything as soon as they get home. They can't help themselves. It's a combination of fear, habit, and much of it is sheer stupidity. Sometimes wives have to trick their husbands, but most of the time the men both consciously and unconsciously feel guilty – often at the same time. That's the essence of marriage. Husbands are always feeling guilty about something, as they should be. (Everybody has something to feel guilty about. All successful men - used car salesmen, or any lawyer and even drug dealers know how to completely sublimate those guilt feelings. Telemarketers and time-share salesmen are born without the guilt gene.)

Guilt. Guilt. Guilt. That's the bedrock of any marriage. It's the reason all men, in love, a little in love or with no love at all, or for money, power, influence, propose marriage. Love, true love, makes them feel even more guilty. And that guilt will crescendo. That's the special nature of a loving marriage. If you're not really in love, you still feel some guilt, otherwise you wouldn't have married her. But if you never feel as guilty as you should, that eventually leads to divorce. In a loving marriage, you do feel as guilty as you deserve to. And that leads to divorce.   All married men in love with their wives need absolution for knowing they said or did something that their wives have told them not to do or to do better – often much better. And, as often as not, they forget to do what their wives told them to do. Because all men only half listen to their wives and they know they're not listening carefully enough. They know this as soon as they get out the door in the morning. So, as soon as they get home from work, they just blurt everything out. Sometimes before they take their coats off.

A good wife will go down a mental check list to see what her husband did, question him specifically on what he accomplished, and take the first opportunity they can tell them all the things he forgot or screwed up. This unfortunately gives him not only the opportunity but the incentive to lie to avoid further confrontation.

The really great and talented wives will let their husband confess as soon as they get home, then make a mental note in their indelible husband-errors and screw ups memory of all the things he forgot to do or did wrong. She saves it all for the next morning and reminds him to do them the next morning at breakfast. If what needs to be done is really critical, then the instructions will come either before or after morning sex, depending on their husband's brain blood flow retention physiology. He associates the tasks with reward(s) and eventually everything gets done with the least amount of conflict. It takes patience, but considerably less effort (husbands always on top in the morning doing all the work) and it avoids husbands lying about things they really did forgot to do. Soon they forget about lying. (If a man is married long enough, he never stops lying, but loses that edge on a vital skill. Another reason why married men are so easy to prosecute and make up a vast majority of local, state, and federal prison populations.)

Wives learn these techniques by watching their mothers handle their fathers. It takes years of observation to absorb the subtleties, nuances, and little verbal and nonverbal tricks wives employ against their husbands. It's the essential part of growing up for little girls – part of learning about the 'birds and the bees' except it starts as soon as they learn how to walk and talk. That's what makes two-parent homes so important to bring up little girls. Boys usually don't learn anything anyway, so that doesn't matter that much. If they need to learn anything to grow up, they can always join the military.

Husbands never wait to discuss any of this over dinner. They're the kind of men who want to enjoy their meals pleasantly in relative suffering peaceful silence. And their wives can enjoy their silent suffering across the dinner table. That's why at dinner they're smiling. It's not undying love, it's watching the suffering of their spouses. All this makes for a better digestion and a peaceful after dinner bowel movement for both husband and wife.

And you can't learn these things from a marriage counselor at hundreds of dollars an hour. And once your wife suggests counseling, you know she is just laying the groundwork for a divorce that will cost you all your worldly goods, an organ you will have to sell to pay both you and your wife's legal fees, and your future earnings.

Just look at PaPa and great grandmama. After their one and only marriage counseling session, no wife in our family, in fact no Kremlin wife ever suggested they go to marriage counseling. The couple settled their differences between themselves, or she poisoned her husband, or the wife and her entire family were disappeared.

Apparently, one of PaPa's NKVD colleague's first wife demanded a divorce. PaPa generously offered his Lubyanka basement 'conference room' to his best friend and trusted subordinate, Major General Vasily Blokhin for that first divorce settlement meeting his wife absolutely demanded. She brought her divorce lawyer, her lover – a younger Russian Army captain for moral support. She sat between the two men. Major General Blokhin, who by the way was the Soviet Union's chief executioner, brought his lawyers, Mr. Nagant and Mr. Korovin.

The lawyer, the wife and the young Army officer sat on one side of the table, and General Blokhin, in his full-dress uniform with all his medals, sat across directly from his wife. The General pulled the two pistols from inside his uniform jacket and put them on the table in front of him. He stood, put one round in the chamber of the Korovin automatic and removed the clip. With a smile on his face, he looked the lawyer straight in the eye, reached halfway across the table with the seven-round Nagant revolver in his right hand. Close enough for a clean shot, but not too close for the lawyer to reach the General's hand and deflect the pistol. In one smooth much practiced motion, and before the lawyer could stand and either take evasive or defensive action, the General put one round in the absolute center of his forehead, splattering his brains on the wall behind the table. Blood and brains splashed on his wife and her boyfriend bouncing off the wall behind them. Only a few drops from the entrance wound splattered on his wife and boyfriend faces and clothing in the front. Just a single but noticeable drop stained the general's right sleeve. The lawyer still had that surprised look on his face as he slumped over, eyes open. The divorce was finalized, and amicably and permanently for the General without the need to sign any documents. Thus, obviating the need for the lawyer or any of his legal fees.

"Captain Stupid. And you are stupid." General Blokhin pointed it at the young captain's head. This time he stepped back to avoid any spray. "I'm your superior officer, correct?"

The captain stood. His voice quivered. "Yes sir." Except he said it in Russian.

"Pick up the Korovin. It has one round in the chamber. I'm ordering you to shoot my wife in the head. If you don't, you're a dead man."

The captain was frozen.

"Reach very slowly for the automatic on the table in front of you. Make sure all your motions are slow and deliberate, otherwise I'll empty this into you, and then shoot my wife anyway. Do I make myself clear?" General Blokhin paused for the captain's answer. "Well? ...If you can't answer 'Yes sir' or No sir', just nod."

The general's wife stood and was about to say something. In the time she hesitated and turned to her husband, the captain picked up the automatic and shot her high in her abdomen. The woman grabbed her belly and began moaning and gurgling in pain. Then she began to vomit blood, bile, and her last meal.

"Captain, I'm disappointed in you. For an officer, a captain, my god, you can't even follow a simple instruction. How did you ever get passed in marksmanship? How are you ever going to lead men in combat?" The captain was frozen with the general's wife still clutching his arm, with one hand slumped on the table in front of them. Her other hand still held tightly against the bullet wound with bright blood seeping between her fingers. Blood and vomit were pooling on the table, which clearly upset the general.

The general looked down at the blood that was streaming to his side of the table. Blokhin thought to himself that the table legs weren't level. And sure enough, when he grasped the ledge of the table nearest him, he could wobble the whole heavy conference table with one hand, even with his wife and her lawyer slumped over on the other side.

He stepped back. "I can't get that on my shoes." Without another word, the general put two rounds high enough in the captain's chest and one in his forehead, dead center, before the captain hit the table after the first rounds exploded his heart and had finished him off. Then, he thought for a moment to just let his wife bleed to death, but he had another appointment, and it would be unseemly for him to let someone else find her gasping and then finish her off. Especially if it was the night janitors. And then they would have to call their supervisor who would have to call the basement night duty officer who would then, by protocol call the NKVD officer shift supervisor. That was the next person up the chain of command that could order an execution. And now it became a matter of pride, honor, chivalry, and efficiency. So, to be sure, he put two rounds in the top of her head. The bullets went through her skull, exiting out her face blowing out both her eye sockets and her nose, and ended up putting two holes in the table. (Under Stalin, marriage vows were sacred. The term '...till death do you part...' was always taken literally.) And it was a very nice conference table. He made a mental note to have the conference table replaced with one with screw levelers in the feet of the table legs. It was very possible that the basement floor at Lubyanka was uneven and not the tables fault. Before the general left, he checked the conference table again to see if it wobbled with all the bodies on it. It still did. That reassured him that the conference table had to be replaced anyway.

The janitorial staff knew enough to clean everything else. This was not their first rodeo, if they ever-had rodeos in the Kremlin. And besides, it was a week before Christmas. Having to clean up a mess like this always meant a little extra in their personal Christmas envelops from PaPa and General Blokhin. The leadership at Lubyanka was always considerate and generous with the janitorial staff, especially around peak execution time – usually after the spring student protests, and the Christmas and New Year's holidays. A special time of the year at Lubyanka. The basement had its own real Christmas tree. There was the smell of the live pine tree, cookies that the NKVD wives gave their husbands to bring to work mixed with the smell of fresh gunpowder, blood and guts that was always hard to get out of the air. Spray air fresheners hadn't been invented yet in Moscow. The janitorial staff hung the western-style car air fresheners in the shape of pine trees from the bare bulb light pull chains. But they really didn't help.

As a favor to General Blokhin, PaPa personally arranged for the lovers and their lawyer's transportation to somewhere more suitable for their permanent 'honeymoon'. That's exactly what PaPa put in the memo to General Blokhin. PaPa knew and General Blokhin understood, never put anything incriminating in writing. General Blokhin sent PaPa the Korovin he used that night as a thankyou present. That Korovin with PaPa's Nagant was passed down through generations from great grandmama and finally to me. Every year I tell my wife the story of the Korovin and the Nagant on our anniversary. I'm a sentimental man, and family traditions are important. You must always remember where you came from. To this day, I carry PaPa's Korovin in my waist holster and the Nagant on my right ankle the way my father did, the way my grandfather did, and the way PaPa did until PaPa was arrested and executed. I sigh when I think of my family's traditions and how this tradition goes back four generations.

We husbands need to always proceed with caution, least we become too complacent and overconfident in our marriages. Husband's 'll eat anything their wives put in front of them. And they'll eat it with relish and profusely thank their wives until they're told to shut up – or the poison his wife fed him shuts him up. That's why poison is a woman's weapon of choice. Men will eat anything their girlfriends, wives, secretaries, lap dancers if they bring you a sandwich with your drink, or even female acquaintances throw in front of them.

And that's why PaPa always had great grandmama serve him out of a common serving bowl or plate both their food came from. And it wasn't just being polite that PaPa made great grandmama take the first bite. She always smiled across the table as she chewed, and PaPa waited until she swallowed before he would start eating. That ruled out cyanide or any other fast acting agent. Grandpa and my father did the same. And so, do I. It's only being polite, always letting ladies go first. Wives should always take the first bite and swallow before any husband begins to eat. The only flaw in that table etiquette is if the wife planned a homicide-suicide. But she would have to be both pretty angry and self-destructive at the same time. And women never have two strong emotions or plans for that matter, all at once. It just doesn't happen. My father told me as I was growing up. His father told him. And PaPa told my grandfather this great truth about all women. I've been told that Stalin shared this wisdom with PaPa, and PaPa always considered Stalin a very wise man, especially when it came to the ladies.

All wives listen to every word said, always remember verbatim what is said, the context, their husband's tone of voice and expression on their husband's, boyfriend's, date's, or any male companion's faces. Everything is stored in the wives'- any woman's - uniquely female indelible memory – the revenge memory - stored away ready at a moment's notice to strategically throw back in their husbands' faces.

And the husbands deny that they ever said what they said. Men usually don't remember what they say to any woman. Especially husband's usually only half listen to their wives and never listen to what they're saying themselves, and barely listen to themselves telling their wives anything. That's one of the immutable laws of physics that makes being a prosecutor so easy. You just must learn how to take advantage of it. (These are the laws of God and nature. PaPa taught this to my grandfather who taught my father who passed the wisdom down to me.) And that's why it's so easy to prosecute a married couple. At least a married man.

And what was worse, Buonarotti never really knows when he is saying something he shouldn't say until he angers his wife. He doesn't know until she explodes when he tells her about it when he gets home. As soon as the words leave his lips, unfortunately, he knew he shouldn't have said what he said hours before at work, and shouldn't have told Rose what he said, not ever. But he said what he said and said it to Rose, and she finds out anyway. It's too late to do anything about it. It's long after the fact that Rose hears about it.

And it's so remote from the incident, he never learns any lessons. Like house training your dog. You have to use rewards and punishment at the time of their good or bad behavior, never hours later. Husbands are no different than your pet dog. Except dogs are much easier to take care of and they listen to every word you say. And husbands, like your pet dog, if you keep the commands simple and repeat the commands exactly the same way and often enough, they will obey. And if you decide to poison your dog, there no need for an alibi, complicated explanations, and it's so easy to dispose of the body. I really love dogs.

Like your dog, husbands are loved – but not as much as

your pet dog, but they're still a dog – only they're usually not treated as well, or with as much affection and understanding. I guess that's why after all the years of marriage, Buonarotti has learned nothing. (PaPa gave these gems of wisdom, to my grandfather who told my father who told me. PaPa got it from the Kremlin marriage counselor after interrogating him in front of his wife, that is great grandmama. PaPa made his wife execute their marriage counselor to remind her that the two were happily married and did not need a marriage counselor. That was the only time Mrs. Biera ever visited PaPa at his work – the basement of Lubyanka.)

The marriage counselor's blood splashed back onto great grandmama's evening gown (there was a formal reception upstairs), but great grandmama thought it wasn't the time or place to complain about it to PaPa, especially with his Nagant out of its holster. PaPa smiled and apologetically told his wife, "I should have had you don something to protect your gown. Sorry about that, my dear. I'll buy you a new gown." And PaPa, always a man of his word, bought great grandmama a new gown the very next week. They still went back upstairs to the reception. This wasn't the first time someone at a Lubyanka reception saw a woman with a blood-spattered gown emerge from the basement of Lubyanka on the arm of her NKVD husband who decided to spare his wife and settle his wife's debt with her divorce lawyer or marriage counselor or both.   The NKVD officers would laugh as the married couple would emerge from the elevator. The officers always said, 'their Nagant was the best marriage counselor'. Most of the lower ranked NKVD officers couldn't afford a new gown for their errant wives they decided to forgive and keep a little longer. All of the wives passed around great grandmama's secret for getting out blood stains from taffeta. That secret was no longer a secret, and all the NKVD wives were told about it as a practical matter and a little bit of a warning.

Great grandmama smiled and said, "The stains will

come out dear. Just with a little bit of seltzer. It's not like it's red wine." The stains did come out and great grandmama had a new gown to boot.

Those were the only words she spoke as she waited to follow her husband out of Lubyanka's basement. He made her walk and the marriage counselor walk down staircase, but only PaPa and great grandmama took the elevator up. The elevator operator had heard the gunshot and was glad to see the woman PaPa walked down the winding steps that opened into the elevator lobby in the basement, was coming up again. He was not surprised at seeing the blood spatter on her gown. He's seen many emerge out of the stairwell, heard gunshots, then fewer arrive with blood-spattered clothing at his elevator to ride up instead of walking. He assumed executions were exhausting for all parties concerned.

Almost everyone was dispatched with a bullet to the brain. With one exception, those who returned to the elevator never had clothing soaked in blood. That one time was when PaPa returned to the elevator, and with a smile on his face, he told the elevator operator, "I had to cut his throat. Next time I do that, I'll wear an apron." He never did wear an apron and stuck to the simple bullet in the forehead for the remainder of his career's basement business.

When we tapped Buonarotti's phone, he told a friend that he was like a bomb disposal technician with a bomb with too many wires and the detonator with only seconds left on the clock. He was talking about living with his wife, not his job. But with all his troubles, Buonarotti doesn't seem to age. He must have exceptional genes to look as good as he does. Of course, that's only matched by his exceptional bad luck picking a wife - or rather being picked as a husband. And I'm quite sure, Rose did all the picking.

Colonel Buonarotti is guilty of nothing – a truly innocent man in word, thought and deed – an innocent soul who his wife tells exactly what to do and speak. He's a bit too stupid, no not stupid, but too naive to be truly criminal. (Buonarotti is imperfect, though. He can never follow her instructions precisely enough. He couldn't be a successful criminal. He couldn't even be an unsuccessful criminal. He would get lost on his way to the crime scene.)

She's better than any Philadelphia lawyer I've ever met. With Rose running interference, getting him indicted, convicted, and incarcerated will be a real task, a real challenge for my legal skills. But I'm sure I'm up to it.

As a prosecutor, putting away the guilty is relatively easy. Judges and the jury pool, any venire, see the guilt at voir dire before the trial even begins. The trial is usually a formality just to affirm our preconceived conclusions. Prosecutors laugh at the concept of 'innocent until proven guilty beyond a reasonable doubt.' Defendants are guilty the first step they take into the courtroom. The law does say you have to go through the motions. If you can't get a plea bargain, the secret is to paint all your defendants, their witnesses, their spouses, children, unborn children, dead parents, grandparents, all their ancestors, and especially their lawyers, as evil and guilty.

Nobody likes lawyers anyway, especially lawyers who defend criminals. You can always have your assistant prosecutor ask some witness if the defense attorney has ever defended some murdering rapist child molesting treasonous traitor. As long as the jury hears the question, it doesn't have to be answered. It will be objected to; the judge will give you a warning and it will be stricken from the record. You don't ask it yourself, just in case has the person asking the question is found guilty of contempt of court and banned from the trial. Then you can take over for the kill. (In PaPa's day, that colloquialism had real meaning.)

Now you've shown how evil the defendant and his entire defense team is and how prejudice the judge is. This lays the groundwork for a plea bargain before there is an appeal of the inevitable guilty verdict. You clear more cases with a plea bargain. You avoid the risk of a crazy jury verdict, and even with a guilty verdict from the jury, there's the bother of a sentencing hearing. Much more efficient. You clear more cases (successfully), and the defendant, especially an innocent defendant, is admitting to being guilty of something. And that's all that matters.

This is especially important when the defendant is innocent of everything and is in sympathetic circumstances. For guilty defendants, limit the witnesses and exhibits. Less to challenge on appeal. Don't use expert witnesses. Their testimony is usually the easiest way for a defendant to have grounds for an appeal and eventually getting another trial. (Guilty defendants always, but always file an appeal. That's part of their original trial strategy. Innocent defendants less so. They lack that criminal drive. They lack the criminal's financial resources, and the legal talent used to defend the guilty. They all genuinely believe if their innocent, then the truth is on their side. The truth is never on the defendant's side. They don't know that the only truth is the truth I present to the judge and jury.)

It never looks good on your record to retry any case. That's when you hope for an in-jail accident or suicide especially when you leak the defendant is cooperating with law enforcement. Suicide and accidental falls and such are not uncommon especially for high profile or midlevel criminals with someone to give up. Prison showers are the least surveilled and most dangerous places. Even with closed circuit television, the steam fogs the camera lenses.

But the innocent, locking them up takes a lot of effort and real ingenuity. The fact that they have the facts on their side always, and most always makes them look sympathetic and innocent. This is especially true when they have no access to means, motive or opportunity to commit the crime. That's when you send long witness lists and as many expert wit-nesses and exhibits as possible. For every expert witness you put on, the defendant has to hire one if not two at his own ex-pense. Make sure your opening statement is especially lengthy and your witness questioning is detailed and prolonged. Run up the defendant's hourly legal costs until he throws in the towel and goes for a plea bargain. Always postpone anything you can until the next day. Defense attorneys are paid for the number of days they spend in court, not how many hours in court they are actually in court attorneying. And when the de-fendant runs out of money and loses his house, the defense attorney stops trying, returning the defendants calls, and pushes for a plea bargain so he can get on to the next paying client.

Sometimes the truly guilty try an entrapment defense. An entrapment defense means three things: (1) the defendant has admitted guilt; (2) any appeal is always futile because the defendant has admitted guilt, and: (3) the defendant picked a stupid attorney. You don't need witnesses or even have to try to win that case because they have just admitted guilt. Just tell the jury the harm the defendant caused. Judges and juries don't even have to consider the facts, they can just get even for society with their guilty verdict and sentencing.

As a prosecutor, your first and foremost obligation to your prosecutor's office, and the task that takes the most skill, time, and only improves with experience is to first find some-one you can probably convict of something. You can't learn that from a book.

If you know he is truly innocent of the crime, remember what PaPa taught grandpa who taught me – 'Show me a man and I'll show you a crime." Once you believe in your heart, your innocent defendant is guilty of something – even if it's not re-lated to your prosecution, you'll convincingly convey the guilt to the judge and jury through your facial expressions, gestures, tone of voice, and even posture. (I'm the best at this. I can do all that and seem as friendly and truthful as an Eagle Scout. Early in my career I practiced in front of a full-length mirror for hours before a trial, then every day during the trial. Now, I only rehearse my opening statement. The rest comes naturally.)

If you're really good, you'll convince the innocent defendant, their attorney, and their loved ones that he is guilty. This never happens with female defendants even when they are guilty. (Women, in general are much better criminals than men. They almost never get caught. And when they are caught, they almost never go for a plea bargain. Juries find it hard to believe any woman is guilty of anything. Beautiful women are to pretty to do anything wrong. Pretty women don't need to commit crimes to succeed. Juries pity ugly woman for being ugly and their lifelong competition with pretty women. And whether pretty or ugly, fat, or skinny, old women look like mothers. In the rare case of a woman found guilty of anything, judges find it hard to harshly sentence them. That's why men occupy so many more prison cells than women. Women commit as many crimes as men or are the root cause of their man's criminal behavior. And, for the most part, they get away with their crime. And after their man is caught, they immediately go on to the next man to commit the next crime for them. It's Biblical – the circle of life!)

Keep in mind, whether the defendants are guilty or innocent, we prosecutors – at least all the special prosecutors who have a reputation to enhance, are always inventing evidence. Guilty or innocent, if you believe the defendant is guilty, the defendant accepts it in the end, will try to cut a deal, or turn on someone up the food chain. What's fun is when they usually turn on a trusted friend - someone who has confided in them. And you'd be surprised how many people who commit crimes, many of them don't know they're committing crimes, especially people who are not really criminal, will innocently confide in someone. You just have to look for them. Human nature is a wonderful thing for prosecutors and the entire penal system. A best friend, a spouse, ex-spouse, child, cousin, uncle, aunt – you get the picture. Ex-spouses are the easiest to get to testify. They're always angry at their exes about something. Rich or poor, wives never think their husbands provided enough materially for them. Not to mention, didn't pay them enough attention, forgot a birthday – you get the picture. Wives are generally not happy with their husbands. And they never forget anything – even things that never happened.

Female cousins, aunts or any female relative are a little tougher sells. Women will clam up for fear of a conspiracy charge, or just don't want to be bothered. Unless they want to get even on the defendant, they know there's only a downside to testifying.

But to lock up a truly innocent man – ruin their lives – is a real challenge. At least I get to pick the judge and jury. I do that by controlling the jury pool and blackmailing the administrative judge with whatever I have on him. And I've collected dirt on everyone. And everyone has dirt to hide. As a last resort, I use his IRS filings.

Everyone assumes as soon as you are accused of a crime, you are guilty. If the state brings you to trial, you are already guilty beyond a reasonable doubt. Innocent men are always complaining and appealing. Prosecutors have human nature on their side. Even when an innocent man persists on complaining he's been wronged; people get tired of hearing it. The judge, jury and the public easily bore and just move on to the next injustice. And after a couple of appeals, if they haven't run out of money, they begin to believe they were guilty - or guilty of something they should be punished for. Just knowing what I know, being a prosecutor is so fulfilling and personally rewarding.

And Buonarotti is an innocent man and in the military. That makes it even a more pleasurable task. I don't like or respect the military. By the way, I don't really have to give him or anybody immunity no matter what I tell him. That's in some of the fine print of the Special Prosecutors two-thousand-page legislation – the exceptionally fine print – in fact, it's in a microdot. If we have to, we just erase that part from the transcript recordings where we mention an immunity proffer, and nobody ever reads the transcript very closely. Even if the immunity deal leaks out, proffers, like contracts, are made to be broken. There's always a loophole in everything. That's the second thing you learn in law school. The first is, if you know your client is guilty, get your fee up front before you go to trial and leaves the country for someplace without an extradition treaty.

But this case is more complicated. That's why he is one of the targets I'm handling myself. Number one, he's innocent. And not only is he innocent, but he's also a sympathetic innocent. His position at the White House, his relationship to General Merriwhether, and Rose, of course.

Rose is going to be the problem. So, this prosecution will need a special lack of a sense of fair play or the finer points of the law, much attention to detail along with a killer instinct. These are my inherited gifts I bring to the Special Prosecutor's office. Not every prosecutor has that. Most have the fairness gene. It's a human quality PaPa told my grandfather, who told my father who told me to fight the urge. If we ever felt it creeping into our thoughts or decisions, it was time for more vodka and to step back and take a cold shower – after the vodka. They try to teach you to subliminally fight the fairness gene in law school. The good law schools are the most successful.

I'm modeling our Special Prosecutor's office after the Stasi. The Stasi considered everyone in East Germany a guilty suspect and always a potential target of the secret police. They never bothered with 'person of interest'. It was Stalin's head of the Peoples Commissariat for Internal Affairs – the NKVD, Lavretity Pavovich Beria who said, '*Show me a man and I'll show you a crime!'* (If you haven't figured it out yet, he's actually my great grandfather – my PaPa. His official title made him sound like he was in charge of all of the national parks. Well, we had to change our name to escape Stalin's loyalists, war crimes courts, and others PaPa crossed, like everyone in Poland. After Stalin died of a stroke, PaPa claimed he had killed Stalin in a power play, sure he would be rise to the top at the Kremlin. There was a minor miscalculation on PaPa's part. Well, nobody's perfect, not even PaPa. Even though the family was on the run, we were always taught to admire PaPa's initiative and accomplishments. PaPa even made the cover of Time Magazine in July of 1953.

Once I became a prosecutor, I wanted to emulate PaPa and the way he ran the NKVD. It was almost as good as the Stasi. But there's no secret police in the world, even with computers, as good as the Stasi. Trying to be the Stasi would be a 'bridge too far', even for PaPa. In the end, PaPa went out in real NKVD style. He had the honor of being arrested by the world-famous Marshal of the Soviet Union Georgy Zhukov, tried by Marshal of the Soviet Union Ivan Konev, and executed the same way as the last NKVD chief Nikolai Yezhov in the basement of Lubyanka Prison. But PaPa died on his knees begging for his life with greater dignity than Yezhov – he was shot through the forehead by General Pavel Batitsky, Hero, and later Marshal of the Soviet Union. This was a great honor. Batitsky was hand-picked by Khrushchev over Uncle Vasily – Major General Vasily Blokhin, the NKVD's chief executioner. Nikita, if anything was considerate of PaPa's feelings by not having him executed by one of his own subordinates, and best friend.

And just for the sake of honest and open disclosure, my first deputy special prosecutor, my executive officer so to speak, is Andrew Wolsstein. His great grandfather was Major General Blokhin and close friend of PaPa. (His family also changed their names before coming to America. But that was easy for the whole crew. They had access to the NKVD passport printing and documents office. No one even had to apply for US citizenship. The NKVD obtained social security numbers, U.S. passports and seven years of income tax returns with substantial refunds so they would have enough of laundered money – directly from the US Treasury - to start their new lives.

I watched with admiration how Andrew put the completely innocent heads of a world-famous accounting firm in federal prison, ruined the firm, and cost twenty thousand people their jobs. All the people he sent to jail were absolutely innocent. He's the only other prosecutor I let handle the cases of our innocent targets.

Of course, I can tell he may be getting overwhelmed with work. With so many innocent targets, he's had to resort more often to perjury traps just to clear cases. It was much easier for grand juries to understand and quicker for them to return indictments than the phony and boring tax fraud charges. He did tell me he knew he was a success when he could feel the real pain of all the people he ruined. Then and only then he could congratulate himself on a job well-done.

As a child, my grandfather told me stories of his father, PaPa's wife's rose garden where PaPa buried his rape victims, he had picked up off the Moscow streets, and of the basement in Lubyanka Prison where he himself tortured and executed many of the state's and his and Stalin's personal enemies. Not nearly as many as Uncle Vasily. Uncle Vasily was a real killing machine, while PaPa had so much time occupied by administrative chores for the NKVD, his personal torture, and interrogation time was limited. He had to cut back on personal executions, reassigning them to more than willing subordinates so he could free time to go on to the next target. The problem was his subordinates were much slower and less efficient with the extracting of information before execution. In a spare moment, he was known to stop one of these torture/executions, have a short conversation with the prisoner, then look him in both eyes before shooting him in the forehead. This was just to keep his staff on their toes and show them that 'the old man' still had what it takes. PaPa could get what he wanted from the prisoners in a fraction of the time it took everyone else.

How exciting for a young boy to be regaled by such a family history. I even made sure my wife has a rose garden just in case I ever needed it. Apparently, growing roses is essential for burying bodies. (Or is it roses grow best where there are bodies buried?)

And the Stasi, God bless them, took my PaPa's wise words to heart. I had my great grandfather's wisdom translated into Latin and made those words the motto of our office. *'Ostende mihi homo ego ostenam tibi crimen'*. It's embossed on my stationary and the stationary of the office of the Special Prosecutor. It's on a plaque over our office headquarters in Orlando and engraved on plaques on our 'suggestion boxes' outside the Senate and House of Representatives' chambers. My father insisted I use the original Russian in Cyrillic but that would have been politically incentive. But I get ahead of myself.

Those were the good old days where the only oversight was from Stalin himself – and he couldn't be everywhere. No human resources departments – just wonderful free-wheeling organizations. Stalin invented political correctness. Being politically correct meant being completely loyal and believing everything Stalin said, doing exactly what Stalin said to do. To be politically incorrect meant to be disappeared. So, no one was left that was politically incorrect. That's the same thing the politically correct people want in this country. Think how dull things would be. No doubt, there would be fewer innocent people to prosecute. Only the guilty would be left, and there would be little challenge in that.

Anticipating Stalin's wishes could be dangerous. If he changed his mind, you would find yourself on the wrong end of a silenced Nagant M1895 revolver. PaPa's Nagant and his Korovin TK semiautomatic was passed down generation after generation after they were returned to my great-grandmother with his other effects by a faithful NKVD subordinate (who was later executed for that act of kindness). When they returned PaPa's corpse, his office staff sent a sympathy card. It wasn't signed by everyone in the NKVD headquarters' office, but they executed everyone anyway, whether or not they signed the card. There was a separate card from Khrushchev. She gave them to my grandmother who gave them directly to me. It was actually her wedding present. We had a real Russian Orthodox wedding, but that's another story.

PaPa told my grandfather, who told my father who told me never to anticipate Stalin's wishes. And my grandfather told me to never claim you murdered someone (especially if that someone is Joseph Stalin) if they died of a stroke. Even if you did murder them, keep it a secret. Having to brag about the murder is a sign of weakness. You as a suspect will be more feared and powerful than if people know for sure. Victims all have friends and many of them want to take over where the deceased left off. And if they are certain, especially if it comes from your own lips, that relieves them of any feelings of guilt, making revenge an even pleasant and satisfying duty, and garnering the admiration of those who hear of the deed.

In cases where there is a power vacuum, it's better you remain an unknown quantity to be suspected and feared while letting the situations naturally evolve. Important life lessons from PaPa. It's a shame he didn't 'practice what he preached'. It's still good advice for those making a career in politics, the corporate world or organized crime no matter where and at what level. (Actually, politics should be called 'better organized crime'.) The problem is in the modern world with all the new technology, especially all the automatic surveillance and DNA tracing, it's too hard to get away with murder, especially political murders. But this presents another life challenge for the most determined and gifted career-goal directed individuals.

In the old days, nobody was 'woke'. And if anyone was,

I don't think they even had a Russian word for that stupidity. They and anybody they told, and their entire families never lived long enough to talk to anyone else. Classic times. The Stasi did it better without computers. The Stasi had an index card system with cross references on everyone – every man, woman, and child in the German Democratic Republic, all their relatives no matter where they were, and probably all of the West Germans. The Stasi's goal was the unification of all Germany under their control.   Before computers, it was the 'Stasi standard' aspired to by secret police organizations around the world. The 'Stasi Standard' was taught in every secret police academy. They all – to this day – the world's secret police organizations - stand on the shoulders of the Stasi giants. I went to a secret police convention last year. They told stories about the Stasi. They had seminars on the Stasi, and even a panel discussion on the NKVD and PaPa as the Stasi's predecessor. I was so proud, you can't imagine. I want my Special Prosecutor's Office to stand with them. I want my agency to live up to my PaPa and his motto and now my agency's motto – 'Ostende mihi homo ego ostenam tibi crimen' - our ideal, our goal. (It brings tears to my eyes.) I shouldn't wax nostalgic.

The big difference is, I have computers and access to all the government computers including the IRS, and no one realizes that. No other secret police or agency has that capability. I just don't have enough trained personnel to take full advantage of my blessings. The computers allow us to do more with less staff, alter and erase records without endlessly hunting through thousands of files. I can make anyone look guilty of anything. I have so many prosecutorial blessings sometimes I just don't know where to start. It's especially easy with access to the IRS files. I can potentially convict anybody who files a tax return of tax fraud. And that's just for starters. What I do is if the perjury trap doesn't immediately work, I accuse them of tax fraud without even looking at their taxes. If they don't capitulate, then I have to do it the hard way by slogging through their tax returns.

Except for going after them for taxes, I live in a perpetual prosecutor's Christmas morning opening all my beautifully wrapped presents. The convictions are all wrapped in beautiful shiny blue paper with red ribbons.

I only use the tax dodge as a foot in the door for the real criminal prosecutions or as leverage to flip whoever needs flipping. I already have the FBI, my own armed police. It's just you can't really use them like the NKVD. Unfortunately, I don't have not enough time and staff to really take control of the whole nation. Not yet. But the plans are in the works. It's still a lot easier than fixing elections.

Stalin relied on paper records and airbrushing people out of official photographs to make them disappear. And Uncle Vasily made sure their entire families disappeared with them. To be sure, it routinely took NKVD at least two weeks until all the targets in one pod were gone. Later the NKVD agents would inquire whether anyone knew the subjects in question. You learned to deny ever hearing their name. Anybody who slipped and said yes, they and their families met the same fate. And all this was done without overcrowding Lubyanka jail cells, any jails, or the gulags.

Maybe not as well or completely or with the finality that Stalin did, but I can disappear people into the witness protection program. I create a credible threat, like telling them the person they ratted on was part of a Mexican drug cartel. Then they beg to be disappeared. I do that with witnesses for the defendants, or any potential enemies that could do anyone in our organization damage.

Now, I can convincingly alter voice recordings to have people say anything we want them to say, Photoshop any visual record, alter or erase any bank, personnel, medical, credit, or purchase records. The trouble is, everyone knows we can do it, so they are less likely to believe what they're hearing or seeing. (In a true democracy, we never erase anybody's identity completely. Whether alive or dead, we use that identity to swell the voting roles in selected swing jurisdictions. I do it for both the Democrats and Republicans, so no one comes after us. For now, though, fixing elections is a tedious labor-intensive sideline. But like any industry, survival is dependent on diversification of skills and products.)

We can have anyone confess to anything with just a keystroke. It's still less hassle to get people to actually confess. True or false confessions, if they confess, they're less likely to make a fuss when convicted and sent to jail or testifying against someone else, or both.

With another keystroke, you can be erased forever from everyone's memory by erasing your social media presence, your credit records, all your purchases, anything. We can even erase you from other people's social media and emails. The only exception we make are for voter rolls. And unfortunately, the far corners of the Internet. There's always some remnant fact floating around the Internet, true or not, that someone looking real hard discovers. In the old days, you can easily burn the index card records. And that was good but erasing people with a keystroke is better. Sometimes, when I'm about to drift off to sleep, I sigh and realize what a lucky man I am living in this modern and enlightened world. Then I wake up in a cold sweat thinking about the Internet.

But I learned from PaPa's fate, power must be used incrementally and judiciously. Time must be allowed to pass between power plays to look out for unintended consequences. Even if you don't think so, time is really on your side during any power grab. That was the one mistake PaPa made and was his undoing. (He only realized that when he was on his knees begging for his life.) We must all learn from our elders' errors, even when you are all powerful – as PaPa was as the head of the NKVD, there's always your personal Joseph Stalin. And I am as the Special Prosecutor, all powerful. I want to be a more powerful than Joe Stalin and really make my PaPa proud. I'm just haven't identified my personal Joseph Stalin. But I know he's out there just waiting for me to screw up. Given the opportunity he, whoever he is, if he can bring about my downfall and even demise, he will do it, if for nothing more than to demonstrate and solidify his own power. That's the nature of politics and the natural law of power.

"Rose told me to cooperate. She said I didn't have any choice." Of course. The infamous Rose. Buonarotti smiles every time he mentions her name. Rose's no frail, either. She's one hundred percent Army. Career Army daughter and Army wife – Army brat and spouse-hardened. She thinks she's untouchable because of who she is, what she is, and who her father is. She thinks her husband is untouchable because of her. Why else would she send him in here without a lawyer. (Not that I couldn't outlawyer any lawyer they can get.) This will be a real challenge for me. I must be on my guard. Both of them have only been married once, and only to each other. That means they're less likely to make mistakes in judgement.

The heightened sense of danger facing a threatened lioness - and what is more fulfilling in life but the adrenaline rush of the hunt. I'll get to her through her husband. Then I'll get her father. Then General Merriwhether, then up to the President (except if it's Joe Biden).

Classic prosecutor tactics – threaten to destroy a loved one. But you have to focus on one loved one at a time. You threaten too many loved one targets, it dilutes the fear. And you're not sure if they're all loved ones of the same intensity or really a loved one at all. No one can equally love too many people at the same time, anyway. PaPa said that was one of the lessons you learn working in the basement of Lubyanka.

But Buonarotti should be easy pickings – at least for a perjury trap. Colonel Buonarotti always tells the truth. A perjury trap is always easy to spring on absolutely honest truthful trusting people. Perjury traps are dime a dozen now adays. But an old and classic standby like "Stardust" or "Honeysuckle Rose" - a good and easy last resort to get people to turn on one another. It certainly takes less effort than using the IRS. I used to think it was a sign of a lazy prosecutor. But with so many targets, you have to cut corners to save time and for the sake or 'organizational efficiency'. (My old boss at the New York Southern Districts Office always said, "My son, my son, it's the body count for which we will pass judgement on you." He also said, "Use the shotgun approach. The more people you investigate, the more you will indict. And the more you indict, the more convictions you will achieve.")

Indict your targets before they get too old or have nothing to lose, like their jobs, marriages, fortunes, or reputations. If someone has property, a happy marriage, school age children and an excellent reputation, they will be the easiest to come up with a plea bargain, especially if they're completely innocent and going broke.

And I know the Colonel really loves his wife. Why else would he put up with the way she treats him. And I know she really loves him. Just look at him. True and mutual love. That's got to be the only reason. But he's like a lost puppy who can't find his master and had an accident on the living room carpet. As we proceed with the investigation, I'll separate him from Rose for longer and longer intervals. Like chess, you have to think many moves ahead.

Anyway, watching that perjury trap spring is one of the true perks of my job. When we have the subject cornered and they're about to crack, I replay the tape for the entire staff. Just so they know what they're accomplishing, and also as a warning, it could be them, next! And once the target cracks, I play that tape back for him and the person or people he implicates. All the pieces fall into place as each person descends into my prosecutorial abyss.

You did really need to play back the confession, even when it's a false confession. When they hear themselves confess, they begin to believe they really did commit the crime. And it's just so much fun to watch the target's suffering. I guess in this modern day and age this is the closest thing I can get to the fun the ancient Romans had with the Christians and the lions. It's not even close to the entertainment PaPa had in the basement of Lubyanka prison. Unfortunately, staff never gets to see the final result. They can't be trusted not to prematurely leak the information.

"I know Rose told you that you had to testify. Remember, Jean Paul Sartre said you always have a choice. And bad faith is hiding the truth from oneself. Colonel Buonarotti, you do have a choice." Buonarotti looks perplexed. "Let's get down to business. I'm turning on the recording camera now and our stenographer is sitting behind you. You do understand?" Not that it matters whether he does or not. He's nodding. "Do not nod. Answer yes or no." I have to be more patient and remember to use a gentler tone this early in the interrogation. It's way too early in the investigation to put the target on guard. Fear is a weapon we need to use gradually until we bring it to the crest of the hill and have it hold there before our target slides or tumbles down.   Just like the last movement of any of the great symphonies. I like to believe that my prosecutions are symphonies – works of art, many musical instruments playing together in complex harmony and counterpoint. All culminating in that single finale – the sentencing. It's when the distraught defendant, especially the innocent ones commit suicide that destroys our moment of triumph.

"Yes." Now we've gotten Buonarotti to follow my instructions instead of Rose. Baby steps, but the beginning of any interrogation is especially important. One must set the right tone.

"Let's have our stenographer introduce herself – Mrs. Defarge, please state your full name and the date and time of this interview for the video record." She's already in the frame with Buonarotti – with the lit cigarette dangling from her wrinkled lips and the bulge of a soft pack of cigarettes in her bra strap. No ashtray. There are none as this is a non-smoking building. Instead of answering, she just flicked her ashes onto the carpet. There are always burn marks around where she sits in all the interrogation rooms we use. And all the carpets smell of stale cigarette smoke. Everyone has stopped asking her not to smoke. She's been around so many years, she can't be fired. (Well, it's the government, nobody can be fired.) No one can even find her original employment records. Someone said they were moved to the National Archives during the Eisenhower Administration. She's the only one left in this section of the government who knows how to access paper files. She's also the only one in the Department of Justice who knows how to take dictation on a stenograph machine. No one knows why we need any of this when we can use our voice recognition technology for any printed transcript copies.

"Fuck off, shithead!" Defarge cracked a smile before taking another puff of her cigarette.

"Mrs. Defarge, please state your full name for the recording. This is an important formality."

"Keep it up, shithead, and I'll tear your heart out through your throat!"

"For the record, Ms. Therese Defarge is our stenographer." One day, I swear I'll get her out of here, either vertically or horizontally. "Now, Colonel Buonarotti, do you swear or affirm to tell the truth, the whole truth and nothing but the truth, so help you God?"

"I do." Buonarotti, now I can get you for perjury!

"State your name for the record."

"Camillo Archangelo Buonarotti, Lieutenant Colonel, United States Army, Army Intelligence. ... And no jokes, please." Buonarotti doesn't know I'm never joking. I have no sense of humor. I may lie, cheat, or steal to get a conviction, but I never joke. (PaPa said to my grandfather who told my father who told me, joking got good people in trouble When they tell their joke they think is funny, some people don't find it funny. And if Stalin didn't find the joke funny, or even if he did, they were disappeared. Apparently, Stalin didn't have a sense of humor. So, PaPa told my grandfather, who told my father who told me.)

I do have principles and a code that I live by – punish the guilty and innocent with equal vigor, talent, cruelty, and skill to be used to the limits the law will allow, without sending me to jail myself. (My incarceration would be my personal limit of the law.) With federal courts and prisons overbooked and overcrowded, sometimes we even run short of holding cells. Summary execution would be the obvious solution for us. It was PaPa's solution to most of his logistical and administrative problems. That's why there was no overcrowding at Lubyanka. No shortage of office space either. Now a days, I can't really execute anyone after we're done with the interrogation the way PaPa did. Most of the time you can't even execute them with finding them guilty after a death penalty trial.

"Let me remind you, everything spoken here is classified at the highest level. You cannot share any of these proceedings with anyone, including your wife. In your own words, tell us how this got started." I already know he's going to tell Rose everything. Another offense he can be indicted, convicted, and jailed for. That's ten years in Leavenworth for revealing classified information. And that's ten years for each fact he tells Rose. A great bargaining chip I can use against Rose. And I can indict Rose for just listening to him. 'Receiving classified information by an unauthorized individual.' The law is a wonderous thing. But it will be difficult to convict her. Rose will tell the jury she never really listens to her husband. And any jury will believe a wife who tells them they weren't listening to most if not all of what he was telling her. And if she wasn't listening, she didn't receive any classified information. And without an exchange of classified information, I can't get a conviction, at least for that, on either of them.

"Thank you, Mr. Seplechre." (If he thinks I won't tell Rose everything, he's crazy. If I don't tell her verbatim what went on, I will face a painful prolonged life only wishing for a quick death that will never come. Even at the end, Rose won't unplug my respirator just to watch me suffer if I disobeyed her.) "I understand perfectly."

"Let me check that the video is running. There, now go ahead – at your own pace. Don't feel rushed. If you need a break, just let us know. Don't worry or be ashamed of anything. You have complete immunity." The elderly Ms. Defarge behind her antique stenograph machine smirked when I mentioned immunity, before returning stoic with dead sharklike unblinking eyes back staring at me through the smoke swirling around her head and her thick glasses, absolutely motionless. "Are you ready, Therese?"

"Ms. Defarge, please. We're not going out on a date." She flicked the ashes of her cigarette on the rug, then barely nodded without blinking, not even once. As the room was filling with her smoke, you can imagine her killing and eating bleeding baby seals. I go home at night after every interrogation smelling like I spent the day in a smokey bar. Even though the stenographer is unnecessary, her presence adds gravitas to the interrogation. Not as much gravitas as a twelve-volt car battery and jumper cables to the testicles, but enough to let the target know this is serious.

"Colonel Buonarroti, the floor is yours."

The Colonel checked his wristwatch. I was told he also carried a railroad conductor's pocket watch. The man loves his wife and loves trains. "Today is March 22, 2021, 9:17 AM. Well, I had finished my breakfast, that first day of a new post-

35

ing-breakfast Rose prepared for me – special – so my stomach wouldn't rumble or produce any gas. I can be very gassy when I'm nervous. ..."

"Now, Colonel, just go ahead, please. You can skip what you ate for breakfast."

"But Rose said that's the most important meal of the day. She said to include all the details just to show my testimony is as complete and truthful as possible. That's what she told me to do and I must do that. Even the intimacies, ..."

"Please, Colonel. That isn't necessary. Just so you know for the future, the recording is date and time stamped throughout. Only Ms. Defarge needs to state the date and time at the beginning of each interview so we may accurately scale the recording to her stenographic transcript." I don't want him giving us any dates and times. It's not impossible, but just another step we would have to go through to doctor his recordings, and another chance we have of our skullduggery being detected. I like that word, 'skullduggery'. Maybe as part of the Special Prosecutors Office we should have a Directorate of Skullduggery – the 'DOS'. I have to mull that over.

"Rose told me to do it. She said trust no one! No offence."

"None taken, Colonel." I knew Rose is the smarter half of this pair. I certainly cannot be trusted. It's just easier to change a time stamp than a voice and video recording.

"Mr. Seplechre, Rose wants daily copies of the transcripts. I was told not to come home without them, no matter how long I had to wait."

"Unfortunately, she can't have them. All of this is top secret, and no one can see them, not even me." Buonarroti almost looked surprised that anyone would deny any of Rose's requests.

"Mr. Seplechre, that isn't going to fly with Rose. I'll tell her exactly what you said, but it might be easier on you and your staff, and me, for that matter, if you just gave me a copy." Buonarotti wasn't threatening. He just looked fearful of having to face Rose without the transcripts. You could see, feel, and hear his fear of Rose. Buonarotti was beginning to visibly sweat. I had him off guard. And as Ms. Defarge's smoke swirled around him, his eyes began to tear. This wasn't good. I didn't want him defensive. Not yet.

"No, Colonel. You can't tell your wife anything I said. Telling her the transcripts are classified is classified. And telling her I told you that you can't tell her that I said is as classified as the first thing I said is classified, is classified. It's all classified. All these proceedings are top secret. You can't even tell her you're here. That's classified." I don't know if anything is really top secret, but it sounds good enough to at least put him off and get on with his testimony. I will eventually lose this battle. Rose's terrifying reputation precedes her. I may have to give her a copy, but I'll fight her just for the hell of it. But her copy won't contain any promise of immunity for her husband.

We never put any of the immunity deals in writing. There are written statements that our targets – and their lawyers think are immunity deals. But they're not. I bet you think we couldn't do that. Well, we're lawyers, the masters of not saying or writing what we mean or mean what we put in writing or anything we say to your face or behind your back. The only ones better at this are the members of Congress. And on the floor of the House and Senate, they can lie about anything without consequence. But God forbid you lie when giving Congressional testimony. It always seemed unfair to me that if the members of Congress can lie from the floors of the House and Senate, we should be allowed to lie to them while testifying from the same place. Seems only just. In fact, that's where I draw a line on who I will prosecute. I'll put any innocent man in jail and ruin his life, his wife's life, and his children's lives – *show me a man and I'll show you a crime.* But I will never, not ever prosecute anyone for lying to Congress! It's not a crime, it's almost sacred duty!

At least the Colonel knows how to follow his wife's instructions. He'll do well in prison. Prison is the closest thing to marriage on this earth, except more pleasant and there's an end in sight, especially with good behavior. In marriage, good behavior gets you a longer not a shorter sentence.

In prison, you're automatically in a lower income tax bracket – at least for most inmates. There's the exercise yard, free meals, the prison canteen for special treats, laundry service, library books delivered to your cell, free medical care with no copayments, free cable television and...and then there's prison itself where he would only have to see his wife on visiting days. No need for an alarm system. You never have to worry about someone breaking in. It's as close to a socialist paradise you can get. No stress. No shopping. No preparing meals or washing dishes even if you're on kitchen duty. All prisons have institutional dish washing conveyors. No decisions to make about anything. The only question you consider are if the horizonal stripes are more slimming than vertical strips. The striped uniforms have always been the penitentiary's equivalent to the classic white tie and tails. The orange jump suits tend to be too informal. Stripes, whether horizontal or vertical are more slimming. Either prison uniforms are more comfortable than my suit or his military uniforms. And you're dressed for work or play every day. Again, no one worries about whether your clothing is in style. And there are no color clashes.

Not that I am prejudging, but when you do my job day and night, you need to learn to appreciate the accoutrements. Visiting the guys, you put away to try to get them to turn state's evidence on one of their most trusted friends or relatives is a real treat even if you're not successful. Just talking with your desperate victims of your prosecution is like gazing at the stuffed trophies hanging on your hunting lodge wall. And seeing them in their prison uniform, that's almost as satisfying springing a perjury trap.

It's all the thrill of the hunt and the eventual kill. It used to be real fun when there was a more frequent use of the death penalty. Life without parole is not the same as life without parole anymore. More and more, some coastal elite governor comes along anytime and commute a sentence, even for cop killers - like the governor of New York. I'll give you a plan to decrease the cost, endless appeals, and the problem of prison overcrowding. Just execute everyone on death row, right in their cells. That could be done by the weekend. That's what they did at Lubyanka. (But I shouldn't take credit for the idea. That came from my first deputy prosecutors. He said that '... *even the innocent are guilty of something for which they should be punished...*" Maybe that should be translated into Latin for our letterhead. *'etiam innocens reus aliquid pro quo esse poena'*. I know he uses it on his personal stationery, and it's been on his Christmas cards for years.)

Buonarroti sighed. I can tell his anxiety level is increasing. He's now anticipating getting this whole ordeal behind him. Then having to face Rose's interrogation, and without the transcript she demanded, I think he would rather confess anything to me here and now than face Rose at home. He won't though because Rose would kill him before I could put him safely in jail.

"Colonel Buonarroti, just take a breath, and know you're among friends." Ha! Every time I tell a target that, I have to stifle a choking laugh. And so, does Ms. Defarge. I'm always amazed how many of the targets believe me. Ms. Defarge shakes her head. Unfortunately, her grimace and silent disbelief are in the camera frame.

"I had just completed my assignment with the NSA Nightmare Computer section and I still had my top-secret clearance. I was promoted to Lt. Colonel and sworn to absolute secrecy about what happened there, when General Merriwhether called me. I was still on furlough and I was planning a surprise vacation – a cruise to Alaska -for Rose and me."

"How did he reach you? Did you receive written orders?" I mustn't show I'm too anxious or becoming inpatient with the Colonel. I mustn't let him become defensive, not yet. You need to save that for latter in the interrogation. I have to keep him relaxed - off guard. Later, I can make use of his defensive posturing and trip him up. Even if he never lies, I'll get him to twist his own words. It's something I learned from my father, who learned it from his father, who learned it from PaPa Levy Beria. And PaPa just did it for sport. He always knew his interrogations ended with a single round from his Nagant in the forehead no matter what anyone said.

"This was going to be something special – unforgettable. Rose would never expect a cruise and never to Alaska, especially at the end of November. I wanted to pay for it myself. I booked an inside cabin below the water line. These cruises will be discontinued after November, and this was the very last cruise of the season. In fact, they told me this cruise would be historic. It would be this was this ship's very last cruise.

The ship was to be used for cattle and sheep transportation from Australia and New Zealand before being scrapped. All the furniture, accessories, equipment would be for sale at incredible savings. They told me savings you couldn't believe. I even reserved one of the main lounge couches as an anniversary surprise for Rose. The color and pattern went with our carpets. We could finally refurnish our home, and maybe if things were cheap enough, put them in storage for when we moved into bigger quarters. Not only could Rose enjoy the cruise, but she could also shop while strolling around the ship. She only had to clip the price tags and turn them in to the bursar's office at the end of each day to claim her purchase. Everything automatically went on our cruise credit card, and the furniture or object was immediately moved to the cargo hold at the end of each day at sea. And for every twenty-five dollars spent, you got a free deck chair and towel. I knew she would love it. She could bring her mink and lambskin coats and wear them on deck while shopping. Rose loved shopping and loved wearing the fur coats – she just never had the occasion to do so."

"Colonel Buonarotti, did you receive any orders – any written orders? And just know we can check everything for anything you might have received."

"About the cruise? I received my reservation confirmation and my receipt for the couch and four free deck chairs." Buonarotti has a one-track mind. Everything revolves around Rose. "Colonel, did you receive any orders about your assignment?"

"Did I receive orders? I get orders all the time. Written and verbal orders. Rose tells me what to do all the time. Sometimes she gives me written orders. My 'to do list'. At the end of the day, I check off what I completed on her list, and give it to her, including things she tells me to do at work – Army-related tasks I must complete to 'enhance' my career. Anything not completed gets a note in the margins. If she approves, she tears up the list. Before bed, I get her written orders for the next day. She will only answers questions I have just before bed, and only once. Rose said this is to keep my reflexes sharp for when I'm sent into real combat. And, Mr. Seplechre, that will be a cakewalk after the way Rose has trained me."

I do feel sorry for Buonarotti. Prison will be like a vacation for him. "She said it gets too rushed in the morning before work. She doesn't want me rushed or anxious before my day begins. She does the same thing on the weekends so I can get an early start and she can sleep late. She told me she does this so I would have no excuses. She wants me to dream about what I had to do the next day. Not waste a minute, whether awake or asleep. But really, Mr. Seplechre, I've given up making excuses to Rose – it's useless even trying.

But this trip. That's why this was going to be such a surprise for her. She never said or wrote anything. You can imagine, Rose is a girl hard (and very risky) to surprise. ..."

(PaPa said Stalin was risky to surprise, too. No one ever surprised Stalin and lived to talk about it. You have to admire Rose, though. She has some of 'Uncle Joe's' traits without the penchant for genocide.)

"... I was really pleased when our reservations for the flight to the west coast were confirmed and the cruise ship was still afloat. And let me tell you how I surprised her. ..."

This is going to take forever. I don't know how he ever gets anything done. He's always sidetracked by something. And that something always leads back to Rose. "Orders, Colonel. I mean orders from General Merriwhether or anyone else in the military or government. Anything that might be an official communication – from the US Army, from the Government. Not from Rose. Colonel Buonarotti how did General Merriwhether communicate with you concerning your new assignment? Did he clarify the mission of the new assignment?" I think jail for him will be a welcome vacation from Rose.

This has been and continues to be a very painful interview. It will be even more painful for the transcribers. Not that I care if Mrs. Defarge is in pain, but there are other transcribers who have to listen and watch the video.

"No. General Merriwhether said put nothing in writing or in emails. No phone calls. Somebody may be recording them. Only talk in interior rooms. Conversations can be read from a considerable distance from the sound vibrations on the glass windows. General Merriwhether is my immediate commander and the commanding officer in charge of the operation. Except for Rose, no one else can give me orders. General Merriwhether said so, and once Rose confirmed it, I knew it was so. If anyone else gave me orders, Rose said I was to ignore them. And I ignored them, didn't hear them or forgotten them.

Someone may overhear and/or be recording anything we may mutter. General Merriwhether told me this, especially for this operation. And Rose has been telling me this since we got married. So, there's no talking, especially among or to ourselves. And certainly, no social media. And this was so secret, when speaking of it, we had to be sure the interior room was swept for listening devices and there was sufficient background noise, to block anything that might be missed or could be heard through the walls. I was instructed to close all my social media accounts and he told Rose to close hers, too.

General Merriwhether said anything that has to be communicated must be done verbally in person or on the secret section's secret computers, secret and secure telephones, fax machines (they had one fax machines and no fax machine to send anything to), telegraph stations throughout the offices (they had them but nobody knew Morse Code or any code they could use,), a half dozen old Enigma Machines from the Smithsonian, and a couple of other things that were so secret, nobody knew what they were, how they worked, or what they were called. Messages were piling up from these devices from somewhere, but no one knew where they came from or what they said. And no one knew where the messages were sent or stored. But there were other devices not in any of the groups I told you about, even more secret than anything I described, so I was told in the strictest confidence. And no one knew anything about them."

"Did you have a SCIF – a Sensitive Compartmented Information Facility?"

"Mr. Seplechre, the whole secret unit was a SCIF inside a Faraday Cage, inside a lead-shielded complex of eight offices to prevent interference from an EMP – electromagnetic pulse that usually accompanies a nuclear detonation. We were already fifty feet underground. And inside the unit was another

Faraday Cage with a SCIF in that. No one had access to the SCIF inside our SCIF unless the person or persons with that access let them in. No one ever knew what happened in that inside SCIF who went in or out. That's all I know about that. And no one knew anyone who went in, and certainly, all who went in, never left."

If he has that straight in his head, he's better than me. And with all that, he still doesn't understand or know how to deal with his wife. "Let's get back to your mission and orders." It sounds like typical government over classification. That's what our military prosecution targets use to stimy subpoenas and contempt charges.

"My instructions were, that under any circumstances, consider anything I was told by General Merriwhether to be official orders. Do not take notes. Do not write anything down. Record no conversations. Do not trust any telephone messages, even from General Merriwhether, and especially do not trust your cell phone for anything. All official orders would come face to face from General Merriwhether or Rose, especially now that Rose was part of the team. I was to carry out the official orders in the reverse order given, then forget that I was ever told to do what I was told to do, in the reverse order, of course. Never try to anticipate. And always deny anything that was done, as if it never happened. That's how secret everything was. Nobody was to know anything. And nobody did!"

"Yet, Colonel, you're talking to the Special Prosecutor!"

"Yes. Rose told me to!"

The Colonel is amazing. He can talk in circles without knowing what he is saying. You would think he attended law school. "And there are – there must be written orders and documentation somewhere. Where are these kept?"

At least I've gotten Buonarotti to skip ahead past his morning sex with Rose and his breakfast, the way he testified during the last investigation. I know I had planned to milk this, but this is excruciating. I had always wanted to retire from this position as Special Prosecutor. But I was hoping to interrogate more and more interesting targets than this poor schlump. "Colonel, what is the section's secret designation?"

"The White House designation for our section is 'THE WHITE*HOUSE', of course. It is obvious and easy to remember." I don't know why Mr. Seplechre looks so puzzled. Maybe not puzzled – more annoyed. "Mr. Seplechre, that is exactly how General Merriwhether explained it to me." When I explained it to Rose, she seemed perplexed. ... Well not perplexed - more aggravated and inpatient. Just between you and me, Rose was annoyed that I accepted the assignment. (Rose is annoyed with most things I do, anyway,) "Anyway, all communications, and that included any internal emails had to be done on their equipment at the White House exclusively inside the WHITE*HOUSE section of the White House on White House White*House equipment – that is THE WHITE*HOUSE devices. No cell phones, tablets - nothing. Everything had to be kept internal to the White House's WHITE*HOUSE."

"You're repeating yourself, Colonel. You can skip ahead if that will help." That would certainly help me. During the pause, Ms. Defarge dropped her glowing cigarette butt to the floor, pulled another unfiltered cigarette from the pack under her bra strap, and lit it.

"But Rose told me to tell the truth, the whole truth and skip nothing. Rose warned me about this turning into something less esteemed than what General Merriwhether promised." (Rose said the whole operation should be called 'Operation Small Intestine' and she referred to the intelligence product as 'Large Bowel Output'. Rose was especially upset when I accepted the assignment from General Merriwhether without asking her first. Rose always told me the worst assignments were at the Pentagon. Bad traffic, lousy parking and you and your career would be just lost in the crowd."

It's like getting assigned to the Kremlin as a junior officer. The difference between the Pentagon and the Kremlin, if you're an assistant to a rising star, there may be some career advancement. If your boss falls out of favor, the both of you may get executed, or if you're lucky, end up a guest at a Siberian gulag. At least at the Pentagon, most of the time you go nowhere fast, but you will survive the tour.

"Rose always told me, given a choice, I was never to accept anything at the Pentagon. But I really thought she would be pleased with me being stationed at the White House.

I think Rose had something more prestigious in mind – something like military envoy to our Paris embassy or military liaison to the Court of St. James – an assignment directly to Buckingham Palace. There is no such position, but she said she could get them to create it for her – or rather her father would have done it for her if I hadn't already accepted the position from General Merriwhether. And Rose was not fond of General Merriwhether, her father's West Point roommate. Rose's father, Lieutenant General Jefferson Davis Jefferson, retired (FFV – First Family of Virginia) sold discount computer systems to the Pentagon, the CIA, and the NSA. And he sold General Merriwhether, the NSA's Nightmare computer system. Now Rose's father is a sought-after consultant – which means he is a highly paid lobbyist.

"Mr. Seplechre, between you and me, Rose was not happy with my assignment. I told her I could back out of it if she really wanted me to - and she really wanted me to - but she said you can never break your word as an officer and a gentleman, and never ever to a general. The entire military is just like a small town. Word gets around and nothing can repair your reputation if you even once go back on your word.

I hated myself for making Rose unhappy. I couldn't wait to tell Rose I accepted an assignment at the White House. I really thought she would be pleased especially after the last debacle. I never anticipated her reaction. Now, just reliving her anger and disappointment brings the lump back to my throat that I can't swallow my own saliva."

I'm thinking PaPa said the same thing about how dangerous it was to anticipate Stalin. As far as not keeping your word, I'm glad that's not true in the Justice Department, or Congress or politics or the legal profession. No one would survive. "Colonel Buonarotti, this is good that you're expressing your feelings. This can be the beginning of a beneficial cathartic that will help us both." I have to keep from choking on my words. "Please, go on."

"I was upset by her reaction I told her I can manage my career on my own and I have my pride. I knew the second the words left my mouth that it was the wrong thing to say. And she said, 'If you keep this up, that's all you'll have!'..." (Actually, Rose's expression was a little cruder, but I wouldn't want those words recorded.)

(Rose must have threatened her father who convinced General Merriwhether to make her part of the intelligence team. But I'm not going to tell that to Mr. Seplechre.) "...Rose spoke briefly to General Merriwhether who felt she would be a valued-added member of the team. Those were the General's exact words. In a day, she had her top-secret White House clearance, and the next morning the two of us were driving from our Fort Meade quarters to the White House together for our first day of work – together in Rose's little vintage two-seater Mercedes sports car. Rose drove. Rose always drove". Rose and I would be together forever, for every waking moment of the day at work, and at home, at night, too. What bliss. And Rose always drove."

(For all this to happen so quickly, that short conversation with General Merriwhether must have been a serious and to the point threat. I'm not sure what Rose threatened General Merriwhether with, nor could I even guess at all Rose's unknown powers. There have been so many Rose-threats over so many years, you learn to both accept and ignore them. I really should say, she never threatens me, as I follow her instruction immediately and exactly as expected. She knows she has me trained. That is unless I forget, misunderstand, or just didn't hear her. Then, I just get yelled at – never threatened. Rose knows that, for me, threats are never necessary. Its other people who don't know her she has to threaten. I can't say for sure; she may have hurt one or two people just to set an example.)

"Colonel Buonarroti, there must be more you can tell me." I have to keep reminding myself to be patient and at the same time keep him focused. Some interrogators just let their subjects' ramble. The old OSS man, the Director of Central Intelligence and the CIA under Ronald Reagan, Bill Casey said that people will always tell you more than they want you to know.

I could have the colonel go on and on and on. It will be mostly about Rose but I'm sure eventually he will talk about others in his circle of unsuspecting friends and acquaintances. His ramblings are bound to reveal a myriad of offences I could indict and convict all of his colleagues, friends, acquaintances, distant relatives, and future generations in his blood line as coconspirators. But who has the time? At the same time, it's too early in the investigation to get any mileage from pushing him and increasing his anxiety. The proper technique requires skillful and patient slow and steady increase in threat intensity.

That comes directly from PaPa. What PaPa did to reduce the level of threat anxiety, at least in the beginning of his interrogations, was to tie a tight ligature around each toe. This reduced both the bleeding, and if he waited long enough, it would numb the toe enough to reduce the pain at amputation. It always amazed me that he used the same hand plant shears his wife used in her rose garden. And he always brought them home to her, still blood stained in a paper bag. She really needed them only on the weekends to trim the flowers in her garden. PaPa wanted her to know he didn't forget the shears at work, and how he used them.

PaPa was old school. He considered cutting off toes one at a time, followed by the pinky fingers a slow escalation. Pulling out teeth caused the person you were questioning to garble their speech and choke on their own blood. It always made it difficult getting information or recording a confession problematic. He stopped extracting teeth when in the middle of the questioning, his subject aspirated and died choking on his own blood then vomiting his stomach contents all over PaPa's uniform fresh from the cleaners.

(When torturing someone, PaPa always said you must give your victim hope of a reasonably functional survival – and always wear a plastic protective apron. That's why pinky toes first. Fingers, starting with the pinky finger are cut off with the same pruning shears, one digit at a time. PaPa told grandpa who told me you must give your subject time to consider his alternatives, feel the pain, and if possible, leave the last person (alive) you questioned in the room, so your subject knows where the whole exercise is going and there's real hope of survival. You need to be especially careful not to amputate both lower limbs, at least not too high up. But it rarely comes to that. Usually, they'll talk first before they're dead from blood loss. About half of the time, they linger after you get the information you wanted and the confession, and you have to finish them off with a bullet to the brain.

My grandfather was a skilled interrogator and said he never went beyond ten toes and the fingers on the left hand and the ring finger on the right before questioning was complete. Finally, with the information and/or confessions obtained, the suspect was told to plead for his life on his knees. Then he was finished off with a bullet to the forehead – or for the squeamish interrogator, the back of the head. PaPa taught his interrogators to, one, wear a plastic apron, and two, stand back several paces, close enough not to miss, but far enough away not to get splashed with blood. A Lubyanka tradition. But now I was being nostalgic.

And as far as torture not giving a person accurate data, other than any confession, any important facts only need to be verified by torturing your target's associates. And remember it's impossible to get perfect congruency of facts after the target passes out from pain or blood loss. And you can control for excess blood loss. PaPa tried using transfusions or intravenous saline to keep the targets alive, but he said at that point there were diminishing returns. Sodium pentothal didn't always give you accurate information and was reserved for targets that had to be returned to their families. You had to start an intravenous line which could be difficult if your targets are struggling and fighting their restraints. That why PaPa, grandfather, and my father always taught us the classic methods are classic always for good reason.

"About Rose and me? I am flattered that you are taking such a personal interest…"

"Yes…and no Colonel. I know how important Rose is to you. And I feel she is so important to me, our entire investigation, to THE WHITE*HOUSE mission, and the entire national security structure. And that you certainly can tell her – from me and from all of us in the Special Prosecutor's Office. But you really need to proceed a little further – at least before we break for lunch." I can hear his stomach growling from my side of the interrogation table. And every time I look past him to Ms. Defarge, I see the corner of her upper lip turn up revealing one yellow canine in a silent snarl before puffing out some smoke then flicking more ashes on the rug. Now the rug is beginning to burn enough to smoke with an artificial fabric smell. That annoyed Ms. Defarge enough for her to stamp out her embers with her right foot.

"I can go on for hours and hours and hours about Rose. She's the most amazing woman I've ever met. She's the absolute smartest, intelligent, and more decisive than any woman I can think of. She's as decisive as any man. She's far out of my league. ..."

"Please, Colonel, ..."

"Rose was already upset with the traffic on 198 getting to the BW Parkway. You could take the Beltway, but it's further and the traffic is worse. Then the bumper-to-bumper traffic on 295 to US 50 until you get off at Sixth Street. Then you're practically at the Treasury, where they told Rose and me to report. The White House is just across the way, passed Massachusetts Avenue, K street.... I really never like to see Rose upset. And traffic upsets Rose, especially with her stick shift. I don't know how many clutches we put in her car, and now it's hard to find the parts. I know she's going to blame me when this clutch goes. She's going to blame it on me for taking a job I should have known would make her unhappy. And this was the White House she was upset with. Who would think?"

The colonel is a man in love, I don't know why. Very few men would put up with nonsense. "Colonel let's try again to skip ahead. Start with your first day at the White House, in the secret WHITE*HOUSE section of the White House. Precisely what went on at the White House's WHITE*HOUSE. Start with when you arrived."

"It's really the 'Ultra-Secret Section WHITE*HOUSE' of the White House – the USSW*H. That's how we signoff of any of our communications."

"Colonel, it sounds more like a navy warship."

"The inside slang for our section is 'USEWOW' for USS-W*H. Mr. Seplechre, what about lunch?".

"I think we all need a break."

*   *   *   *   *

51

CHAPTER TWO

"Once more unto the breach, dear friends, once more; ...
Stiffen the sinews, summon up the blood, ...
Disguise fair nature with hard-favour'd rage, ..."
[*King Henry in William Shakespeare's Henry V, 1599*]

"Well, Mr. Seplechre, Rose and I pulled up at the guard house at the 1500 Pennsylvania Avenue Entrance of the Treasury Building at 0700 hours exactly, just as General Merriwhether instructed. The Marine guards were about to ask for identification when General Merriwhether just came out of the morning shadows behind the gate's thick black iron bars. Even though it was a clear morning, he was surrounded by a mist that partially hid his face. I told Rose that this was a sign. Rose told me to shut up and never mention that nonsense to anyone ever again. I tell you, when Rose and I first met at NYU, she told me she loved when I waxed poetic. Now the only thing that gets waxed is her faint mustache. Anyway, before we were married, at NYU, ..."

"A very keen observation, Colonel. That tells me you're a man of feelings and deep emotion who will do anything, tell us anything to help his country...help us get to the truth. You can skip your college and just get back to that morning. If you, please." I had to stop him from rambling. But I should probably take a second look at his and Rose's days at NYU. You never can tell. It sounds like the two of them may have been some sort of rebels. NYU is known for that.

"General Merriwhether had to shout over our car's bad muffler, 'You're not to identify yourselves out here. From this moment on, never identify yourselves to anyone.' General Merriwhether nodded to the Marines. One of the Marines returned to the guard house to throw a large black plastic rotating handle attached to a solid brass lever forward to open the motorized gates. It looked like someone took it out of an old elevator. The Marines saluted the general in unison and with a second snappy salute they saluted me. We were waved into the Treasury Department's south courtyard. With Rose driving, I could easily return the salutes. Rose nodded, approving my return salute. That made me feel better.

This was the strangest thing. Neither of the guards asked for my military ID, asked who we were or what we were doing. The General instructed us to park at the right curb side of the driveway, shut the ignition and leave the keys in the car behind the driver's sun visor."

"General Merriwhether, they don't know who we are. How do I know I'm going to get my car back if they don't know who I am." Rose's questions were more threatening than inquisitive." (But General Merriwhether was a combat veteran and was used to incoming fire. Rose may have frightened him, but he didn't show it. Generals never show fear, even in front of a firing squad. You don't get to be a general by showing fear. My problem is, I'm too easy to read my fear of Rose." (I'm glad Rose is not with me when I'm in front of the promotion board. I was glad that during my prior duty assignments she was home. Now (joy of joys) we'll be working together, all day, every day until our mission is complete (or she murders me). I do and I don't wish she were here during my deposition with Mr. Seplechre.) Somehow, I know, whatever I say will be the wrong thing. And no matter how classified this testimony is, no matter how secret, Rose will know exactly what I said. She knows I'm here and I have to say something. So, there's no denying I said what I say and will say. I might as well just tell her as soon I get home.

"'We're going directly to the White House Medical Office.' Keep in mind, we were the only car parked in the courtyard driveway of the Treasury Building. General Merriwhether's big mustached smile made me feel welcome and warm. I felt good until I saw Rose's scowling reaction to the General. I knew just from her heavy sigh – more a growl - Rose wasn't happy about leaving her car keys and her car where someone was going to move it. Having someone else park her car always starts Rose's day the wrong way. And she certainly wasn't happy seeing General Merriwhether. After my last duty station under General Merriwhether, well..."

Buonarotti doesn't know it, but General Merriwhether was always a target of mine since the last investigation. He was the one that got away. Now he's jumped to the top of my new list. "Please go on, Colonel. Now we're on the right track." I know I can bag the Colonel. General Merriwhether is a general. It won't be hard to find the skeletons in his closet and get him indicted. Rose, on the other hand, is another story. She's too smart, too slippery, a woman's woman, and too threatening – I should say dangerous and moves too fast to get off a clean kill shot.

"Thank you, Mr. Seplechre. Anyway, I saluted the General, and after he returned the salute, he said, "This is where the two of you will report every morning. Rose don't worry about your car. It will be as safe here as the three of us in the White House WHITE*HOUSE. Just leave the keys in your car and when you're ready to leave, you'll find your car in that same spot in the evening. They'll know when you're leaving and when you will arrive back here. In bad weather, a Marine lance corporal will meet you with an umbrella and slicker. We will even fill it with gas from our motor pool just to save you the time and energy. No need to call ahead. We want nothing diverting your attention from your primary mission."" Then General Merriwhether told Rose, "Only your keys will be returned to you after you pay your parking fee to the parking attendant." Rose couldn't believe her ears, that we were going to be charged for parking. Then the General explained, "The entire White House staff has to pay for parking out of pocket, and that includes the President, Vice President, and even the Secret Service. Everyone pays for parking."

"Colonel, and what was that mission?"

"Rose was seething. That's when Rose told me, and not so quietly, she was driving us to work tomorrow in my car."

"I know, Colonel. Rose loves her car. She loves to drive the stick shift. She loves the feel of the road through the mechanical unassisted rack and pinion steering. I also know her father gave it to her on her twenty-first birthday, and that was a long time ago."

"Mr. Seplechre, I really wouldn't mention anything like that. Ever again!"

"Colonel, this is all classified. She'll never hear the recordings or see the transcript."

"Mr. Seplechre, Rose is all knowing. Once you utter the words, it will get back to her."

"What a coincidence. When I was on the phone with Rose from the PX doing the shopping, those were her exact words." We were listening in on his cell phone and his home phone. Those were Rose's almost exact words – that she is all knowing. And the Colonel is not even suspicious. This just gets better and better. But I have to redirect his focus otherwise it will be cars and Rose, NYU and Rose, Rose's instructions for shopping... "Colonel, let's get back to your mission. Please go on from that point."

"To provide vital intelligence for the President, Cabinet, the Pentagon and..."

I'll need to rephrase my question. I can't have him reverting to rehearsed answers. "I get that, Colonel. Let's go back to the White House's WHITE*HOUSE. You need to paint a picture, a complete picture of what you and Rose were doing." Whenever I interrupt the Colonel, he gets sidetracked. He was about to recite the Army Intelligence Corps mission statement.

He had to be refocused, again. I am slowly beginning to understand why Rose treats him the way she does. Just as an aside, he'll probably be promoted to full bird colonel, especially with a friend like General Merriwhether and Rose as his wife.

But he's far too frightened of Rose to be promoted to general. I guess, if the promotion board is as frightened of Rose half as much as Buonarotti is, they might just approve his appointment as a general officer. For the record, I'm not frightened of Rose, I just know to treat her with due caution and diligence. Like a circus lion tamer with a pistol, whip, and chair.

"General Merriwhether made us welcome and began by explaining some of the amenities and perks we were going to enjoy at the White House's WHITE*HOUSE. He said if we let the motor pool know the night before or even the next morning, weekday or weekend, we can change your oil and replace any worn or all of your tires and balance them, of course. Leave a note with what maintenance you want performed with the keys behind the visor. 'We will do it for any car you drive here. If you get stuck on the road, we will come and tow you back to the Treasury Building and provide you a loaner until we repair your vehicle. That is, as long as you pay for the parking. And by the way, when we say 'tow' we mean we will put your little sports car on a flatbed to prevent any in transit damage or wear on your tires or the rear differential. And we know it's a vintage vehicle. Any essential parts that can't be repaired and must be replaced, the CIA's Vintage Vehicle Repair Directorate, the VVRD, will find the part, if they have to steal a car like yours and then strip the part to make your repairs. And with your permission, if you leave your car overnight and use our loaner, we will repair all of the body work that it needs, including repainting, with a minimal overnight parking fee. You'll need to leave it here for two days after we paint it for free, except for the parking.'"

And this is all at government expense. That's why I don't feel the least guilty about running my Special Prosecutors

Office the way I do. In fact, the entire Federal Government is like this – completely without guilt about spending money on themselves. I asked some of my congressional friends (and don't say it, nobody in Congress is anybody's friend, and Special Prosecutors' only friends are friends that he can use and then betray), we don't use tax money, we just print it. "Colonel, I think I'll bring my car in for service. Just as an aside, General Merriwhether seemed to spend a lot of time on amenities? These are very important, but more to the central purpose and operation of the WHITE*HOUSE."

"Mr. Seplechre, you mean the White House's WHITE* HOUSE."

"Colonel, is there another WHITE*HOUSE not at the White House."

"Mr. Seplechre, you are referring to 1600 Pennsylvania Avenue?"

"You know what I mean, Colonel. Now, go on. Just forget what I just said. Just go on where you left off." Ha ha! Buonarotti let it slip. There's another WHITE*HOUSE other than the one below the White House at 1600 Pennsylvania Avenue. I have to make a note to track everyone in and out of the Treasury Building. I'll find it, no matter what.

"Mr. Seplechre, as much as this has to do with amenities, it's all central to the security operation. General Merriwhether went on to say, 'There'll be tracking devices that we use that will locate you. Just call our toll-free emergency hot line (1-800-TOPSECRET, Extension WHITE*HOUSE). And we were instructed not to use our cell phones. We're to find a pay phone, and never use the same pay phone twice. Then just ask for the motor pool master sergeant, Sgt. Bilko. He, like everyone else here, is available around the clock, seven days a week. Just one of the White House's WHITE*HOUSE perks. We want you to love us, love the organization, and we want both of you to love your jobs. And most importantly, we want your loyalty.

Except for parking, we take care of everything."

PaPa was like that, too. No one who was disloyal, suspected of being disloyal or was unenthusiastic about the NKVD survived to retirement. The NKVD really didn't have much of a pension obligation.

"General Merriwhether emphasized – 'And we'll do anything and everything to accomplish that sub-mission always for the sake of our primary mission. This is our sacred responsibility to the nation, for the Pentagon, and the President for our principal purpose.'"

"Colonel, try to make the connection for me. What kind of role did Rose play in all this?"

"Rose explained to the general, 'My car easily floods when you go to start it cold. They need to be careful.' Rose paused, but not long enough for General Merriwhether to say anything. "See if the motor pool can do something about that. The carburetor float sticks...'"

"I'll make a note of that and leave it with your car. I'm sure it will be attended to before you go home this evening." Nothing phased General Merriwhether, including getting an old car fixed. I was going to have my father drive down from New York, with my mother for the weekend and fix her car, but we couldn't find parts anywhere in the Washington DC vicinity. The General knew that fixing Rose's beloved car would make Rose happy and make my life and his worth living again. Mr. Seplechre, there's no finer a man, maybe except my father and Rose's father, than General Merriwhether. And that includes George Washington, Abraham Lincoln and Donald Trump!"

I think I would rather Buonarotti go on and on about Rose than talk politics. And he certainly knows the wrong thing to say. I've spent years investigating the evil Trump. And there are valued members of my staff whose direct descendants investigated Washington, all of the founding fathers, and everyone else on Mount Rushmore and probably any politician who has a statue, monument, or plaque in Washington. Now there's a motto worth coining – 'Show me a man with a statue, monument or plaque, and I'll show you a guilty felon who died before conviction.' It has a nice ring to it. 'They'll never be prosecuted because they're dead.' That's something my great grandmother passed down to my grandmother who told my mother. 'If they're dead, they're not worth hunting down and punishing.' My mother told me that when she told me fairy tales about wicked witches pushed into ovens, evil goblins, and other bedtime stories.

The more time I spend with the Colonel, the more I understand Rose. I would almost feel sorry for her, except she's such a bitch.

In this town, investigating politicians is as much a cottage industry as politics, lobbying, law, and professional bag men. We all know about gangsters, organized crime, the RICO act. But politics is truly 'better organized crime.' And the last presidential election proves that.

Buonarotti has no sense of Washington realty or history. The Special Prosecutors go further back than 'The Birth of a Nation'. DW Griffith's got his movie title from the special prosecutors who investigated all the founding fathers. That's what they titled their very first Congressional Special Prosecutors report to the Continental Congress, 'Corruption and Interference by the Deep State into the Founding of the United States of America – The Real Birth of the Nation'. And yes, the deep state dates back to when Columbus discovered the New World.

In the Bible, God was his own Special Prosecutor for anyone who crossed him. I think of myself in that way. 'In the beginning…Let there be light…' A story as old as Adam, Eve, the apple, and the serpent. And remember, the serpent won that round.

I bring plague, pestilence and could take your first born

if need be. It's just that I'm limited to just putting them in prison. Of course, if I leak that they are cooperating with my office, then that's the Special Prosecutors equivalent of 'smiting the sinners'.

The signers of the Declaration of Independence were worried about being hung by the British. What they really had to worry about was being jailed by their own government for being on a list they signed with their own hands with other subversives. The Declaration of Independence gave the infant nation's first special prosecutors (one each or everyone who signed) their very first, their inaugural list of targets. All the founding fathers were known to the Founding Special Prosecutors as 'The First People of Interest'. In colonial times, those Special Prosecutors wore black hoods. Now we all wear the three-piece pin-striped double-breasted suits always with a handkerchief that matches our bow ties and suspenders. The handkerchief folded as a double triangle in our breast pocket. And every special prosecutor carries two blank signed Federal subpoenas, one in each inside jacket pocket he can personally serve as the need arises. The single sheets of paper don't spoil their suits lines. You have the extra subpoena when your target defiantly rips up the first one you hand him.

Somehow when you can look directly into the eyes of your victim when you serve your subpoena, it's as close to an orgasm a lawyer can get without having sex. Of course, most special prosecutors have been offered sex as a bribe when they serve the subpoena. All of them have sex with their subject, then serve the subpoena. If the sex was really good, they leave without serving the subpoena themselves and just have the process server do the job the next day. The rest serve the subpoena after they put their pants on. But the subpoenas are always served no matter what.

"Colonel, we'll get back to General Merriwhether later. Now, why was Rose upset about leaving her car? It's an old car, and I'm sure it has some sentimental value, but it is an old used Mercedes with over 160,00 miles, not particularly rare or valuable." We searched the car while it was parked at the Treasury Building. When we took it out of its parking space and returned it, we were charged a double-parking fee. The door panels were removed and put back without a mark. We know it needs brakes, a new muffler, clutch plate, floor mats, new upholstery, a new driver's seat mechanism, the driver's side window crank replaced, and the rusted dings in the right fender filled in and repainted. It's so old, it still had heavy metal chrome-steel bumpers and bodywork. It still has a vacuum tube radio that makes noise but can't receive any radio stations. At the time we checked, there was 168,715.6 miles on the odometer.

"Rose has a thing about cars and especially strangers driving her cars. They change the mirrors, the seat distance, the radio presets. Everything in the old car is manual. All the mirrors are wobbly, and the driver's seat ratchet already had broken teeth on one side so it would always sit crooked to the left no matter how many times you tried to get it straight. The clutch and brake pedals were bare metal where the rubber foot pad was once attached. The driver's side window wouldn't roll down. If you rolled it down, to roll it up, you would have to remove the entire inside door panel. And if anyone smoked in her car, especially if they left ashes in her ashtray, she would track them down and...

Well, I've seen Rose in one of those fits after she found I was driving her car. You can never get the mirrors back to where Rose wanted them. And you would never dare touch the right outside rear-view mirror. Even if it didn't wobble and have a worn ball joint that couldn't be tightened, it takes two people to get that right. And it's never right enough for Rose.

Rose finally never drives her car anywhere where there is only valet parking. If we were going somewhere where we can't self-park or find street parking, we would turn around and go home to get my car or just stay home and make excuses later.

We were forever looking for street parking. And you don't know how difficult it is to parallel park without power steering and a manual transmission – especially on a hill. Otherwise, if we knew there was no street parking – embassy events, special affairs at exclusive venues – you know what I mean - we took my car. And she still drove." Apparently, Buonarotti not only become animated – enthused – talking about Rose, but also Rose's car.

I don't know how many times he's going to repeat himself. "Let's get back to the General at the Treasury Building. Details, Colonel. Details about that. If Rose's car comes up, just talk about it in relation to the mission." I have to encourage him, making him believe I am hanging on his every word.

"The General led us passed the parking attendant's booth to the Treasury Building's bank of four ground floor freight elevators that stood hidden around a corner away from the main passenger elevators. To the right of each elevator was its own up and down black plastic call buttons in old ornate polished brass frames. The left most elevator, the elevator marked "4 FRIEGHT". It was wider than the others. Its doors were triple wide vertical opening with rusted steel where the battleship grey paint had scraped or peeled away in long strips where the guide wheels met the metal doors above and below the elevator's framing. The General pressed that elevator's down call button that signaled the elevator doors to open revealing a brass scissors gate. There was also a brass rotary manual levers and folding jump seats below the call button lights, both front and back.   The General opened the scissors gate, stepped in first, waited for us to enter, then closed the loose-fitting gate. He moved toward the farthest end of the elevator where another scissors gate and set of rusting vertical doors stood shut. There were no monitoring cameras, visible microphones, motion detectors, antennae, or modern lighting. Only an old fashioned large base bare clear light bulb in a cage in the center of the elevator ceiling. He checked that we were behind him and asked me to close the scissors gate. He then pressed the B button four times before the vertical doors behind us slammed shut like a guillotine.

General Merriwhether pushed the large, polished brass lever forward, partially instructing the elevator to slowly descend. (This was the exact duplicate of the lever at the front gate of the Treasury Building.) We watched the floors pass by through the cage-like brass gate. We passed three levels each of the vertical doors marked 'B-1', 'B-2' and 'B-3' with the black lettering split exactly in half in the center between the upper and lower doors. We approached the fourth set of doors marked with the same block lettering except in red 'B-4'. General Merriwhether abruptly stopped the elevator. The elevator car vibrated and made a dull thud sound. The elevator failed to level with the floor. The General pulled the lever toward him, then pushed it away trying to level the elevator with the entrance floor. On the third try, he was close enough to open the elevator scissors gate, then push the two outer doors apart far enough for their motor to take over and complete the outer doors' opening process. The rear floor doors opened with what seemed to be much less effort and no noise.

The doors in front of them were the problem. There was a creaking muffled high-pitched screams of steel on rusting steel obviously needing lubrication. Behind us was a pitch-black passageway. In front, after a couple of seconds, open bulb single tube fluorescent ceiling lights in industrial wire cages flickered on. The only piping seen anyplace was the single power feed going from light fixture to light fixture.

General Merriwhether opened the scissors gate. He was genuinely embarrassed for the elevator and I guess for the poor lighting in the tunnel. "Just needs some grease. And this is the newer of the elevators. We're just beginning to use this entrance to the White House. The tunnel takes us directly below the East Wing – its' sub sub sub-basement. Just follow me.""

"This is remarkably interesting, Colonel. Is this 'USE-WOW' proper? I didn't even know these tunnels existed." I knew about the old tunnel from the White House to the Treasury, but I didn't expect it to be so extensive or as deep as it appears to be. I have to get my staff on the inside to document all this. If I look close enough, I can probably identify some crime connected to these tunnels. Every edifice, every monument, every road, bridge, overpass, underpass, or full deep tunnel in Washington DC is, was or continues to be a criminal enterprise – even the street signs. I can and attack someone's legacy and even their estates and their beneficiaries. I think to myself, 'So many prosecutions so little time.'

"The tunnels aren't really secret. The Treasury Tunnel dates from 1941. It's just nobody uses them."

The Colonel states the obvious. That's in every Washington DC tourist guide. "Colonel, you teach me something new every day. Now, please go on."

"General Merriwhether has a knack for finding unexpected uses for otherwise ignored infrastructure."

(Yea, that's original. There's a tunnel between the White House and the Treasury Building you use to go back and forth between the White House and the Treasury Building. Genius. And nobody knows who's entering and exiting the White House and not just the Treasury Building. Except there's cameras everywhere so you know who enters the Treasury and who turns down the freight elevator corridor. I'll tell Ms. Defarge to have someone send for the surveillance tapes. And that's another thing that upsets me. There are so many closed-circuit television cameras, just gathering the recordings from DC takes a full-time staff. Even with facial recognition, you can't process all the information. I think of all the people we could be watching and prosecuting but for lack of manpower. 'Show me a man, and I'll show you a crime.' It's really an unattainable goal. PaPa, I say a prayer to you every night, and no matter where you are, and I know it's somewhere special, up, or down, please help me not be overwhelmed.

"After you've worked with him, you're not surprised by anything he does. You are amazed at his ingenuity and original thinking. There are two additional emergency escape and utility tunnels from the White House that lead to the surface. They were built specifically for USEWOW access. One tunnel travels south and surfaces inside the sub subbasement of the Langley CIA Headquarters' main building and the other travels north to the third level subbasement of the NSA main building at Fort Meade. The tunnels go below the Potomac, zigzag four times each. Both tunnels have a double track small narrow gauge third-rail electric railroad with multiple interconnecting manual switching points without any blind sidings, and a two parallel walkways on either side of the tracks wide enough for two golf carts. Each tunnel is complete with vertical venting and escape shafts at every change in direction. All escape shafts are fitted with ladders, and manual and electric winches. There is an extensive ventilation system, closed circuit tv monitoring, hard-wired emergency telephone boxes and internet and cell phone reception throughout. Very impressive engineering, and no one ever detected it was being built. Power and communication hard wiring are carried on the walls of the tunnels in lead-shielded pipes exclusively to this subterranean section...."

Something else I'm sure I can investigate find criminal activity. Anything that involves a Federal contract for building something is a criminal enterprise. Some would say 'until proven otherwise.' But I can always prove it, even if I have to invent evidence. I can call it 'Tunnelgate'. "Colonel, why the lead shielding?" I have to look interested and I need this on the record. That's why I asked him. It has nothing to do with this investigation. He volunteered it without coercion or even a question from me. I have to remember what Bill Casey said when the Colonel's thoughts begin to wander, that eventually, given the opportunity, people will tell you more of what they shouldn't say. This type of detail means something, though he should have never revealed. It will look great when I present it to a jury. The prosecution will be difficult. I'll have to make him look like a criminal mastermind, an evil genius. Making Colonel Buonarroti look smart will be the challenge.

He is so assuredly on his way to prison; he doesn't even need a trial. At the end of this interview, I'll have Ms. Defarge give him orange jump suit. – Don't laugh. I'm not kidding. The targets are handed the jump suit marked 'PRISON' in black letters. Whether guilty or innocent of the crime we are accusing them of, some will immediately start talking plea bargain even without their lawyers. With everybody being guilty of something, especially in Washington, the prison jumpsuit gambit works enough times to give it a shot.

"Mr. Seplechre, the lead protects against any EMP, especially from a nuclear blast. That's obvious."

"Colonel, thank you for explaining that. I had no idea this was part of our nuclear preparedness." As much as I hate when anyone treats me like I'm stupid, I just tolerate it because I know they're only digging their own graves. As soon as anyone mentions 'nuclear' it all becomes pure prosecutorial gold. The first thing you learn is everything that is nuclear or related to nuclear weapons is 'born' top secret'. And there are a whole set of prosecutions that are now on the table. "Colonel, keep going, you're on a roll."

"Thank you, Mr. Seplechre. Well, there are no electrical or communication connections going up to the White House proper. And no wireless communications anywhere in the USEWOW complex or tunnels. And all of USEWOW including all the tunnels are wrapped in one giant Faraday cage. No communications can leak out. Messages can only be sent or received by Fort Meade and the Langley CIA headquarters through shielded hard wiring. Any communication to the actual White House must go through both Langley and Fort Meade special message sections for this operation.

Messages received from the two military posts are compared at the White House USEWOW office in the West Wing. (General Merriwhether made sure that office had windows looking out at the Rose Garden.) Two copies of the messages are printed on railroad teletype machines linked to teletypes in Fort Meade and Langley. There are two specialist with the highest security clearances who receive the printed copies. They exchange copies. One of the specialist reads a copy to the other. They exchange messages a second time. This time the other specialist reads the message to the first. If the messages are verified genuine and identical, then they are passed only to the White House chief of staff and the President. USEWOW never communicates directly with anyone. And all this is classified at the highest level. It's TOP SECRET COMPARTMENTALIZED – EYES ONLY FOR POTUS!"

"And you have no qualms about talking to me?" And I know what his answer will be.

"Rose told me to cooperate completely. I wasn't to hesitate about telling the whole story – the whole truth." (For Buonarotti, only Rose has a higher security clearance than the President of the United States. Rose knew something wasn't right and she didn't want her husband between a general and a special prosecutor, or a government special anything.)

Buonarotti was calm because he knew he was following Rose's instructions to the letter.   "This morning, Rose told me just to tell the truth, and I would be alright." (I can't remember her ever telling me I'd be alright. I don't know whether or not to be frightened or happy. But there it is, after all these years of marriage, she finally has faith in me. What a good feeling. I felt good saying those words to Mr. Seplechre and have them put into the permanent record.)

The Colonel is an innocent lamb being led to the slaughter – just like in the Old Testament. We have to keep him that way. I need to preemptively deflect his suspicions. "I have to say, no one is usually greeted at the White House by a general. To be treated like that on your first duty day. You and your wife must be incredibly special. Everyone assigned to the White House is considered VIP, but the two of you must be among the aerified elite. You can't imagine how impressed I am."

I got Buonarotti to smile. I know he can't wait to tell Rose what I said. He and Rose are among the 'aerified elite'. How wrong she was about him taking this assignment. He needs to prove Rose wrong without rubbing her nose in it. (He knows that if he tried, she would break his nose first, then both his arms and legs.) What he doesn't know is that Rose was right all along. This assignment is going to end his military career and put both Buonarotti and Rose in federal prison. It just goes to show you men never learn to heed their wives' instincts.

"Rose will be pleased to hear that." Buonarotti is smiling like the Cheshire cat.

No, she won't. It's telling Rose she was wrong about her husband taking this job without her permission. After all the years he's been married, he hasn't learned anything. Maybe that part of his mind is marriage-learning disabled? "Remember Colonel, you can't repeat a word I'm saying. It's all classified. And you can't tell Rose I said it was classified, because what I say to you is classified. But I am impressed." I'm sure this will be the first thing he tells Rose and then he'll repeat my words to her over and over. He'll want Rose to know how special I think the two of them are, and how I trust him with such highly classified information.

"Were you taken to the medical office for an intake physical examination? I'm sure you've had your annual officer's physical, so I question why this was necessary. Did Rose need a physical?"

"Mr. Seplechre, it's not what you think. General Merriwhether led us out of the elevator. We turned right at the first intersecting corridor which ended abruptly with a green door marked 'White House Military Office – White House Medical Unit – *WHMU USSW*H:* Security and Identification Section. General Merriwhether knocked twice then once again, opened the door, and was greeted with a snappy salute by a young very fit and blonde full figured busty comely female Marine captain. Her class A uniform barely hid her figure with her narrow waste, generous caboose, and muscular calves. Her uniform jacket had to be at least one size larger than her skirt to accommodate her – large upper frame. As soon as she stood, you could see her M1A1 Colt .45 in her snap-covered brown leather field holster low on her ample right hip." (You know Rose is not bad looking, either. Look at Rose. I can tell the Colonel likes women with meat on their bones. And probably so does General Merriwhether. So, does everyone in the military. Not like lawyers, who like their women to have no curves like skinny flat-chested adolescent boys. Lawyers think they should have sexless fashion models on their arms – trophies to show off without any other obvious purpose.)

This too is unusual. You'd expect an Army or Navy nurse, not an obviously combat trained Marine captain. I'm sure this woman was personally chosen by General Merriwhether. "Colonel, I could tell you we're extremely impressed by the captain." I'll bet the old man was impressed, too.

"General Merriwhether hand-picks all the personnel for all parts of his command. He waited for me to return her salute before he returned her salute. The general formerly addressed her as Captain Rogers.

As she stepped from behind her desk you could see she was wearing black patten leather pointed toe stiletto heels and seemed stockings. She swayed back to one of three doors at the back of the reception area, waved us into the examination room and told us to make ourselves comfortable. There was a single examination table with a large operating room style examination light. Electronic instruments with what looked like scanners were attached to two walls. A large computer screen with a keyboard was on the grey laminate counter. The overhead cabinets with clear glass doors were filled wrapped disposable needles, syringes, sterile gauze, rubbing alcohol, Betadine skin disinfectant, and spray bottles of topical anesthetic. At the right of the door were two floor standing glass cabinets. One was filled with sterile-wrapped surgical instruments and the other vials and bottles of medications. Beside them was an old double x-ray light box. A red and wall-mounted rotary-dial telephones were to the left of the door. Against the back wall were six tall lockers. The General had us sit side by side on the examination table facing that wall."

"Colonel Buonarotti, is this medical office part of USEWOW?"

"No, Mr. Seplechre. You can't get into USEWOW until your 'chipped' – just like your pet dog."

"General Merriwhether kept smiling. He said, "Archy, Rose, take off all your cloths including your underwear and put on these scrub suits." And there was no screen to step behind.""

"I gather this wasn't for a physical?" General Merriwhether is a strange person. And so is Archy. But let's see where this goes. "Colonel Buonarotti, you don't need to pause between thoughts. This is all being recorded for posterity." I forced a smile to warm him back up.

"I'm sorry, Mr. Seplechre. I was just gathering my thoughts to try the get the correct sequence of events in the correct order correctly – for the record – for the recording.

Let me tell you exactly how General Merriwhether explained our accommodations. What General Merriwhether said was "I'll step outside while you change. Put your clothes, keys, wallets, pocketbook, everything in the two lockers in the corner. Lock the door and take the keys with you. You'll need them at the end of the day to change into before you go home. We'll be taking those lockers to your assigned USEWOW offices and wardrobe changing rooms. You can even use these rooms, day, or night, if you want to stay on premises without going home. There's a shower, minibar, wakeup, television with all the premium cable tv stations, and maid service. You'll each be assigned another adjoining room for all your uniforms, any necessary costumes and anything else you need for the mission. There will be a hamper for your laundry and a cloths rack for your dry cleaning. These will be collected every morning at 0700, and 1700 hours, seven days per week and returned the next morning and that evening at the same time your soiled clothing is collected. You can even bring any laundry and dry cleaning from home if you wish.   You'll have everything you'll need, at least until the end of this fiscal year. I'm still working on the budget for next year that I can advance for this year. There have been some unexpected expenses for the operation that will require an increase in funding and/or cutting back on some of the personal amenities. But that's a story for another day. Under any circumstances, though, the Federal Government won't reimburse anyone for parking."

I could see Ms. DeFarge, smiling and shaking her head. She took the cigarette butt from her mouth, took another cigarette from her pack, put it in her mouth and lit it from her glowing cigarette butt. Then she flicked the butt to the rug before she resumed taking dictation on her stenograph.

"I remember the General's exact words. He said, 'Archy, once you get your feet wet, you can help me with all that. As always, you'll be my right-hand man – officially my executive officer.' Being a general's executive officer is a big deal.

Mr. Seplechre, General Merriwhether walked over to Rose and patted her on the shoulder. She doesn't like it when men are condescending, but he was a general and she knew she shouldn't say anything. She flinched, just a little. But she learned being brought up an 'Army brat' and being an Army wife, these things had to be expected. Her lip turned up in the corner, but she still said nothing to offend the general. "Rose, soon if all goes well, you'll be the loving wife of a full bird colonel. Won't that be grand." Rose tried so hard to smile. I don't completely understand it when someone gives you good news, ...You know how modern women are about those things." Buonarotti could only shrug. I didn't really understand it either. I sympathetically shrugged.

At that point, looking totally disgusted, Ms. Defarge said. "Yes, tell us how 'modern women' are and how you think they should be. You and Merriwhether are both pigs. Seplechre, you're the biggest pig of all."

Of course, Buonarotti was right about modern women and Ms. Defarge was right about Buonarotti and Merriwhether. I'm on their side in this one, but I'm not really a pig. I just know how women really are. I know in the old Soviet Union, women were soldiers, fighter pilots, effective cold-blooded ruthless assassins for the NKVD, KGB, FSB, SVR, FSO, and the GRU and front-line soldiers in the 'Great Patriotic War. The beautiful women, or at least women whose looks were within an acceptable range, were set aside to be trained as spies and/or 'morale builders' for the more senior officers. But they were never in charge of anything. They weren't even in charge of other women. And that's the way it was in the Stasi, and in today's Guongu. No one ever talked to them or about them, and they were rarely executed at Lubyanka – just not important enough - unless they were married to the wrong person. And those women were executed even if they turned in their husbands. It was in the Soviet state's official marriage vows right after 'till death do us part.' It was the 'execution as a couple' clause printed right on the marriage certificate – and not even printed in small letters.

"Well, Mr. Seplechre. We were both in our green scrub suits when the White House WHITE*HOUSE doctor came in. He was a full bird colonel without a smile, frown, smirk – nothing, not even disgust. His Colt .45 M1A1on his hip bulged under his white coat. He explained who he was – a West Point graduate and a graduate of the F. Edward Herbert School of Medicine of the Uniform Services University, subspecialist in his subspecialty who had an MD, two PhDs, and an MBA from Wharton. He had trained for sixteen years in Medicine alone and had authored seventy-six original research papers, co-edited two textbooks in his sub subspecialty, served in combat multiple times, was wounded when a grenade exploded outside his aid station, he was awarded the Purple Heart, and served three unaccompanied tours after that. As a reward for a career, he sacrificed everything for, he was divorced twice and was broke. He was excited to meet some rich divorcee or widow in White House circles and get out of debt. Then he ended up down here. And this is so secret, he's not allowed to show his face in the White House proper. And what put's the cherry on top of everything, he has to pay for parking.

He told us he has been waiting for years to receive his orders promoting him to brigadier general and a major hospital command – in fact, any hospital command anywhere. Now this was his only assignment – his only mission – his only task – to 'chip' everyone who becomes part of USEWOW. He emphasized that he wasn't a vet – a veterinarian, even though he chipped pets as a favor to the staff with the USEWOW location chips. Anybody at USEWOW who lost their cat or dog, would call the White House WHITE*HOUSE, and they did. Either the CIA, Army Intelligence or the FBI was sent out to find the lost animal. And it was easy because the USEWOW chips were better than anything you could get at PETSMART, PetCo or from your own veterinarian. Our doctor's security clearance was just below that of the President. That's why he had to chip himself because no one else had the security clearance to handle and place the chips. That meant all the dogs and cats he chipped had the same security top Presidential clearance. He told us, 'Every woof and meow was classified. It was a violation to pet your dog or cat after they voiced anything.' Mr. Seple-chre, I can't emphasize how hush hush this all was."

The doctor explained how he was injecting two microchips for tracking and two microchips for identification for each of us. Everything was redundant to guarantee there would be no mission failure on his section's part. The tracking chips were in the back of our necks and on our chests between our clavicles. The identification chips were on the palmer surface of both our wrists. They wanted him to put the tracking chip at the top of our skulls, but that would have been itchy, uncomfortable, and would have excessively bled.

The doctor told us General Merriwhether would explain everything to us in a moment. The doctor swabbed our wrists and the back of our necks and a small area just below the sternal notch with betadine, sprayed them with something to numb any sensation and quickly injected the microscopic chips at each site. All the time he kept muttering curses with his resume - something about sixteen years of training, seventy-six research papers, and a lifetime of front-line clinical experience, multiple combat assignments, all leading to this moment. Before we could exchange any pleasantries, he was out the door still muttering to himself. The last thing I heard him say was, 'And after all that, she left me, and I still have to pay for my own parking!' The door slammed closed, then opened immediately for General Merriwhether.

General Merriwhether had a big smile for me, but knew he had to get serious and first directly address Rose. "Rose, let me explain. This was all your father's innovations. His company sold us the entire chip location and identification system. You won't need a security pass for any part of the White House including our special section. You now have an all-access proximity detecting pass for the entire complex in your wrists. And I just found out this will get you through any E-Z Pass and automated bridge, tunnel, and highway tolls anywhere, and the tolls are charged to the government. I haven't had the chance, but I can't wait to try it out at COSCOs self-checkout.""

"Mr. Seplechre, between you and me, Rose was not happy about this whole thing, and after we got home, I was in for it. General Merriwhether escorted us out of the medical examination rooms to the special elevators to take us down below to a lower level below the East Wing of the White House. He pressed the down brass call button. In moments, the two polished brass eight-foot-high doors, each with 'Otis' cast in raised letters at eye level across their width opened without a sound. Inside was a very old man in a grey uniform with a red strip down the outside center of his pant legs, a jacket with single red strips around the lower sleeves of his grey uniform jacket, and six tightly closed polished brass buttons on the front. His grey-billed uniform hat had a single thin-red chin strap. He stood from his little stool by the left wall of the elevator car and slid open the brass scissors gate.

'Down.' He had a gravel voice. His standing and announcing the elevators direction caused him to wheeze and become short of breath. General Merriwhether mentioned he's been operating the same elevator since Nixon took office. He's waiting to retire, but Watergate intervened and with some of the evidence against Nixon, his original employment records were 'lost'. Apparently, they've been looking for them since Bush the father was president.

General Merriwhether let Rose and I enter first. As soon as we stepped back inside the elevator car and turned facing the door, our elevator operator slid the gate closed, sat, and pushed his large brass rotating lever forward, first partially to give the elevator a smooth start then fully forward so it could gain speed descending. Judging by seeing the unmarked floors flash by through the scissors gate, the elevator was fast but took us at least ninety seconds to reach our destination.

As the elevator door opened, we were met by another older but more spry man in a similar uniform as the elevator operator except he had two red strips around his jacket
sleeves and a gold braided rope looped under his arm and
through his right epaulet. "Welcome to the Thomas Joseph 'TJ'
Pendergast memorial elevator.'

General Merriwhether greeted him. "Jonas, how
are you today." General Merriwhether turned to me and Rose.
"This is Jonas our elevator starter. This elevator was built during Harry Truman's White House Renovation. Jonas's grandfather was the elevator bank's first starter, followed by his
father, and of course, now Jonas. The family is an American – a
White House tradition. This will be the only time I'll mention
his name. Jonas is our elevator starter and Ira is our elevator
operator. There are others on different shifts, but you'll never
hear or utter their names. By the time you have occasion to
meet them, your chips will be activated, and after that, no
names may be spoken – not anyone's name and not ever. This is
the only time I will say their names. Ira, say hello."

Ira smiled at us, said, "Up." He shut the brass
doors, then we heard the scissors gate rattling closely followed
by a jerking sound then the hum of the ascending elevator.

General Merriwhether led us down a dark corridor lit only by low wattage clear incandescent bulbs inside
small steel cages. We all turned a corner and walked a few
paces to a plain grey sheet metal government-issued desk that
sat in front of a counterweighted sliding concrete fire/blast
door hung from rollers on an inclined steel track above the
opening. On the desk was two flat screen monitors. Behind
the desk was a middle-aged woman with short but stylishly
coiffured grey hair, heavy but strongly built in a man's suit,
plain white shirt, and red-plaid bow tie. Her chair looked uncomfortable, she looked uncomfortable, and she made all of us
uncomfortable.

"Rose, Archy, this is Ms. Haversham. Ms. Haversham, this is Lt. Col and Mrs. Buonarotti. Mrs. Haversham monitors all the video feed inside USEWOW, the Treasury feeds, and all the tunnel feeds. All the feeds are hardwired because all of USEWOW and all the tunnels are shielded from any electronic or microwave transmission. They are shielded from any electromagnetic pulse from any source including a nuclear explosion.

Mrs. Haversham is very important. And this will be the only time we will exchanges names. Once she activates your chips, no one is to address any one of the staff at USEWOW by name.

I automatically saluted and stated who I was, and I was reporting for duty with Mrs. Buonarotti. A moment passed before she looked up. She said, "I am the concierge. You don't report to me. You don't need to salute me. I'm just here. Remember, from now on, no names. No names ever. If we cross paths on the outside, on or off duty, no matter what we have to communicate to each other, no names. And remember, I'm always watching you and watching everybody.

When you arrive at your appointed time, I will be here except when I'm not here and someone else is here. I will read your identification chip, activate it for your day's activities. Wave your right or left hand anywhere in front of either the door on the right or the door on the left, depending on which hand you waved. All rooms are sealed shut, airtight, soundproof, and shielded from any radio, microwave, or cell phone transmission. You will be able to enter or exit rooms you are cleared to enter or exit with your handprint combined with your identification chip. Our security system requires both forms of identification to open the security-sealed doors. Here, only one of the doors will unlock. You will distinctly hear which the door to use. Which door is hard to say? It may or may not be the same door each time. Then turn the knob either to the right or the left, whichever way the knob will allow. Just push the door away from you and go through the door to my left or my right, behind my desk. Each door will bring you to one of your tasks for the day. And the tasks will be different for the doorway on the right from the tasks for the doorway on the left. This is for security reasons, so no one is sure what you are doing, and neither are you. You complete your task, then go on to the next one until all are completed. The tasks behind the two doors the next day will be a different set of tasks from each other and different from the tasks behind either door the day before, but completely dependent on what you did the day before. But the choice of doorway is yours each and every day.

You will have entered USEWOW. The door must close before we can read your wife's microchip. Then she just waves her left or right hand, but not the same hand you used. The door unlocks and she follows you through. But the door pulls open. She must pull it - just the opposite of what you did. Any errors, all your microchips will be erased. Then the whole process has to start all over again. Commit these instructions to memory. They will not be repeated. And these instructions only apply to the two of you. Each person, couples or related groups all have different protocols. This will be your protocol until it isn't, or we cancel it for a mistake on your part or on our part. Is that clear?" She paused but didn't wait for an answer. "Don't answer, there is no right answer. There's never a 'right' answer at USEWOW."

The concierge stood, came from behind the desk and starred at us for at least ten seconds. To the right of her desk was a coin operated rotary telephone in a brown booth with two half-glass folding doors. "Sit inside. Put a dime in the coin slot. If you don't have a dime, I can make change. But you're better off bringing your own dime. Two nickels will also work. Put the dime in the slot. Wait for the dial tone. Dial your telephone number, your home telephone number of record. Wait for the recording. It will give you a code. Write the code down then hang up. Pick up the receiver, put another dime in – by the way, make sure you bring plenty of change when you report for duty. – dial the code and wait for the recording to tell you to hang up. It may say something else before it tells you to hang up. Just ignore everything except the hang up order. Once you hang up, wait for the lights in the phone booth to blink before you open the doors. It is especially important to wait for the phone booth light to blink. If you don't wait, your chips will be erased, and we will have to start all over again.

Once the light in the phone booth blinks once, and it will only blink once, then you may stand, open the door, and exit the booth. Walk toward the USEWOW entry.

"Where do we go, once we're on the other side?"

"Colonel, Mrs. Buonarotti, please bring plenty of nickels dimes. We use the rotary dial telephone booths through-out USEWOW for encoding messages and instructions for our agents."

"And once we go through the door, do we wait for one another? And where do we go?" Rose was asking the questions, but I knew that General Merriwhether was going to make every clear. I had faith in the General, where Rose didn't."

"I am the concierge. I am the official concierge for USEWOW. I am the concierge captain. I am the most senior concierge. Others who may sit behind the concierge desk are all assistant concierges. I will not, cannot nor have I ever, or will ever pass through the doors. No concierge may ever pass through those doors."

The concierge rose from his desk, walked in front of us and waved her right hand in front of the door's proximity sen-sor. The concierge pushed the door open for the Colonel and Rose. "This is the only time anyone will open the door for the two of you, and this is the only time you will be allowed to go through the door together, as a couple. I'm smiling because I'm a romantic at heart. You can skip the telephone booth for today. You're only getting your room assignments." The concierge had the look of a sad executioner who didn't get a clean kill on the first try.

The door creaked open. It was the sound of rusting steel on rusting steel. Apparently, every door in USEWOW needed lubrication. In profile, the doors were solid metal with interlocking teeth and more than a foot thick. Every door in USEWOW was Cold War era nuclear blast proof surplus. No lubricant was ever used because the heat generated on one side of the door would cause the lubricant to smoke or catch fire, or just become gummy and glue the door shut. The horizonal scrape marks in the paint belied the slow warping and their poor fit after years of neglect.

General Merriwhether put on his serious face. The same face he put on when he was talking to Rose. "We are now entering USEWOW. Use no names. In USEWOW, we never use any names."

*　*　*　*　*

CHAPTER THREE

**"He who controls the present, controls the past.
He who controls the past, controls the future."**
[George Orwell]

Moscow Rules and the Kahuna Kilokilo

"General Merriwhether, welcome. Thank you for making the time to speak to us." Now I got the big Kahuna. "I hope all is well and your mission at USEWOW is going well." "Mr. Seplechre, I've always liked you." The general is so full of shit.

"Thank you for appearing for testimony without a lawyer."

"I just couldn't find a lawyer with a high enough security clearance to be part of any investigation." I don't know how Seplechre got away with carrying out this investigation. I sent a message to the White House through the NSA and CIA. The response I got back was "...background only...". And that's all I'll give him. The President knows, at least the people who received and answered my messages, and I know...and we all know, that's all any prosecutor wants, is to be able to cut off the head of the snake, no matter who is the President. The ever-present threat is the ultimate power of the Special Prosecutor. In the Federal Government, it's always the threat that's the power over anything else. Archy's little Rose works the same way. To say the least, she has both me and Archy buffaloed.

"We all at USEWOW want to look forward to answering all your questions that we're permitted to answer – by regulation and to the limits the law and our security clearances allow us – within the range that our firsthand knowledge – as speculations whether or not true, accurate, inaccurate, and whether or not within the range of our expertise will not be part of our testimony at any time, now or in the future. And, for the record, that's my provisional answer. As Commanding Officer of USEWOW, that is the organization's provisional nonbinding response." Just to be sure I wouldn't get tripped up by my own words, I wrote the statement, had it reviewed by USEWOW's security advisor and legal staff, then I memorized it word for word. You may think it doesn't follow logically. That means you were actually listening to me. It meant everything that was said and wasn't said in the statement.

"Of course, General. This is the provisional investigation with only provisional questions." The idea is to put the target at ease. Make him believe that anything he says doesn't count against him. "And since this is a provisional investigation with provisional questions, we only want and expect provisional answers, whether these answers are provisionally right or provisionally wrong, or both – depending on context, voice inflection and punctuation. General, do you have any questions or wish any clarification?"

"Thank you, Mr. Seplechre. Thank you for being unambiguous in your explanation and thank you for being clear in your intent." I'm watching the General's facial expressions. He is taking me seriously. Behind him, Ms. Defarge is quietly chuckling at the same time puffing great clouds of smoke. "Our request for striking from the record facts, true, false, or purported speculation reflected in the record, should be placed in the record for future consideration of all or part of the record, thereof."

"General, is that request on the record or off the record?

"Mr. Seplechre, we wish to provisionally place it on the record but review the right to have it stricken from the record."

"Thank you, General. So, noted. Do you have all that, Ms. Defarge?" Ms. Defarge grimaced, flicked the ash from her cigarette to the floor, and grunted some sort of answer.

"General, at this point, it's still not a formal request. Nothing is official until you are sworn in and Ms. Defarge and the camera record your statements." Actually, we record everything. From the moment the general walked in the room's hidden ceiling cameras and microphones are motion and voice activated. This goes for all the interrogation rooms, conference rooms, and selected offices of my colleagues, and the toilets. That's always a good place to pick up unguarded conversations or cell phone calls made from the stalls. The toilet stales' microphones are activated when the stall doors are shut, as is the small wide-angle cameras that will pick up anything the subject is holding with views from above and two cameras to the left and right of the toilet flusher infrared sensor. (I personally sweep my office for bugs or cameras every morning and after I come back for lunch. I don't bother with the conference rooms. Everything is recorded in the conference rooms, even when they are dark and empty – because sometimes they're not. I just make sure I segregate any tapes I might be on from everyone else's.)

"General, let me introduce you to Ms. Defarge." They seem to know each other. Ms. Defarge took the cigarette out of her mouth and warmly smiled at the general. This wasn't like her. The last time she smiled like that was when President Kennedy was shot.

"General, it's been a long time since we were both at the Pentagon." With her cigarette still smoking in her left hand, she got up and walked to the general at the head of the conference table, put her right hand on the side of his face and gave him a light kiss on his cheek. "I'll be glad to swear you in." She went back to her stenograph machine.

"General, ... "

"Yes, Mr. Seplechre." I can tell by the general's smile that he's distracted. That may be good. He won't use all his concentration on avoiding anything incriminating. Who would have guessed Ms. Defarge would be the key to the General's interrogation and undoing?

"General, now we have to get down to business." He's still smiling. That's good. He's still distracted by Ms. Defarge.

I guess she got around. She's buxom, not fat, has a boxy figure now which, I guess could be very attractive, depending on how high her high heels are, even in her grey business suit. The tight jacket made her look like she wore a bustle. Ms. Defarge's cigarette cough is not too bad, and her face is not too wrinkled from all her smoking. But I guess with your eyes closed... "General, Ms. Defarge, are you both ready?"

"I would love to swear in General Merriwhether." Without hesitation, she said, "Honey, do you swear to tell the truth, the whole truth and nothing but the truth, especially when we talk later?"

I had to interject, "...General Merriwhether, for the record, do swear or affirm to all of the above, so help you God?" Now both of them sighed deeply, still smiling.

"Yes, Mr. Seplechre. I do." Maybe if Ms. Defarge was enough involved with the general, I'll be able to indict her, too. Something more to look forward to. In fact, everyone in the office would like to indict, convict, and incarcerate her.

"General Merriwhether, for the official record that will go to Congress, tell us how this USEWOW got started."

"Mr. Seplechre, this cannot go anyplace except deep in your files. This especially can't be sent to Congress. ..."

"General, we can edit out anything sensitive - national security is and will always be our primary concern." Ms. Defarge is beginning to choke, smoke and laugh, all at the same time. I shot her a nasty look, she paused long enough to stop laughing, pull the cigarette from her lips and flick the glowing ashes on the rug in front of her.

"Consider this as background only. It's still classified at a Presidential level. Nothing I say here can be shared with anyone." General Merriwhether lost his smile. Even Ms. Defarge grimaced and put the lit cigarette back in the left corner of her mouth.

"Trust me. General, I promise you none of what you tell me will leave my custody." I stifled my laughter, but Ms. Defarge couldn't completely stifle hers, and started clearing her throat to disguise it. "You can tell me everything – in this way we can record it for the historical record. Remember I and the Special Prosecutor's Office have 'Presidential' security clearance for everything." Sure, we do.

"Well, Mr. Seplechre, this whole mission started March 5, 1953, the day Joseph Vissarinovich Stalin died of a left sided hemorrhagic stroke. The courteous Georgian seminarian, poet, shrewd intelligent leader, always well informed, grasping all the detail of every situation, of surprising human sensitivity and sentimentality, and mass murderer left behind his beloved devoted and obsessed English translator. Stalin's NKVD agents recruited him along with many other Cambridge students. His was a brilliant student, his English was flawless, almost Shakespearean, as was his Russian – his spoken Russian was as elegant as Tolstoy's writing. He began teaching Russian Literature at Cambridge, specializing in Count Leo (Lev) Tolstoy. He had his name legally changed to Lev Niolayevich Tolstoy, when the NKVD thought he might be more useful as General Secretary Stalin's English translator.

By that time, he was already delusional and thought he was Count Tolstoy. Stalin was amused by the translator, especially when he insisted, he be addressed as 'Count Tolstoy.' Stalin made all his subordinates address him that way. They all thought this was some sort of code name that Stalin wanted to use. 'Count Tolstoy' impressed everyone in the Kremlin with his knowledge of Tolstoy and all the greats of Russian literature. He impressed the secretaries, in particular. They all thought he was a real count from the time of the Tsars. He dated many of the secretaries, married one and dated more secretaries. Then he had two children – one with his wife and one with one of the prettier the NKVD's typist – not even a secretary. And she was skinny, so the NKVD agents weren't really interested in her. He…"

"General, thank you for the background. But how does this have anything to do with USEWOW's operation?" Sometimes you have to put general's back on track. If they're not attacking something, their minds wander.

"I'm sorry, Mr. Seplechre. This is as interesting a story as the one about the translator. Well, this is still about the translator. Anyway, the CIA's station chief was driven to Sobornaya Square-Cathedral Square where he visited, walked to three different cathedrals or churches – the cathedrals of the Dormition, Archangel and the Annunciation, and the churches of the Deposition of the Robe and the Twelve Apostles every evening between six and ten PM. He entered three of the five of them in succession, but in a different order each night, and knelt and prayed in the last pew of each. In one of these places was that evening's dead drop and sometimes nothing was left for him to pick up. It was like three card monte - every night different combination of three churches, and dead drop signals varied from week to week and was different for each church visited. Either before or after his visit to Cathedral Square he would be driven to St. Basil's Cathedral in Red Square, sit in the last row and pray. He never used St. Basil's for a dead drop. He just liked St. Basil's Cathedral, and this would add to the confusion being the only church that was consistently visited. It was during these sojourns on March 5, 1953 that the CIA's Moscow station chief who found the translator wandering in the subzero cold in front of Saint Basil's Cathedral.

The station chief in Moscow at the time was an old OSS man recruited by 'Wild' Bill Donovan, directly out of Yale. He was sent to occupied France, then to Nazi Germany to the V-1 and V-2 slave labor production facilities, and then tracked them to their deployment sites on the French and Dutch coasts. Once the Nazi's went to mobile V-2 launchers, he began taking more risks to try to locate where they would launch their missiles. And always he was just one step ahead of the Gestapo and the Abwehr. At the same time, he was the handler of the Abwehr's chief, Admiral Wilhelm Canaris.

With his attention split between the V-2s, he never forgave himself, always wondering whether he took enough precautions Admiral Canaris. His once in a lifetime asset when Admiral Canaris was arrested by Heinrich Himmler's SS in 1944 and hung at Flossenburg Concentration Camp, April 9th, 1945, less than one month before Nazi Germany surrendered to the Allies. April 9th every year is a dark anniversary for the Moscow station chief.

Despite that the Moscow station chief was the best CIA officer the organization had. He trusted no one with the most risky and high valued intelligence gathering and ended up spreading himself too thin. He trusted no one with any of the Moscow assets and personally covered all the dead drops himself, even the one-off pickups.

Getting closer to midnight on March 5, 1953 when our station chief was walking from St. Basil's Cathedral in Red Square, a man in a red bathrobe staggered toward him. The confused pale man muttered he was not dead. The station chief approached the man without even looking around. He knew never to check if he was being followed. Moscow rules dictated that someone was always following you and watching anyway, so why be distracted. And this was more than fifty years before all the closed-circuit television surveillance.

"Who are you? Who's not dead?" The station chief immediately recognized the hat and pipe as being exactly like Stalin's.

"I'm not dead! You don't recognize me?" The translator spoke in a quivering voice, his entire body was shivering from the bitter Russian winter cold. He spoke perfect English with a slight Russian accent.

The station chief asked who he was, in his best Russian, of course.

"Kind sir, I am Joseph Stalin. The Joseph Stalin. Joseph Vissarionovich Stalin. Look at me. You don't recognize me? You must have cataracts." But this living 'Joseph Stalin', our translator, looking many years older than he actually was, wore Stalin's actual red robe, slippers, Lenin-style mariner's cap, and puffing Stalin's unlit bent briar pipe held tightly between his teeth. The translator said in perfect English. "You don't know? You don't recognize me. Are you one of those East German tourists? I'm the Joseph Stalin."

Whoever this was, the station chief couldn't ignore the man and let him freeze to death the way the few Muscovites walking past the two of them did at that late hour. This could still be a set up. No doubt he was being watched by the NKVD and this was a sacrificial lamb he was taking in and not a Trojan Horse. The station chief's car and driver were nearby. He waved to them, and when they pulled up, he pushed the poor translator in the back seat. The next day, the world learned that Stalin was dead.

As soon as they returned to the US Embassy, he alerted the ambassador. The two of them went to the Embassy's basement file room and pulled every picture they had of Stalin, both published and unpublished to try to identify who they picked up. They found the crazy man's face in pictures always behind Stalin between either Churchill or Roosevelt at the Tehran, Yalta, and Potsdam war time conferences, and behind and between Stalin and Churchill to Stalin's left (Stalin's good ear) at the Moscow Conference. He was absent from other pictures with Stalin including all pictures of Stalin with the Kremlin ruling elite reviewing parades in Red Square.   And these were photos the CIA had both before and after Stalin's air brushing. Judging from all the photographic evidence and his near perfect English syntax and Russian accent, he was Stalin's English translator. To be that near to Stalin all those years, he was trusted and knew many Kremlin secrets.

The next morning, Stalin's death was announced from the evening before. An immediate coded cable went out to Beetle Smith that they had Stalin's English translator and he thought he was Stalin. CIA director Smith before the war attended a Yale sponsored lecture by Dr. Heinz Herman who described the delusional syndrome of *fievre Jerusalemienne*. The key was it generally disappeared once the subject was removed from Jerusalem. Director Smith's cabled coded instructions. They were simple and curt: "Keep him until we send for him Stop." The director knew he could be dealing with the Russian version of the Jerusalem Syndrome and this would be an intelligence gold mine. In a day Stalin's Kremlin mock office and his living quarters were readied in the basement of CIA Washington, DC headquarters, and the translator was packed in a vented diplomatic trunk, driven in the trunk of the US Embassy's limousine, and placed in a US State Department chartered aircraft.

The ambassador, the station chief and Beetle Smith didn't know the Russians were reading all of our secret communications – until the aircraft was shot down over Russian airspace. At the same time, Deputy Premier, Lavrenity Beria had NKVD -MGB-MVD round up that translator's family and friends and had them disappeared. Beria's instructions were to be thorough – which was in secret police parlance, enquire with friends, neighbors, and distant relatives if they knew what happened to the person. If they knew, didn't know and/ or wondered what happened, they and their families were disappeared until everyone's answer was, "We never heard of him." People in the Soviet Union learned early in life, usually from their mothers, never admit you know anyone or question where people might have gone. As a reward, the fighter pilot (and his entire family) was not disappeared but reassigned to the Dolinsk-Sokol military air base in Sakhalin Oblast. His in-laws, close friends and several neighbors were sent to Magadan and Pevek for new 'employment' opportunities.

After the diplomatic protests over the downing of a State Department aircraft, just to prevent any other diplomatic incidents and embarrassing loss of life, Beria had all of Stalin's translators, their families, and friends (a special 'friends and family' package) brought to Lubyanka prison. This was a central location for their 'final debriefing' as they were conveniently (convenient for the NKVD) all in Moscow. And Beria made sure this all got back to the American Ambassador and the Moscow station chief, just as a warning.

General Walter Bedell 'Beetle' Smith and Allen W. Dulles when they were CIA directors saw the tremendous intelligence value in this crazy translator. The Kremlin's over the top reaction convinced Director Beetle of the value of any of these translators who were suffering from their own form of *fievre Jerusalemienne*. He put into motion the world-wide search for other affected world leaders' translators. He brought the Moscow station chief back to the old CIA headquarters on E street in Washington DC. After all, these translators were with these heads of state day in and day out, translating as needed, and most often having to anticipate their words and thoughts. USEWOW was thus born. To this day, we don't know the name of that Moscow station chief. After the loss of Admiral Canaris, the downing of the State Department aircraft with deaths of all on board, including the translator, and all the disappearances of all Stalin's translators, their families, friends and acquaintances, his rule for his section at the CIA and lettered on his door in Latin instead of his name, title or section was 'NON UTIMUR NOMINIBUS' - USE NO NAMES."

*   *   *   *   *

CHAPTER FOUR

"And so, from hour to hour, we ripe and ripe.
And then from hour to hour, we rot and rot;
And thereby hangs a tale."
[Othello in William Shakespeare's The Tragedy of Othello the Moore of Venice, 1565]

"General, is there science behind this experiment?" Remember, prosecutors only ask questions they know the answer to. There is no science behind this operation. No matter what he tells me, it's a lie. And prosecutors count their blessings every time a defendant lies to them. It's a wonderful thing. If the prosecutors were Catholic, they would light a thank you candle to their favorite saint every time someone would lie to them. And with almost everyone lying to a prosecutor, they would burn down the church.

Generals lie all the time and do it well. That's because they know they're always right and believe they're telling the truth. And if they're always right, then nothing they say could possibly be a lie – eventually it's got to be the truth. Stalin told that to PaPa, who told my grandfather, who told me directly. And even if they know it's a lie, it's for the success of the mission, and then it's not really a lie, but part of the mission. And there's never anything that comes before the mission. That's why they're promoted to general. And that's what makes them successful – lying to the enemy – attacking unexpectedly, and always winning in the end. (Stalin's general's lied all the time. They lied to Staff Headquarters, their fellow generals, their subordinates, their troops, the public, and the press. They just told the press what to print or broadcast. And the news media dare not deviate. But those who lied to Stalin were quietly but immediately dispatched with a silenced Nagant M1895

7.62x38mmR behind the right ear.)

"Mr. Seplechre, the science all comes from the descriptions of the fourteenth and fifteenth century Dominican theologian during his travels to Palestine and the religious mystic Margery Kempe. The *fievre Jerusalemienne* was recognized and named in the 1930s. The 'fever' becomes an intense religious experience, obsession, and delusion after being exposed to Jerusalem, Mecca, Rome other places of religious or a cultural obsession while in the artistic centers of importance, such as Florence. What our Count Tolstoy had was a combination of *fievere Jerusalemienne,* and obsessive admiration for the world's premier homicidal political leader – one of the few dictators with absolute power who personally exercised his penchant for ordering murder. Genocide as a term for Stalin, or even PaPa, is not that it's too strong, but the wrong term. Stalin saw murder as the efficient means to an end. He murdered individuals because they betrayed him, were about to betray him, or he thought they might betray him. He committed genocide out of patriotism for Mother Russia. In fact, all genocidal despots commit their mass murders for purely patriotic reasons. There's not one of them that did it for the fun of it. And in general, the genocidal despots were not really fun people.

Stalin felt his genocide was not murder but adjustments in population densities to optimize the state's economic outlook. It was a 'future's market' with human lives. At times, in order to be efficient, he would order mass murders usually but not exclusively by starvation of large populations, if that turned out to be more efficient, economical, and convenient than targeted killings. And Stalin had a cadre of informers who made sure all the murders were carried out. The secret police looked up to Stalin, but some of his victims got away. The Soviet Union was just too big a country in people and land area to be as efficient as the East Germany Stasi. That's how we found out what was going on. Only the Stasi had absolute control. The only reason anything was discovered about the Stasi, was the complete fall of East Germany. It was amazing how..."

"General Merriwhether, we appreciate your historical insight, but we understand…"

"Mr. Seplechre, this should be on the record when these accounts are read far into the future, when they will eventually be declassified. I hope they will someday be declassified, but sometimes that never happens. There are classified documents from the American Revolution still sealed in the National Archives. But I digress." General Merriwhether took a deep breath. "Did you know that Franklin Roosevelt and the press referred to Stalin as 'Uncle Joe' just to humanize him and make him a more lovable ally?"

"That I didn't know. The only 'Uncle Joe' I know is Joe Biden. That's what the press and Democrats called him to make him seem warm and fuzzy instead of just senile."

"And Stalin buffaloed a sick Roosevelt at Yalta and plunged half of Europe into slavery." Merriwhether is a man who loves history. Or is he just living in the past.

"Yes, you are right, General. But don't be dismayed. The world corrected itself." Let's try again. "I am hanging on your every word. Please continue but try to get back to USEWOW." I have to keep telling myself to be patient. All generals are like this. I have to keep telling myself. "Let's get back to the science behind USEWOW."

"But the world hasn't corrected itself. That's why we embarked on USEWOW more than fifty years ago."

"General, you still haven't explained to me how or why it works." And the more he explains, the more things he can be indicted for and everyone else he mentions. And chance are that most of them are innocent and more likely to go for a plea bargain and testify against someone.

"It was the continuous almost intimate proximity to Joseph Stalin's words, personality and thoughts pushed our delusional translator over the edge. I've had a few on my general staff – actually just one who was so dedicated, he assumed my personality, my gait, my mustache. Mr. Seplechre, you get the picture." General Merriwhether smiled and waited for applause. "Generals, and especially me, we are all very charismatic."

"I still don't understand. Your Count Tolstoy translator is long gone, and you said you can't wait around to find someone else roaming Red Square." And remember, someone in the Pentagon or several administrations green lighted the funding of USEWOW for over seventy years." Actually, government projects only have to be approved for funding once for a project like this – any government project, department, agency, commission, committee – anything can and will continue forever. This is true even when there are 'sunset' provisions built into the enabling and funding legislation. There's never anyone around with the authority, security clearance, nerve, or even cares if something comes to an end.

It's secular immortality without the second coming – it's the Federal Rapture. It only stops when someone fails to appoint replacement for retired or dead participants. The exception is for top-secret projects. Even with no one left, whatever it is, the top-secret project will continue forever. First, if there is no one left, everyone either retired or dead, nobody knows anything because it is all top-secret. The money just piles up in separated accounts – forever. I looked at some of the military funding accounts. There are still accounts growing every fiscal year secretly funding George Washington's invisible ink research. It was Martin Van Buren who insisted that the accounts be interest bearing. No one alive today has the security clearance either to end the funding stream or investigate whatever was done or being done since Garfield was president. Because they are so secret, no one is even sure whether or not someone is working on the project. The reporting chain of command has long retired and died off, so there is no one to check anything. And the offices are so secret, even their locations are secret, and no doubt disguised, that nobody can find them. There is one office in the basement of the Commerce Building still ordering quill pens. And the quill pens are being ordered through NASA.

As a rule, with top secret agencies, projects, departments, divisions, committees and commissions, anyone with the authority to revue or deny funding doesn't have security clearance high enough to study it to decide. Those with a high enough security clearance to decide on funding, if and when they read and study it, don't understand it. They don't ask what it's about because that would entail more work. And they don't want to look stupid by asking. Asking someone puts that person at risk for prosecution for breaking security protocol, because their never allowed to talk about it – ever. Everyone else involved, it's either in their interest to keep it going or not their job to do anything except what they're doing or are dead. They say for some of the most top-secret projects, people have been found dead at their desks, sometime for weeks when the janitorial staff finally came around to collect the burn bags. Everyone involved usually doesn't have anything better to do anyway, except wait for retirement or death.

"That's the wonderful thing about USEWOW, we have all the time in the world, and there's no end in sight."

"General Merriwhether, I know you are in charge of USE-WOW, but who is in charge of 'acquisition' of the delusional translators?" If he gives me a name, I can increase the 'indictable targets' and add charging him with revealing the name. In the Special Prosecutor's office, we call them the ITs. They may even be 'indictable coconspirators' – ICCs. We do try to limit the number of 'persons of interest,' POFs. And you can use the threat of revealing someone as POF and ruin their lives as a threat. If for no other reason as the sport of it. If you can't indict them, and don't use them as witnesses, it's just a waste of time. But it was still fun and set an example of the raw power you had to convince other potential witnesses to lie for you.

In the old days, you had to find three women to keep track of the ITs, ICCs and POFs – one each. Now with computers, you need just one young pretty thing to do the whole job, plus the three IT people to keep the system from crashing. I really preferred the old way. There are no attractive IT girls out there, even if you could find the few girls in the IT department with a high enough security clearance. The ones with the necessary security clearance are usually old, fat, obnoxious and... But what are you going to do?

"It's important, that this name be kept from everyone. But I only mention it here so he will be remembered for posterity for his service to the country he loved so dearly." The General, who was always smiling, now changed his face and tone of voice to a stern gravel. "His name is Silas Barabbas. He's famous throughout the CIA and the entire intelligence community."

"Never heard of him."

"All his contemporaries think he retired. We even threw him a classified retirement party and put a plaque over the Russia Desk at CIA headquarters for 'He who will forever remain nameless, faceless and incomprehensible'. Then we had him drop off the map."

"No one has ever heard of him. Not ever. Everyone who knew him or knew of him has retired and died. He doesn't use his real name in his Florida retirement community he's been living in for the past thirty years. He runs USEWOW Acquisitions – USEWOWAQ – from his one-bedroom condominium in Naples, Florida. He has a beautiful view of the Intercoastal Waterway and he's high enough up to see the Atlantic Ocean. He's still very good at what he does. He runs all his agents using two lap top computers – always in duplicate – both differently encrypted, and he uses no names. He personally speaks to each of his agents every day, and each of their assets at least once per week. They all know who is in charge. Everything goes through him. Right up to the time the new translator asset arrives on US soil."

"He sounds like that Stalin-era Moscow station chief."

"Mr. Seplechre, that's who it is. And he's just as mentally sharp, cunning, intuitive, and devious as he was those many years ago in Moscow. He invented the 'Moscow Rules' they teach at The Farm, to this day."

"General, I find it hard to believe. He can't be the same man, No one would be alive and have served in World War II and be in shape to…"

"It is the same man! He's become a germophobe. He never leaves his apartment."

"General, I've never heard of him or anything that even suggests his very existence."

"Mr. Seplechre, to the world, he is a nonperson. His condominium is owned by a CIA dummy corporation who pays all fees, taxes, utilities, and anything else, except for the parking. Everybody has to pay for parking, and I don't know why. He even pays for two parking spaces, and he doesn't have a car. Any needed plumbing, electrical repairs, painting, rug cleaning, window washing is done by the CIA operatives. The CIA owns the condos across the hall and on either side of his. And the CIA pays for those condo parking spaces. But at least they use them, sometimes. They usually remain empty except for a rotating security detail.

Doctors, his barber, his housekeeper and his delivery people are the only people who enter his apartment. And they're all CIA agents with Presidential security clearances. Everything else, groceries, medications, any clothing, any item he needs, is delivered. Anything he orders through Amazon or any other retailer goes to CIA headquarters in Langley, is unpacked, checked for explosives, toxins, or biohazards before being brought to him by our agents. He's got all the cable channels, the Cadillac of sports packages – everything, and it comes out of our budget. He's been in the government so long, with the incremental raises over eighty-five years, he makes four times the President of the United States salary. And in the enabling legislation, his salary, and all the salaries of assets he recruits, and runs are federal and state and local tax free. The only out of pocket expenses is their parking. There can be no records of any of these people. The biggest problem he has is what to do with the money. We buy everything for him. He can't use it for charity – that would attract attention. He can't have any bank accounts. We bring him the cash and store it in the apartment next to his. We already have one other apartment filled with currency. And he can't figure out what to do with his money."

"If what you say is true, and I don't believe it is true, he must have incredible genes."

"No, Mr. Seplechre. For the record, when I last spoke to him, which was only two days ago, he said it was his guilt over his murdered intelligence assets." The General's face relaxed, but the sigh told me I was about to hear Silas Barabbas's secret to longevity. "He is alone. He has outlived all his immediate family, friends, colleagues – and enemies. It is his unforgivable self-guilt over the death of those in his charge that won't allow him the peace of death. And he was never married."

Without saying another word, he rose from his chair, smiled at Ms. Defarge, and patted her on her shoulder as he left the interrogation room.

*   *   *   *   *

CHAPTER FIVE

**"Clothes make the man, especially
with Two Pair of Pants
Naked people have little or no influence on Society"**
[Mark Twain-Samuel Clemens, and Israel Beilin]

I know this whole thing having my Archy work for General Merriwhether is a mistake. A big, big mistake. I take the blame for some of it. I've been trying to give Archy more confidence in himself, and in me that I will always back him up. He must learn to have confidence that he is in command of his surroundings – that there isn't any one person, place, thing, or situation he can't turn around to his advantage. Archy has never been very forceful or adaptable. He tends to do things repetitively, in the preconceived perfect sequence that worked the first time – just like his computer programing. And there are just as many times he repeats things in the same sequence that didn't work the first time. That's when I hit 'high C' and have to become unpleasant. I have to shake him out of his complacency so he can finish one task and go on to the next. Otherwise, he's stuck, like in one of his computer program do-loops.

I don't even attempt to get Archy to multitask. His mother even told me after she wished me 'Good luck,' at the end of our wedding reception that Archy was like his father, he could only do one thing at a time. And then she said, 'That's why Archy's an only child.'

Let me give you an example. When he drives someplace, he always starts from home. In between destinations, he goes back home then to the new place instead of taking a direct route. I yell at him. For that one time he alters his course – instead of going from home to point A, and then return home before going to point B, with my harsh words ringing in his ears, he goes directly from A to B. But he only does that when we're in the middle of an argument. The next time, he goes back to his routine of returning home before going to the next destination. It's something he's been doing since childhood. Something Archy's mother taught him. Trying to reteach Archy habits he's acquired from his mother is as impossible convincing him not to love his mother. That, I'll never be able to do, but getting him to drive directly from one place to another, I still hold out a glimmer of hope – like getting him not to put my bras, wool sweaters and anything marked 'dry-clean only' in the dryer. The problem is with that last thing, it requires him to read clothing labels, which he never has and probably will never do.

He's been exactly like that in our marriage. I've done almost all the adapting, but I'm chipping away around the edges. I do lose ground every time we go to Brooklyn to see his parents – especially his mother. She's never liked me. But now that she's gotten older, she's more forgetful. She seems to think her Archy made a better choice than she first thought, and she's a lot more tolerable.

When Archy has been away from his mother for a while and comes home for a visit, Mama Buonarotti finds her son a little annoying, although she won't admit it. Archy's father looks forward to his son's visits. It's mostly the undying love between a father and son, and a little is diverting the constant suggestions (nagging) from his wife on everything he does. She interchangeably nags Archy instead of his father.

His mother always said she didn't like the way I talked to Archy or her. She said I should learn how to be a dutiful wife. I was disrespectful. I said I was standing my ground. Now, she's hard of hearing. Before she had to work hard to ignore what I told her and what I was constantly telling Archy in front of her. Now she misses half of the conversations, and at least is assuming I have only the best of intentions toward her and her son. This new lack of understanding between the two women in Archy's life seems to work well for all parties concerned. Archy's father always seems to be in another room when I'm with Archy's mom. And he spends a lot of time in the bathroom when we're eating dinner together.

His father like Archy, hasn't really changed. Women need to realize that the man you marry is the man his mother trained for you and she expects her training to be your 'life sentence without parole.' Once they're trained as puppies by their mothers, there's nothing you can do about teaching 'an old dog new tricks.'

Archy is a master programmer. But this assignment is different. I'm still not sure exactly what we're doing here, but it's not computer programming. I knew he would have to get away from his computers once he was promoted and had to command troops, or at least start running a larger part of whatever Army organization he was assigned. I had to start preparing him to be a staff officer. That's a completely different skill set, the real skills necessary that they don't teach at The War College. Men only learn that through years of marriage. Female officers, though, are usually born with those talents – it's something to do with two X genes and estrogen, then losing the estrogen edge at menopause and overcompensating for it that makes women better staff officers at all levels except one. Women just lack the testosterone that would make them effective commanders.

I've been letting him make more decisions around the house. Giving him compliments no matter how stupid he acts. I figured these were just little things that didn't matter much, that would eventually self-correct – like the way he loads the dishwasher, or just can't load it properly. And his laundry peculiarities. He always sneaks in the colored wash with the bath towels just to save time. I can never get him to wash my dishtowels separately. And I only recently trained him how to fold bath towels in thirds instead of in halves, then quarters. He still slips and puts my bras in the dryer, and everything in the dryer goes on the highest temperature for the longest cycle. And when I'm not looking, the washing machine is always run on 'Heavy Load'. I have disciplined myself to keep quiet about the little things, so I'm not always correcting him. I can always buy new bras and I've learned never to leave things that can't be dried in the dryer out of the laundry basket and well hidden from Archy.

Archy does laundry every day and goes around the house looking for my dirty cloths. I thought this was such a good habit. You can't keep anything hidden from Archy that needs to be washed or dry-cleaned. Then I realized that he's obsessed. He's already shrunk most of my wool and cashmere sweaters. I hide my dry cleaning and anything that doesn't go in the dryer. Now, I'll secretly wash them and hang them in a closet in the garage – the closet I keep telling him to clean out – I know he'll never go in there. He says I make him nervous. But he drives me crazy – Archy drives me crazy in a loving way, and he's always trying to be helpful and attentive.

He just doesn't know how to be helpful and attentive without being minorly annoying or committing a major faux pas. He's a very good person. His heart is pure. And he is a very original person. He has the genius to see things differently from everyone else. And this makes him a genius for the way he solves problems. His success is at the cost of him being mistaken, annoying, socially embarrassing is so many ways, you would think he would have run through his whole repertoire of malaprops misconceptions, misinterpretations, and poor judgement. But he hasn't. He always has a new way to embarrass himself, me, and anyone who accidently is involved with him at that moment, while at the same time, clearly defining a challenge and coming up with a unique and often, the very best solution. Archy just doesn't get the credit because of his journey to the solution, not the solution itself. Archy seems to always look bad doing something he is eventually a success at.

When he told me what he had done, he was so pleased with being able to surprise me with the White House assignment. Not even my father was ever officially assigned to any

White House command – and Archy knew that. Him doing the wash, shrinking my good cloths, unloading the dishwasher, and putting everything in the wrong place constantly surprised me that he could never get it right. But this White House business. I'm sure it sounded good to Archy. And I'm sure it sounded good to General Merriwhether, him being a general. I'm sure General Merriwhether's dreams about being on the Joint Chiefs of Staff, or even Secretary of Defense was now a possibility being that close to the President of the United States. But Archy. Archy. Archy. Archy. What have you done?

General Merriwhether may have fooled Archy and may have fooled himself. But not me. It's not even the real White House with the real President of the United States – not the real Ruffles and Flourishes and Hail to the Chief. General Merriwhether usually has his own hairbrained operations that everyone ignores and are soon forgotten. But putting him in charge of a questionable operation at best that goes back almost seventy years – this is going to be hard to ignore and harder to forget. It's TOP SECRET, so I'm sure everybody knows a little something about it. Washington is like that. (And for that matter, so is Moscow, Beijing, Tehran, Pyongyang. In London they have MI5, MI6, and GCHQ. All the secrets have better names, and all the TOP SECRET secrets have an English accent. Everything sounds more important, so much more official, and more TOP SECRET. And the English are always threatening everyone with the 'Official Secrets Act', even if you don't have your dog licensed.)

And the longer a project is around, the more different versions of its mission are circulating, even among those assigned to and in charge of the project. The only people with a clear idea of what is going on are the Communist Chinese and Russians. And only the CIA and FBI counter-intelligent code breakers know this from reading their espionage agents communications to and from their embassies and consulates. That is, if the CIA and FBI are reading the coded messages correctly. But they can never be sure because they rarely compare notes.

And when they do, the same messages are read differently by different codebreakers in the different agencies. The only thing that lets me sleep at night is that the Russians and Communist Chinese have a multitude of agencies reading our coded cables with probably the same bureaucratic inefficiency and inaccuracies.

If I had known it was General Merriwhether I would have stopped Archy, White House or no White House. Neither Archy nor General Merriwhether know this isn't even the White House. First, we can't enter or exit the White House through the front door. Even General Merriwhether is not allowed to use the usual White House entrances. We have to sneak in like moles underground through the Treasury Department Building. And nobody important ever goes to the Treasury Department. The Secretary of the Treasury has his important office in the White House. His office in the Treasury Building with bookcases, paper-filled file cabinets and the big wooden desk and leather chair are just for show. All he needs is a laptop, a small desk, and a place for his secretary. And his secretary isn't even in the same building. She is in the Treasury. He has the civil service people counting the money for him, anyway.

"Rose, isn't it thrilling being at the White House." Archy has that stupid clueless grin on his face when he is waiting for my approval. Well, it's too late now to chastise him or punish him for the mess he made. Like a puppy, you have to punish them and push their face in their mess immediately, otherwise they just won't understand. After all my years as an Army brat daughter of a general, and an Army wife, you learn that about husbands and generals. And there's not much difference between them, either. Sergeants are the only one's in the entire military that learn from their mistakes and remember everything they learned.

Now, I can only smile dutifully and try to put him at ease – that's the only way he'll focus on the job in front of him. Otherwise, he puts all his efforts into worrying about me being angry at him. I'm always angry at or with him. I know I will be angry at or with him for something in the immediate future. It's our usual state of affairs, but I am determined that it doesn't become nonproductive or counterproductive. So, I've learned how to hide it. It's not too hard. Archy is not very perceptive.

"Yes dear. Anything you say. I can't wait to get a new gown for our first state dinner." Yea, like they're going to invite us to a state dinner if we can't even go through one of the delivery entrances. If everything we do is so highly classified – so secret we're not even allowed to address people by their names, they're not going to bring us upstairs to mingle with the Washington elite or those trying to be the Washington elite who got into the dinner because they're a friend of a friend of a relative.

"See, Hon. I knew you would find a silver lining to this. Now aren't you a little happier I didn't turn down a White House assignment?"

"Of course, Archy, darling." In the Army, you follow orders. You can't just turn down assignments. Orders are orders. If that were the case, Archy would be blameless. But the one time he was given a choice. The one time – and he picks wrong. If I didn't love him so much, I would stab him in the throat.

Now, we're just following General Merriwhether down this miserably lit ugly tunnel. On top of all that, we even have to pay for our own parking. The peeling paint on the ceiling and the walls tells me this operation is not a very high priority on anyone's part. I've seen this color before. This is World War Two surplus battleship grey lead paint the Defense Department couldn't give away. I'm depressed enough to start eating the paint chips, which won't be difficult the way they're falling off the walls and ceiling.

Now we're at a hallway that meets the tunnel at a perpendicular. There is a whole series of doors. The door directly in front of us is flanked by two plainly printed signs on old wood sign boards with dull weathered black lettering with faded gold-leaf trim and a grey background that one time in the past was white:

Kleyder makhn dem mentsh **Shnayder Krom**

Gegrindet 1892 beshas di mikhuss fun Csar Alexander III, Tolotshin Imperyal Rusish Imferye

Riloukeytid 1917 tsu Vilyamsburg, Bruklin, Beshas di hershn fn Frezident Voodov Vilson

Ishral aun Rkhl Beylin, Prapreyaterz

[Mumkhh shnayder aun Neytorin - Tsvey hoyzn mit yeder pasn mit a vesti

Frwy oltereyshanz mit ae pertshasaz]

[Original Wood Sign from the Beilin family's Tailor Shop, at the corner of Kent Avenue and South 5th Street, Williamsburg, Brooklyn]

And

In Shotn fun der Vilyamsburg Brik Teyler shop

Bespoke Teyleringaun aun Khat Kutur

Ishral aun Rkhl Beylin s Shnayder Krom

Mumkhh shnayder aun Neytorin

[Hant gemakht mjhg suts dresiz, gaunz, aun formal ovnt ver – Frey lifetime enderungen aun tsvey hayzn mit yeder pasn]

Riloukeytid 1917 tsu Vilyamsburg, Bruklin, Riloukeytid 1956, Manhetn

---

[Wood Sign from Israel and Rachel Beilin's *In the Shadow of the Williamsburg Bridge* Tailor Shop, at the corner of The Bowery and Delancey Street, Lower East Side, Manhattan]

The door was half frosted glass with gold lettering: **"BY APPOINTMENT ONLY – WE ARE ALWAYS OPEN: SHIRTS STARCHED AND PRESSED – WASH AND FOLD SERVICE/ONE DAY TURNAROUND - DRY CLEANING DONE ON PREMISES-1 HOUR AND 24-HOUR SERVICE AVAILABLE"**. The double door to the immediate right was marked **"DELIVERY – LEAVE YOUR CLEANING IN THE BASKET – LEAVE YOUR LAUNDRY IN THE LAUNDRY BAG - WITH YOUR TICKET(s) FILLED OUT with Your Department Code - Note any Special Instructions: _USE NO NAMES_."**. In front of one of the double doors was a stack of black plastic laundry baskets, one inside the other, and a white laundry basket filled with grey laundry bags marked **"LAUNDRY – TOP SECRET – USE NO NAMES"** in black lettering with the White House seal. Above each stack of baskets and bags were open boxes marked **"Top Secret Laundry Tickets – Use Your Department Code – _USE NO NAMES_"** and **"Top-Secret Dry-Cleaning Tickets– Use Your Department Code – _USE NO NAMES_"** The door to the immediate left, which was two half 'Dutch' doors was marked **"ALL TOP SECRET PICKUPS – HAVE YOUR CLAIM TICKET READY – _USE NO NAMES_"**. Further down the hall was another double door marked **"TOP SECRET COLD STORAGE – WE CLEAN, BOX AND STORE YOUR WEDDING GOWN, ANY FORMAL WEAR, PROM GOWNS, BRIDESMAID GOWNS – _USE NO NAMES_"**. A fourth double-wide door at the end of the hall, on the perpendicular wall was marked, **"EMPLOYEES ONLY – DO NOT ENTER [Employees – do not identify yourselves as employees – _USE NO NAMES_]"**.

"Rose, this is another USEWOW perk. We will do all your dry cleaning, laundry, press all your cloths. If you don't mind carrying your laundry to the Treasury Building and down to here, you'll never use your washer and dryer again." General Merriwhether seemed so pleased with himself. "If there's a particular brand of detergent or softener, we'll get it and use it. Our cleaning service checks all your clothing for stains, lose or missing buttons, damaged zippers and repairable tears like it never happened before it goes into the wash or for dry cleaning. Not so much for you, but for our special USEWOW agents. Blood stains and gunpowder burns are hard to get out unless it's done prewash. When the agents over oil their Glocks, or Colts, we use a drop of Dawn on their shirts and spot dry clean with Tide Stain Sticks their pants before we put their suits through the entire dry-cleaning cycle. We can even get out invisible ink stains when their pens leak with the developer in their pockets. Sounds minor, but it's an important National Security service we provide. Of course, we replace anything that can be replaced or repaired, or we'll replace the entire suit within a day. USEWOW agents are weighed in at the Medical Office monthly. Any change in weight of more than ten pounds requires the agent to be refitted with a new suit with vest and two pair of pants. Old suits are kept if the agents weight returns to its baseline. Old suits are used in the unfortunate event we need to bury them."

"Rose, this is great. I'll get a little shopping cart we can put it all in my trunk. You can roll the laundry into the Treasury Department, through the tunnels and to here. This will save us money on laundry soap, wear and tear on our washer and dryer and make life easier for you. No laundry, and we have to come to work anyway. Win win for everyone."

"Rose, I'm thinking after I've saved the country and the world, I'll develop a new military branch of service – The National Laundry Service. All members of the service will be armed with M1A1 Colt .45 caliber side arms along with their holstered stain sticks ready at a moment's notice. I'm sure I could run it out of the basement of Federal Government buildings across the country and use the US Mail for pickup and delivery. There's lots of surplus basement space and the US Mail could turn a real profit on this. Of course, Archy would be my chief of staff – as a full bird colonel. And once I retire, Archy will be promoted to Brigadier General with an office in the Pentagon and a seat on the Joint Chiefs of Staff.

We can call it 'The General's US All American Free Wash

and Fold and Dry-Cleaning National Service – USAAF', Our motto – 'Patriotically Clean Your Cloths with The U.S.A.A.F. – Support our military, veterans and the US Post Office and Save Money on your Cleaning Bills'. Our service will have its own uniforms, all white with brass buttons and a high collar.

"Rose, I am excited about the General's idea. I'll have a readymade position – a nationally recognized title. And then maybe politics. A run for the Vice Presidency. And General Merriwhether, you could be another General President - George Washington, Andrew Jackson, Harrison, Grant or Eisenhower."

"Archy, I am honored to accept your nomination." You won't believe this. The two of them are staring blankly at the peeling paint on the ceiling as if they're seeing a vision of their future. "Rose, dear Rose. I can see you at Archy's side at the western front of the Capital Building looking out on the National Mall on Inauguration Day. The National Mall filled with Americans in their cleanest of clean laundry and dry-cleaned coats admiring you Rose as Archy's Second Lady in your cleanest cloths. And someday you'll be the First Lady." I love it when the General has one of his real delusional smiles. Even his mustache smiles.

I could see promising everyone in the country, clean laundry." Actually, that's not one of Archy's worst ideas. No other politician has run on a platform of promising that we become a nation of clean laundry. Another national entitlement. Unique. I have to remember how people laughed at Social Security and Medicare.

"Combine your national Laundry and Dry-Cleaning Card with your Voter ID, and it would actually be workable. Great Britain has its National Health Service – popular but full of problems – people waiting for months for care. We'd have our National Laundry Service – how many problems could you have with laundry? All we would need is to produce more washing machines to meet the demand.

And hiring more postmen. It would be a boon to the

Post Office. I bet Benjamin Franklin never thought of anything like this. He insisted on a national postal service to unite the country. And not only will we unite the country but clean their clothing."

"General, Archy, before the two of you get carried away, the USAAF has already been taken. That's the acronym for the United States Army Air Forces – you remember, from World War Two. And the Navy wears all white for their dress uniforms."

I haven't done any laundry since we were married. That first week after the honeymoon, I had to show Archy who was boss. I let the laundry pile up until he quietly asked about it. I told him to do it himself, and he's been doing the laundry – the wrong way, always the wrong way, ever since. No matter how many times over how many (many) years I've told him how I wanted it done, he still can't get it right. He always does it wrong, but at least he does it without me even asking.

I told him to spot any stains with Dawn or any dish-washing detergent. One day, I was out shopping, he couldn't find the laundry detergent, so he used Dawn in the same amount as washing machine detergent. He was sitting watching television when I came home and could hear the washing machine making a racket in the basement.

"Archy, that's the washing machine making a lot of noise."

"I know, Rose. That's why the TV is turned up so loud. It was even making more noise before."

"But how could you do wash? I just bought the laundry detergent."

"I used Dawn, dear. Just the way you taught me."

At that moment I knew what he did. He filled the laundry detergent hopper with Dawn. When I opened the cellar door and turned on the lights, I could see the suds already at the first stair step. Suds were spreading all over the basement floor.

Even when Archy listens to me, he can't get things right.

Now I know why his mother kept him away from any household tasks, especially if it involved appliances. I yelled at him in the proximate time frame he filled the basement with soap suds. This is a lesson he learned, and I have him still doing the laundry. Halfway there is better than nothing.

You know his mother ruined him for any woman. All mothers, especially the first born, and if they're an only child, then women out there, be warned it's hopeless to try to teach your husband anything. And if they have sisters, their still an only child, except its worse. Then they have more subservient women to cater to them. And as soon as a son is born into any family, all women become subservient. The boys learn that from birth, all the men learn that, and all the women learn that. And that's the way has been. Just read your Bible.

But Archy is so happy and he really thinks I'm bringing my dirty laundry to work every day – in fact, my dirty laundry is not leaving my house. What if someone sees us? The cleaning, well, that will be a convenience. I still don't want to tell him that the laundry stays home, and the laundry is still his responsibility. Why spoil his moment to shine? Laundry and putting out the garbage – man's work he was always proud to do. His father did the laundry and garbage, and he was determined to do the same.

"Rose, I only wish we had a PX for you to do your shopping." The general thinks I like to shop. I just order out or have what I need delivered. Archy never suspected that none of his meals were home cooked. And I don't have to clean the stove. I do transfer my in out orders to my own dishes, otherwise he might become suspicious.

No. I take that back. I could serve him Chinese take-out right from the white cardboard cartons. Tell him I made it and put it in the cartons for authenticity, and he'll tell me it's even better than the Chinese restaurant. Husbands are all alike. They'll eat anything a wife puts in front of them and love it. They're always afraid if they didn't and didn't eat everything, the wife would stop cooking for them. And then they'd starve to death, slowly but surely.

Wives consider reheating leftovers cooking dinner. God eventually created microwave reheating for all women. If He had created it with – well with his first crack at Creation during those first six days, Eve would have ordered dinner out, Adam would have eaten reheated take-out snake meat he thought Eve prepared herself, and we would still be in Eden.

"It's time to go in and get fitted for what you will both need for your assignments." Now I have to be fitted along with Archy for new clothes. I don't mind custom clothing, but I insist on picking out my own. Archy is different. He hates buying clothes, or even uniforms. He hates trying on cloths. Archy, as brilliant as he is with his programming, he is lazy and stupid about everything else. This is especially true about dressing himself. His mother did it for him, and this is just part of the Hell she's left me.

General Merriwhether knocked. The door was opened by an elderly hunched over man in a pinstriped vest and pants, starched white shirt, and a black and white flowered bow tie. His hair was a younger salt and pepper and didn't match his older wrinkled face, with his tailor's tape measure around his neck. Behind him stood what I assumed was his wife, stooped over, head bowed, appearing silent and assuming the classic female subservient posture of an old married couple from a bygone age. She was wearing a nondescript high collared faded print blue dress that went down to her ankles. Over that was a hideous white (slightly off color) kitchen apron with faded pink and blue ruffles. At least I could see they both wore matching yellow gold wedding rings.

"This is Mr. Israel Beilin. He will fit Archy for his four suits and twenty-four uniforms – dress uniforms, class A uniforms, fatigues. All uniform insignia will be Velcro-attached for flexibility. We make them think they have a big staff by just changing your rank and insignia. They only look at the uniforms, not the faces. They don't even check your nametag. They all only address you by your rank. They are forever rank-conscious, and nothing else. These national leaders believe they don't need to know the names of their subordinates – only the names of their enemies – or possible enemies who are 'permanently and forever demoted.'" General Merriwhether stopped smiling. "Don't let them get to know your names. That's another reason to 'USE NO NAMES'.

"Archy, your suits will be in the style of the national leaders you are assigned to, plus a tuxedo, morning suit, and white tie and tails for White House affairs or formal dinners at the other national capitals – the national capitals we invent down here at USEWOW." General Merriwhether turned to Israel. "Israel, my old friend, just so we're prepared and have to stand in for Rose with the Iranians, please fit both Archy and me with your black burqas."

The General looked pleased with himself, believing he thought of everything – except who are we dressing for. Maybe we're going to get to travel, and we will get invited to White House State dinners and diplomatic receptions. Maybe this was not as bad an idea that I thought. The exposure will be good for Archy's career, and for me, too.

"General Merriwhether. and why am I here?" If he just tries to palm me off as a secretary...

"Rose, you will be each leader's secretary and the waitress in the dining hall. On special occasions, you'll be our cocktail waitress, and Rachel will make special outfits for that. Seamed stockings, bustier, rabbit ears. You know, casino style. For the Iranian, you'll just use the same burqa, and worse comes to worse, Archy and I could step in and help out. Nobody gives a woman a second look in a burqa. What else - well. You'll be assisting your husband handling..."

I'm not assisting anybody. With these two boobs, I'll have to take over early on to make sure they don't shoot themselves in the foot. "Why General, I'm here to help you and Archy any way I can. Just tell me what you expect of me." I said that all with my best and softest Southern drawl. They're both smiling. I can tell that they just don't know I'm faking being subservient.

"Rose, I'm so glad to see you're coming around. This will be exciting for both of us." Archy is still clueless if he really thinks being someone's secretary is what I wished for all my life.

"Not much to do for you but gain these leaders confidence, dear sweet Rose. You'll be fine just being there and yessing them." That's all a woman ever gets to do until... "You'll get two grey tweed business suits, tight at the waist, below the knees in length, high collars with a plain white blouse. You'll be fitted with a taffeta low-cut backless strapless black evening gown. You'll only need one pair of shoes: high stiletto heels, and a couple of pairs of seemed stockings, no matter what you're wearing – that includes the burqa. I know all women love to wear high heels. That makes them feel more feminine, especially with the seamed stockings. In the burqa, you'll have to work at feeling your feminine best." If I don't kill him now, I will later. "You'll need a couple of pairs of work sneakers when you're their waitress."

"Rose, just listen to the General. He told us both that, 'All will be revealed'." I'm going to kill Archy and bury them both together if they keep up this sexist condescending crap.

"Just be their secretary. Offer to take dictation. Bring them cups of coffee, tea, whatever they want until they have to pee it out. If they accept the drinks, one after another, that means you are gaining their confidence and they want to please you." Now the General's mustache turned downward, and he took on a serious tone. "After all the coffee, tea or whatever their drinking, after the first time they have to leave to empty their bladder, you know you've gained their complete trust. They'll tell you things, make the most sensitive phone calls with you in the room and dictate highly classified information instead of writing it out themselves. They'll start getting lazy in front of you. All men do when they have an obedient secretary. When they tell you it's confidential or secret, that's to impress you. And that's how you'll know you're succeeding in your mission. Or they just forget you're in front of them. Just encourage them to talk and talk and talk. And just know, audio and video is being recorded." Now that he laid out my task, the General took a sigh of relief, and he excused himself to empty his bladder. I was to be a pseudo-honey trap. But he's out of his mind if he thinks I'm going all the way.

And who the hell does the General think he's dressing, and then ordering my wardrobe for me? The General is back from the bathroom, now more relaxed. "Rose, you will look fetching in a subdued way. For these men, maintaining your feminine mystique is what it is all about. For the Iranian, though, you'll switch off between your black full-length burqa and face veil and your harem girl sheer high-waisted harem pants, cropped belly shirt, and cap with attached veil." Apparently, he's given my costume a lot of thought. "And don't forget the tassels." And where to you think he wants the tassels?

Take my word for it, the General doesn't know what it's all about if he thinks I'm going to put that on in public. And Archy is smiling. I can't say anything I want to say to him in front of the General, or these two people. But I can't wait until I get Archy home.

The old woman just smiled and shook her head. Apparently, she's heard all this before.

"My dear, Archy. I'm thinking of that last costume and I can't wait until I get you home…tonight, home alone." Archy, the General and the little old man are all smiling. I'm going to kill Archy tonight for the way he's acting. The only saving grace is at least I know I still have what it takes to…

The old woman stepped out of the shadows. Her husband stepped aside with deference. "You look unhappy dear." The old woman smiled at me, came forward, grabbed my hand. "I had to wear an outfit just like that years ago. It was for the job. Just remember it's your duty. It's how you'll get the results you'll want to get for your nation's security." Her husband smiled thinking of his wife those many years ago just the way Archy was smiling thinking of me dressed that way. "I think you should have three of these outfits, one in sheer black with red trim, red with white trim, and white with black and red trim – all to accomplish the mission." Apparently, this old woman was more in charge than her husband. "You'll also be issued black waitress uniforms, knee length skirts and white aprons. For each leader, you'll need change only the Velcro shoulder patches to indicate your part of that nation's food service. If we decide the leader is eating at a different restaurant, you'll get a different shoulder patch."

Rachel smiled at Rose. "I had the same type of assignment for the Mossad years ago. I had to blow the man's brains out while pouring wine with one hand over his right shoulder, all while trying to recite the dessert specials. The people who were having dinner with the 'guest of honor' were stun, but not surprised who had the ultimate migraine or not to ask which desserts came with their dinner specials. And the three remaining dinner guests used the fourth dinner guest's credit card to pay the check and generously tip me. It's usually not necessary to eliminate everybody. Nobody will remember your face. All they will remember clearly is being splashed with brains and blood and be happy the bullet didn't go through the guest of honor's skull and hit one of them. And that's why you use a .22 caliber. Usually, but not always no exit wound. And if there is an exit wound, it's not too big or messy. Something to remember. Also, there is no need to kill everybody. Then there will be nobody left to pay the check. Usually your tip is extra generous – the diners are only glad they weren't the ones shot." Rachel was more than a Mossad seamstress.

It's obvious that Rachel was now taking over. "I suggested to the General, and he agreed, keeping the dinner and dessert specials the same for each day of the week for all the leaders. Also, we know you're not a professional waitress, so trying to remember different specials for four different settings, three meals a day, and the possible need for an ad hoc assassination during dining service will be difficult to pull off smoothly."

"And don't forget the gold tassels." I don't know if the General really meant to say that out loud. His mind was wandering again. "Tassels is the distraction that will make any execution easier." Rose and Rachel cleared their throats disapprovingly. "I'm only thinking strategically. The only problem is, where to hide your gun. You'd probably be restricted to a two-shot .22 caliber short Derringer. Any larger caliber would make too much noise. Just thinking strategically and practically. One should always be practical, I say!"

"Rose, if you don't have a silencer device, pressing the gun against the back of the head will muffle the sound of the shot, even though you will probably get splashed if you're not standing directly behind your 'subject'." Rachel was a wise woman.

For a second, the three men began to walk toward each other to congratulate themselves when the old woman very sternly said, "Gentlemen, it's time we got down to business." General Merriwhether and Ruth's husband's body language showed her great deference. Archy was just bewildered. "For Rose, may I suggest for our North Korean guest, she be outfitted with Choson-ot. The variations for men and women's traditional Korean apparel will not be enough for these delusional men to know who's coming or going, so I will produce identical outfits for General Merriwhether and the Colonel."

"What I meant to say, Rachel, was that if the need arises, she could permanently neutralize anyone either over dinner or desert, especially if she use a tray to carry the cocktails with her left hand. I know Rose is a right-handed shooter." General Merriwhether smiled and so did his mustache at the thought of me dispatching an enemy.

"And who are these 'leaders'?" This better be good.

"Rose, Archy, this is the most amazing demonstration of the 'Jerusalem Syndrome'. The CIA began abducting translators for world leaders of our enemies more than sixty years ago. Over the years, we've gotten everyone from the USSR, the entire Eastern Block, Communist China, Yugoslavia. They've all come and gone. Some have been crazy enough to think they were their country's leaders, others just faked it to get into the US. And many were crazy, thought they were their countries' leaders, stupid, and useless.

All the translators we couldn't use went into a special branch of the Federal Witness Protection Program – The Directorate of Terminal Translators Organization – DITTO." I would have thought this was the General's craziness, but it was not. "It was Bill Casey who got the major and permanent funding and set up the infrastructure. The resettlement program for used translators was President Jimmy Carter's idea that he bankrolled it under his presidential library discretionary funds. Carter didn't have anything too interesting to put in his presidential library anyway.

We had to send the translators some place where they wouldn't be noticed. All of them were settled in Hollywood, where they did very well making made-for-TV product commercials and Hallmark Movies. And the whole operation is run out of the Environmental Protection Agency – where nobody would notice, and nobody really knows what they are doing or what's going on."

Bill Casey is long dead and gone, but like anything in the Federal Government, the program has a religious immortality. Life after death without the Second Coming occurs every four to eight years in Washington, every time Congress, and the Presidency changes party hands. The minority party won't let go of anything that was part of their past administration and blocks the majority party from ending the funding. With a new election and new majority, the old majority, now the new minority clings to these questionable programs because it was part of their old administration. And that's how continuity of government works in the American Democracy. My father taught me that when I studied civics in high school. They stopped teaching civics and now there's an entire generation of Americans – of politicians especially – that don't know how the Federal Government really operates. So, with each election, the new politicians add new programs, and the old politicians are sure to fund, and expand the old programs. And any National Security designated programs live in a nirvana, that aerified heaven of unending money, time, and lack of any oversight only the Supreme Court possesses. And the Supreme Court doesn't care unless somebody complains to them. And nobody is going to complain and bring a case to the Supreme Court.

Well, Archy gave his word to the General. Secret or not, between Archy's and the General's big mouths everybody in the military community knew he was working for General Merriwhether at the White House before I could start to brag about it. I forced my way in to protect my husband. Now, I have to make the best of what's going to be a bad situation and not let Archy see my disappointment.

He knows I was angry, but he thinks that's because he decided to take a 'White House' assignment without my approval, and not the decision itself. Otherwise, he'll show his unhappiness with my attitude, and he'll stop cheerfully trying his best. It's not that he's angry at me, only worried that I'm unhappy with him. He can't be cheerful about anything unless I'm happy about it. We go out to restaurants, if I don't compliment him on his choices from the menu, he won't enjoy his meal, and stiffs the waitress on the tip.

He'll still try his best. He at least always thinks he's trying his best. He always does, but it will be a different less enthusiastic best. He's been that way since we first met. He's unhappy about what he's doing when he knows I'm unhappy about it. And when I'm unhappy, he's unhappy, his performance suffers, at work and at home, if you know what I mean. And that I can't have. I have needs that technology is really no substitute for. It's an impossible situation to be in. I have to be at least outwardly cheerful all the time, and you wouldn't think it, but I'm really not like that.

I better cheer Archy up, a bit. "Archy, I'll make sure I'll take one of the outfits home one night to model it for you." Not only did Archy stand at attention and smile more broadly, but so did the General and so did the old tailor.

"Now, you're in the spirit of the moment." The old seamstress smiled at me, patting my hand then my shoulder. "Israel, don't be a wise guy." I didn't know it; Israel was reaching to give me a pat on my ass. "I'll break all your fingers. Enough!"

"Rachel, I'm too old for anyone to take offense. They'll think it's cute and that I'm probably senile." Israel had a disarming smile, then just shrugged his shoulders. "Rachel, you act senile too, to get people to ignore you, put them off guard, before you have to complete an assignment. You're certainly humane about it."

"These are things you're taught at the Kidon Caesarea. The Metsada is just an 'old boys club' where you just pat the girls' asses and they let you get away with it." You could tell that Rachel was proud of she and Israel being a part of the Mossad, even though she knew the Kidon was the more elite unit.

"You been here a long time, Rachel. You used to have your shop on the Lower East Side of Manhattan and Williamsburg, Brooklyn."

"My husband and I love our trades. Being a tailor for my husband and a seamstress for me is all I ever wished for. My mother taught me, and Israel's father taught him. My mother escaped from Poland to Palestine in 1946, and Israel's father escaped from Romania to Palestine in 1947. I was raped by two Palestinians. Israel was strangling one. When the other one went to attack Israel, I had a .22 caliber revolver I pressed it to the back of his head and pulled the trigger. I was surprised that it didn't make much noise, and luckily there was no exit wound. The bullet would have no doubt shot Israel in the forehead. As that man fell away, I dispatched the second man the same way. The bullet went through his head and took off the top of Israel's left ear. Look at it." Rachel pointed to the missing part of Israel's top left ear." Rachel loved her Israel and loved Israel.

"We were both arrested." Rachel smiled warmly at her husband. "That's when I met David Ben-Gurion. He asked me very quietly what had happened. I told him. He nodded, looked at the bloody bandage over Israel's ear, but said nothing. He motioned to the policeman who had us handcuffed together and to the arms of the chairs we were sitting in. We were quickly released. Both Israel and I stood to thank the elderly Ben-Gurion.

"That's when he said, "I would like both of you to work for the State of Israel.""

"I'm a seamstress and my husband is a tailor. He is a very fine tailor."

"Israel needs tailors and seamstresses. Israel needs the both of you. Call me in the morning. I will set you up." Ben-Gurion gave me a fatherly kiss on the cheek, kissed my husband on both cheeks, shook my husband's right hand with both of his and instructed the police officer to drive us home.

The next morning, we set out to find the man who set us free. We had no phone, so the two of us walked a block to find a pay phone. We told the story to whoever answered at Mr. Ben-Gurion's office. She gave us an address, and as we had no money for either a taxi or the bus. We walked for three hours to get to a building marked in Hebrew, "Government of Israel.""

General Merriwhether interjected, "These are very special people. My old friend, David, had me bring them to Washington."

Israel hadn't said anything up to this point. Now he was becoming more animated. "We were taken to a small office marked in Hebrew, 'HaMossad leModi'in ule Tafkidim Meyuhadim- Reception'. Inside we found out we were being recruited for something called the Mossad. Rachel was being recruited for the Kidon, a special unit of Caesarea Department of the Mossad, and I was assigned to the Metsada, an antiterrorist unit. The thin older man in charge of this reception office said we didn't need any special training, especially my wife. We would be sent directly into the field. Our assignment was a tailor shop in Williamsburg, Brooklyn where we would receive further instructions. He had a son in England at Bletchley Park who worked for someone called Alan Turing.

We were to become part of the World-Wide Web of Nazi hunters and Dispensers of Justice for Israel and all the Jewish people. We were given American passports, steamer passage to New York, clothing, and enough money to rent the apartment over our tailor shop. Between our stipend from the Mossad and the tailor shop, we were doing well."

General Merriwhether was very proud of the part he played in all of this. "I first got a call from the CIA, actually George Levin, a very old OSS officer now too old for any field operations. Ben-Gurion called both of us to look after Rachel and Israel. Little did I know, our government was never officially notified, nor did they sanction any of this cooperation with the Mossad. Ben-Gurion only delt with me and George Levin.

Rachel worked well and efficiently as a lone assassin. She was given neutralizing assignments by the Mossad, particularly for troublesome UN enemies of Israel (which was just about everyone). Israel wanted to do the old Nazi's, but Mossad did not want to risk exposure of one of their antiterrorist operatives. When one of the subjects of her mission was a Russian that was part of the Katyn forest massacre, that was just a bonus. She was disappointed and dejected when she found that Lavrentiy Beria died of 'natural causes.' But the tailor shop was doing so well, they opened a second shop on the Lower East Side, just on the other side of the Williamsburg Bridge.

Naturally, these hostile governments knew what was happening to their UN staff. They would mount a revenge action. Israel was to run interference and coordinate with the Mossad's Brooklyn and Manhattan antiterrorist team. And that team was Reinhard Kaltenbrunner, Ernst Heydrich, and Otto Steinhausl (their code names), also sent to New York City by Ben-Gurion and the Mossad. Otherwise, Rachel was on her own. There was no closed circuit tv cameras like today, and one more corpse on a Manhattan sidewalk did not raise police suspicion or make the tv or radio evening news. And these UN diplomates and their staffs were never very popular with New Yorkers anyway.

But the Mossad's UN informants heard that particularly Iran, Russia and Turkey were planning an aggressive mass extermination at the Williamsburg tenement where Rachel and Israel lived along with torching the tailor shop and the tenement itself with white phosphorous. That would burn long enough and hot enough to destroy any evidence. Mossad ordered both tailor shops closed. That's when Mossad contacted George Levin and me to find a place for Rachel and Israel. And now they're here.

Ben-Gurion called the UN the center of worldwide anti-semitism dedicated to the destruction of Israel. Just the General Assembly's one resolution, 'The right of return', was to achieve the internal destruction of Israel from within using its own democracy against it. Just the way Hitler used the Weimer's Republic democracy to destroy Germany."

Rachel turned Rose. "The Mossad and Israel has more appreciation for women than any American. I'm still operating as a lone assassin, and very successfully. Look at that sign on the back wall – behind our assistant making casket pillows."

Behind the large pattern cutting table with the giant overhead industrial jig saw sat a man at a small pedal operated Singer Sewing Machine – Still black with distinct Teutonic lettering quietly sewing casket pillows embroidered with 'Mother' on one side. "That man is sewing my silencers. No one suspects an old stooped over woman carrying a casket pillow. You hear practically nothing if you have to shoot your target on the street through the pillow. It's just that I'm not that tall, and I have to reach with both hands to shoot him in the back of the head, and not drop my purse from its shoulder strap. But I learned."

"Rachel, the signs behind the man must mean something." I pleased to see a woman in charge instead of a man.

"Rose, the signs tell the whole story." We keep copies of the store signs of our stores across from the United Nations on the east side of Manhattan.

> **RSHA Wansee Butcher Shop, Delicatessen and Charcuterie**
> [Directly Across from the United Nations Headquarters, New York City]
> **"We serve the Excellent Aryan"**
> **Reinhard Kaltenbrunner (chef garde manager), Ernst Heydrich and Otto Steinhausl, Certified Butchers and Proprietors**
> **Fresh-Frozen, Cooked, Cured, Fermented, and Emulsified Sausages, Katyn Kielbasa, Vienna Sausage-Wieners, Frankfurters, Straight Forced Meat, Country Style Forced Meats, Gratin, Mousseline, Pate, Terrine, Galantine, Roulade**
> **Apprenticeships Offered, Inquire Inside**

[Sign in the window of the RSHA Wansee Butcher Shop, Delicatessen and Charcuterie, across from United Nations' Headquarters, NYC]

> **Aryan Custom Suits and Military Uniforms of All Nations**
> **Two Pair of Pants with Each Order, Custom Tailoring Cleaning, Dry Cleaning and Cold Storage on Premises Israel and Rachel Beilin, Proprietors**

[Sign in the Window of Aryan Custom Suits and Military Uniforms, next door to the RSHA Wansee Butcher Shop, Delicatessen and Charcuterie, across from United Nation's Headquarters, NYC]

We target our advertising, and when our target comes in, we take his measurements, custom make the suit, suits, or uniforms, all with two pair of pants. When he comes back for a fitting, we have him try everything on, while Israel runs his credit card, I give him one .22 caliber through the casket pillow to the back of the head. Then wrapped in dry-cleaning clothing plastic wrap, we put him a laundry cart, and out the back door to the butcher shop next door.

There, Reinhard, Ernst and Otto turn him into sausage, delicious perfectly seasoned Aryan sausage in casing made from all his intestines, even though we have to purchase sausage casing for the excess filler. We sell all the sausage back to the UN. The UN is as corrupt as New York Democratic Politics, but even more anti-Semitic. And before you know it, especially with our secret Kosher seasoning, the body is deliciously gone. They can be baked, fried, taken home by the UN staff for backyard barbeque, and the kielbasa or hot dogs can be just boiled.

The clothes we made for our 'subject' we return to the legation with a bill which they pay usually without question. Once he goes missing, the Mossad has the CIA plant a story of his defection and his placement in witness protection. No video of the murder, no body to dispose of, and pure profit from the tailor and butcher shops. One of the few government programs either in the US or Israel that pays for itself.

Rose, you come with me so I can get your measurements. All your cloths will fit you so well, you won't believe the way you look when I'm done. By the way, I also do makeup and hair, if you're invited upstairs to the real White House for a formal dinner or ball. We'll be done with you rather quickly. We want to fit you with your sidearm so there are no unsightly gun-bulges. If you didn't bring one, we can lend you your choice of sidearm and holster, unless you would just rather carry it in your purse. You're choice. It's Archy that'll take longer with all the suits and uniforms. He gets the M1A1 original Colt .45 caliber.

Rose was credulous. "I thought we were to mention no names."

"We don't worry about that, here. If someone hears our names that shouldn't, that's the last thing they hear." With those final words, Rachel motioned Rose to behind a curtain, where she undressed, stood in front of three mirrors and watched Rachel take her measurements

Archy followed Israel into a dressing room, undressed for his measurements and General Merriwhether sat with Abraham, the man sewing the coffin pillows. Abraham was blind and sewed the pillows perfectly from seventy years of memory.

*   *   *   *   *

CHAPTER SIX

**"For there is a time there for every purpose
and for every work"**
[*Ecclesiastes 3:17*]
and
"Any excuse will serve a tyrant"
[*The Wolf and the Lamb, Aesop*]

"All will be revealed."

"You said that before, General." Rose was becoming more and more inpatient with the General. Sometimes I think I get inpatient with the General. But then I've been taught, no junior officer is ever or should ever get inpatient with any general. They can sense it and that's bad for your OER, your career. Lieutenant colonel is not exactly junior, but at the White House, that's pretty low on the totem pole, pecking order or whatever metaphor would apply. (Rose doesn't like when I don't speak directly and use metaphors. I still slip sometimes and that makes Rose cross with me. But I've never been as eloquent or direct as Rose. She's amazing, the way she speaks, the way she smiles, even the way she gets angry at me.)

When you're actually under the White House, deep under the White House that it's so secret, we can't even be seen entering or leaving the building. Maybe that's why Rose is inpatient with the General. I'm sure Rose told everyone we're at the White House. And everybody at Fort Meade, everybody she knows in the Army knows people at the White House or were at the White House. But nobody at the White House or anybody who knows somebody at the White House knows we're here. We maybe not at the White House, but at least we're below the White House. You would think that it's called the

WHITE*HOUSE would be enough for Rose. But Rose said, more than once, "If you can't be seen, then you're not really there! And if you're not really there, then saying your there is even worse than not being there at all."

I think I probably feel that way because that's the way Rose feels, and I feel that Rose feels I should feel – that is, feel that way about the general because she feels that way about the general. I know she's not happy with me working for General Merriwhether, but it's the White House, and I know I made the right decision and she'll realize that in the end. I hope. And to me, it is the White House no matter who knows it or doesn't knows it. That's just the way I am. I think? That's what Rose told me, anyway.

"Rose, Archy, all will be revealed." I think all generals tend to repeat themselves. It's something they learn at the special generals' seminars at the War College, just to make sure they're not misunderstood. As part of the General's staff (actually I'm his only staff), I must understand what he says, what he means, and what he intends every time he changes his mind and didn't really mean to say before he changed his mind. Rose told me that's an important quality for a general staff officer.

"Now, or as of noon, Washington DC Eastern Standard Time – 1200 hours Romeo, we are operational. Our mission has the highest priority and National Security Clearance – The Presidential Security Priority One Clearance. And only the President and his chief of staff know anything."

The President and White House Chief of Staff communicate with USEWOW solely through General Merriwhether. "The 'world leaders' we're assigned are dangerous men who think they have killed and could kill with impunity. They may be more dangerous than the people who they think they are, because on top of everything else, they're crazy. Be sure you carry your sidearm with a full clip and one round in the chamber. Don't be afraid to shoot any one of them if you think you're in imminent danger. And down here at USEWOW, you can shoot anyone you want. And you don't have to clean up your own mess."

I'm sure the General was half joking. He said it with one of his big smiles. It was still music to Rose's ears. She once told me shooting a bad guy relieves a lot of tension. Meating out justice is very soothing – at least that's what Rose said.

"I wouldn't mind putting a bullet in any one of these characters." Rose was snarling and speaking without her drawl. I knew she was serious and was ready to take out her 'inconvenience' on whomever she could.

The general just smiled at Rose, totally ignoring her threats. "Remember Rose, Archy – we're here to gather intelligence. But if you think your threatened, don't hesitate…"

*

"If you can't bite, don't show your teeth."
[Yiddish Proverb, ed. Hanan J. Ayalti, 1949]

"Take my word for it, General Merriwhether, I won't hesitate to either feel threatened or put one round between their eyes." Rose wasn't smiling when she said that. Rose was better than anyone else with a Colt .45 caliber. She's been shooting the Colt since age five and got a Gold Cup .45 caliber ACP competition Colt for her tenth birthday. It was a present from her mother. After her mother died, she carried the pistol everywhere in her purse – always loaded with one round in the chamber. (It was a big purse for a little girl.) At twelve, she had a woman's figure of twenty, natural blond and a little on the meaty side. She attended a Catholic School off base in her Catholic School tartan knee-length skirt and white blouse, always buttoned to the neck. She would often miss the school bus and, instead of calling her father, took public transportation. On a Friday, she was particularly late after hanging with her girlfriends at the only candy store – delicatessen-pizzeria within walking distance of her school. She missed her school bus by an hour, and it was getting dark. She boarded a near empty bus when two older men got on, and in seconds pushed her off the bus forcing open the rear door. The bus hadn't fully stopped, and the driver pulled away without really seeing any-thing. After the bus pulled away, they hit her in the face and shoved her to the ground. She was bleeding from her nose and her mouth. Rose instinctively reached into her book bag. She hesitated for a moment.

"Your money, your wallet isn't going to save you from the both of us. Don't scream, or it'll be a lot worse for you!" The bigger of the two men started to say, "Little girl, you're going to enjoy this." Before he finished his sentence, Rose pulled her Colt out of her book bag – she didn't bring her everyday hand-bag to school. Rose emptied half of the clip into the tall one in front of her. The first two rounds went into the center of his chest, almost through the same hole. He seemed surprised and didn't fall over immediately. But before he fell and she had to roll away from him, she put two more into his forehead. The other man was stunned, hesitated before he turned and ran. She got to her feet, took careful aim, just as she was taught by her father at the firing range, and emptied the rest of the clip into his back – a close grouping considering she was fright-ened, and he was already fifty feet away. She reloaded with an-other full clip, policed her brass, walked a mile to the next bus stop and took the next bus back to the base. She had blood over her white blouse but tried to hide it with her jacket. She never checked whether they were still moving. By the time she got home, her split lower lip was swollen, her nose started bleed-ing again and both eyes were blackened and bloodshot.

When her father got back to their on-base housing, she broke down in tears. When she told her father, he said he would fix everything. He was calm, but after seeing his daughter like this, he formulated several alternate plans for justifiable homicides. First, he had to investigate to see if they survived. He always carried his own Colt and an unregistered throw-away. If either of them survived, Rose's father's plan was to finish them off his .45 and plant the throw-away on them – no matter where he found them – ambulance, hos-pital, back of a police car, police station, in the operating room.

Rose's father was angry but never showed it and would never lose control. You can't execute a strategic plan in anger. By the time he drove to where his daughter was attacked, he had worked out the details of the scenarios he imagined and would improvise for any other situation. And he knew that even in front of eyewitnesses, eyewitnesses are the most unreliable testimony.

The man Rose shot in the back had crawled to the side of the road and bled to death on the shoulder. The other lay where he fell. The state police and the coroner's van were already there, and a photographer was taking pictures of the crime scene. There was a spot of blood and a blond hair near the first body. Rose's blood and hair. And even though they hadn't survived, the projectiles remained in the two bodies.

The hair, her blood and a ballistics match to her Gold Cup .45 would be a slam-dunk case against his little girl. Her father was in his Class A uniform with all his battle ribbons. He told the troopers he wanted to make sure it wasn't one of his AWOL troops. They let him approach the first man and lift the sheet. Even though they had already photographed the blond hair and blood stain on the gravel, he ground them both into the dirt, rubbed the ground with his sole and heel of his shoe until the blood and hair disappeared into the gravel. He moved the plastic number marker with his foot, far enough away from the original site, but not so far as to be noticed. He thanked the troopers and left the crime scene knowing he did exactly and successfully what he set out to do.

He still had to take away the young girl's gift from her mother. Rose cried even more but understood the implication of matching ballistics. Her father replaced it with a standard issue .45 caliber M1A1 Colt. Rose's Colt from her mother was never registered. Her mother was always thinking ahead. So, when it disappeared, no one was the wiser. Rose's knew neither Colt was registered either. Her mother taught her never carry a registered traceable handgun. Always wipe off the ammunition and clip before loading, just in case the young girl had to use it, in an emergency. That day, Rose broke one of her mother's cardinal rules by loading the spar magazine without wiping it off. She didn't think about that, but her father did, and he thanked God she wasn't stopped by the police.

*

"All assignment, rendezvous or event times will be Zulu Time – Greenwich Mean Time. That means, our noon, 1200 hours is 5 PM or 1700 hours ZULU Time. All operators need to set their watches to Zulu time to avoid confusion. Just like the tide tables, we don't use Daylight Savings Time." The General checked his own wristwatch, then his antique railroad pocket watch. His wristwatch was set to Zulu Time and his pocket watch was set to Washington, DC local time.

"We're a little short staffed. Bill Casey didn't allow enough for inflation, military pay raises, pensions, and health insurance. Some of the marines assigned to security will be assisting us. They've all been fitted with burqas. Rachel and Israel, once they've completed their days uniform and clothing production, will assist us while you two go home to get a shower and a change of clothes. You can actually live out of your assigned dressing rooms and take your meals in our common dining hall. Rachel and Israel have their own burkas and a selection of civilian cloths and military uniforms they can use at a moment's notice. Everybody's uniforms, civilian clothes, and burqas – and everyone has their own burqa, go on and off with Velcro, just to cut the time it takes to change clothing.

But you should still get home, at least to pick up your mail. Forwarding your mail will be a dead giveaway that you're assigned to the White House. Everyone knows, if you forward your mail to the Treasury Building, it's because you're using the secret tunnels to the White House. Even the Post Office knows. And once they see the change of address pasted on your mail, everybody in the local sorting room will know you're at the White House.

Anyway, when you go home, we'll send you home with at least two large bags of kitchen garbage you can put out, so people know you're still living there. And the enemies counter-espionage operatives will go through every bit of garbage you put out. Our counter-counter-espionage agents have pictures of them going through the garbage. And don't think we haven't gone through their garbage."

"Archy, we're taking your car to work from now on. Nobody is putting garbage in my car." Now Rose has another reason to be unhappy with the General – and by extension – a very short extension - unhappy with me, the love of her life.

The General was oblivious to what Rose just said. And she wasn't speaking softly, either. "This is what we've learned so far. We've made dummy phone calls and rerouted any calls they've made to Rachel and Israel. As I said, we're short staffed and everyone has to do double duty. Israel and Rachel can still work in the shop, supervise the cleaning and pressing, and engage these leaders in conversation as needed. And they don't have to say much. These leaders just love to talk and give orders. More than once, the Ayatollah, and The Dear Respected One demanded that the person they were speaking to be brought to them for personal execution. The Dear Respected One wanted them brought to the courtyard behind his office, where he would dismember them with a Bofors 40mm anti-aircraft gun at one hundred yards, the way he dispatched an elderly uncle. With his uncle he tied him to a stake too close to the reviewing stand, and his audience was covered in bloody body parts, blood, and full intestines. They mistakenly gave the uncle a last meal. They never did that again. The Dear Respected One had those guards executed the next day the same way – except the stakes they were tied to were much further away. The Dear Respected One never made a head shot on anyone.

When the Ayatollah ordered a personal execution, he had them brought to the entrance of his home, Beit Rahbari Compound on Palestine Street. He ordered the front driveway gates opened to the public so the faithful could witness the Ayatollah throw out the first stone and then invite his followers to finish the execution. His servants would arrange the throwing stones in one of two semicircles around the execution guest of honor. The outer circle for men, and the inner circle, six feet closer for women. Just like in golf, with the further tee off for men, and the closer tee off for women.

Israel and Rachel assumed a new telephone identity, and the Ayatollah never knew the difference or noticed they spoke with a Yiddish accent. When Rachel slipped and called him a 'mensch', the Ayatollah wanted to know, 'What's a mensch?' When she said, "A Jewish Ayatollah," he laughed, and hung up, He placed another call and instructed the woman on the other end, who was Rachel again, to cut the first woman's throat on the spot. Then he impolitely slammed the phone on her. Of course, how polite can you be when you order someone's throat cut.

*

Putin and Xi just ordered who they were displeased with to be disappeared. Mass murders were never personal, and they never gave details of how they wanted their subjects dispatched. But Putin and Xi, if they knew your name, they would order some special execution, that if they could fit it in with all their meetings, they would attend and often personally participate in. And nothing as simple as a bullet to the back of the head. And if either of them personally dispatched someone, especially from their inner circle, they wanted their coworkers present, just to send a message.

The real Putin was a traditionalist. Lubyanka basement was favorite site. No bother about cleanup. Lubyanka had a dedicated cleanup crew available at a moment's notice. He never showed anger, even when he was angry enough to shoot the person that needed to be shot as he sat behind his office desk and that person sat comfortably in front of him. Even though he had good people to clean up, he's had to replace at least three oriental carpets, and cleanup ties up his personal office for an entire afternoon, especially if it's a head shot, or with a large caliber handgun with a gaping exit wound. They replaced so many chairs, they've stopped buying fancy chairs and now all the replacement office chairs are comfortable Naugahyde faux leather with a special bullet proof back to prevent splatter behind the chair.

Our Putin and Xi never got wise to the fact they were always talking to the same two people, Rachel, and Israel. Every time either one questioned Rachel or Israel about only speaking English, they would only tell them that it was their request so they could practice speaking to the world leaders at the upcoming opening UN General Assembly meeting.

Now, our Vladimir Putin is finished his dinner and is just reading his essential papers in front of his television set. Tonight, he's trying to sell more gas to Germany and screw NATO. President Xi Jinping is just dozing off, dreaming about more completely enslaving his people to increase his country's production of cheap crap and Apple products he can sell to the West. He's planning on more slave labor re-education camps for dissidents, ethnic minorities, all of Nepal and Mongolia totally isolated from the rest of China. He hasn't told us his special plans for India, only that he as special plans for the entire Indian subcontinent. Xi still wants to get even with Japan over World War Two. He has an especially inventive enslavement and reeducation plan for the Japanese.

That's the second reason he wants his nation to get to the moon. Primarily, Xi can place a large part of his nuclear force on the far side of the Moon, far beyond striking distance of the US. He plans to demonstrate it once against Guam, say it was fired in error. Then threaten the US with overwhelming retaliation if China is attacked. He needs to do this before the US develops the capability of targeting far-side moon-based nuclear weapons or intercept them before entering the earth's atmosphere.

The first and real reason is to put his slave labor camps there in complete darkness. A special treat for the Japanese. If there's a problem at one of the Moon slave colonies, just remotely cut the power from their nuclear power plant. Shut down their nuclear electric generating plant, and in less than a day, no oxygen, no inmates. Then you send up another group of dissidents to clear the bodies, stack them on the dark side of the Moon outside the colony where they'll freeze solid, and then use the frozen meat to feed the new slaves. And the machinery for the manufacturing will remain unharmed. With multiple camps, Xi can segregate his workers by age. The older and less productive they become; the power is cut remotely from one of the satellites orbiting the moon to the aging far-side geriatric labor colony. Machinery saved, useless or less useful slave labor eliminated, and they become a high protein food source for the new slaves. The same moon-orbiting satellites can be used to launch their dark-side of the moon nuclear strike force.

*

It's 10:30 PM, and time for the Ayatollah Ali Khamenei warm milk and stool softener so he can fall into a peaceful sleep dreaming of the sinners he can stone to death. It was a special nighttime treat when he dreamt of adulteress women and how they committed adultery with evil Westerners. Then he could behead them as a couple. Apparently, throwing homosexuals off roofs is not the fun it used to be and very messy. With everyone having a cell phone, videos leak out, then it's just throwing people off the same roofs for leaking the video – and it never seems to end. And after a good night's sleep with these pleasant dreams, he'll start the day with a good bowel movement before any of the scheduled executions. Afternoons were reserved for the ad hoc stoning, which always took longer.

And stoning takes so much effort. There are only a few designated stoning parks in any major city. Stones can't be too big that you can't throw them far enough, too heavy that it takes one direct hit to the head to be fatal, nor too small that they can't cause a painful injury. They have to be between baseball and softball size to be able to throw them accurately and be comfortable to pick up. The stones placed along the inner circle are baseball size for the women and girls. The softball size stones in the outer circle are for the men. The circles are not one inside the other, but side by side, with men and women socially distanced.

These stones are relatively hard to come by being always in demand. All the stones eventually end up in the center of the stoning circle where they lay blood stained – nobody bothers to pick them up after they were done. The Ayatollah was always bewildered how good people meeting out justice could on the other hand be so inconsiderate. It's as bad as littering. He is dreaming of forming the Ayatollah's Stoning Monitors, to be sure that once you throw your stone, it is eventually cleaned and returned to the official outer or inner stoning circle from which stones must be cast. No stone may be thrown either closer or further away. So, it is written. That is the law!

The Ayatollah wants stoning to remain the popular pastime of the faithful and patriotic Iranians. Stoning is the way the Ayatollah eliminated divorce. Unfaithful wives were stoned to death with their divorce lawyers. There are still unfaithful wives, but no one is practicing divorce law.

The Ayatollah reserves beheading for political prisoners, or people who served the Ayatollah faithfully and then fell out of favor. They are usually accused of disloyalty or treachery. And being unsure, the Ayatollah has them beheaded by the person who made the accusation, and then beheads that person as well, never being sure of who's telling the truth. In any case, no matter who is telling the truth and who isn't, justice is served.

The very first 'secretary' we had assigned to our Ayatollah was actually our Marine Captain from the medical office. He liked her. He told her he liked the way she filled out her burqa. He told her about his dreams, and when she forced a giggle and told him how interesting he was, he took it as flirting. He called her an infidel, an apostate whore who dared to speak to his name and speak to him in a sinful voice (the captain's Southern accent). He yelled for a guard. Ordered her to be stoned to death at dawn, and he was to be awakened so he could cast the first stone after his prune juice and bran breakfast, but before his morning bowel movement. Those were his exact orders. The real Ayatollah likes his morning executions early so he can take his time with his bowel movement and read his newspaper at the same time.

Casting the first stone is the Iranian equivalent to throwing out the first pitch on opening day of the baseball season. The guard entered and took the captain away before she had a chance to strangle the old man. On the way out, the captain had already hiked her burqa up past her hip with her right hand on her Colt .45 service side arm. The next morning, the Ayatollah was just told that she hung herself in her cell by her burqa. Her body was then chopped up and fed to the dogs. In truth, the medical division kept a 'service dog', a poodle-cocker spaniel six-month-old puppy. The Ayatollah only arrived a few days ago, and no permanent staff has been assigned to him since that incident.

*

In Pyongyang, The Dear Respected One, The Shining Sun, The Supreme Leader, Kim Jung Un has been in a sugar-carbohydrate coma for hours and won't wake up until his first bladder call. We feed him a high calorie diet, with lots of port – supermarket port. We pour out whiskey out of single malt labeled bottles, but the stuff is COSCO's off brand on sale whiskey and paint thinner. Our budget isn't what we thought it would be. The Dear Respected One gets pizza with extra cheese and three toppings when we have the coupons.

It's delivered to the White House south lawn entrance where the helicopters land and brought through the elevators, through the tunnels down here. Just to make it simple, when we order pizza for the Dear Respected One, President Putin gets pizza, the Ayatollah gets pizza and President Xi gets pizza. Our Chinese leader's pizza has rice and Chinese noodles, snow peas, and water chestnuts as a topping and is seasoned with soy sauce. And yet they're all crazy enough to believe they're in their respective capitals at the center of their governments. You wouldn't believe how isolated these despots are. We learned all that from the translators who think they're the rulers of their sacred lands.

One night we ordered out Chinese for President Xi. The best Chinese food is more than a mile from the White House. Security, Medical, and Rachel and Israel wanted Peking duck. We were going to get it for everyone and our guests, but we had only limited coupons. With our budget, we got a whole Peking Duck for each member of the staff, security, and ancillary staff, including the janitorial and dry cleaning and laundry staff. Our special guests got pizza that night with no extra toppings. We told the Ayatollah that the plain round pie was invented in ancient Persia by Cyrus the Elder, the unifier of Persia and inventor of take-out food. President Xi was told that the plain pizza was brought back from China by Marco Polo, who also brought back the plain pie back from ancient Korea. That's what we told the Dear Respected One.

*

As far as President Putin goes, he just enjoys plain pizza once in a while. Pizza was something very hard to find after his last purge of the Kremlin pizzerias. The real Putin thought it was a CIA dead drop. He ordered the FSB to keep it under surveillance. The surveillance team was eating two meals a day, and one of the members began dating the pizza chief's daughter, who also made pizza. The pizzeria did so much business with the FSB, when the agents insisted on vodka with their pizza, the pizza chief was more than happy to comply and served the good Russian vodka with crackers and Russian caviar.

With the FSB as regular customers, people seeing more people eat at the shop, encouraged more business from the tourists, other foreign spies, the CIA especially – and everybody was ordering whole pizza pies with extra toppings, vodka and caviar, and more and more customers ordered caviar as the extra topping instead of anchovies. Word of mouth passed from senior FSB agents who started in the KGB to old, retired KGB agents living in Moscow that this was the place to have pizza with their vodka. The pizza chief added two more ovens, expanded with tables to the two empty store fronts flanking his shop, hired more waitresses, two more pizza chiefs, and two delivery boys for takeout. He was doing so well, that the pizzeria was open twenty-four hours a day, seven days a week. He delivered all over Moscow but did an especially brisk business with Lubyanka prison. His pizza with caviar topping and a vodka to go, became a favorite request for a last meal, if you bribed your jailor and were allowed a last meal.

All was going well until this was reported to Putin by the FSB surveillance team watching the FSB surveillance team. The photos they took from across the street identified almost all the known foreign agents in Moscow, all sitting next to the FSB agents. Even with the additional tables, everybody was sitting close to everybody else. And when everybody is a secret agent of one government or another, there's no place else to sit.

No body from the FSB superior officers considered that the restaurant was popular, and the tables were crowded together. And ordinary Muscovites couldn't really afford to eat there anyway. You had to have the extra income as a spy to pay for it. The original FSB surveillance team just put everything on their expense account, which they padded anyway.

Putin decided that the pizza chief's pizza making daughter was part of a CIA honey trap and that his whole KGB team was compromised. The original FSB teams were executed in the Lubyanka basement, as tradition dictated. The pizza chief and his daughter were transported to a Siberian gulag. The gulag's commander had actually heard of the pizza topped with good Russian caviar. The pizza chief and his daughter were to spend the rest of their days making caviar-topped pizza for their camp commander and his officers. The other foreign agents and the American CIA agents were well known to the FSB, and Moscow rules dictated that not only they remain unharmed, but not harassed or impeded in any way.

It was so cold above the Artic Circle where the camp was located, he had the chief leave pizzas outside to freeze, then boxed them and made a good deal of money selling the frozen pizza and shipping it across Russia. But this was a very generous camp commander. He made sure everyone in his chain of command had their share of the cash profits shipped with their frozen pizza. Pizzas with caviar were regularly sent to the Kremlin's FSB offices who shared them with President Putin. The camp commander ended up divorcing his wife – she couldn't cook except for Russian borsch - and marrying the pizza chief's pizza making daughter. We learned all that from Putin's translator who thinks he's Putin.

*

"General, we have four different leaders from four time zones." Rose saw problems and not solutions.

"Rose, Archy, each one of these leaders has a suite of three rooms, no windows just video screens to simulate what would be outside their offices. They have one office, one outer office and one sleeping and lounge area. We couldn't afford much else. We have one dining hall in the center of the four suites. Each suite has a locked door to the dining area, and only one suite is unlocked to the dining area at a time. To keep them out of the other doors, each is marked with "Asbestos Contamination – Cancer Danger - Enter at Your Own Risk". The other doors are locked under any circumstances. When none of them are in the dining hall, all the doors are locked. These signs are shifted depending on which world leader is having dinner, leaving his door as a safe door he can return to his suite. And at all meals, from now on, they'll be eating with and having a conversation with their staff assistant – that's you Archy. Rose, you will be our waitress for everyone except the Ayatollah. All you need to be is an acceptable waitress. These guys don't tip. Try to get their orders mostly right, sway when you walk away from them just to distract them, and please don't poison them.

When the dining hall is empty of any of our guests, our

staff is invited to help themselves to meals from the kitchen and eat in the dining hall. It's comfortable, roomy, serves a whole variety of beverages, both alcoholic and non-alcoholic. Everyone is welcome to anything in the kitchen. Food in the refrigerator marked 'Kosher' is for anyone who observes these dietary restrictions. There's a separate food cabinet and refrigerator and freezer for gluten free." The General obviously took a lot of time planning the kitchen and dining hall and was proud of what he accomplished.

As far as the Ayatollah is concerned, we can put anyone in a burqa to be his waitress. Rose, you will be everyone's secretary except for the Ayatollah. We can put anyone in a burqa for that job, too. I plan to take my turn, just to see what he's up to. During the time you would normally be the waitress or secretary for the Ayatollah, you'll sneak into their suites and change their clocks. If they ask about the bedroom clocks, just say there was a power failure. You will always be setting the clocks ahead. Over the next three nights, advance Putin's, and the Ayatollah's clocks ahead by one hour. Then for the next eight days, everybody's clocks are advanced by one hour, until everyone is near Washington, DC time. Putin will be the easiest to fool. He drinks like a fish, keeps a glass of vodka at his bedside in case he wakes up thirsty. He loses hours under normal circumstances. Do you have that Rose?"

"I've got it, General. But do you expect everyone to keep this straight, especially with one dining room? And who's handling the video screens?"

"Rose, we set up their video screens well in advance of their arrivals. It's all on a continuous loop. We have four loops, all generic scenery that could go with any location. And even if it doesn't, these guys are delusional anyway. Anything that doesn't make sense, they'll figure it's just another part of their delusion. And as long as they know they are running everything with the power of life and death, they won't care. They all, in their heart of hearts, as long as they have absolute control of their countries, they'll live forever. With the power of life and death for all their nations' peoples, they really believe that they have the power to conquer death for themselves."

"General, do these guys think they're going to live forever?" Rose looked at me. "The translators are crazy and so are the guys their translating for. That's exactly what they believe."

"Xi, the Ayatollah and Putin have a whole host of compatible prisoners that are actually treated very well, not knowing they're the transplant donors for their leaders.

The Dear Respected One, the Shining Sun thinks that his people have volunteered to donate organs to keep him alive forever. He really believes it. That's why he doesn't have any prisoners he keeps as organ donors. But in North Korea when you seek any medical care, someone always draws blood, and you are tissue typed and your lab number is tattooed on your abdomen. They don't use any limbs in case their amputated when questions by the Dear One's secret police. And all medical care in North Korea is paid for by the state. It's their form of Obama Care."

"General, I'm worried about keeping all these schedules straight, and have time to change clothes and uniforms." Archy looked confused already.

"Archy, there will be three clocks on the entrance to each suite. The one to your left as you face the door from the outside about to walk in, will be Washington, DC local time, whether Eastern Standard Time or Daylight Savings Time. The clock in between the two other clocks will be Zulu time – Greenwich Mean Time. And the last clock will be the time that is set on the clocks inside the suites. Rose, be sure to reset the third clock on the right, not left, not center, but right, every time you change the clocks inside. Archy, you will get two additional wrist watches. The lowest watch on your wrist will be Washington time. The center watch will be the time in your assigned suite, and the upper watch will be Zulu time. That means every time you enter a suite, you have to synchronize your middle watch with the clock on the door to the right, as you're facing the door from the outside. Not the clock on the left as you face the door, which is actually the door's right, especially when looking from inside.

Your fingerprint, Rose's fingerprint, and anyone with USEWOW clearance fingerprints will unlock the door to each suite, and you can enter the dining room from within the suite if it is unlocked for your 'guest'. It will be one guest at a time in the dining room. After your guest leaves the dining room, change the Asbestos signs, and unlock the next door. Then lock your door behind you. Exit, and go to dinner with whomever your next assignment is. Don't worry about leaving your last dinner companion. Putin will be half stoned on vodka, even though he won't show it. Kim will be going into his post prandial carbohydrate coma, and the Ayatollah will not know who is under the burqa. And we have plenty of people to wear burqas. The problem is President Xi. He's too smart, and too sober. His translator who thinks he is Xi is not stupid either. Rose will have to double back, put a business suit jacket over her waitress uniform, let him take a phone call with Rachel or Israel, then double back to the dining room to serve the next course to whomever. What we'll need to do is schedule Xi to eat all his meals last, but that may not be possible.

"General, I assume it's our index finger that unlocks the doors." Rose asked the question for a reason, although I'm not sure why.

"Rose, Archy, your index finger will open the doors, in fact any finger on either hand will work, in case someone cuts off one, you can always use whatever fingers are left to get into the doors. In fact, if your captured and questioned, as long as they leave you one finger, you can come back to work. If you lose all your fingers, you can always go through the kitchen to the dining hall, and then enter any of the suites. The doors between the dining hall and the suites open without a fingerprint going into the suite, but you will need your fingerprint to bring your guest into the dining hall.

Archy, each suite has a study/conference room with four

flat screen TVs to watch the American News Channels, Russian News Channel, Chinese News Channel, and Iranian News. Kim suite has two TVs. One is for the American News Channel and one is for anything he wants to watch. He's usually asleep a half an hour after eating. He has serious sleep apnea that will end up killing him sooner than later."

"And General, I didn't mean to interrupt you, but when do we start really engaging these men?"

"Rose, Archy, for now, you need do nothing but yes them. I want to see how they react to the news from the television and newspapers we supply them. We bring in the papers from Moscow, Tehran, North and South Korea, Beijing, New York, Washington, London, Berlin, Rome, and Cairo. These are the subscriptions Bill Casey left us with. It's a good representative sample of the world press, but he left out so many, that we wondered why."

"General, they're not going to confide in their secretary or waitress."

"But, Rose, they will talk to their Chief of Staff. And they will speak more freely on a telephone call between like-minded heads of states. We are going to have them call each other, and then arrange a summit for Nuclear Nations that Hate the US - the NNHUS. We have Archy suggest it to each of them – the NNHUS – pronounced 'the NEWS'. It'll roll off their tongues. Just tell them they need a catchy phrase to get the world's attention. And you have to make it seem like it's their idea, each individually. That shouldn't be a difficult task. They're already delusional megalomaniacs who think they are delusional megalomaniacs."

"And what makes you think that they're going to band together?"

"Rose, darling…"

"You don't have to 'darling' me, General. Never, ever 'darling' me. I'm nobody's 'darling'. Rose said that in a soft monotone that was more frightening that her screaming, or her screaming holding her .45 caliber Colt.

"Our video people have been monitoring the news, all day, all night and every day. Recording everything. For our guests, we just let them flip between the live news broadcasts. It didn't make the news yet, but the UN General Assembly opening is coming up, and all the world leaders, including the real Putin, the real Ayatollah, the real Kim and the real Xi will all be speaking. Once they hear that, I'm betting they'll want to talk to each other and start plotting a strategy against the West, and the US in particular. With that impetus, their meeting will be in the bag and we'll have a glimpse into what our enemies are planning before they even know themselves."

"General, that seems to make sense." Archy was smiling at the General, the genius of the General's plan, and the fact that General Merriwhether include him and Rose in this top priority national defensive and offensive strategy.

"General Merriwhether, you know you're just listening to the ravings of mad men. And your plan is to put them together to amplify their hallucinations." Rose was more talking to Archy than General Merriwhether.

"Rose, Archy, remember, 'There was never a genius without a tincture of madness.'"

*   *   *   *   *

CHAPTER SEVEN

"But evil men and seducers shall wax worse and worse, deceiving and being deceived. But continue thou in the things which thou hast learned and has been assured of, knowing of whom thou hast learned them;"
[*The Holy Bible – authorized King James Version, 1611 – II Timothy 3:13 & 14*]

General Merriwhether always has a positive attitude. Rose, not so much. As Rose requested, actually ordered is a better term, we were to use my car my car every day for our commute from Fort Meade to the Treasury building. This morning, to my surprise, she was far less sarcastic than usual. Normally I say nothing during her rants. But this was, maybe not a new Rose, but a different Rose, at least for today. It must have been the incredible sex we had last night, finally in our own bed. It had been a while, with work and having to stay at USEWOW. She was so different that I thought she might want me to not only contribute to or commute conversation but lead it – pick the topic.

"And don't think it was because of the sex. That helped. You were certainly adequate. I just needed to be home." You see, I was wrong as usual on all counts. Rose she still drove even though it was my car and she hated automatic transmissions. She said that you can't feel the road unless there are solid gears between you and your tires.

Rose always drove unless she told me to drive. And when she told me to drive, she gave me our destination and exactly how to get there – turn by turn. The only time I was allowed to drive with Rose in the car was if we were going anyplace – the O club, the PX, anywhere on base or an off base official military or diplomatic function where we might be seen by other officers and especially their wives. The diplomatic functions were usually when we were her father's guest, retired Lieutenant General Jefferson Davis Jefferson. In case you've forgotten, he was General Merriwhether's roommate at West Point and life-long friend.

Anyway, Rose always said, it wasn't manly for a husband to allow his wife to drive him around. Her father told her that as a young girl when he wouldn't let her drive his stick shift. Her father taught her how to drive just after he taught her how to shoot her .45 caliber Colt. By the time she was thirteen and could reach the pedals without extension blocks, she could double-clutch with the best of them.

Rose, and her father told both Rose and me on many occasions after Rose forced herself behind the wheel of her car, that it was as important for my career to appear competent, knowledgeable, decisive, and manly as it is for a wife to be meek, deferential, and obedient to her man. For if a man cannot command his wife, he could never command troops on the field of battle. And marriage was the ultimate field of battle for every married man. And so, said General Jefferson, and so said Rose!

My mind does wander. Rose always says that. Well, this morning she was far less sarcastic. I don't mind the sarcasm, but when you have a break from it – it's just like if you keep banging your head against a wall, you really don't mind, but when you stop, it feels so good. It's the same with Rose's sarcasm, snarls, nasty quips, and deadly silences. I suffer just as much during these awful silences as any other time. The only time you wish for any of her usual conversational repertoire is when she's yelling. Rose doesn't scream or get hysterical – she raises the volume of her voice and changes its entire tone, speech rhythm, and tempo when she yells. And unless you have a wife like Rose, you'll never appreciate the difference between tempo and rhythm. And only women, just certain women can do that. There is no man on earth that is genetically engineered with this ability.

And Rose does this amazing thing, uses this amazing weapon of hers without using any foul language. No one, not even Lawrence Olivier reciting Shakespeare had the command of the King's English as Rose when she chose to yell. When she got started, she could quote English literature, French literature in French, and Cicero in the original Latin. She could not only make you feel bad at whatever she was screaming at you about, but make you feel both especially stupid at what you did, and stupid in general about all the things you don't know. And that's both frightening and awe-inspiring for friend and foe alike.

This morning, Rose almost wore a smile as she entered the Treasury Building. Last night was the first time in the eight days we began to incrementally change the clocks and alarms in each of the leader's suites to get everyone's time zones close enough that we could run all the offices and serve all their meals at a more synchronized, convenient, and disciplined time. Last night we were home for the first time at a regular hour, showered in our own bathroom, slept in our own bed, and I put out the garbage just as General Merriwhether instructed.

It was our first night home, and both of us were exhausted after a hectic work week and sex, but too curious about someone rifling through our trash to fall asleep. With the lights out in the living room, Rose and I sat quietly in the dark, watching out the front window. About one AM, strangers completely dressed in black with black ski masks, picked up the plastic garbage out of our garbage pail full of the garbage from the USEWOW kitchen and drove away in their nondescript black four-door foreign intelligence agency generic sedan. I've seen these vehicles before. They're all over the Washington and cruise outside of every military base in the nation – like Ubers.

I wouldn't doubt if some of the poorer spy's double as Uber drivers using their company car. This is especially true of the Chinese Ministry of State Security. The Communist Chinese use cheap labor for everything. And their spies consider themselves lucky. They get to live in the U.S. get to keep most of the money they make at their second job and send a chunk of the money home to their families being held hostage so they can bribe their jailors with US dollars.   The generic cars they drive must be the last autos on the market with fender skirts and a hood ornament - a big chrome 'GM', for Generic Motors. The cars are imported from China under GM, but it's not our General Motors. The Chinese Communists give the cars to other nations' spy agencies. Our CIA has studied the cars. They all have bugging devices and GPS so the Chinese can keep track of everyone who uses their 'gift'.

Rose said, there are so many of these cars around, they must be leases. The less experienced spies follow too close and end up rear ending the surveillance target. All of these cars are followed by our counter intelligent agents, who are all followed by lawyers who leave their business cards with both drivers even before the police arrive. Everyone exchanges licenses and registrations, even though they are all forgeries. All parties play by Moscow rules, no one is harassed, and no one is particularly upset. I should say, except for the lawyers, who never can generate a case. They give up, and now the only lawyers following the GM cars are new law school graduates who don't know any better.

Originally, cars needing repairs were just junked by Chinese counterintelligence. The Chinese Communists never brought any spare parts to the U.S. Now with all the junked Chinese spy cars, there's a big secondary market in junked spare parts. You see junk yards all over the country advertising spare parts for 'GM' cars. I know my Uncle Jimmy runs a junk yard in the Bronx that specializes in these 'GM' junked cars.

Russian spies drive around in used American made – union-built automobiles they buy from GRU fronted used car lots. The GRU car dealers all advertise 'All American Union-Built Used Cars – Money Back Guarantee'. Uncle Jimmy rents some of his parking lot space to 'AAUB Cars'. And with CIA, MI6 and the French DGSE counterintelligence agents watching the AAUB Cars, there's no street parking anywhere near Uncle Jimmy's lot and gas station. Since MI6 and the DGSE are cheap, they buy their spy vehicles from AAUB Cars, sweep the cars for listening devices, remove the GPS tracker and change the oil and oil filter. AAUB Cars never changes the oil or oil filter on any of their cars. MI6 and DGSE usually drive their purchases right off the AAUB Cars' lot into Uncle Jimmy's gas station and parking lot next door for the oil change. Uncle Jimmy will plant a CIA GPS tracker, listening device and front and rear micro cameras he bought in bulk at BJ's electronics. That actually saves the CIA surveillance time and money. They can track whomever MI6 and DGSE are tracking. For MI6, for every three oil changes, they get the fourth free. Uncle Jimmy doesn't like the French and won't work with German BND and MAD counterintelligence agencies. He figures they're in with the Russians, or at least are trying to play both sides of the street with their Russian pipeline. German's never can be trusted, anyway. Uncle Jimmy say, 'Just look at history!'

Uncle Jimmy doesn't need to pay for his own security and Uncle Jimmy's adjacent parking lot is always full. He still has to kick-back a very small percent of the parking fees to keep his parking lot, and him and Aunt Anna safe. Some sort of tax, he said, from the parking lot gods.

Uncle Jimmy has already raised his hourly rates twice, put in a twenty-four-hour hot dog cart and snack stand, Starbucks opened withing walking distance, and everyone concerned is making money. I have on good sources – sources inside the CIA, deep deep inside CIAs counterintelligence service, that the way the CIA is able to spot spying hotspots, active dead drops, and spy recruitment sites is to look for the cluster of chain coffee shops and fast-food establishments. McDonalds had the best intelligence service here and overseas in discovering these locations. McDonalds beat the CIA, the GRU, MI6 and everyone else to be the first to put in a franchise at these prime high traffic locations. Uncle Jimmy said Godfather pizza was also pretty good. And no matter who they are, everybody pays for parking. But that's another story. And so is Uncle Jimmy.

By two thirty AM, the men dressed in black returned with the full garbage bag, put it quietly in the garbage can, and checked the recycling container again, which was still empty. One of the two men, I assume they were men, and a woman who must be in charge to get anyone to act so stupid and be so demeaned as to go through someone's trash, I imagine the smarter one took notes, and the other one took pictures of the garbage can with the full plastic bag replaced exactly as they found it, and the empty recycling container, again. They had both before and after pictures to prove we didn't sneak any other classified garbage out for the next day's pickup. Apparently, they returned every Sunday night before the Monday morning garbage pickup, and every Wednesday night before our Thursday morning pickup. They would watch the garbage be put out. Sneak the bag out of the can, go through the contents, placing it on a table in the exact sequence it was put into the garbage bag. They placed the garbage bag back in the can with the garbage returned in the same order it was found and stayed to watch the garbage until it was picked up. These espionage agents were specialist in garbage and returning the garbage pristine after a thorough search and photographing each scrap of ...crap. This was all reported to us by our garbage counter intelligent agents who watch these agents watch the garbage.

Some of the less informed espionage agencies decided it would be more practical just to run the garbage trucks themselves. Some of them did. And wouldn't you know it, their trucks ended up at the bottom of the Potomac off the end of one or another pier, and their agents accidentally broke their kneecaps. At least those that didn't fight back. Those that did, at least those we assume that did, ended up with their seat belts still fastened when they accidently drove their truck off a pier through the barriers, or were just never seen again. This happened twice. The third intelligence agency gifted their fleet of six, two-hundred-thousand-dollar trucks to a local 'carting' charity and promised never to enter the carting business again. As a consolation, the carting company delivered the full garbage bags directly to their offices, the first month free. After that, they had to pay an additional monthly fee for the carting company to stop the carting company from delivering the garbage. These espionage agents turned themselves into the FBI, ratted on their entire network and were put into witness protection. And that's how they escaped the carting company. Eventually they got jobs in different cities under assumed identities working for other carting companies.

Garbage disposal, like espionage is a very competitive business. Uncle Jimmy taught me that, and that's why he never got involved in the 'carting' business. That is unless you do them a favor and they owe you one. And Uncle Jimmy said that he learned that from the Bible, the Old Testament, Exodus, the second book of Moses. Uncle Jimmy said that was how Moses got in trouble with the Pharaoh and his carting company.

*

Once our garbage was picked up, I brought in the garbage can and empty recycling container and we left for the U.S. Treasury. When the elevator door opened in the sub sub-basement of the White House, Rose and I were greeted by our concierge, without using any names, of course. We went through all the formalities and procedures for entering USEWOW and once through the secret door that had a brand-new sign that read, "Secret Door – Use No Names", we were met by General Merriwhether.

We all walked to our changing rooms. General Merriwhether waited anxiously right outside the doors which were side by side. It was General Merriwhether's turn to wear the burqa but wouldn't put on the black veil and head piece until the last minute. Rose's secretary and waitress uniforms only needed substituting the white apron for a business suit jacket. Someone else was assigned the burqa duty every day, so Rose didn't have to bother with that. As far as I was concerned, I only needed a change of uniform jacket. I wore one uniform jacket and carried the three others over my left arm. There was a clothes tree inside the staff hall entrance to the kitchen where Rose left her suit jacket or apron, which ever she didn't need, and on another nearby clothes tree, I hung my three uniform jackets I would change into – for each of our guests. I left a tweed sports jacket there to wear with the uniform pants in case I had to be chief of staff and then go back quickly to military aid de camp. As our guests' chief of staff, I wore my one suit, with two pairs of pants for the entire day, making changing unnecessary. Just for economy of time's sake, I had just the one three-piece suit. And with two pairs of pants, I would probably be buried in it. The sports jacket was mine I brought from home. I've had it for years.

None of these 'world leaders' ever noticed me or that the uniform pants didn't match any of the uniform jackets. Twice a week, I would show up in a business suit, and they always assumed any one in a suit was their chief of staff. And any one in any sort of a uniform was their military attaché. I know, more than once I walked into the wrong suit with the wrong uniform.

The one day I really had a problem was when I was assigned the Ayatollah. I had to wear the burqa over the uniform. Very warm and extremely uncomfortable. Even with the Velcro ties, you get tangled in all the cheap polyester cloth of the burqa with all its static cling from out of the clothes dryer, even using dryer sheets. The dryer sheets don't work with burqas. When you're rushing to strip it off or try to put it on again, it's a real mess, and never hangs right. And these are all custom-made burqas. You can't get those burqas off the rack.

And when you're not wearing your burqa, there's no place to hang it except in the kitchen. And it doesn't fit inside the biggest attaché case or any reasonable carry bag or briefcase, so you stuff it in the file drawer of the desk. It's hard to retrieve it without drawing attention to yourself, so you start with a new burqa, (did I mention they're cheap wash and wear polyester blend – the good ones are a polyester-cotton blend – and you don't always get a good one). We have maintenance change the desks full of old burqas for identical empty desks. USEWOW has a lot of desks and burqas. I suggested we take our used burqas and make it a part of our foreign aid to the Middle East and Afghanistan. But that has to go through Congress, and if it doesn't cost the taxpayers money, it will never be approved. And besides, this was all highly classified, and no one could be told what this was all about. And no one would allow highly classified burqas to be exported to potentially hostile countries. And if it competed with in-country burqas, it could become a nasty top-secret classified international incident.

"Rose, Archy, before you go into your morning assignments, we're going to meet in the dining hall with Rachel and Israel. Things are getting hot. The news is carrying the story about the opening meeting of the General Assembly and the world leaders that are arriving in New York. We'll see our guests' reaction to the news and what they say on the phone to their subordinates. They'll be speaking to Rachel who will receive the call as Israel's secretary, and Israel who will play all the parts of our 'leaders' junior staff'. Rachel, of course will be everybody's telephone secretary."

"And nobody is going to notice their distinctive Yiddish accent?" I could tell the way Rose asked the question, she didn't think this was going to work."

"My darling little Rose…" General, that's no way to address Rose. She's going to store away your words and figure out how to get even. It goes into her female 'get even' memory bank. Another anatomical site in the distinctly female brain, unique especially to married women. That's something I learned years ago and not at the US Army War College, although that would be of greater value than some of their courses. "…it will work. No national leader ever listens to a subordinate on the telephone, unless the country is being attacked, or they've lost an election and have to plan a coup. Even when they've been told they're the victim of a coup, they're only half listening and don't believe it's happening to them. That's the way it is when you are at the top of the heap."

"I know how important this is, General. But I'm due to wax Putin's back and chest today." I'm genuinely concerned about disrupting Putin's routine beauty care. "General, Putin wears a shirt and tie and a two-piece suit in the office, but the last two days has gone shirtless in the dining hall for all his meals. He stands and poses when Rose brings each course and tries to rub up against her. And lately he's asked Rose how nipple rings would look, and would she wear matching nipple rings for her President!"

"General, I wasn't going to bother you with this little Putin detail, but I already asked Archy what he was going to do about it. All he did was stammer and then said nothing. Absolutely nothing!" The General and I both knew Rose wanted us to do something. Rose wanted revenge for Putin's insults, insolence, misogyny, and having to serve him with a smile while he sits there shirtless like it's a real treat. But both the General and I knew that the entire operation was coming to a climax. In fact, those were the General's exact words.

"Dear Rose, dear dear Rose. Our mission is coming to a climax with the opening of the UN General Assembly. ..." The General was trying to sooth Rose, but she interrupted.

"Putin thinks he's coming to a climax. I'll climax him when I twist his tiny pecker off his ball sack and shove it up his left nostril. And I bet it's so small, he won't have to mouth breath. And that's important after I knock out his capped teeth. Now, are you or Archy going to put up with the way he treats me?" This was more of a challenge to me and the General, than any sort of question as to what we were going to do. Before either of us could say anything, even though our mouths were wide open and we were about to speak, Rose said, "Well, don't just stand there, tell me what you two are going to do about it."

"Rose, darling," Just between you and me, you never "… darling…" an angry woman who carries a loaded Colt .45 – even if you're a general. "Rose, engage our 'Putin' in friendly banter. Moments into his breakfast, Archy will come in with a phone message he must return immediately. And now we'll see how well this will all pay off."

"So that means the two of you are going to do nothing. You're both useless! He's a disgusting piece of shit. Today, he's going to get his scalding hot soup in his lap." Rose became more serious. "Archy, let me do his waxing. Let me put in his nipple rings, then let me yank them out. He's disrespect-ful, disgusting, and he's only a translator, not even the real thing…"

"Rose, but he thinks he's the real thing. They all think they're the real thing. That's what makes this such a perfect plan. This could go down as the best intelligence-gathering operation in the CIA's history. Remember, this was Wild Bill Donovan's brainstorm, the father of the CIA. The father Rose. The Father!" I wouldn't have the nerve to say anything like that to Rose. But the General did. Probably more out of stupidity than malice. I knew he was fond of Rose. He still thinks of her as a little girl. A little girl with her own Colt. And I didn't mean a pony.

That's one thing that's consistent with General Merri-whether – he's always pleased with himself. I don't know many generals, but my guess is they're all like that. Rose knows a lot of generals. I'll ask her in the car on the way home, tonight if that's the way they all are.

"Look I need my morning coffee and some breakfast. We all need a real Army field breakfast. Hot black coffee and chipped beef on toast. I know Archy will have the same. He's been an Army man all his life. His father-in-law, my best buddy, told me so. Israel, how about you?" Israel and Rachel snuck up on the table without saying a word. I learned later that this was standard procedure for the Mossad. Israel took the seat at the table to the left of the General, and I sat to his right.

"General, I'll have the same, except put a shot of whiskey in my coffee."

"Now boys, that's a real Army breakfast." The General was enjoying the comradery of me and Israel. Rachel and Rose were silent.

"General, IDF tradition when you have your first breakfast with your commanding general." Israel smiled at General Merriwhether. The General acknowledged the smile with a powerful slap on the back. You could tell the General was happy with the way things were progressing.

"Girls, it would be nice if the two of you brought us or chow, just like in the old days."

Rachel and Rose looked at each other, without a smile or frown, without a grunt or even the sound of a deep breath. They walked quietly to the kitchen with heads bowed and the sound of their shuffling feet. Rachel came out first with two full plates balanced on her right arm and the third plate she held in her left hand. She placed each hot plate in front of the men. The first went to General Merriwhether. The second to me and the third to her husband. Rose was next out of the kitchen, with eating utensils and napkins in her apron pocket, her right hand held three coffee mugs through the cup handles and in her left hand was the coffee pot from the kitchen restaurant drip brewer. After she put down the cups, she put a napkin beside each plate and the utensil for each of the men. She then poured the coffee. All this time, Rachel stepped back from the table, her head bowed, and a curious smile on her face. There was no cream pitcher and no sugar. Army men drank their coffee black, strong and without anything in it, maybe except bourbon whiskey. That was Army field coffee the way it should be.

"Archy, my boy. Israel. Dig in." The General took the first bit of the chipped beef and seemed to approve of the taste. "You two aren't hungry?" The General looked at Rose. With a chuckle he told Rose, "Bring us all the hot sauce, woman." I saw both Rose and Rachel reach under their aprons for their side arms. Israel nodded 'No!' to his wife, and I just moved away from the General to avoid any blood splatter if Rose lost her temper.

I looked at Rose. She said, "Go ahead Archy, eat it."

"I'm really not hungry, dear." I was afraid to eat it. I was both too guilty to have had Rose serve me and then try to eat it while she is standing behind me. And I'm too frightened.

Israel looked at Rachel who was across from her husband, standing behind General Merriwhether where he couldn't see her. She was just nodding "NO".

"Rachel, dear. I don't have time for breakfast. We have the shop, and we have to be ready for the telephone calls." Israel walked to the dining room door, waited for Rachel, then he stepped aside politely to let her exit first.

The General ate with the gusto of a man having his last meal, which Israel and I thought might be the case. Only Rose and Rachel knew for sure. The General finished the last bite of his chipped beef on toast, slammed his knife and fork down hard enough for the utensils to bounce. He was pleased with his breakfast and pleased with the progress his plan was making. His words as he was getting up from the table that Israel and I thought might be his final words were, "The strongest of all warriors are these two – Time and Patience."

*　*　*　*　*

CHAPTER EIGHT

"All the world's a stage
And all the men and women merely players,
They have their exits and their entrances,
And one man in his time plays many parts,
His acts being seven ages."
[William Shakespeare's As You Like It,
Act I, Scene 7, 139-141, Jaques]

"Archy, Israel, today is the day we put our plan into high gear. We have no choice. I want you to remember this day. It will be the most important day in the world history espionage and our national security practices. No one else has attempted let alone thought of doing. The only thing that was as momentous was the Trojan Horse. And once the world knows of what we have done, years from now whence this is declassified, we will become Odysseus and you, Archy and Israel his men inside the horse breaking the siege on the free world in our modern age."

This old fart of a General still doesn't address me directly when there is something important going on. He doesn't talk directly to Rachel either. If it's important it's 'Archy this,' or 'Israel that,'. He doesn't utter our names to give us the heads up that we might be involved in an important way. He's always talking over Rachel to Israel, too. We were both meant to just look pretty – well I was meant to look decorative and Rachel was just a necessary stage prop - assume whatever female role is expected of us and listen very carefully to his every word in complete silence. And if our husbands' spoke, I'm sure the General wanted us to listen with our heads bowed. That is, except for a smile of devotion and a nod telling him we understood or his 'complex' concepts that could easily be over our poor women's head.

He only looks at us directly when he asks, "Does everyone understand?" I know for a fact that he used to treat his female staff officers the same way, at least when he had a staff. All the women at USEWOW are ignored, but we're still expected and required to hang on to every word very respectfully and subserviently any man utters.

I actually heard him say that once to one of his former military secretaries before he was reported for the third time for harassment and her reassignment. And his explanation was that it would help her with her OER and getting promoted. He actually meant no harm. He was only trying to be helpful to the young 'dear'. That's when the military personnel officer decided not only to transfer the woman, but not replace her immediately. And that was two years ago. Eventually every member of General Merriwhether's staff was transferred until the only one ever assigned to him was my Archy. And my Archy is a general staff of one, and suddenly I'm Archy's assistant. Well, in the Army, all Army wives are their husbands' unofficial assistants. That the way it is today, and that's the way it always was, starting with Martha Washington. You would think, if she only put her foot down with George, things would have been different for all of us women.

"First things first. Archy, we have to call your Uncle Jimmy. He's the only one with the contact in the Broadway Stage Carpenters' Union that could have our mock airplanes and any other sets built to continue our illusion as we move our 'guests' from their suites to 'our New York and our United Nations.' I'm sure your uncle could arrange with Actors Equity to hire some out of work actors to be 'our UN General Assembly delegates'. In fact, I'm sure your uncle could arrange for anything. You told me that he told you that, 'He knows people.'

Rose, you have an important task. You need to go home after your done here, shop for Uncle Jimmy's favorites, especially the deli Italian imported prosciutto, hearts of artichokes, and whatever so he feels right at home when he arrives. Set your table for Easter Sunday dinner, prepare an acceptably elaborate meal, and make him and Aunt Anna welcome. Prepare a guest room for him and Aunt Anna. That's especially important. I wouldn't want him sleeping in a hotel. We don't have the budget – hotels being so expensive near the White House. Every hotel, motel, bed and breakfast and temporary lodging is wired for video and sound by our intelligence services, the Chinese Communists, the Russians, and the Albanians. Every other nation has a subscription to the Albanian recordings. That's how Albania balances its trade deficit. I understand that with the Albanian surveillance subscription, you get a one-month free cell phone plan. But their listening in on all those cell phones, too.

Having Uncle Jimmy and Aunt Anna stay with you and Archy also saves us arranging for transportation. You and Archy could drive both of them hear the next morning, and every morning. Archy, you and I will pick them up at Union Station, just to save Rose the time. Dear, we can't have you rushed with your preparations. Put everything on your expense account, but please save all your receipts and any copies of coupons you used at the supermarket. And please use as many coupons as possible. I have some in my desk draw you can pick up before you go home, tonight. And for securities sake, don't have any of this delivered. People are always watching. Especially for deliveries. Remember – Moscow rules! Your only out-of-pocket expenses will be your parking.

Rachel, your part in it is to make Aunt Anna some new dresses and maybe some formal wear. I know that Uncle Jimmy doesn't waste any money on frivolities like women's frocks, but something like your custom-made dresses that would finally fit her correctly will make her happy. And if she's happy, Uncle Jimmy will be happy with the free clothing – alterations included - for his wife. Whenever you get the chance when Uncle Jimmy is near the shop take his measurements. I promised him two three-piece suits with two pairs of pants for him to take home with him to New York. I'm sure Israel won't mind. Uncle Jimmy will be armed with a shoulder-holster Colt .45 and a .38 Smith and Wesson revolver on his right ankle. Be sure to allow extra room for them in the jacket and right pants leg. I want the suit to hang perfectly when he looks in your full-length mirror. I want him to have nothing to think about except the mission in front of him." What did I tell you!

"Today there's been no natural disasters, no terrorists' attacks, at least none with more than a few people killed and minimum loss of limbs. Nobody has invaded anybody – at least anyplace that's important or anyone heard about. Nobody cares about the refugee boats that sink on their way to the EU. It only makes headlines when they actually arrive. And all the political scandals are just a continuation of the old ones, except on the continent, and nobody can figure out anything that actually happens with EU politics – who's screwing who, both literally and figuratively, and Germany is screwing everybody. Maybe not everybody equally since Great Britain left the EU.

What made the local news in New York City was that it's been an entire day without a fatal traffic accident, even with the three dozen bicycle riders clipped by turning cars as they disobeyed all the traffic signals, and the seventeen pedestrians the bicycle riders hit by blasting through all the cross walks. I really never understood it. In New York City in particular, pedestrians have the right of way. There are signs up all over. It's just that the New York drivers and bicycle riders don't believe it. And all the bicycle paths have caused more congestion by narrowing the streets. And they're not used all winter. Actually, I'm told the traffic congestion in the city hasn't gotten worse because fewer and fewer people go into Manhattan." At least that's one thing the General and I agree on.

"All of a sudden, the opening of the UN General Assembly made the front page of the print media and the lead story on cable and broadcast news." It makes New Yorkers hate the UN even more. All the diplomats parking illegally causing traffic jams by blocking travel lanes. The street closures, and that's besides all the tax revenue lost to the tax-exempt United

Nations on the best piece of real estate on the East River.

"The General Assembly meeting for this year won't convene for ten days, and we're not prepared for the news broadcasts suddenly reporting on it. We had to wait for the right moment, the correct world event to test our theory. I was waiting for the right moment, but I waited too long. I've had many women in my life who always told me, 'Timing is everything'." And I'll bet they told the General his timing was always off.

"Now we have to get our world leaders into high gear. If they're even half predicative of what the real Putin, Xi, Kim and the Ayatollah do at the UN, we know we're approaching them the right way. I will immediately go to the President with our results. I'll have him watch our tapes and he can compare them, practically side by side with the news broadcast tapes. We'll have written transcripts of our dictators and their real counterparts that the President can compare against one another. They're the real leaders' translators. I'll bet they say word for word what their real counterpart says."

When you're a general you have to be sure of yourself. And General Merriwhether is certainly sure of himself about big things, small things, insignificant things, and things he usually knows nothing about. But that's no different than every Federal department supervisor, right up to the cabinet secretary. And the President's cabinet probably knows the least about what they are in charge of. In fact, that's no different than newly married man. At least until his first anniversary – if there are any more anniversaries after that.

"Telling the President – our President is one thing but listening to the words of our dictators – our dictators doing what the real dictators will do at least days before they do it. It's jaw-dropping – even though I never knew anyone who actually dropped his jaw and then had to pick it up." General Merriwhether had a quiet chuckle. He always laughed at his own jokes. All generals laugh at their own jokes in order to signal their subordinates that they're just kidding, and they too should laugh at the right moment. They learn the technique at the War College – they think it helps humanize them. General Merriwhether unfortunately doesn't have the timing nor the delivery to be any kind of a standup comic. It's a good thing he's a general or he'd be standing in the bread line. And I wonder, do they still have bread lines, especially if you're on a ketogenic or gluten-free diet?

"I think we have it. We've made our time adjustments just in the nick of time. That's sort of cute – time adjustments in the nick of time. I'll have to remember that one.

Our guests, our world leaders have their office clocks as well as their internal clocks only an hour apart. Archy, be sure to get into Putin's office first, turn on the four TVs to his preset news channels. Exchange some pleasantries. Rose, once Putin leaves the dining hall, you don't have to clean his table. Just change the Asbestos warning signs so the Ayatollah doesn't come out of a door with the Asbestos warning sign or exit into someone else's suite. I'll be in my burqa to clear Putin's table and serve the Ayatollah his morning tea, prune juice and bran flakes with virgin goat's milk. Get into Putin's office immediately. You only have to wait for a call from Rachel and Israel. Formerly announce the call and the urgency of the message. Israel will tell our Putin there's a plot to disappear him and replace him with a look alike who will be at the UN. Israel will tell him it's imperative to get him safely out of the Kremlin."

You know, this isn't going to work. Our Putin is no halfwit. "Rose, our Putin is no halfwit. Every absolute dictator always has his ear to the ground and semi trusted informants that have a vested interest in keeping them in power. Even our delusional Putin will buy the story. All dictators, delusional or not are paranoid. For that matter, so are our Congressional leaders. The others in Congress are too stupid, inconsequential or both to be paranoid. And if they were, nobody would notice." If you say so, general. Now, what could go wrong? "And whomever he decides to call, one of them is bound to be a CIA asset and will tip off our CIA who the real Putin's true allies are in the Kremlin." This is getting hard to follow. Listening carefully, I don't think the General follows it himself, or just is talking to hear himself think out loud hoping to clarify the whole mess in his own mind.

"Archy, it's your turn to engage our Putin. Tell him the plan for his safety is to fly him to New York and get him to the UN to confront the Putin imposter – who is in reality the real Putin – and embarrass him in front of the UN General Assembly and the world on live television. Hopefully, the networks and cable won't cut out for a commercial."

I am surprised that anyone carries the UN General Assembly. It's a drone of boring speeches to an auditorium full of diplomats with their earphones on, either listening to some soccer game, music, or are asleep with their eyes open. They all learn sleeping with their eyes open at diplomat school. You can tell who's sleeping because they don't blink. The one's listening to music are moving their lips ever so slightly singing along. The rest are listening to soccer with clenched fists waiting to cheer for the one goal in the entire game. As boring as soccer is, it's still less boring and useless as the UN General Assembly.

"Our Putin will be snuck out of our 'Kremlin' tomorrow in a steamer trunk and loaded on a commercial Aeroflot flight to New York. The flight will be empty except for him. That's what you're going to tell him. Today, he I am sure he will spend all his time talking to his Kremlin allies to tell them about the coup and his plans to thwart it. Israel's Yiddish accent is close enough to a Russian accent for our pretend Putin, that he won't notice the difference. He will only be half listening anyway. We'll find out who his most trusted allies are. It'll be key to find out who our Putin orders to be executed and who he orders to execute the executioner. That's the way the GSU operates, the KGB operated, and the traditional, steeped in history and lore, the most secret of them all, the famous NKVD. Our Putin will actually be speaking to Israel after Rachel poses as Israel's secretary. I know the Mossad will have Rachel add some of some of these gentlemen to their Moscow Kidon's agents' Christmas - or Hanukkah gift list. This will become a gold mine for our Kremlin intelligence." The General is counting his chickens too soon.

If I were either the real or make-believe Putin, I would invite the suspects into my office two at a time. Shoot one, and then question the other. If he doesn't like the other's answers, he shoots him, and invites the next two deputies in. They can dispose of the bodies, and the questioning begins again. Whoever breaks for the door first is shot in the back, enough times that he falls, then Putin asked the other one to put one round in the back of the head, assuming the first man fell forward in the direction he was running. If he shoots the first one in the back, the man is almost for sure to fall forward. And the second man won't hesitate to shoot the first man on the floor because Putin has his automatic pointed to the center of his chest. There won't be an opportunity to turn his gun on Putin. No one's draw from a waist holster would be fast enough. I'm anxious to see how this plays out. I'm not sure the General has thought it through. He's rushed and is trying to justify taking an action while being forced into a corner. I just hope General Merriwhether wasn't stupid enough to give these guys loaded weapons. Even if they loaded it with blanks, at short range, the wad from the blank could kill you.

"Rose, while Archy manages Putin, you get back to the dining room to serve Kim. I'll handle the Ayatollah myself. I'll wear my burqa, serve him his morning tea at his desk, and exit, and come back as his right hand in my Revolutionary Guard uniform jacket.

Archy while Rose is serving Kim breakfast, you get into his office, turn on the TVs and check that their tuned to the correct news broadcasts. Before Kim returns to his office, you need to put on your North Korean Army Uniform. Tell Kim the same story you told Putin. Is that clear?"

"It's important for Kim to know that there's going to be a coup attempt against Putin?"

Archy's voice had a positive intonation, but he got the whole scenario wrong.

"No, Archy! You tell Kim that there will be a coup attempt against him by substituting a look alike at the UN General Assembly. His life is in grave danger and will be eliminated here long before…" Do you really think this is going to work? This is just too entertaining for me to try to straighten out.

"I get it now, General." I doubt Archy understood what was supposed to happen if the General's plans worked. I doubt Archy or the General had any inkling of what could go wrong. Neither of them had not an idea of the consequences. Fortunately, our Kim, Ayatollah, Putin and Xi really didn't know what was happening, and nothing, not the General's plan nor any scheme they come up with, was going to happen the way anyone expected. I knew this, and so did Rachel. That's why our sidearms were never fastened in their holsters, and there was always one round in the chamber. Our four translators are as big and objectional pigs as their real counterparts, and I know Rachel will finish them off before this is all over, but I especially want Xi for myself. He the smartest, most vicious, condescending and most misogynistic. He needs to be knee capped before the bullet between the eyes. Especially after all the people he killed with the China virus. - - - Shit, I have to remember he's not the real Xi.

"Rose, you get back to the dining hall to serve Xi his breakfast. As soon as he's done, you need to clear the dishes, and when he leaves change the Asbestos warning signs on the doors to get ready for the lunch rush. Make sure all the tables are set, and for lunch, like dinner. Use the cloth napkins, not the breakfast paper napkins. In fact, we should be using cloth napkins for all the meals, after all, these men are their countries' leaders. Remember, two place settings at each table. Archy, me or Israel will be one or the others' companion for this important meal. I'll take the Ayatollah in my Revolutionary Guard fatigue jacket. We'll have to get Rachel to serve us wearing the burqa. It's sort of her turn in the burqa.

Then when Kim's meal is done, go to Kim's offices to wait for Rachel and Israel's calls. Archy, as soon as Rose arrives, you go to Xi's offices with the same message. Rose, while Kim is on the phone with Rachel and Israel, you go to Xi's office to help him place the calls to whom he believes can be trusted in his own government not to assassinate him. Every leader has two lists, those who are to be trusted, and those to be shot through the back of the head by those who are to be trusted or shot in the back of the head after they finish their assigned executions. Occasionally, these leaders are frequently revising their lists, and add too many people to one list and forget to remove them from the other list. And when they have the same people on both lists, it leads to some embarrassing moments and unnecessary violence, with the bloodshed in places where it's more difficult to clean up. And if you point out the error of the lists, you're executed first." It's a good thing we're the only ones with loaded handguns.

"After Rachel calls Rose and Rose puts Israel through to Putin and tells him to pay attention to the news, you go in to Xi and while Rose goes to Kim to get the call from Rachel to put Kim through to Israel. Archy, your job is to get President Xi to watch his news broadcasts, at least until Rose gets to his office to get the call from Rachel who will put Israel through to Xi as soon as he's off the phone with Kim. The 'he' being Israel. Now is all that clear? It's important to keep everything straight in your heads."

"Who's off the phone with Kim?" Archy was getting confused.

"Israel, Archy. It's Israel who's going to give these would-be dictators the warnings about the coups against them." I had to tell my husband what was going on. I don't think anyone noticed what Archy said and that he was thoroughly lost. That's when it's better that I correct him. I knew he appreciated the help when he gave me a little smile.

"Archy, Israel will deliver the message to our dictators. Kim tends to go on and on. That may put our timing off a bit. Do we all understand, now? Are we all in synch?" General Merriwhether was still smiling but you could hear the anxiety in his voice. It's like a lightbulb was turned on over his head. He had just realized how confusing it all sounded and that it was going forward, then, and now, and without a rehearsal.

"Archy, dear Archy. You know General Merriwhether over plans things. But don't worry. General Merriwhether's overplanning will spell success in the end." I smiled, flipped my hair, and tried to act coy. But, has everyone listened to this? This is why I didn't want my husband to get involved in another of General Merriwhether's schemes. And this scheme is not even his, it's a fifty-year old counterintelligence scenario dreamed up by Bill Casey, hopefully before he had his stroke.

"Rose, now pay attention. You look like your mind is wandering off to cloths shopping or preparing dinner or re-arranging the furniture in your living room. I know how women think. When things get too complicated, they retreat into planning their domestic, and even sometimes their marital duties, or something. Rose, this is important. I know you'll try, but please don't get distracted. Not that your dinner tonight for Archy's Uncle Jimmy and Aunt Anna isn't very very important. Your dinner will be his first impression of how well we do things at USEWOW. Not that I want to put you under a lot of pressure, but..."

You know you crazy old General, I still have my .45 Colt, and if I shoot you, nobody will know because this is so top secret, it can only be shared with the President. Firstly, who's going to believe I shot you. Secondly, who's going to bother the President with someone shooting you. Thirdly, the President will tell his chief-of-staff to do something about it, but the chief-of-staff can't because he can only talk to the President about anything we do because the only other person besides the chief-of-staff that has the security clearance to even know what we're doing is the President. And he just can't go back and tell the President what the President told him. And lastly, not only are we so secret, but we also don't exist anyway, and if we did, nobody would care.

"Don't worry General. I'm paying attention. Everything

on my end will get done."

*   *   *   *   *

CHAPTER NINE

**"Discipline is the soul of an army. It makes
small numbers formidable; procures success
to the weak, and esteem to all."**
*[George Washington, Letter of Instructions to the
Captains of the Virginia Regiments, July 29, 1759]*

"Aunt Anna, let me have your coat." Anna was standing behind her husband. Uncle Jimmy was dressed in his best suit. One of his two best suits. Both were Israel Beilin suits- one tweed and one pinstriped – both with two pair of pants. Jimmy wore his pinstriped suit. It fit so well, he felt like he was lawyer in it. He wore it with great pride today just to show Israel he still prized his Israel Beilin suit he bought from Israel's original tailor shop in Williamsburg. He bought it to be married to Aunt Anna. It only had to be altered twice by Israel, and that was still when he was at the Williamsburg shop and before Israel and Rachel opened their shop on The Bowery on the lower east side of Manhattan. As far as everyone in Hell's Kitchen was concerned, in fact, everyone on the lower west side of Manhattan, Israel and Rachel's tailor shop was the only place buy and be properly fitted for a Sunday suit, a suit to be married in, or buried in, appear in court – all suits were three-piece suits with two pair of pants.

Even if your suit had bullet holes and your own blood's blood stains, and you survived, Israel could repair the suit, match any fabric usually from the suits original bolt of cloth, and dry clean the blood stains out of it. Israel and Rachel guaranteed free alterations for as long as you owned the suit. That included bullet damage or blood stains. The cleaning was included in the lifetime guarantee. That was the best lifetime guarantee for the suit anywhere in the five boroughs of New York – your lifetime only, not Israel's lifetime or anyone else's lifetime.

If you didn't survive, the widow could have the suit repaired and used for the wake, free of charge. If the suit weren't too badly worn, she could have the suit removed before burial and sent back to Israel and Rachel's Williamsburg shop for dry cleaning and resale. Israel and Rachel felt that the poor widow had enough tsuris and the entire sale would go back to her. If she was the one who did in her husband, whether or not the widowhood was justified, or for a big insurance payoff or not, they kept the proceeds of the sale. It was usually common knowledge in Williamsburg who was a self-made widow and who was not. This was the way things were done in Williamsburg, anyway.

For a long time, Williamsburg, Brooklyn was the only place you could find an Israel Beilin suit – three piece with two pair of pants. It was the only real reason to ever go to Brooklyn. But there were rumblings on Tenth Avenue at the Twenty-Third Street corner candy store that Israel and Rachel's shop at Bowery and Delancey Street wasn't as good. Different quality in the bolts of cloth. That was the rumor. But the rumor was started by the other tailors along the Bowery. At the time Israel and Rachel opened their second shop, the second shop struggled until Israel had Rachel ask Aunt Anna to ask Uncle Jimmy to 'spread the good word'. And Uncle Jimmy 'spread the good word' among the other tailors on The Bowery, and Israel and Rachel's shop in Manhattan flourished. Uncle Jimmy was rewarded with a second three-piece suit with two pair of pants, and Aunt Anna was given a new frock and apron. The same apron she wore to Washington today. And Jimmy was given the promise of another favor.

*   *   *   *   *

If you win, you need not have to explain. If you lose, you should not be there to explain.
[Adolf Hitler, 1889-1945]

It was a day; Aunt Anna was bringing her cleaning into Israel and Rachel's Manhattan shop. She walked all morning with her shopping cart full of her dry cleaning from Tenth Avenue to The Bowery. That day, Israel was behind the counter when a very disturbed Aunt Anna told him about the Puerto Rican child in one of the three upstairs apartments who was beaten, raped and was still in a coma at Beekman Downtown Hospital. The child's mother told Anna she knew who did it. They showed up at her apartment and threated her, slapped her around until she fell to the floor and then robbed her. Anna saw them climbing the stairs the very day they broke down the door into the apartment and beat and robbed the girl's mother. They said they would be back and if she didn't want more of the same or worse, she should come up with some substantial cash. And the next time, besides her getting beaten, they would finish off her daughter in the hospital and no one would care because they were Puerto Rican foreigners.

Except Anna said the mother told her they were far cruder. What the mother told Anna -the whole story angered her. And Aunt Anna never really angered, not at anyone, not at Uncle Jimmy, not at the politicians on television. Aunt Anna had her loaded .25 caliber Iver Johnson in her purse and knew the mother wouldn't be returning until the evening. Anna was determined to protect her without telling her husband. She wanted to do this and keep Jimmy in reserve in case everything went south and she, herself needed to be revenged.

Israel just asked Anna one question, "Is the girl Jewish?"

Anna repeated that the girl was Puerto Rican and the mother and daughter always walked every Sunday to St. Francis of Assisi Catholic Church on Thirty-first street with her. Israel excused himself and came back with Rachel.

Rachel looked at Anna and new she needed to help her friend. Anna told the story.

Rachel asked, "Is the girl Jewish?"

Anna told her no, she wasn't. That's when Israel angerly

said, "This girl is Jewish!"

"Anna, when are they coming back?" Now it was Rachel who moved to the front of the counter and took charge.

"I don't know. It could be anytime. I'm sure they're watching the building. I saw them across the street as I was leaving. The mother isn't home now. She's at the hospital with her daughter and will be there until visiting hours are over. I knew I had time to come here, drop off my cleaning well before she got home. I had planned to stay with the woman all night if necessary. Jimmy doesn't go to work until midnight tonight anyway." Anna took breath hoping Israel would offer some help. "I was going to leave the cleaning ticket on our kitchen table just in case something happens to me."

"Is there a father on the scene who may want to take action himself?" Rachel asked the question. Neither Rachel, Israel nor Anna ever mentioned the police as a course of action. On Tenth Avenue, the police were never a serious consideration. They all knew it's not that the police didn't know who these guys were. But the girl was in a coma and couldn't identify them. She's in danger as long as she's alive and we don't know how long the police will post an officer at her bedside. And even if the mother had them arrested for what they did to her, with the new 'no bail' law, the two of them would be out before the evening news picked up the story, which they probably won't because, well just because nobody died yet."

"The father is dead. Dead after some unfortunate business deal." Anna knew the business deal involved the two men who raped the young girl but wouldn't say.

"I'll come back with you so you can introduce me to this woman when she comes back from the hospital." Rachel looked at Israel.

"I'll report this to Kidon while you're on your way. I'll tell them the girl is Jewish and they're Nazis. And we have proof. I have a few SS insignia and Swastika flags you can take with you to plant on the bodies. Take enough photos and everything will be fine. We'll get a preliminary OK from the local Mossad branch office. If Mossad pursues it further, we'll have the photos and say they snuck into New York from Uruguay. Just make sure the woman we're helping mentions that they spoke with a Uruguayan accent."

"What's a Uruguayan accent?" Anna already knew what the plan was, but just wasn't sure how she was going to explain a Uruguayan accent. "Rachel, you know for sure she's at the hospital?"

"Anna, both Rachel and I know this mother is at the hospital every day and all day. These two are watching the front of your building for her to return to rob her again. Introduce Rachel to this woman, and the two of you can keep her company." Israel looked at Rachel. "Rachel, I'm coming along."

"Israel, just let me go alone with Anna. I've handled tougher quarry. I'll have the element of surprise."

"Your other assignments were carefully preplanned. You were familiar with the location and you still had the element of surprise. Doing this on the fly is not a good idea." Israel was very concerned even though Rachel was already considered elite among the Kidon agents.

"Just Anna and I walking into the building with her shopping cart will be less likely to raise suspicions and make them more cautious. In fact, let me take a shopping cart with me. I need to get my shopping cart in the back. I just need my purse, and my little coffin pillow. You watch the shop. I don't know when I'll be back, but I will help Anna and this poor mother settle this annoyance. And Israel, closing early with both of us away is bad for business." Rachel gave Israel a little kiss on the cheek. "If all goes well, since I'll have my shopping cart, I'll stop at the Kosher butcher. Dear, is there anything you want?"

"A brisket. Just a brisket."

Anna and Rachel both with their purses and shopping carts, and Rachel with her pillow walked across town to Tenth Avenue. That was the entire afternoon. They stopped at Anna and Jimmy's apartment to quietly leave the dry-cleaning ticket on the table and not disturb Anna's sleeping husband before he had to go to work at midnight. But it was too late. Jimmy heard the door open, came out of the bedroom which was adjacent to the kitchen with just an airshaft and windows in between the rooms. Anna put her coffee pot on the stove to perk for her husband.

"Jimmy, when the coffee is done, shut it off, but save me a cup. I'll be down before you go to work. There's cold corn beef in the fridge if I'm late. Just heat it in the oven at three hundred seventy-five for fifteen minutes. Any longer and it will dry it up. If I'm not here, save me a slice."

Rachel nodded to Jimmy and the two women shut the apartment door behind them and walked up the flight of stairs to check if the woman was home. Jimmy didn't know what had happened to his neighbor's daughter and Rachel squeezed Anna's hand to silence her and told Jimmy they were there just for a visit upstairs. Jimmy, usually only half listening to any woman, grunted as their apartment door slammed shut.

The distraught mother opened her apartment door, so relieved it was her downstairs neighbor that she threw herself into Anna's arms for a reassuring hug. Anna introduced Rachel as a close friend. Of course, the woman knew of Israel and Rachel's shop in Williamsburg and the new one on The Bowery. Every man on Tenth Avenue knew of the store. Her late husband was buried in an Israel Beilin suit, the same suit he was married in, the same suit he went to church in, and the same suit he was shot dead in. She put on a kettle for tea, put out three cups. While she was cutting lemon wedges with her one large kitchen knife, there was a pounding on the door.

The woman didn't want to open the door, but Rachel told her to stand back and motioned Anna to open the door and stand behind it. Anna opened the door, and Rachel already had her little coffin pillow embroidered with "Mother" in her left hand and her .22 caliber revolver in her right. Two men pushed through the door just as Anna turned the knob.

Before Rachel could get close, the woman rushed toward

the first man, rammed the carving knife into his belly. She kept pulling it out with a twist, plunging it back in, again and again. She always pulled it out with a twist. It took at least a half-dozen blows before the man fell forward before she could stab him one last time. Before the first man fell on his face, Rachel had her pillow by the second man's temple and pulled the trigger of the double-action revolver twice. One shot creased the top of his skull, but the second missed and just spread pillow feathers in the air. Anna already had her .25 caliber out of her purse before she opened the door. The second man was still standing when Anna scattered the small caliber rounds into his chest and abdomen. The second man was on his knees trying to stop the bleeding in his chest and abdomen moving both hands from one hole to another.

The mother, who was distraught and visibly trembling at first, walked calmly behind this second man pushing Rachel to one side with enough force to almost knock Rachel off her feet. She grabbed his long greasy hair in her left hand, and before his black hair slipped through her closed left fist, she cut his throat ear to ear with the calm steady even slicing motion of the deli butcher slicing a freshly baked pastrami. She wasn't a particularly strong woman, and his head was still attached to its gurgling stump of his neck by the intact spinal cord. Both bodies were shaking on the floor for several minutes before blood stopped pumping. All movement stopped simultaneously, and their bowl sphincters relaxed in their inevitable terminal state.

"Anna, it's time to call Jimmy to help us clean up this mess. I hope I've been a help, but I have to get back to the shop. It's a long walk back to The Bowery and it's dark out. It's a dangerous walk." Jimmy came to the door before Rachel left.

"I heard the gunshots, dear. I knew from the sound it was your Iver Johnson." Jimmy was annoyed at having to step over the bodies in the doorway to get into the apartment. He dragged them both in so he could close the door.

"Jimmy, I have to get back to Israel. Sorry about the

mess. It's a long walk." Rachel was about to leave when Jimmy stopped her. "I still have time to make it to the butcher. Israel wanted a brisket."

"Rachel, next time bring some plastic from your dry-cleaning supplies. This is a mess you left me." Jimmy thought better of being annoyed with Rachel. "Rachel, I should be thanking you. I understand you did a kindness for our neighbor. I heard what happened to this woman's daughter from our neighbor's downstairs when everyone opened their doors when they heard the gunshots. They looked up here but didn't looked surprised that there were gunshots. They knew these guys were coming back. I could tell, none of them wanted to get involved, but were glad about hearing the gunshots. I think they knew what happened when they saw you and Anna going up the stairs together."

Considering the blood on the floor and the smell of blood mixed with excrement strong enough to make your eyes water, Jimmy had softened his tone. "Rachel, I'll call you a cab. It's too long a walk in the dark." Jimmy was genuinely concerned. "I would take you home myself, but I need to tidy up in here." Uncle Jimmy's car was at his parking lot in the Bronx. He walked every night from Tenth Avenue to the railroad and back again. He would get a gypsy cab to make the round trip to the Bowery or to Brooklyn, wherever Rachel wanted to go. No one on Tenth Avenue ever used any ride share services. They were just unreliable.

"Not a good idea, Jimmy. I can't really be traced to this address. That's why I walked here. And I'll walk back. Don't worry. I'll be fine." With that, Rachel grabbed Jimmy's arm as she slipped in the puddle of blood that was pooling around both their feet. The splashing blood spotted her dress and shoes.

"Rachel, not even a gypsy cab?"

"There can be no hard evidence I was here. I'll get rid of my gun on the way back, anyway." Rachel smiled at Uncle Jimmy. She always liked him and knew he was a standup guy.

"If strangers with an accent inquire as to what happen, all you know is the family is Jewish and these were Nazis." Rachel was out the door and down the stairs without looking back. Uncle Jimmy shut the woman's apartment door before anyone else could see what was happening.

"Anna, take this woman down to our place. Make her some tea. I'll call in some favors and get this cleaned up."

"Jimmy, do you want my pistol to dispose of?"

"Anna, did you reload?"

"No, dear." Anna only rarely called her husband 'dear', and when she did, she was usually being sarcastic. This time it was a warm, loving and a sheepishly shy 'dear'. Not at all what you would expect from a woman who just emptied her revolver into some stranger, without even an introduction.

"I emptied the entire five shots into this guy and still couldn't kill him. I'm sorry, Jimmy. I panicked. I was upset. I'm so sorrow about not getting the head shot." Anna felt dejected.

"Anna, dear. Everybody has an off day. The next time it will be better." Jimmy lifted the jacket and tore the man's shirt partially off his back. No exit wounds. When Jimmy rolled the body over, there were three widely scattered small holes in the man's shirt over his chest, one hole in his shirt to his belly, that was already oozing bile mixed with blood. The man's fifth bullet whole went through his belt and wasn't bleeding at all, at least not outside his pants. "Anna, it's probably better you didn't shoot him in the head. If it didn't blow the back of his skull off, there would be no retrieving the bullet, I would have to dispose of your gun. And if it did, we would have to re-paint the entire kitchen, just to get everything to match. Even though, it looks like it needs a painting, anyway."

It took a minute for Uncle Jimmy to formulate a complete plan. "Girls, just go downstairs and have some tea. I'll come down with you, get my long needle nose pliers, destroy the entrance wounds enough that nobody will be able to figure the caliber of bullet. I'll have the bullets extracted before I have to leave for work. The apartment will be pristine, and the bodies will be gone forever before I finish my shift at the railroad. Have your friend stay with us tonight. The cleanup will take a couple of hours." Uncle Jimmy smiled more broadly when he told the women, "It'll be like the two of them never existed. They'll never find the bodies."

"Oh, no Jimmy. After all we went through. The world must know these two got what they deserved. You can't just make their bodies disappear." Anna was calm but emphatic. The angry vengeful mother of the rape victim was just smiling contently looking at the two corpses and smelling their blood, bile, and shit.

"Don't worry, Anna. If you want me to make an example of them, I'll make an example of them that will be the lead story on TV and the story above the fold in the New York Times."

And Archy's Uncle Jimmy was a man of his word. The bodies disappeared and Uncle Jimmy was on time for his shift at the rail yards as yard master. The apartment was cleaner than it was before the incident, and what made the news – two cleanly decapitated heads, one with a superficial bullet wound were found on the steps of Beekman Downtown Hospital. The surveillance cameras all malfunctioned, and it remains a mystery to this day how they got there. And that's the way Archy told me the story. So, it turns out Aunt Anna is not as meek and mild as anyone thought.

* * * * *

To conquer a nation, first disarm its citizens.
[Adolf Hitler, 1889-1945]

Today, Uncle Jimmy even wore his spats. Looking at him, with his jacket buttoned, he must have gained a little weight. Israel would have to alter the jacket again to have it perfectly hang on Uncle Jimmy's broad shoulders. You could see the slight bulge of his shoulder holster, and that wasn't acceptable to Uncle Jimmy. But his pants hung perfectly. His ankle holster was undetectable.

"Aunt Anna, you're still wearing your kitchen apron over your pretty dress. Why..." She had obviously bought the dress new for this trip. Her apron was the same apron she was given by Rachel and she this was the apron she always wore on special occasions. It was bright white, cleaned, pressed, and starched. It had fancy ruffles and her name embroidered in script across the front.

I told Rose about my aunt's purse. I said she had her same purse she carried ever since I could remember. She always had a piece of butterscotch hard candy for me without me ever asking. She would have to take out her little .25 caliber Iver-Johnson breakopen five shot revolver to get to the candy at the bottom of the small now cracked-leather genuine alligator purse. I held the gun gingerly for the first time when I was five years old and she gave me my very first butterscotch hard candy. What a taste experience. I remember her saying, "Is that a good taste, my little Archy." Then she would sternly say, "Keep your finger away from the trigger. Just enjoy your candy." Anyway, it was Aunt Anna's best purse, the butterscotch candy was the freshest she ever gave me, and her revolver had mother of pearl handles. The purse was a Christmas present from Uncle Jimmy for their first Christmas. The Iver-Johnson was her first anniversary present along with flowers and a box of good chocolate - not drugstore candy, either. It was candy from a real German-Bavarian chocolate shop in Brooklyn a few doors down from Israel and Rachel's original Williamsburg tailor shop. The chocolate shop is still there. Uncle Jimmy and Aunt Anna made the trip themselves to Brooklyn before coming to our house at Fort Meade to bring us a two-pound box of assorted chocolates as a hostess gift for Rose and a pound of assorted dark chocolates for General Merriwhether. They had become great friends with General Merriwhether when they met me and the General at the NSA working on my father-in-law's Nightmare Computer system. But that's another story.

"Jimmy told me to wear my apron, that's why. He said I should be ready to help however I can. And he wanted to let everyone know I was ready to help. And Jimmy always said, when a woman wears her kitchen apron, you know she's really ready to help. And that's when her husband will be the proudest."

And Aunt Anna would never sit at the table with Uncle Jimmy if there was another man waiting to be seated or another domestic task to be done. And it wasn't that Uncle Jimmy would demand it. No one knew if he expected it, or if he said anything to Aunt Anna ever in their marriage. Aunt Anna knew her husband and knew her place. She knew how to comfort Jimmy and comport herself, especially in front of her husband when his friends or anyone he brought home was present. This is the way she was taught by her mother. Her mother said over and over again, "If you respect your husband, everyone will respect him. Those that should fear your husband will fear him even more. And if they respect your husband, they will both respect and fear you, my little precious one."

And this is the way her father expected her mother to conduct herself as his wife in their home or anyplace in his presence. And I was told by Aunt Anna that her father and mother were kind and loving, but everyone knew what their place was in the home. No one raised their voices – at least not about the 'trivial' domestic issues, and Aunt Anna's mother always wore her clean white starched apron with ruffles and her name embroidered on the front, everywhere. And my Aunt Anna told me, everyone respected and feared her mother more than her father. She never did say why.

Aunt Anna's mother requested that she be waked and buried in her very best white kitchen apron. Her husband was waked and buried in the same Israel Beilin three-piece suit he was married in. And it had two pair of pants. Aunt Anna looked at me, and I knew she was about to ask, where was Rose's apron, when Uncle Jimmy interrupted.

"All right, Anna. Enough." Uncle Jimmy ignored Rose and his wife and greeted me with a slap on the back. "Archy, you're looking well, spiffy and successful. When you're ready to leave the Army, come work for me. Working for me, every-thing you earn is 'tax-exempt' except for the tribute you owe to…" Then Uncle Jimmy put his finger to the tip of his nose and bent it slightly. "My accountant, three-fingers Louie, of course after last tax season, he's two fingers Louie, … he's working on a 401 3B plan for everyone in my organization. It's a sort of an offshore retirement fund."

"Uncle Jimmy, I don't know if anyone followed us here." I led everyone from the Treasury Building to the concierge, who obviously knew Uncle Jimmy was coming. Uncle Jimmy greeted her by name. "Moscow rules, Uncle Jimmy. Moscow Rules. Please, use no names while you are at USEWOW."

"Archy, we invented 'Moscow Rules on Tenth Avenue. Flora knows that," Uncle Jimmy always had a warm smile when he talked to me. I always said he was the best uncle there ever was.

"Well, Flora Haversham. How many years has it been? It's been a long time since our Tenth Avenue days." Jimmy was smiling. He was about to approach Mrs. Haversham for a kiss when Aunt Anna stepped between them.

"Not enough years!" Aunt Anna wasn't happy.

"Flora, this is my wife, Anna."

"The last time I saw you Anna was at your wedding." Mrs. Haversham smiled at Anna.

"I remember very well." Anna didn't smile back. All she remembers is the kiss Mrs. Haversham gave her new husband, and it wasn't a good luck sisterly kiss, either.

"Now, let's get everyone into USEWOW." Mrs. Havers-ham led us to the telephone booth, recited the instructions, then led us one at a time in and out of the booth. She used her fingerprint to open the secret door, still marked secret. She held the door open so we could all enter at the same time. Alarms went off.

"The system doesn't approve of more than one person entering USEWOW at a time. I'll just reset it at my desk." It was hard to hear Mrs. Haversham over the alarm bell. "Now remember everyone, especially you, Jimmy. Use no names in USEWOW." Mrs. Haversham couldn't help smiling at Archy's uncle Jimmy as she closed the door behind us. Aunt Anna paused, didn't smile, which for Anna was a snarl, then turned and was the last one into the inner USEWOW.

General Merriwhether was waiting on the other side of the door. As the door closed, he came to attention, made a snappy salute, then relaxed and approached Uncle Jimmy with both hands for a warm, almost loving handshake. Then he walked over to Anna, greeted her with a silent smile and a kiss on both cheeks. Anna smiled and giggled.

General Merriwhether wore his dress blues. He wanted Uncle Jimmy and every know how important this man was to the mission, to national security and to the United States of America. To General Merriwhether, Uncle Jimmy was as central to our secret mission, so secret that only the President and the President's chief of staff had a high enough security clearance to think about it, let alone talk about it. It was so secret, they could only talk to each other about it, and no one else.

And now there is Uncle Jimmy. General Merriwhether says that even the President stands in awe of Uncle Jimmy. And nobody knows why, but everybody is afraid to ask because if they find out, it could be 'curtains' for them, their families and damn their generations of descendants forever!

And that's exactly what General Merriwhether said. "I want you to know Jimmy, how important you are to our Presidential secret mission, national security and the United States of America. Anna and Rose, be it known, you are in the presence of greatness. Jimmy Buonarotti, I am so happy you are on America's side in this one." Even for General Merriwhether, he's laying it on a bit thick.

"General Merriwhether, my whole life has been on the side of 'truth, justice, and the American way. I am always and forever on the side of the United States of America. And I will always be on your side, my dear, trusted and revered friend." Now Jimmy came to attention and saluted the General. I knew they were both laying in thick for the women, whom they barely acknowledged with a nod after that.

When I used to visit Uncle Jimmy and Aunt Anna at their tenement apartment on Tenth Avenue, Uncle Jimmy explained to me after he sent Aunt Anna out for prosciutto, other cold cuts, and a fresh loaf of Italian semolina bread that this was the way you treated your wife with respect. You treat your wife like I treat Aunt Anna, she will forever love you and forever be sure of your love. She knows you have nothing to be guilty about. And women who love their men, love being obedient and performing all their domestic and wifely duties, including being the consummate hostess at their husband's command. I was about to tell Rose but thought better of it. It doesn't work for WASP wives, even though she went to Catholic school.

"Jimmy, I know what you are going to say next." And I thought Jimmy would first duck into a telephone booth and come out in tights, a trailing cap from his shoulders, and wearing his shorts on the outside of his body suit. I guess this whole thing isn't as urgent as everyone said it is.

"Rose are you alright. I'm a little worried about the way you look." I thought Rose was in some sort of trance. She's in such awe of Uncle Jimmy, she can't get two words out.

"I'm fine, Archy." I guess it was more boredom than the trance of an adoring devotee. She was actually rolling her eyes and swaying. I'm just not sure what that was all about.

"Dear, women always swoon over my Jimmy."

"Aunt Anna, you need your medication if you think any modern woman is going to swoon over Jimmy Buonarotti in his spats." Suddenly, Rose woke up.

Uncle Jimmy had tuned out the girls a long time ago. "And General, I know you have your time in for a full military retirement. Working for me would be a new chapter in your life. And you're a good-looking dog in your uniform. But we put you in one of Israel's three-piece pinstripe suits with two pair of pants – you'll have to beat the women off with a stick.

I'm sure your main squeeze might enjoy New York a bit more that stogy Washington." Now Uncle Jimmy is trying to recruit General Merriwhether, again.

"Jimmy, I've really thought about this offer when we talked while Archy and me were at the NSA. The only thing that stopped me then, and the only thing that stops me now, is my country – our country needs me here. And our country needs you here with your mind on our mission."

"General, more than anything, more than any foreign intelligence victory, the United States of America needs honest politicians. With all the top-secret stuff you know, and I don't mean any military or national security secrets. I love our country and would do nothing, absolutely nothing to put it at risk. Never reveal any military secrets to me. I, like everyone else – like every loyal and patriotic American – as far as military secrets especially here and now for our mission, I'm on a need-to-know basis.

You, me and Archy are men of the world. We don't have to tell the girls anything for them to do what we need them to do – for the mission. It would probably be way over their heads anyway and would no doubt confuse their little estrogen-soaked brains." Now Uncle Jimmy said this out loud and everyone heard him.

'Just to be clear, I would think with all your years in Washington, in command, you must have a wealth of knowledge, all the dirt, I mean on Congress. We could spend a lifetime on Congress without even thinking of the Pentagon. With all you know, we wouldn't have to invest in any 'opposition research' firm. Save money on achieving our end goal. And our goal is always honest politicians, at a modest profit for us. At least cover our expenses. Especially since parking has gotten so expensive.

All the congressmen and senators are multimillionaires, and they didn't get that way by being alter-boys. And they didn't get elected to Congress by being boy scouts either. And the beauty of it is, they have all the money in the world and the power, to at least grant 'small wishes' or do 'little favors. Nothing big enough to say 'no' to or temp them to turn us in or worse. Just small favors, minor pieces of information, small amounts of hush money so they don't have to bother with us. Better they consider anything we ask for, small as it is, as charity rather than that ugliest of words, extortion.

Anything we ask for, always politely, and only as a favor they could turn down if they wished, would be so small that it just wouldn't matter to them. And we always tell them they could always say no at any time. They can say no even in the middle of granting the favor. And it wouldn't affect our friendship for them or our respect of them in any way, 'probably...'

And then there's so many of them, you can hit them up, and not get back to them for years. They won't feel a thing. Most won't remember because they want to forget the details as much as possible. The beauty of the whole operation is that once they 'grant a wish', they're admitting they did what we said they did, and we didn't even have to show our hand. Even when we're bluffing, they're admitting guilt whether or not they're guilty. And that's the way all politicians are in their very souls. Remember, General, 'You can't cheat an honest man,' but he can be bluffed.

I've been doing this with New York City's government all my life. And with each election and each new administration, more opportunities. In New York, there's so much corruption, no honest man even tries to get elected anymore. And the corruption leads to the turnover, and then more of the exact same corruption, just with different politicians. And in a city government, no matter how big – like New York City, the biggest – there is just a limited amount of ways corruption can be corrupt. None of these crooked politicians, and they're all dishonest, because even the most honest ones lie to themselves. Neither the most crooked nor most honest, anywhere on the spectrum of being a politician can think of new ways of being corrupt. You would think if they had any pride in their chosen profession, they would try to be original.

You don't even need to hit the same 'clients' twice. In New York, the political opposition research opens the door, and I – my friends in our enterprise just walk through the golden gates of opportunity. The only limiting factor is that the New York City government, as big and useless as it is, is much smaller the Congress of the United States of America.

Congress on the other hand, and the Federal government takes corruption to a whole new level. Congress will be different. More money, more power, bigger payoffs and favors, but with incumbents being re-elected over ten, twenty, thirty and forty years – it's the incumbents that always will have new things to hide.

With over four hundred members of the House and Senate, that would be very infrequent to even go after more than one misstep that bends the law – no more than once per term in office. And you would have to work hard at it every day – including weekends and holidays - to make sure you get around to everyone. Even with senators' six-year term, it will be hard to get around to them more than once considering how slow the Senate works. It's a daunting task for us to look over Congress's shoulder at every turn to try to keep them honest. We not blackmailing anyone, not really. We're performing a public service that we need to be compensated for.

When they announce prematurely that they will no longer seek election, that usually means they are without real or imagined power, and their dishonesty winds down to something not worth pursuing. We have to wait to see who is nominated for the Senate or House seat. There's no use wasting our time and financial resources on losers."

No one understands Washington as well as Uncle Jimmy. I just don't know how he has time for everything he does, and still hold down a full-time job with the railroad. Uncle Jimmy always said, and so did my father, railroad people are the best people and can always be depended on to get the job done. No matter what the job was, and especially if your life or someone else's life depended on it. Their devotion to duty can only be compared to that of our military. And that's who he called upon for General Merriwhether's job.

"Jimmy, I want your people build for me an aircraft cabin with four sections. One for Air Koryo – national airline of North Korea; one for Iran Air; one for China National Aviation Corporation; and one for PJSC Aeroflot. We have photos of the interiors for all four airlines. We need hydraulics to simulate in takeoff, inflight turbulence, and landings. We also need a mockup of the UN General Assembly. We'll do that in one of the large hangers at Joint Base Andrews."

"This sounds like Bill Casey's old scheme with the translators. I thought that was abandoned years ago. When Bill told me about it, I told him I thought it was a good idea. But we were eating prosciutto hero sandwiches and finishing my last bottle of chianti. I had to send Anna downstairs to get more wine, bread and cold cuts."

"And I remember that day, Jimmy. It was very hot in the apartment. When I came back with the wine, bread and cold cuts and some other groceries, Casey's driver and bodyguard got out of the limo and asked if they could carry the packages upstairs. I felt sorry for Bill Casey's men parked out front. I went down with two cold cut sandwiches and cans of beer. They were very kind men. They thanked me profusely."

"No, Jimmy. Like the rest of the Federal Government, especially top-secret projects, they go on and on. And now they gave it to me. And I will make it work!" General Merriwhether was wound up. "We'll go to our dining hall. Israel and Rachel Beilin will meet us there. We can all have a light brunch and finalize our plans."

We all entered the dining hall through the kitchen. Israel and Rachel sat at the table nearest the kitchen's double swinging doors. Mugs of coffee, and large cloth napkins were in front of each of them. Under Israel's napkin was his right hand and his Colt .45 caliber automatic. Under Rachel's napkin was her .22 caliber revolver and on her lap was her coffin pillow embroidered with the word, 'Mother'.

All the asbestos warning signs were in a pile on the table next to Israel and Rachel. When General Merriwhether looked at them, Israel very quietly said, "They tore them off the doors and threw them on the floor. I think we're in trouble."

Israel motioned to the far end of the dining hall. Around a fairly small table sat the four translators who believed they were the Ayatollah, Kim, Xi and Putin. And Putin had no shirt on and needed his chest and back waxed except where his back at the base of his neck and the center of his chest was partially shaved for the two-by-two-inch bloody dressings. All had bandages around both wrists. Each one had a peanut butter and jelly sandwich – grape jelly- on a paper plate and a small brown sandwich bag they had taken from the kitchen. One or two spots of blood had soaked through the paper bags.

"General, they removed their tracking chips. Look at their bandages. And the paper bags."

"There's usually grease leaking through brown paper sandwich bags, not blood. They must have made themselves rare roast beef sandwiches." General Merriwhether is always an optimist. But none of us saw any rare roast beef on the electric meat slicer in the kitchen."

"I'm afraid to know what's in the paper bags."

* * * * *

CHAPTER TEN

"The Moving Finger writes; and , having writ,
Moves on: nor all your Piety nor Wit
Shall lure it back to cancel half a Line,
Nor all your Tears wash out a Word of it."
[*From The Rubaiyat of Omar Khayyam as
translated by Edward FitzGerald, 1859*]

"Before you try to explain anything, first, where we are? And I mean you with the fancy blue uniform and the stars on your shoulders. Now answer my questions before I decide to alter your state of being, forever." That must translate into Mandarin to something much more threatening. He doesn't know it, but from him, not so much. The question was is this a real threat from the President of the Peoples Republic of China and the head of the Chinese Communist Party or was it a bluff of this usually meek translator who knew he, and everyone on President Xi staff was always in danger of being executed. That was President Xi's employee incentive plan. It was the employee incentive plan for President Putin and the Ayatollah. For the 'Shining Sun-The Dear Respected' one, he would pick a staff member to execute by someone also on his staff, just to set an example and remind them all of the importance of promptness, loyalty, and efficiency. No body presently on the Dear Respected one's staff was ever late. Anyone who was late, well...To say the least all his meetings started right on time.

I interrupted our translator who thought he was President Xi of Communist China, hoping he still thought he was President Xi. I had to know whether the shock of discovering he wasn't in his office in Beijing had broken the 'Jerusalem Syndrome' spell, his useful and very important delusion.

I'm stalling for time to come up with an entire fairy tale that would at least have its own internal logic. I figure in terms of intellect, our Xi and the real Xi, are the smartest of this group. Our Putin is a close second. The Ayatollah and the 'Dear Respected – The Shining Sun', we can't stress them too much, but you never can tell whether the weaker and weakest minds might not hold onto their delusion as strongly as a stronger mind. If Xi is convinced he's Xi, then I've probably fooled the rest of them. It's just that I know they've found their tracking devices, and now obviously know their way around and out through the kitchen.

Our Xi, like the real Xi dominated. He seemed to take charge of his little group. Our translator thought he thought he was the most powerful person at the table – the leader of the most powerful nation in the world – at least that's what our strategist believe the real President Xi believes. And at least half of the world believes Communist China is as powerful, if not more powerful than the United States. And that includes some NATO countries like Germany. (Nobody knows what Belgium, the Netherlands or Luxemburg think, and nobody really cares.)

"Sir, before we proceed, you need to self-identify yourself. We will certainly believe everything you tell us. Our expectations are that you are here, and here is the correct place you should be, at least for now and the near future. And that sir, at least answers the first of many questions you have. Now, sir, identify yourself, please, Mr. President."

I thought I would give him a hint and hope that addressing him as President might assuage any doubts as to who he is and where he is. If he believes he is President Xi, he won't have any anxiety. He is the leader of the most populous nation in the world in possession of a credible nuclear force, the largest standing army. Our President Xi and the real Xi are confident men. The real Xi is a confident, resourceful, and cunning leader, mass murderer, and a serial killer in his own right. Our Xi thinks he leads Communist China, and thinks he is a successful mass murderer, and serial killer. Everybody at the table with him have a remarkably similar resume. If our Xi believes, the others believe and will continue to believe as long as Xi believes, especially if Xi believes the others believe.

"Sir, I'm asking the questions for all of us, now. Who are you?" Our President Xi stood and pounded his fist on the table. He was trying too hard to be threatening. I don't know if his delusion is slipping. I could tell he was more confused and bluffing than angry. The other three sat stony faced, just as confused as our President Xi, and scratching at the bandages on their wrists. They were all more than happy for Xi to take the lead. Putin must have been getting cold. He grabbed his shirt off the back of his chair and put it on over his head.

None of them showed any anxiety considering they watched as, who they thought were their doubles, arrive at the United Nations and declare themselves the leaders of their respective nations. At their level and the way, the constant power struggles played out in their countries, they were all used to internal threats. Was this coup against the four nations most opposed to the Great Satin, the US? Was the US getting even for all the mean things Xi, Kim, the Ayatollah and Putin said. Or was this a long thought-out power play to throw the entire world off guard while the Great Satin makes some momentous move in international power politics.

The absolute leaders of absolute dictatorships are long winded in their speeches because they believe their people love standing for hours in either the heat or cold to hear their speeches. And their people know, anyone who sneaks out early is executed. Anyone who faints is revived, given a drink of water, then executed because they are too weak to serve the state or their leader without possibly using valuable medical resources. In the same way these despots are long winded in their private thoughts because they are so taken with themselves, they amaze themselves with their own ponderings. Thinking about their own thoughts, profound thoughts they were sure, was as pleasurable as sharing their wisdom with their people for hours upon hours. At one point all of them, the Ayatollah in particular despaired that there wasn't enough time to listen to their wisdom and slave for the state.

"President Xi. You are the President of the Peoples Republic of China. You are 'The Great and only President Xi. I will identify myself now, even though over the years, the many times I met you and warmly greeted you with my U.N. salute at the entrance to the United Nations Headquarters, this was the first time you noticed me. And this is the very first time you spoke to an usher. It is a great honor and privilege that you chose me to be the first usher, ever, you spoke to." Now I better explain the uniform. "President Xi, I am General Merriwhether, I am sure you recognized my usher's uniform. I am the chief – general of all the United Nation's ushers, and most senior usher at the United Nations building. I was sent here to escort you, the most important leader in the world, and certainly the most important leader to speak at the United Nations General Assembly. Yours's will be the keynote address." I saluted stood at attention and saluted President Xi again. "Wherever and whenever you speak, it is always the keynote address. That has been part of the United Nation's usher's manual. And so, it is written for now and posterity."

"And why do you wear what looks the uniform of the armed forces of 'The Great Satin', as my dear friend and head of China's most important client state, Ayatollah Ali Khamenei, Supreme leader of the Islamic Republic of Iran, calls 'The Great Satin'? Ayatollah, I have to hand it to you, calling the United States 'The Great Satin' was a wonderful power ploy. Did you think that up yourself or did your public relations department come up with it first, and then focus group test it?"

"President Xi, thank you for the compliment." The Ayatollah entire tone was jovial after he was recognized as achieving something over the United States, especially from the President of the Peoples Republic of China. "I have to admit it, it was my idea, but we did focus group test it, first. Those who didn't like it were sent into exile in the dessert, and those who thought it was too harsh, well they were stoned along with their lawyers and the adulteresses. The whole 'The Great Satan' campaign became a national hit. Thank you, President Xi for those kind, warm and true words, and thoughts. And that's why we sit around the table of the first meeting of NEWS (NNUS) – Nuclear Nations against the United States." The Ayatollah stood, bowed his head toward our President Xi, then turned and bowed his head individually toward Kim and then Putin. Putin and Kim returned the acknowledgement with barely a smile. This told me, at least now, all their delusions were intact. But it bothers me they found the tracking devices.

"And, General of the United Nations ushers, explain why your uniform is so much like the uniform of the American Armed Forces. Is the UN trying to insult me and the rest of the world? I suspect you're no usher. Explain, sir!"

"President Xi, of course I am an usher. I stand in awe and tremble in fear of you and everyone at this table. And so, does every usher at the United Nations. I could never lie, nor would I ever lie. No United Nation's ushers ever lie. I wouldn't lie to any of you and risk my life, the lives of my family or any of the loyal ushers at the United Nations." I paused dramatically looking for something else to say that would be believable. I came to attention again, made one salute to everyone at the table and said, "The Americans donated their surplus uniforms to the United Nations' staff. Many of those staff members are here to serve all you gentlemen. And all of them look like they're in the American military. But, believe me, they're not."

"Our collective second question is why are we here? Out third collective question is how did we get here? And finally, why are there imposters impersonating each one of us at the opening meeting of the United Nations General Assembly? Do you know, man in the elaborate usher's uniform? You, the general of all the United Nation's ushers – tell us what you know!"

I still had to be sure they remained delusional. "Gentlemen, the United Nations Uniform Code of Usher Conduct – UNUCUC- or at the UN we shorten it to UCUC – the codes demand that all of you identify yourselves definitively." I was standing closest to the table with the four translators seated at the four points of the compass.

The other three turned toward Xi and nodded in unison. "Let me do the introductions. Firstly, I am the leader among all our leaders here. And in a short time, I will be the leader of all the world leaders. I am Xi Jinping, President of the Peoples Republic of China, Chinese Communist Party General Secretary and Military Chairman. Of all the important world leaders that sit before you, I am by my very presence can act here and now to change the course of human events across the globe, at my mere whim."

I haven't figured out how they all got out of their suites and are here at the same time. They obviously know this is a ruse, but at least our Chinese-English translator still thinks he is Xi Jinping. I still can't be sure that they believe I'm an usher wearing the dress blues of an American general officer.

"I have no recollection of even getting on an airplane." Our Xi was adjusting his glasses. "You're in the uniform of an American Army officer. You're no usher, are you?"

"And I don't remember the flight here. I don't believe you." Xi was becoming agitated. "I want to talk to my staff at the embassy."

"President Xi, you, the Ayatollah, President Putin and The Dear Respected One, The Shining Sun all flew nonstop from your capitals to New York on your national civilian airlines. Air Koryo and Iran Air all had their planes fitted with oxygen concentrators made in the Chinese funded aviation business the Chinese started in Sudan to compete with Boeing. It was the Sudanese company's first and last attempt to build airliners by starting to build parts to airliners. The company couldn't sell their oxygen concentrators to any of the world's international carriers, domestic carriers, FedEx or even the drug smugglers. Amazon Prime refused to carry it on their sale's sight. The company went broke, the executives only making in the millions instead of tens of millions in US dollars. All the employees went unpaid. The employees took the stock of oxygen concentrators home, and individually sold them on eBay. Some of the concentrators worked, some didn't work, and some only intermittently worked.

The one's they sold to hospitals killed all the patients that used them. Those hospitals or some of their employees after the hospitals removed the concentrators also put them on eBay. But they were even cheaper because they were listed as 'gently used'. And because there were so many on eBay, and they were so cheap, Air Koryo and Iran Air fitted all their domestic and international fleet with the used Sudanese concentrators, selling the original equipment oxygen concentrators that came with the airliner from the factory on eBay for a profit. The eBay oxygen concentrators from Air Koryo and Iran Air came without the original installation instructions included. PJSC Aeroflot and China National Aviation Corporation replaced their oxygen concentrators with what they thought were new ones but were actually the old ones from Air Koryo and Iran Air. That would have worked except the installation instructions were for the eBay Sudanese oxygen concentrators originally installed in Air Koryo and Iran Air aircraft. It's the intermittent anoxia that gave all of you your retrograde amnesia."

"And what is your title?"

"I am the most senior UN usher and general of all the ushers at the United Nations Headquarters in New York City. My duty and assignment directly from the Secretary-General of the United Nations is to escort you into the General Assembly and walk with you directly to the podium for your opening remarks." I could tell that the Ayatollah didn't really understand what I was talking about.

"Do they know in Tehran what happened during the flight?"

"Yes, they do, Ayatollah. Indeed. They're awaiting your

instructions." Let's see if they buy any of this. Rose, Anna, and Uncle Jimmy stood back from the table. Israel and Rachel have their hands under their napkins with their right index finger already inside the trigger guard of their pistols. I turned around just to give Israel and Rachel a smile. I could see them cock the hammers of their weapons to be able to get off a clean first shot. Rachel already told Israel she had dibs on the Ayatollah. Israel was to take out the bare-chested Putin and leave Kim for last. This translator was rollie-pollie just like the real Kim.

Putin was fidgeting. That's so unlike someone who is the so much in command to fidget or show any emotion or anxiety. I can't tell whether reality is breaking through. "Sir let me salute you as the renown and respected world leader you are. In keeping with the higher protocol of the protocol section of the United Nation Headquarters Ushers' Manual, Guide and General Orders, I must ask you to identify yourself." Let's see how far that gets me.

He is standing. At least our Putin is looking me straight in the eye. "I am Vladimir Vladimirovich Putin, President of Russia. I need to call the Kremlin immediately."

The Ayatollah, who was sitting to his right, put his hand on his shoulder and said, "We all need to call our capitals, if anything to adjust with some permanency our national airlines management team as well as our ground airplane mechanics.

If you like, we could do it as a group activity of NEWS. Stoning, as time consuming as it could be, is a very satisfactory way to relieve any pent-up tensions you may have. And I could have my people explain it to your people the proper procedures and stoning protocols. Or I could send them a complimentary copy of my book, "Stoning For Idiots" on Barnes and Noble and Amazon web sites. They can stay at the Russian Embassy in Tehran, and once they're over their jetlag, I'll put on a demonstration with the executives of Iran Air. There are enough of executives, their wives, and children, and even grandchildren, we can make a day of it. My people will be glad to show you how it's done. We'll break for a light lunch, and once done with the afternoon's agenda with the very top airline officials, we'll have a state dinner, that I hope you'll attend."

"Ayatollah, thank you for the invitation, but the Russian tradition is not as bloody or vengeful. I'll just have them all, all the executives, wives, children, grandchildren and whatever nieces and nephews by blood or marriage who happen to be visiting or neighbors brought to the basement at Lubyanka. I will personally have the mother's shoot their children, the husbands shoot their wives, and I'll finish off anyone who refuses to do what they're told or who are left. Nieces, nephews, and cousins – I will spare their lives and just send them directly to a Siberian gulag. If I can have my secret police round them all up, I can be done in one afternoon and be back behind my desk just after dinner and finish up the days' paperwork. You wouldn't believe it, but when you are the absolute power in the country, there is a terrifying amount of paperwork. You would think I was running the Moscow DMV."

"Ayatollah, I would appreciate an invitation. And I would bring my own airline executives. I was planning a mass dismemberment and enjoy watching them exsanguinate, but your way speaks to me as a matter of tradition. I think my nation needs to develop some of its own but ancient traditions." Our little Kim knew he had to say something just to remain relevant.

"Dear Respected One, forgive me, but I thought you knew you always had an open invitation to Tehran, especially for any and all of our public executions. And my invitation also includes any member of your immediate, military, or diplomatic family, and of course anyone you want executed. In fact, anytime you want to visit me in my capital, we will put on an execution in your honor. I have people waiting in a que for execution that my Revolutionary Guard keep in reserve for just such a special occasion. Some of them are in prison, and many are not and don't even suspect they're on my list. They're the best ones to pick up, bury up to their heads and stone to death. You should see the surprised look on their faces."

"Very inefficient." Xi had a look of derision toward his fellow dictators. "Once it becomes clear what happened to me on the flight here, the executions will be completed by that evening. Trains to the work camps will be filled with the mechanics assistants and their friends and families who installed the oxygen concentrators, and my secret police will hunt down those at eBay who placed the online offer. And theirs will be a special gift to all who flew in their accursed aircraft and those who got screwed by an eBay deal. No one will ever know their fate, or even ask. Such is our Chinese efficiency!"

I had to ask – poke the bear, so to speak – "And if anyone is spared, President Xi?"

"When I return to Beijing, my trusted informants will tell me who was spared out of bribe, inefficiency, stupidity or unauthorized mercy. I will find out who they are, have them and their families brought to my office, and personally shoot everyone as they stand in front of my desk. And the unfortunate ones who let them go, their families, friends, business associates – everyone – the secret police will handle secretly so I won't have to give it another thought. We have so many people in China, no one is ever missed. Their empty homes are immediately occupied by our efficient real estate agents, and everyone below them in their employment just moves up one position. Then I will have my office cleaned, painted, and have all the furniture replaced. I hate blood splatter on anything. I will wear an old suit that I will no doubt donate to charity. When you are a great leader, it is important for your subordinates, and your public to know that you are charitable with your personal possessions, even when they are bloodstained."

Uncle Jimmy was smiling as he listened to all the men. It was a smile you didn't want to see if you were the one, he was smiling at. "President Xi, President Putin, Ayatollah, Dear Respected One, Life goes on." Anna grabbed Uncle Jimmy's right arm as he was about to reach under his suit jacket.

"Archy, your uncle smiles at the strangest things."

"I saw it once before when he smiled like that at a particularly unpleasant person who ran a Tenth Avenue collection agency. He watched a man in a cheap suit collect a debt from an old man and his widowed daughter. The man had one hand on the woman's arm, and pushed her very roughly, even though the old man had cash in his hand. Apparently, he often collected debts ahead of time. Debts that people of lesser means, influence, and connections had not even incurred."

By this time, Rachel brought cups, spoons and napkins from the kitchen and placed them in front of the four men at the table. After a nod from Rachel, Rose went to the table and brought out a tea pot and coffee pot. Rose poured tea for the Ayatollah and coffee for the other three. By that time, Rachel had brought back a small pitcher of cream and a sugar bowl. I was half watching the table as I was listening to Archy.

"Uncle Jimmy's tenement on Tenth Avenue wasn't far from the North River. It was unusual for him to walk me there, but he said he wanted to go over there before we stopped at the corner candy store and delicatessen for cold cuts. It wasn't dinner yet, but we could do with a sandwich. There, we watched from the sidewalk as the police with their flashing lights pulled a body out of the water with hooks. They didn't even bother with divers. The body was bloated and burst the buttons and split the pants on the cheap suit. We smelled it even as far away as we were. It was the smell I remembered most. Finally, the New York City's Medical Examiner van came, loaded him onto the stretcher with the black body bag open. He was zipped up, and off he went. On the way back from the river, we stopped at the bakery for a fresh loaf of Italian bread. Uncle Jimmy said nothing until we got to the apartment. Aunt Anna said nothing. She put out dishes, sliced the long loaf in half, one half for me and the other for Uncle Jimmy. She opened the halves to receive the cold cuts. She put the cold cuts on a plate with some sliced tomatoes, an open jar of mustard and a bottle of olive oil. Uncle Jimmy and I made our own sandwiches. I was about to take a bite, and before Uncle Jimmy closed his sand-wich he said, "Archy, I just wanted you to see that life goes on!"

* * * * *

CHAPTER ELEVEN

**"The one means that wins the easiest victory
over reason: terror and force."**
[*Adolf Hitler, Mein Kampf, 1924*]

Rachel was returning to the kitchen for another pot of tea, and Rose was pouring coffees. Putin grabbed Rose's left wrist and Kim grabbed her right wrist with the coffee pot. Without addressing her directly, the Ayatollah pulled a bloody cloth handkerchief out of his robe let it open up in the center of the table and spilled out the bloody sticky chip trackers attached to a good deal of human skin and fat tissue that the translators cut out of each other's their wrists, chest and back.

I was about to attack these crazy shits when Uncle Jimmy stopped me. I wasn't thinking. Then in a second my question was why Rose didn't pour the hot coffee over Kim's lap and break the coffee pot over Putin's head and then cut both their throats with the broken glass of the coffee pot still attached to the black plastic handle. (This was the coffee pot for the caffeinated coffee, that's why the handle was black – just in case you were wondering. Nobody at the table drank decaf.)

Rose could and would have certainly overpowered any of these translators. Once Rose saw the bloody tracking chips, she knew she had to bide her time and play the long game. I knew that Rose knew she would get them in the end for laying a hand on her. The four translators didn't know they signed their own certificate of doom – the 'Rose guarantee'.

"Archy, let me count." Uncle Jimmy pushed me away from the table, stepped between Putin and the Ayatollah, reached into his jacket, and pulled out his Mount Blanc fountain pen. This was a pen I saw him only carry for weddings and funerals to sign the guest books. This was the very pen he used to sign his and Anna's marriage license and wedding certificate. He used the capped end of the pen to push the bloody tracking chips into four groups of four. "General Merriwhether, are they all here?"

"All the chips are there, Jimmy." General Merriwhether's voice was grim. The delusional translators suspected they could be tracked and cut them out probably using a kitchen knife.

Uncle Jimmy said, "This is right out of Bill Casey's game plan." Putin and Kim still tightly had Rose's wrists.

"Archy, before I do something these two will regret…" And Rose still had the hot coffee and was growing angrier and more impatient by the second. I know they didn't frighten her. Rose was warning me and the General if we didn't get her loose, there would be at least two fewer translators for us to deal with. Rose still had her Colt .45 in her apron pocket, and it wouldn't take much to get one hand free and put bullets in both these guys. And for that matter she might not even break the coffee pot, just burn Kim's balls, and shoot them all. Once you start shooting, killing them all with a .45 Colt at close range would take no effort at all. That would avoid all the broken glass and having to replace the coffee pot.

"Archy, let me handle this. General, I have dealt all my life with gentlemen like this. And they are esteemed gentlemen, the leaders of their countries. They've come to the U.N. to spread the message of globalism's peace, prosperity, and tranquility that comes with top-down rule order and discipline. And these four superior men among men are the leaders of tomorrow who will slay The Dragon." Uncle Jimmy turned to President Xi but was addressing all of them. "Esteemed leaders, the woman means nothing to us. Do what you will, but then there will be one less of them for all of us to serve our meals. And if you kill her, she'll probably drop the coffee pot and make a mess on the floor. I'm sure you don't want to be splashed. And I'm sure you can all do for another cup of coffee, and another tea for the Ayatollah.

I try to think practical, and I'm sure you do too." Uncle Jimmy's smile was the smile to be feared. I knew that and knew not to pay attention to his words. The four translators who thought they were the unchallenged absolute rulers over life and death in their countries could only hear the fawning words – the words that came from everyone around them. They heard Uncle Jimmy's words but read his smile the wrong way.

"This is unnecessary and will only delay us reaching our desired and important goals for world peace and stability in the image you all desire. And the first step toward world peace is world discipline. The stability, prosperity is of strong, and formidable Peoples Republic of China, Islamic Republic of Iran, the Russian Federation and of course under the leadership of the Dear One, the Democratic Peoples Republic of Korea.

Let me introduce myself. I am Most Senior Special Agent In-Charge Jimmy Buonarotti of the United Nations Worldwide Security, Intelligence, and International Peace Agency – for short we're known as the UNWWSI and IPA – and for shorter, just the IPA."

The four men seated at the table looked puzzled and shrugged their shoulders. Then Xi said, "We've heard of you, but refresh our memory. You don't make many news articles and my intelligence agencies have only mentioned your agency in passing. Now you can explain more to us." Xi paused and gave Putin and Kim a grim look. "Break her arms, kill her or do whatever you planned, but I want another cup of coffee and another peanut butter and jelly sandwich, in triangular wedges and the crust cut off of the bread."

"Sweety, I want a cup of coffee, too. And I don't have a cup." Uncle Jimmy looked at Putin and Kim. "Well, gentlemen, how am I going to get my coffee if you continue to hang on to the wench?" Without a word, Putin and Kim immediately released Rose. "You can break her arms, break her wrists, break her fingers later. As long as I get my cup of coffee." Uncle Jimmy moved his hand to pat Rose on the ass.

Rose, as she passed Uncle Jimmy paused on her way back to the kitchen, whispered, "You touch my ass, and I break your fingers, then I'll shoot the four of them. Your mission will go to shit, but I'll feel better."

"General Merriwhether, you are the official usher. Instruct the woman to avert her eyes from us, return to the kitchen and bring back, coffee, my sandwich and tea for the Ayatollah."

"Woman follow the orders. Bring a plate of sandwich wedges for everyone, coffee and tea for the Ayatollah as instructed. Now go." I could see and so could General Merriwhether see Rose put her hands in her apron pocket. Both her wrists were bruised. She looked at the bruise on her left wrist and with her right hand in her apron pocket, cocked the hammer of her Colt .45.

It was Uncle Jimmy who gently put his hand on Rose's upper arm to calm her. "Just bring the sandwiches, Rose." Then Uncle Jimmy leaned close to her right ear and whispered, "Without the poison. We need them alive." Uncle Jimmy let Rose's arm loose and Rose went off to the kitchen.

Uncle Jimmy smiled that smile that told me these four were in his gunsights. "We are an ultra-secret agency that we don't even know one another by name or by sight. I, and our agency director, the Director General of IPA, the DGIPA, know who is working for the IPA and who at the UN just work in the mail room, the janitorial services, park the cars, are the messengers or are the ushers. Our agents are mixed in and disguised as the most menial of UN workers. They're even paid that way so as not to arouse suspicion. But we're out there. Our motto is, 'Use No Names'.

When we got wind of this dastardly plot against the four most revered of all the United Nation's nuclear leaders in the world, with universal peace and world control at stake, the UN Secretary-General decided we had to kidnap all of you off your airplanes right in front of your comatose security and bring you here to the UN's undisclosed safe site before the traitors in your country had you secretly assassinated. It was all going to happen on American soil. If the plot was discovered, their plan – the traitors' plan was to blame the 'Great Satin.'

We didn't learn until later that you had trackers when we placed you in your suites that wouldn't allow the trackers to transmit. I was brought by UNWWSI and IPA to see to your safety, get you all to the United Nations so you could confront your impersonators in front of the General Assembly, in front of the press, all their mothers, and the world.

I will arrange for you to use the UN subbasement for your interrogations when they are apprehended. The UN-WWSI and IPA will supply you with leather restraints, implements for interrogation and expert 'interrogation assistants who actually trained with the FSB, the Iranian Revolutionary Guard and the old SAVAMA, the Chinese Ministry of State Security, and the Korean Ministry of State Security. And just so you know our 'assistant' interrogators we make available to all UN member states who think of UN globalism and need their services in the UN basement. Just for your information, they are not well paid, and tipping is expected at the end of your interrogation. Disposal of the bodies is taken care of by the assistant interrogators, but they should be tipped separately for that, depending on if there is the intact body or more than one body part to dispose of. Our assistant interrogators love their work but can barely make ends meet living in New York. All of them had to get rent controlled apartments in Brooklyn or the Bronx. None of them could afford to live in Queens or Manhattan.

Our assistant interrogators are all headquartered at New York UN headquarters. Their emeritus director of assistant interrogators - our EDOAI - is Markus Johannes Wolf, the 'Man Without a Face.' He was reported dead but lives upstairs from me on Tenth Avenue and Twenty-Third Street in Manhattan and commutes every day with me to the United Nations on the East Side. We walk to the cross-town M42 bus and take it to the

UN. He is especially busy when the General Assembly is in session. So many of their citizens that need questioning are asylum seekers in the United States and end up protesting when their national leaders come to attend the General Assembly. It just so much easier to interrogate them right in the basement of the United Nations. If they have to be disappeared, the UN is right on the East River making it convenient. And everyone has diplomatic immunity, so the police don't even bother with involving any of the UN staff or diplomates. Convenient, economical, and it's all paid for by the United States."

Uncle Jimmy was on a role. But when you listen to him, you realize that when I visited him and Aunt Anna on Twenty-Third street off of Tenth Avenue, he did have an upstairs neighbor he introduced laughingly as 'The Man Without a Face,' when he came down to borrow some cream for his coffee. He had one of the rent-controlled apartments in the tenement for so many years since he fled Germany just ahead of the Nuremberg investigators. When he took the job with the Stasi, he still refused to give up the apartment. That's what he told us, and that's why he's the only interrogator at the UN that doesn't have a long subway commute.

Uncle Jimmy invited 'The Man Without a Face' in, and he sat at Uncle Jimmy's kitchen table, spoke with a thick German accent, spoke of the old days in Germany, and how he just came back from his day job at the UN. He was working nights with Uncle Jimmy at the railroad. And Uncle Jimmy always said, railroad people were the best people and the only people you could trust in an emergency. In fact, this 'Man Without A Face' was who Uncle Jimmy called years ago to help clean up the mess Anna and Rachel made in that unfortunate woman's apartment just upstairs from Uncle Jimmy.

As I reminisce, I just realize over and over again what a magical place Tenth Avenue was and still is. But back to the problem at hand. Uncle Jimmy is spinning one of his most entertaining and convincing tails. But it shouldn't be a difficult sale, these four are already delusional.

"We have already learned that this was a plot by a certain Western Hemisphere major political and economic power to take over your countries and stop the globalization you are seeking. Is that right, President Xi! Now you have already seen how the traitors in your own countries sent imposters to speak for you and then return to your countries and take over. The United Nations, the UNWWSI and IPA, and as head of that UN agency, I was duty bound to save your lives, at great risk to my own life and my wife's life..."

"Jimmy, if you're going to keep talking, I'm going to sit with Israel at the back table. My feet hurt." With that, Anna turned, and walked toward Israel's table. She sat, and quietly put her purse on the table, her hand in her purse and cocked the hammer on her little revolver.

Even before she sat, the Ayatollah spoke. "I assume that was your wife. You let your wife speak to you like that. You let your wife speak at all in front of other men. I would have her whipped just for the disrespect. In fact, if you want, I could arrange to have her whipped for you."

"Ayatollah, then who would serve me coffee and my meals. I'm not as well off as a great Ayatollah. Who would do the shopping, clean the house, laundry, pick up the dry cleaning - all the things I need have done for my own upkeep? And after the whipping, how much time would she be unable to serve me at maximum capacity. In marriage, at least in marriages in the environs of the Great Satin, they're up sides and down sides of marriage, at least until the global order is achieved and womenkind can be put in their proper place. And that's why I'm here. To save your lives from the traitors in your country and help achieve the global order." Uncle Jimmy snarled his words through his smile. He was very fond of Rose, even protective, not that Rose needed protection. I'm sure he had something planned for Kim and Putin for manhandling my Rose.

That is if at the end of all this, Rose didn't get to them first. My Aunt Anna only had a small caliber revolver, and she would have to empty it into two of them, then reload. I'm sure she is going to ask Uncle Jimmy for her own Colt .45 like Rose's. And Uncle Jimmy will get it for her, for some special occasion – their next wedding anniversary. And befitting a wedding anniversary present, Aunt Anna's Colt .45 will have pearl handles along with a new and bigger alligator purse to carry it.

"President Putin, Ayatollah, President Xi, President Kim, take note of the date and time. You need to return to your suites and make your important calls to your capitals and warn your trusted few and loyal patriots that there are imposters at the U.N., and they need to warn their nation, warn the U.N and warn the world. Instructions have to come from all of you personally to your most trusted and devoted deputies." Uncle Jimmy looked around and just nodded to Israel and Rachel. They headed back to their shop to receive the calls from each of the translators and pose as their deputies on the other end of the phone."

Putin asked, "And afterward?" The other three translators nodded.

"Gentlemen, as soon as you're done with your calls, we can all convene here for dinner and the first meeting of NNAUS." Uncle Jimmy gave all of them his warmest and reassuring smile. Israel and Rachel had disappeared through the kitchen. "Gentlemen, is there any little snack you would like to bring back to your offices? Woman in the apron, prepare three coffees and a tea and bring it to their suites." As strong a personality as Uncle Jimmy was, it was not in him to be disrespectful to Rose.

Rose made a face, hesitated, her hand still in her apron pocket holding her cocked Colt. I knew Rose in her heart of hearts is going to personally kneecap before she kills Putin and Kim.

"Well, woman. What are you waiting for?"

Rose walked slowly to the kitchen, trying to calm herself down. Her instincts were to shoot Putin and Kim dead – between the eyes. She had second thoughts and just belly shots and watch these two pigs die slowly and painfully. And as the two men lay slumped over the table, she would bring the Ayatollah another tea and President Xi his second cup of coffee and dare them to say anything. Her right hand was out of her apron pocket and rubbing the painful bruise on her left wrist. The four men left the remains of their peanut butter and jelly sandwiches on their cake plates with the black and gold presidential seal but took their increasingly bloody brown paper sandwich bags with the same Presidential seal with them.

* * * * *

CHAPTER TWELVE

Terror is naught but prompt, severe, inflexible justice; it is therefore an emanation of virtue; it is less a particular principle than a consequence of the general principle of democracy applied to the most pressing needs of the fatherland.
[Maximilien Marie Isidore De Robespierre, 1758 – guillotined 1794]

General Merriwhether had a grim look on his face. His stubble beard made him look more worried. Why he hadn't shaved - it wasn't like him. Now that is very unmilitary. I worry he may be off his game. "We have to find out how they got out of their suites undetected. Everything is under video surveillance, yet the four of them got out, made sandwiches for themselves and served themselves coffee and tea. I'm afraid to let Rose go to their offices with the coffees and tea." Generals always shave and never admit they fear anything. He is definitely off his game.

"She should make sure she brings some crackers or cookies. She can't and shouldn't serve tea and coffee without at least offering crackers and cookies. That would be impolite. I'm sure she has an extra clip of .45 caliber treats, Colt cookies and Remington chocolates for our translators." Uncle Jimmy was trying to be subtle, but he just couldn't hide his disgust for these men. Uncle Jimmy hated bullies. And it was not that he hated power. But to use your power just to bully, especially a woman – Uncle Jimmy thought it dishonorable and unchivalrous. And the code of chivalry mandated anyone witnessing the abuse of a woman come to a woman's immediate defense. After the fact, then you were obligated to cause consequences of sufficient enormity as to discourage further abuse by the offender or anyone who witnessed the offense and corrective action. And this had to be done publicly. The modern code of chivalry only caveat dictates that what is done is out of view of surveillance cameras. And Uncle Jimmy along with all of us witnessed Rose's abuse and stood there and did nothing.

I knew it and Uncle Jimmy and Aunt Anna knew it, but our Putin and Kim were oblivious to the fact that they were already worm meals. I could see it in Rose's eyes that as soon as their intelligence value was spent, they were getting a .45 in the back of their heads or between the eyes if not in the knee-caps first. General Merriwhether being a WASP may not seek such severe revenge. Uncle Jimmy, Rose and I will be willing to wait until our mission is complete. But Aunt Anna wasn't even as patient as Rose.

And when it came to a member of his family, and Rose certainly was – they laid their hands-on Rose left marks and hurt her - that was a special and completely separate from any code of chivalry. That had to be revenged. Rose had to be revenged in a manner that was not in any code or practice of chivalry or knighthood. It was a matter of honor, though. The family code of honor and the Tenth Avenue code of honor dictated immediate, swift, and a decisive permanent response. It didn't mean necessarily taking a life and having the body found hanging from a lamp post or draped over the corner mailbox. Permanent responses could range from loss of at least both thumbs or all the fingers on one hand, three fingers keeping your thumbs on both hands, an entire hand or one or more limbs combined with a tongue, one eye, and often if not always combined with loss of a penis. Kneecapping with loss of penis was popular at one time, but with the advances in orthopedic surgery and penis prosthesis, it is less popular as loss of a penis with loss of one or both hands.

And the response had to set an example to others, so it couldn't be done in the shadows. Everybody had to know who did, who was being avenged, and why it was being done. Never too soon after the incident so it doesn't blur into one single horrible event. But never delayed so long, that the people on Tenth Avenue don't immediately connect the revenge with the offense.

That's the problem with the 'legal' justice system. It's not swift or decisive. That's because lawyers aren't swift or decisive, and they bill by the hour. The advantage of having the offender walking around with a missing limb, and knowing he is missing his penis discourages more bad behavior than any prison sentence that is often postponed, or significantly shortened by parole. Even life without parole isn't life without parole after crazy Cuomo pardoned cop killers who were originally sentenced to death for ambushing killing several police officers.

A corpse, even a disfigured corpse, that in days is often forgotten, especially that the city doesn't leave them out on the sidewalk for any length of time. It does prevent repeat offensives. The savings in court costs, incarceration, rehabilitation, halfway houses, the cost of parole officers and the idiot parole boards would be substantial plus. There would be a sense true justice really being served. Even though it's a good idea whose time has come, the idea has only taken hold in a few places – like Tenth Avenue.

It had to be known that you did it with your own hands. That was part of the Tenth Avenue code. It was almost as shameful to hire someone to perform your obligation as the act that had to be avenged. It had to be done by you, personally, but without getting arrested, or at least if you were arrested, you couldn't be convicted and go to jail. The code of Tenth Avenue said to avoid going to jail. If you're caught, even if you're caught in the act, deny everything including being where you were when you were where you were.

I'm betting Uncle Jimmy figures I would do it but get caught. I would do it; I would need Uncle Jimmy's planning expertise. At least I'll need to run the plan past Uncle Jimmy first. I know he could fix me up with an unregistered untraceable pistol and a choice of locations without surveillance cameras. Live witnesses will spread the word. Eyewitnesses are unreliable in court under any circumstances. At best, even if they are willing to testify, once they hear the reason, their testimony will be unsure, shaky, and they'll be wearing their new pair of very thick glasses. On Tenth Avenue, no one really lies in court under oath, but everyone is human, and has human frailties, including eyesight, hearing, clarity of memory, especially under cross examination, if it ever gets that far. It usually ends with the first deposition, and there's never, not ever anyone who will rat out someone seeking justice. And on Tenth Avenue, there's never a need or expectation of a plea bargain. The only downside is you still have to employ a lawyer.

There's a Tenth Avenue family protocol about going to the most senior person in the family about anything as important as something like this. Just like asking who you should buy a used car from. It's something you will have to live with, maybe not forever, but until the transmission gives out, or after your trial and you get out on parole if you're caught and in the very unlikely event you are convicted.

But the practicality of a Wasp which was needed in order to get the most from these 'intelligence sources', the assets who didn't know they were intelligence assets, dictated the cooler course of action, for now. With General Merriwhether not firing on all cylinders, Rose was the one who had silently taken charge, even though these would-be delusional despot-translators didn't know their lives were ultimately in Rose's hands.

"Rose, do you have an extra clip for your Colt?" Uncle Jimmy was very unhappy about not personally doing anything and was genuinely concerned for Rose's safety. At the same time, he had faith that Rose could take care of herself and would do what had to be done if the need arises. "My dear Rose, if your instinct tells you to shoot, don't hesitate. Keep pulling the trigger until they're flat on the ground. If you have any ammunition left, put one in the head. Remember, they think they're killers and think they're all powerful and can't be held accountable."

"Uncle Jimmy, you don't have to tell me twice." Rose gave Uncle Jimmy a warm look and took his right hand and patted it trying to reassure him. "It won't take me that many shots for me to finish them off. You have no faith. My father taught me how to shoot before I had my first period." Now that embarrassed Uncle Jimmy and at the same time made him feel better.

I knew Rose always carried an extra loaded clip in her purse. As did Uncle Jimmy. Aunt Anna carried a few extra loose revolver rounds in the bottom of her purse mixed with the hard candies she brought for me and Uncle Jimmy.

Rose always wiped off her fingerprints off each round before loading them and wiping off the clip before pushing it into the Colt's pistol grip. As did Uncle Jimmy. As did everyone on Tenth Avenue who brought an extra magazine for whatever untraceable automatic, they carried. And now that the crazy mayor practically put a halt to 'Stop and Frisk', combined with no bail for all the criminals, everybody in the Five Boroughs was packing.

Rose's mother taught her that a lady always has a pretty embroidered handkerchief in her purse. Rose always had her very feminine soft white cotton embroidered handkerchief in her purse to wipe the fingerprints off her Colt, and the clip she ejected and the replacement clip, just the way her mother taught her. Rose always thought of her mother whenever she loaded her Colt automatic and put one in the chamber.

"These are dangerous men, but if they're still delusional, the intelligence we can glean from them will be invaluable. Our President will have unheard of insight into these despots' thought processes and a preview of what they are going to say at the UN General Assembly." General Merriwhether was thinking out loud again. "We have to get whatever recordings we have, especially anything from their discussions in the dining hall between themselves. This is the ultimate peak at what our own 'Evil Empire' is thinking and planning." The General

looked so pleased with himself. "And more interesting is what
they think they can do together."

"And what their telling their own henchmen back in
their capitals, how they're going to execute the ones in their
inner circle they think is responsible for their betrayal. More
interesting who they call next to execute the executioners.
That's part of the 'International Despot's Manual'. And the
most interesting is how they're going to screw one another."
Uncle Jimmy turned to me and put his hand on my shoulder.
"What did I always tell you, Archy – and what do they always
say on Tenth Avenue – 'If you can't screw your friends, who can
you screw?'"

Apparently General Merriwhether ascribed to this phil-
osophy as did the faculty at the War College and the permanent
staff at our State Department. "It's that way in international
politics. It's just that our State Department and administrations going back years, maybe except President Trump's administration, never learned how to properly implement it - especially when dealing with NATO." The General thought he put
the icing on that cake. "NATO was always screwing the United
States. And when they couldn't screw the U.S., they would
screw the British. And that is especially true of the Germans."

General Merriwhether barely took a breath. I haven't
seen him this animated since we arrived in the dining hall.
"When it comes to Israel. Israel is the best friend of the US. We
try to screw Israel all the time because we think we can make
friends with the Palestinians and Iranians by showing our vul-
nerable sensitive side. I think the Kerry and his entire State
Department expects a dinner date from the Palestinians and
an invitation to the prom from the Iranians. And the US has
already bought its prom dress. And while this is going on Xi
and the Communist Chinese are stealing our lunch and laughing their balls off.

"Every administration especially Obama and the Democrats have tried to screw Israel. It's the 'faculty lounge' men-
tality." Everyone's jaw dropped including mine. Who thought

Aunt Anna had a grasp of international politics? Who thought she even knew about the figurative 'faculty lounge'.

"Aunt Anna, I didn't know you followed politics like that?"

"Archy, your Uncle rants all day. He plays Fox New all day when he's not sleeping. He talks at me and either doesn't think I'm listening or if I'm listening, I don't understand. Or if I understand anything, I don't have the brains to have a real opinion. Well, I understand, I have an opinion. And if I had a Colt like Rose, I would have shot the four of them dead where they sat. That's the only way you can deal with the likes of these. That's the real Tenth Avenue way. The Tenth Avenue men aren't nearly as efficient as Tenth Avenue women. And we waste fewer expensive rounds of ammunition doing what has to be done!"

General Merriwhether smiled. "Aunt Anna, the intelligence and espionage business needs far more finesse. There are many shades of subtleties that need to be addressed with diplomatic practices and applied knowledge that generations have acquired and passed down to our military leaders, like me."

Anna was about at least to verbally attack the General, especially for not willing to cut Putin and Kim's throats on the spot. Uncle Jimmy grabbed his wife's upper arm. Anna looked at her husband and fell silent. Uncle Jimmy didn't want Anna to say what she or he was thinking. And once said, couldn't be taken back. Jimmy's touch, or actually firm grab brought down the pitch of her anger toward Putin, Kim and General Merriwhether several octaves.

"Well, are they just bluffing, as crazy as before, or bluffing and crazy." Uncle Jimmy was thinking out loud, too. "It's obvious from their body language, they were plotting together. But why didn't they make a break for it?"

Now it was General Merriwhether's turn again to think out loud. I think both Uncle Jimmy and General Merriwhether are in love with the sounds of their own voices. It's like watching the reflection of your fingers in the polished wood as you practice the piano.

"Diplomatic immunity, General. They all think they have diplomatic immunity. Not only are they murderers, serial killers, mass murderers and committers of small and large-scale genocide and decidedly unpleasant to boot, but they believe they have diplomatic immunity." Uncle Jimmy had the answer.

And General Merriwhether had the answer to the answer. "They know they're all powerful in their countries, and they believe that they're all-powerful here. Now they can do what they want just for fun."

At the War College on the very first day, they teach that putting audible words to a dilemma in front of a trusted staff often clarifies the problem. It makes the solution magically appear out of the words floating in the room.

"In the typical locked room mystery, it turned out the room wasn't locked all the time. And I know Mrs. Haversham would have alerted us if she saw them together, here. We're going to need to get to her as soon as possible. When I saw them there at the table together, I feared the worse for her. We have to deduce what happened up here before we separate. I am sure they had outside help and that person got past Mrs. Haversham, our security, and us. We shouldn't underestimate their cunning and lethal potential."

Uncle Jimmy was worried but had a sneaky smile on his face. Anna said, "I'm worried about my niece going to them alone. She a brave girl, carrying on this charade for 'the mission'. She may hesitate to defend herself." As forceful a woman as Aunt Anna was, she looked at her husband to ask permission. "I think I should go in there with Rose. Why take any chances."

"Anna, you mean shoot them in the balls if they make one false move." And Uncle Jimmy wasn't speaking figuratively. "You're not the right person to be backup if we want to keep them alive. If we didn't, then I would hand you my Colt.

But I've seen your temper."

"Exactly! Rose's a patriot. She will almost any risk for America." Uncle Jimmy and General Merriwhether looked at each other.

I was worried about my wife, too. She loves her country and would sacrifice anything for the mission. I know she will serve them at their desks, and as long as they're seated in their chairs and she has the desk between her and these men, she'll do fine. And if anything is amiss, she'll shoot them dead with the first bullet out of her Colt. And then she will go on and roll her cart to the next one with his coffee. "General, I know we had to send Rose in alone, but I was hoping to back her up – at least be outside the door out of sight when she goes into their inner offices."

"That's probably a good idea, Archy. If she knows you're nearby, she'll be less likely to find an excuse to shoot them dead. And that would end our mission before it even got started." I'm glad the General agreed with me. Now, just to tell Rose when she comes back with the serving cart and the coffees, cream and sugar, and the Ayatollah's herbal tea."

"Archy, I know our Rose is going to kill Putin and Kim, just for laying a hand on her. And if were up to me, I'd let her. The only reason I can give you to prevent Rose from killing those two or all of them is that it would deny me the pleasure of doing it myself." Then Aunt Anna turned to her husband. "Jimmy, this revolver won't do the job. I need a .45 Colt or Glock. I'm not as good a markswoman as Rose, and I would need something that can really cause some damage no matter where I aimed."

"Anna, now is not the time." I can tell Uncle Jimmy was annoyed at Aunt Anna. He was angry with Putin and Kim in particular for the way they hurt Rose. Uncle Jimmy acutely felt his niece's pain. Uncle Jimmy also didn't like to be annoyed at two things at the same time. He wanted to concentrate on getting even with the two delusional translators. Anna diverting his attention was annoying. "Anna, your next birthday or anniversary, whichever comes first, I'll get you a .45 ACP Baby Glock."

"Jimmy! Do you even know when my birthday is? Do you even remember our anniversary? You're always forgetting! You are terrible. I just can't believe it. At least make it a new Glock, not anybody's throwaway. And giftwrap it for a change!"

"Anna, we have bigger fish to fry. What do you think?" Uncle Jimmy turned toward me and General Merriwhether. "General, the entire mission is at stake. Something is very wrong."

"Anna, we have to track down our breach in security. Be calm. Here, take my ankle .38 snub nose Smith and Wesson. Keep it as a gift until Uncle Jimmy gets you the gun of your dreams. Give your husband your little revolver. You won't be able to get both guns in your purse. We have to be sure everyone is adequately armed and at the same time find our breach in security."

"General Merriwhether, now I have a choice of ruining the way my suit jacket fits with the bulge of my wife's inadequate revolver in the jacket pocket or ruin the lines of my Israel Beilin pants." No matter what the situation, no matter what the danger, Uncle Jimmy wanted to look dapper.

"Jimmy, my concern now is Mrs. Haversham. She's the one person who will have the answer. She's been watching the monitors. If anyone knows what happened, she'll know." The General walked toward the kitchen door, followed by Uncle Jimmy. "Anybody coming up here has to get by Mrs. Haversham."

I had walked ahead of General Merriwhether, Uncle Jimmy and Aunt Anna. I met Rose as she was coming through the kitchen door with her coffee cart. The cart had four coffee cups and saucers and spoons, all with the White House seal, the coffee pot from the kitchen drip coffee maker, a pot of tea, and a small pitcher with cream and a sugar bowl. There was a small stack of ivory cloth dessert napkins with the Presidential Seal. I thought to myself they would make nice souvenirs and hoped Rose put some in her pocket. Then I noticed Rose's demeanor was disturbed, but with less anger in her eyes. Maybe she thought of taking the napkins for me because she knew I liked souvenirs and then ran out of napkins.

"Rose, first are there any of these napkins we can take home. ..."

By this time, Uncle Jimmy, the General and Aunt Anna had caught up with us in front of the kitchen door. "You all better come with me. And now!"

Rose led us through the swinging double doors of the kitchen past the four restaurant-kitchen stainless steel prep tables. Two tables had puddles of blood that had found their way to the closest table edge and was slowing dripping, drop by drop, to the floor. The floor or the table legs or both must be uneven for the blood to drip in only one direction. She pointed out the blood, and only said, "No knife, anyplace. No bloody knife in the kitchen." Then she opened the door to the walk-in freezer. Surrounded by shelves of frozen meats and bagged fresh frozen vegetables, was the sous chef and the chef in his tall chef's hat, both in their bloodied white uniforms, both hanging from large rolling meat hooks from the 'I' beam rail bolted to the freezer ceiling. The two men hung three feet off the ground, which would have been an impossible task for a single person or even our four translators. The chef and sous chef were both Marines, armed and not about to be overpowered. They had both hands cut off far above their wrists and were missing their side arms from their leather holsters.

"Our translators didn't have a drop of blood on them." Uncle Jimmy as concerned as he was, he was planning our next move.

"It's obvious USEWOW has been breached. And that means that the White House has been breached." General Merriwhether voiced what we have all been thinking. But was USEWOW the target or the President.

*   *   *   *   *

CHAPTER THIRTEEN
"He who fears being conquered is sure of defeat."
[Napoleon Bonaparte, 1769-1821]

"Rose, you and Archy go serve the coffee and tea like nothing happened. Uncle Jimmy, Anna and I will go to Israel and Rachel at the shop. The tailor shop's phones are secure. We can call Mrs. Haversham and find out what she knows." I guess with the dead cooks, the translators conspiring among themselves, and now we know what was in the paper bags, we have given up with 'Use No Names'. "Each of them with the cooks' hands and chips, they have access to everything, including the White House, the tunnels to Fort Meade and the CIA in Langley, and all of Washington, DC. And they still haven't attempted escape."

The General looked to Uncle Jimmy for an answer. It was Anna who said, "They're crazy. They feel safe in their offices. They're not afraid of us and they're not afraid of doing anything to us whenever they wish because they have diplomatic immunity." That's when Anna pulled the revolver out of her purse, cracked open the cylinder to check there was a round in each chamber, closed it and put it back in her purse. Then she thought she said it to herself, but we could all hear her whisper, "Do they really think I'll respect their diplomatic immunity? They're all dead men. For the poor cooks and for touching Rose."

"We're on our way." I pushed the cart for Rose until we got to the first hallway suite – the Ayatollah's rooms. Inside, we went through to the secretary's anteroom. Rose pushed the cart ahead of her to be sure that there was always something between her and the Ayatollah. I waited behind the door out of sight of the Ayatollah.

I could see through the crack where the hinge attached to the door, the Ayatollah sitting behind his desk on the phone, holding the receiver with one hand, and with the other hand studying the chief's hand and bloody stump, obviously looking for the key identification chip. He was relaxed, leaning back, savoring with an Ayatollah-like smile through his beard the advantage he had over us.

Without looking up, the Ayatollah told Rose, "Just put my tea on the desk." Then into the phone, he rattled off four names. Waited for a response. "You can execute the first three yourself. Wait until I return. I want to stone the last one myself. I want to do it privately in my garden. Make the preparations now." The Ayatollah paused. "I'm an old man. Only the smaller stones. My shoulders aren't what they used to be. I have trouble playing catch with my grandkids – trying to teach them the art of pitching their stones accurately enough for the kill shot at the end." He paused again. "I love my grandchildren. And thank you for all your efforts. Put Achim on. I have further instructions for him."

The Ayatollah paused, because Israel on the other end of the call paused as if to call Achim. Israel tried to change his voice. He answered, "You're speaking to Achim here, Deputy Executioner - Execution fulfillment department. Beheading by sword or guillotine depending on the availability of the sword executioner and stoning our premium specialty. Burning to death in custom steel cages upon request. Firing squads by military court approval only. The customer is always right. This is a recording. You may leave a message or wait for our next customer assistance executioner associate. This offering meets all private and public legal requirements under the Laws of the Islamic Republic of Iran and all regulations governing those laws. At this time, there is a (click click click) - three-minute wait - or you can contact us through our on-line service center." Israel had called Achim's number and that was the exact message. He had it written out to read back verbatim to the Ayatollah. The Ayatollah, both Ayatollahs had heard the message before. But neither had heard it in English or with a Yiddish accent.

"Thank you for waiting. This is Achim, the Islamic Republic's Deputy Executioner – the faithful people of the Islamic Republic's executioner, your deputy executioner. Now how can I help you?"

"This is the Ayatollah. You didn't recognize my voice? You certainly don't sound like Achim."

"Supreme Leader, I'm so sorry, so regretful not recognizing your voice. Your call wasn't identified on caller ID and I thought it was just spam. That's why I let it go to our recording. It's our new discounted telephone service you ordered. It is not as clear as the old service, and the caller ID only identifies local calls. But how may I serve you and serve the great Islamic Republic you lead with the wisdom of the ages?" It was obvious, Israel could lay it on thick. I could hear both ends of the conversation because the real Ayatollah is hard of hearing and uses a speaker phone. Our translator thinks he's the Ayatollah and thinks he's hard of hearing.

"Number one, Achim. I am your Supreme Leader. I am infallible – just like the Pope. The only difference is he only has a small city in Rome. I have an entire country, and that country has nuclear weapons. Number two find the person who approved the phone system and have him executed. It is their fault that the phone system is so poor, never the Supreme Leader's error. It makes you sound – Jewish. And always remember 'The Supreme Leader is always correct.'"

"Of course, Supreme Leader."

"Achim, I have good news for you. You're getting a well-deserved promotion. I already know you do all the work. After your boss executes the three on the top of my list, you may execute him – as the new chief executioner, you may choose the method. And while you're at it, the executives running the phone company. But they can be done at your convenience. No rush."

"Supreme Leader, thank you for the promotion. It will all be done immediately. Everything will be done immediately, including the telephone company executives, their wives, children, grandchildren, ..."

"I get it, Achim. Just make sure your boss finishes the executions I ordered him to do. And let him do it himself. Then you may finish him off. Humanly, of course. He has served the Islamic Republic well, but I don't trust a man who would execute the friends and colleagues he has known and worked with for years. If he refuses, it means he is disobeying the Ayatollah and must be executed immediately. Unfortunately, that'll leave you to do all the executions. It may be too many for stoning to death. Just go with beheading. I would make sure our chief swordsman is available, otherwise go with the guillotine. These need to be done before the day is out. But try to go with the swordsman. He needs to keep in practice, especially if we need him for a public event. He always told me that beheading was like golf, you have to practice your swing. And there's no golf driving range to go to for beheading.

Achim, nothing says 'special' like a beheading with a sword. Clean, precise, one cut at the back of the neck, the stump of the neck squirting blood with the heart still beating, and the head falling in front of the block. I love it when it rolls a few feet and the crowd gasps."

"Supreme Leader, do you think we should start using a basket with a pillow in the bottom? It might make a nice touch for the news cameras."

"Achim, we're not the French. The head bouncing off the planks of the wooden scaffold makes a dramatic statement. It tells the world of our resolve. It tells the world of my resolve as the Ayatollah!"

"Of course, Ayatollah. You're the boss. You're the Ayatollah. You're the Supreme Leader. You're wish is my command." Israel is beginning to talk like Aladdin's genie out of the bottle. And with the Yiddish accent and him trying to throw his voice, its comical. All I can picture is Israel coming out of the bottle in a puff of smoke trying to adjust his yarmulke. "I always admired our swordman's strength and accuracy. The blow must be powerful enough to go through vertebrae with the first stroke. That takes real talent. Especially with these old bastards with arthritic ossified spines."

"You're right, Achim. We don't really appreciate our nation's swordsmen, enough. If he performs his executions with a single clean blow, remind me he deserves a reward."

"Again, Supreme Leader, your wish is my command."

"And Achim, I forgot to ask, how's the wife and kids?"

"My Supreme Leader, they will be thrilled with my promotion. And I'm sure my wife won't mind the longer hours. But they are doing wonderfully and confident in their futures, and the future of the great Islamic Republic of Iran, as long as you are leading our nation. They are so thankful you are and will be our Supreme Leader forever."

"Achim, it is important to balance work with your homelife. I get concerned with all my key people. You need to be aware of the danger of burnout. I know you always do your best. Congratulations on your promotion. After this is all over, take a day or two off. Now enough of the small talk. Too work, Achim."

The Ayatollah hung up and looked up at Rose. "You look like my secretary. The only way I could tell the two of you apart is by your apron." The Ayatollah was studying the severed hand more closely than looking at Rose. "Where are my distance glasses. I just can't use progressive lenses I got from our Tehran COSCO." One thing I do know, there's no COSCO in Tehran or anywhere in the Islamic Republic. I'm not sure if his delusion is slipping into reality.

"Supreme Leader, is there anything else I could do for you?"

"You are a woman. You're never to address your Supreme Leader directly. You should never address any man directly. If I want anything, or if your man or any man wants anything, he will tell you. Obey in silence. Silence and obedience is the order of the day for all females."

Now the Ayatollah looked up at Rose without the distraction of the sous chef's left hand. "You're not unattractive, but still your dress is sinful. You make me feel sinful, except I am the Ayatollah and am never sinful nor do I ever have sinful or incorrect thoughts." The Ayatollah lost his train of thought. He went back to looking at the hand. Without looking up, he told Rose, "You make other men think sinful thoughts. You should wear your burqa. All western women should wear burqas, as I have commanded. Now, leave and be out of my sight. Do not return without your burqa!" Rose bowed her head and backed out, pulling her tea cart out of the office in front of her.

Now we were off to Putin's office. Putin was on hold for the Kremlin. He didn't know he had to wait until Israel finished with the Ayatollah on the other line. Putin ordered his executions all to take place in the basement of Lubyanka. He ordered one round to the back of the head from one of the ceremonial Korovins that once belonged to the NKVD director Lavrentiy Beria. Putin was a traditionalist in one sense. But our Putin thought that having them kneel and beg for mercy from their executioner before getting shot in the center of the forehead the way Beria met his exit, was barbaric, and inefficient. Begging wasted a lot of the executioner's valuable time

Then our Putin on the phone, ordered the executioner's assistant to execute the executioner. The Putin never really listened to subordinates. Both the executioner and the assistant had the same Yiddish accent because both were Israel. Our translator wasn't nearly as charming as people said the real Putin was. He didn't promote the executioner's assistant and didn't inquire about his executioner's or his assistant executioner's family. He did instruct the assistant to execute his boss after the chief executioner was done with the first round of executions. And if the executioner refused, he told the assistant to shoot the executioner immediately for disobeying orders and then complete the executions as originally ordered.

Our translators reasoning for terminating the executioner was that he couldn't trust anyone who would execute people he knew and worked with for years. And if he didn't complete the executions, he would have to be executed for disobeying the original execution orders. Sounds familiar?

Rose served him his coffee as the translator hung up the phone. Our Putin looked closely at Rose's bruised wrists. "I bet you enjoyed that, sweetheart." Putin stood, pushed aside his suspenders, and started to unbutton his shirt. "Deary, do you like what you see?" I couldn't see Rose's expression, but I was sure she was smiling as she put her hand in her apron pocket. I could hear the muffled click of her cocking the hammer of her Colt .45. Putin stood and pulled the shirt tails out of trousers and then took his shirt off. "Do you like what you see? Answer me. Now!"

"You're too beautiful a man but you need your chest waxed." Rose turned around and then turned her head to look back at Putin, rapidly turned her head back, coquettishly flipping her hair, and said, "Waxing your chest and back will make you look god-like. Your naked likeness belongs on the Acropolis to be admired and desired for the ages." Rose giggled for effect.

"And I never liked the Greeks until now." Putin laughed. He was looking forward to having a beautiful woman touch him.

"There's wax in the supply cabinet. I'll get it if you like. I can wax your chest and back. If you permit me, I just want to rub my hands over you. If you like, I can do your scalp." Rose turned and put her left hand on her left hip. Her right hand was still in her pocket on her cocked Colt.

Putin nodded yes. Rose turned again, went into the secretary's outer office, sorted through the boxes, and supplies in the stationary cabinet and took several minutes to read labels of the different adhesives. She carefully selected two large jars of fast-drying acrylic-paper cement from the back of the very bottom shelf. In large letters it was marked '**WATERPROOF –**

DO NOT ALLOW CONTACT WITH SKIN, EYES, OR MUCOUS MEMBRANES – DO NOT INJEST'. In smaller print on the back label watermark printed with an orange skull and cross bones and in red letters it said, 'Corrosive to plastic, leather, oil, and water-based paints, finished and unfinished woods, linoleum, ceramic tile, porcelain tile, granite, marble, quartz, and laminate counter tops and surfaces. Keep away from pets. Use only in a well-ventilated room. This product is banned from sale in California, Oregon, Washington and Minnesota.'

Rose took a bottle of Russian vodka from the same cabinet. It was a few quick steps back to Putin. He had an empty water glass on his desk. Before Rose could pour the vodka, our Putin grabbed the bottle, pulled off the top and took a swig. "Sweetheart, we'll both enjoy this more if you take a drink."

"As soon as I'm done rubbing my hands over your body. Then we can both drink it all together. Close your eyes Mr. President. It's important to enjoy the sensation of the body waxing. Just relax and take in the vodka-like aroma of the wax. This has to set for at least fifteen minutes before I come back to take it off." In a second Rose was behind him. She put one jar down on the desk, careful that the label couldn't be read by Putin. It took both her hands to open the first bottle that she rapidly poured over his right shoulder. The contents ran down his back and front of his chest. With one motion she tossed the empty jar into the waist paper basket, grabbed the other jar, opened it with both hands and poured it over Putin's left shoulder. She had to use her coffee napkins to spread the glue over his back and chest, and what was stuck to the napkin, she put on his head. "Now close your eyes tight." He did and she spread the glue over his face, to glue his eyelashes together and his lips shut. Unfortunately, his lips were wet with desire for Rose, and the glue wouldn't work mixing with his saliva.

"Very good, Mr. President. Lean back. Don't worry about the chair. And be sure you keep your eyes closed tight."

"Dear girl, that doesn't smell like Vodka."

"Mr. President, anyone can get Russian Vodka. This is a

rare Finnish Vodka wax. It works better than any Russian wax. It had to be more powerful that the Russian wax because the Fins are so much more harrier." Rose left President Putin glued to his chair not suspecting what had happened.

"Rose, what happens when he finds out he's glued to the chair and can't open his eyes?"

"Archy, I'm going back in there and confess that I did this to please him, and President Xi gave me the body wax. If he doesn't believe me or tries anything, I'll bet you I shoot him before you do, anyway." Rose had that impish smile she had when she was absolutely sure of herself. "I just need any excuse."

I certainly didn't have an answer to Rose's plan. Now on to Kim. We all knew, and the other translators knew that Kim was an idiot - just like the real Kim. It was Kim's sister who was the brains of the outfit. She was probably more blood thirsty than Kim, and she no doubt put him up to his murders and atrocities for her own purposes. Kim just killed people for the joy of murder, bloodshed, dismemberment, and generally trying to be all around unpleasant.

His sister personally killed as many if not more of her enemies, her brother's enemies, (and all their families, of course), possible enemies, or people who needed killing just to allow North Korea to run more efficiently. Kim's sister killed no one unless there was a practical reason. She was good that way. Most of the time you knew why you were in front of one of her firing squads. But occasionally, she would yell, 'Surprise!' and then 'Fire!'. Not even a 'Ready, Aim,' first. And on those occasions, it was a surprise to everyone, especially the executionee.

Rose and I followed the same plan. Her loaded Colt was in her apron pocket. I was behind the door between the outer and inner offices out of sight, and Rose served Kim across his desk. He too was on hold for his Pyongyang. He was actually on the line with Rachel who was the international operator trying to get through to the now North Korea's Israel Beilin. Kim never questioned Rachel's Yiddish accent which was thicker than her husband's accent.

Once Israel got on the line, Kim asked for his most trusted aid by name. That in itself was an intelligence coup, learning who Kim's right-hand man was in North Korea, and it wasn't Choe Ryong-hae, President of the Assembly Presidium and First Vice Chairman of the State Affairs Commission. Israel waited a moment, clicked the telephone receiver, then acted as Kim's aid. Kim said he was betrayed and wanted to know who it could be, and that they should be executed immediately. Their families should witness the executions, then they should be executed. First the children in front of their mothers, then the mothers one at a time in front of the mothers' parents, the grandparents, and so on. Kim did it this way because in Korean society, there was great respect for their elders, even when it came to executions.

Then if anyone was left not in any of those categories, it was Kim's assistant's choice which man should execute the other men first. His assistant could then execute the last man standing. In the non-designated category, it was always the youngest executed first. This way the elders were respected in that they got to witness everyone else's executions before their own.

Kim was in a quandary as to who Israel said would ask Kim's sister about his orders. Israel said that Kim Yo-jong, Kim's sister was in the office anyway. Israel put Rachel on who played Kim's younger sister. Rachel as Kim's sister slipped into Yiddish before telling our Kim in English that she wasn't sure about his orders. Kim rattled off a half dozen names, and Rachel said they were as good as any to execute just to set an example. Kim agreed with his sister. Kim always agreed with his sister. His sister never countermanded Kim's orders unless it was something important. Executing the wrong person or a few extra people wasn't worth having a family squabble. He had great love and respect for her in all matters of state and especially when it came to who to execute, although she left the manner of execution to her brother, 'The Dear One.' That was his field of expertise and he really shined there.

Kim asked to speak to his assistant – Israel, again. Israel was the only person in 'North Korea' who could speak Yiddish and spoke English with a Yiddish accent besides 'Kim's sister', Rachel. Our Kim didn't notice and never realized he was carrying on all his conversations in English. Kim told Israel that Rachel had the names and just proceed with the executions as expeditiously as possible. They were to be no frills executions, with one bullet to the head. They were to do it outdoors, weather permitting, to avoid any cleanup requiring repainting offices, jail cells, dungeons, and furniture repair or replacement. North Korea was a very poor country, and he personally was trying to cut costs where he could.

He told Israel, that trying to expand his nuclear program required cutting costs somewhere. And that somewhere began with executions. To generate a better balance of trade, after the executions, they would harvest and sell the viable organs – even some marginal organs.   As a cost cutting operating measure organs were harvested after the execution. If they harvested the organs before the executions, the State would have to incur the cost of another anesthesiologist, surgeon, OR team, drugs, and supplies, even though they didn't have to be so particular about drug expiration dates and how many sutures were needed to close the incision. In fact, they were never particular about drug expiration dates or sutures on even patients they wanted to survive. Stapling the wound closed would have been faster, but they would have to pay for the staples and the stapling gun. And North Korea was awash in expired suture material from Communist China. In a pinch, they just used sewing machine thread. Besides, the sutures only had to keep the wound closed long enough for the firing squad to do its business. And in the rare cases you wanted to remove the organs before the execution, you still had to use the anesthesiologist, because the screaming during the procedure from an awake patient disturbed everyone in the operating room suite, and in the other ORs on the entire floor.

Both Rose and I knew we had to get all the names from

Rachel and Israel, so the CIA could warn everyone in Moscow, Tehran, and Pyongyang, possibly turn them into assets, or at least save their lives and their families lives. It was the CIA's chance to pump them for inside intel on all their regimes. I'm already sure, Rachel and Israel are sharing the names with Mossad, so it depends on who gets there first with the best offer. Hopefully, whoever gets the prize shares it with their sister intelligence agency.

Kim looked at Rose, looked at her bruised wrists and just asked for another sandwich. When Rose hesitated, he said, "Go, woman. Another sandwich, now. Go! And I want the crunchy American peanut butter and the grape jelly. Cut the crust off the bread, too. Just like my mother did." Kim went back to the papers on his desk. The papers were all random garbage we put there just to fill up the space and make it look like a real office. What he was studying most carefully were the take-out menus we left. Chinese take-out, pizzeria menus, Indian take-out, and of course, all the fast-food restaurants, burger, fried chicken, and fried fish take out.

Now to the smart one, President Xi. He was their leader. And the delusional translator may be crazy, but was as smart as the real Xi, as cunning and probably as deadly with his new persona. He was no longer a mere translator.

I was at my usual station behind the door, I thought hidden from sight. Xi sat with his hands folded behind his desk. No phone calls, no shuffling papers, just looking straight ahead watching Rose's every move.

"President Xi, I hope this is satisfactory."

Xi pulled the bloody hand on the stump of a wrist from the bag. "I know this can get me out of here. I know you're not a waitress. And I know someone is watching us from behind the door behind you. And he is no doubt armed. You may speak if you wish." Xi sat very still. He sat without emotion. His face neither smiled nor frowned.

"President Xi, you are said to be the wisest of all the leaders here, possibly of all the world's leaders. A man among men. A man among nations of men."

"Little girl, you sound like a diplomat. But I know all the diplomats. At least President Xi knows them. And I met them with President Xi. And I know I'm not President Xi."

"President Xi, ..."

"Stop pretending, girl. And tell your friend to come out from behind the door."

"All right, Archy." Rose motioned to me to stand with her.

I came out and stood just behind Rose. But President Xi could see I had my Colt in my right hand with the hammer cocked.

"I saw the way he in particular looked at Kim and Putin when they twisted your wrists. I heard no gunshots. And I do know they're not Kim and Putin. And the Ayatollah isn't the Ayatollah. They don't know it, but I know it, you know it, and everyone I've met knows it, including all organization that attacked your compound and is trying to free us.

"President Xi, each one of your offices is soundproof. You would not have heard any gunshots."

"Young man, I would have smelled the gunpowder from your pistol and the gunpowder fumes on your clothing, and on the young ladies clothing. And I'm sure you would have used more than one bullet on either or both of those men."

"And, President Xi, how can you be so sure I didn't? How can you be so sure I'm not going to shoot you?"

"In Beijing, I've been with President Xi when an appointment he was seeing walked in immediately after an execution. The less experienced man, and sometime the woman, will immediately sit, without asking permission. Without even greeting Xi. Most people who just killed someone with a single bullet to the forehead are usually a little rattled, and often disheveled. The pros, though, come before President Xi, stand at attention, and wait to be addressed. When they are invited to sit, they carefully open their suit jacket, always revealing their shoulder holster as a matter of pride. They still wait for

Xi's first open-ended question to start describing in detail the death scene. President Xi enjoys hearing about the kneeling and begging before the bullet splatters the back of the man's head on the wall behind him.

That's especially true of the old NKVD killers. Putin's father knew them and when Xi and I visited Putin, we were introduced to some of the old timers. They talk about their first kill as if it were their first woman. They described the smell of cordite in their cloths. And in Beijing, the smell of burnt gunpowder was always carried into President Xi's office when he interviewed his personal Charon for the details of how the person usually personally chosen by Xi met his end. Xi seemed to enjoy every detail.

I thought for sure by now Putin smelled of cordite, burnt gunpowder. That's why when you both walked in, I was surprised you or he hadn't already shot both our Putin and Kim dead. You had a better reason to shoot him than me and you hadn't. That's why I knew I was safe."

President Xi looked at Rose. "I see you have your Colt in your apron pocket, and I imagine everyone in your party is armed. But we have made some very powerful friends. You may have the drop on me, but if you don't let all of us free, your four eminent world leaders free, all your friends will die, and some horribly. The tailor and his wife on the other side of the telephone – yes, the two Mossad agents will be turned over to the Iranian Republican Guard. Everyone else in this secret cavern will be sealed in as we fill it with some surplus World War Two Zyklon B gas." President Xi stood and smiled at the both of us. "Remember, there are no friends in international relations, only alliances that can shift at any time. That being said, I wouldn't want any of the Zyklon B to seep upstairs to the White House. That would be a tragedy. No matter who's the aggressor, it would an unnecessary strain – a nuclear strain - on international relations."

"I don't know your real name, and you don't need to tell me. I refer to you as President Xi." Rose was taking charge.

"Why should we believe you about the Zyklon B?"

"I like the sound of that. Maybe I should go to the UN and tell the world I'm President Xi? Or maybe I should disappear into America, become a used car salesman or a telemarketer, or both, and live the good life. One thing for sure, I could never go back to China." President Xi leaned back in his large leather desk chair. "I'm sure the real President Xi arrested my wife, children, parents, cousins, friends – anyone who knew me and were stupid enough to admit it to the Guoanbu – our secret police. They're all waiting in our secret detention centers. They're waiting for my return followed by my debriefing and execution. Then they know they will be joining me soon after for us all to meet our ancestors. Life is cheap in China. Nobody is missed. Pandemics, ethnic cleansing, political cleansing, is all part of the Chinese Communist Party's plan for efficiency, political hegemony, and world dominance. That's just the way of life in China."

For the first time, our President Xi looked sad. "I am homesick. I miss my China. The China of my youth. But as long as I'm free and never returned to China, my family and friends have an outside chance of staying alive. Maybe in a prison camp, but if they're there long enough, they will be forgotten in the crowd of millions and millions of inmates. And if you're forgotten, you have a better chance of disappearing on a work detail and have a chance of starting over. There are so many prisoners, after so many years, they're lost and forgotten. They'll still be alive, but no one gets out. But at least they're alive and they'll forget their former lives and become accustomed to their situation. I've been told that by the few who were wounded and not killed trying to escape.

We interviewed some of the English-speaking escapees for President Xi before they were returned to their original prison and hung by piano wire in the prison yard as an example to others. Prisoners who died of their wounds before escaping were also hung in the prison yard. Some people do escape successfully. If they're not caught and returned promptly, then the guards are hung."

"President Xi, if you help us, we can have you relocated where no one will find you. But you have to help us." Rose will tell me that pleading with him was showing our weaknesses. I'm not sure bravado in face of the threat he made is going to be helpful. He does not look like a tough guy. He knew he was beaten, and his family condemned as soon as he was kidnapped. So, he, like all the Chinese prisoners in the prison camps, tried to make the best of it.

"You know we had help. Overwhelming help. I can't prove to you the poison gas is here without telling you where it is. And I can't tell you where it is because they didn't tell me. You can either take my word for it or not. But if we're not released soon, the gas will kill us all, and very quickly. And don't ask me how much time we all have. I don't know their timetable. If they release the gas, we're all going to die, so I have an interest more than just escape and stopping this tragedy from happening."

"And, President Xi, how much time do we have?" Rose was very calm and very serious. Rose always told me you never give up asking, even when the first answer is no. Sometimes, the person you're questioning let's slip some snippet of valuable information.

"I told you, I really don't know how much time. The people who helped us didn't share the details, but I assure you, I've taken them at their word. If they release the gas, they're not coming back to save me or the other translators. For whatever reason, whether we're dead or free from you people, that's all they want. They made that clear to me. My only purpose is to save my life, the other translators' lives. And if the Chinese Communists find out I'm dead, all my family and friends will no longer serve any purpose and will be immediately executed."

"President Xi, do you want your peanut butter and jelly sandwich?"

"Is it the crunchy peanut butter? If it's going to be my last meal, I want the crunchy peanut butter."

* * * * *

CHAPTER FOURTEEN

**"Treason doth never prosper: what's the reason?
For if it prosper, none dare call it treason.**
[Sir John Harington, "Of Treason," Epigrams, 1615]

Uncle Jimmy and Aunt Anna were the first to get to the USEWOW reception desk. There was puddles of blood on the floor in front of the desk and what appeared to be human hair, brain matter and shards of shrapnel imbedded in the ceiling, brown discolored linoleum tile – old asbestos flooring that was installed with the Truman administration – and spent .222 caliber rifle shouldered shells and rimless automatic 9 mm pistol shells scattered throughout the lobby. There were too many to count. Several trails of blood were smeared across the floor from whoever was dragged through the USEWOW entrance. The door was propped open by someone's lost combat boot with his lower leg still in it. Double aut chain shot from Mrs. Haversham's automatic shot gun was scattered in six tight groups across from the wall and door facing her desk fired from under her desktop between the two pedestals. Three boots with lower legs, one after the other were left in front of where Mrs. Haversham must have fired while still seated. The blood pools around the three lower legs had already clotted and made the floor too slippery to walk on.

Aunt Anna was ahead of Uncle Jimmy at the grey steel reception desk. The front of the desk had bullet holes and dents from shrapnel fragments that littered the floor in front of it. Aunt Anna tried to avoid the puddles of blood but slipped and had to catch herself from falling with both hand on the top of the desk. Where she grabbed the desk, there was another puddle of blood mixed with vomit and short scalp hair still attached to the scalp.

Anna said nothing. She was just ahead of Uncle Jimmy in front of the desk. For a second she had a blank stare on her face as she looked over the desk. "This is what I was afraid of. As soon as I saw the four of them at the table together, I knew."

Mrs. Haversham was sprawled on her back, arms stretched out in a pool of her own blood. There were dozens of both rifle and pistol projectiles that only put superficial holes in her jacket that hadn't penetrated her Kevlar vest. She emptied her fully automatic shotgun from under her desk before anyone fired a shot that hit her. She was hit many times but managed to empty two of her Colt .45 magazines into her attackers. There was a loaded magazine part of the way up the handle of her Colt and two empty magazines were on the floor next to her. The floor and the desk were littered with her sixteen .45 caliber shell casings, and there was another full magazine next to her body. Her Colt .45 was by the side of her body. It wasn't in her hand, because they cut off both hands well above the wrists and took both hands with them.

They had fired many rounds into her bullet proof vest. A single shot to the vest would have knocked any man down. But not Mrs. Haversham. She took two round to the belly below the vest that were oozing blood and gut contents – mostly yellow bile-stained stomach contents-, must have been horribly painful but missed her spine and were not immediately fatal. She emptied her second magazine when she was shot once in the left eye and once in the forehead. Then someone came up to the corpse and place a large caliber pistol barrel against her forehead and pulled the trigger. The impression of the pistol barrel against her forehead with its powder burns and the missing back half of Mrs. Haversham's skull told us what had happened.

Mrs. Haversham put up a valiant fight and did a lot of damage to the enemy. She, and General Merriwhether thought an attack on USEWOW would be unlikely, but if it did, everyone would be wearing Kevlar or similar body armor. Everyone at USEWOW wore body armor, very slimming and stylish body armor. All the ammunition issued to the USEWOW staff was Teflon coated, designed to penetrate any enemies body armor like melted butter on hot pancakes.

By the time General Merriwhether, Rose and I joined Uncle Jimmy and Aunt Anna, Aunt Anna was collecting Mrs. Haversham's Colt and full clip of ammunition in the handle and the empty clips. She went through the reception desk's drawers, found several boxes of the Teflon-coated .45 caliber ACP shells, loaded the empty clips. It was a small purse and a big Colt with the full-length barrel. She couldn't close her purse and the gun butt protruded from the top.

"Here, Jimmy. Put these in your jacket pocket." She handed her husband the two full Colt magazines. "I'll need them when I catch up to these bastards." Aunt Anna wasn't so angry as to be irrational. But she was angry enough to have a long- and short-range tactical plan to kill every one of the people who did that to Mrs. Haversham. Mrs. Haversham may have been her rival for Uncle Jimmy, and maybe Uncle Jimmy dallied with Mrs. Haversham (which she knew he probably did because she knew her husband too well), but that made her family all the same. And family is family. And it was up to her, as Uncle Jimmy's wife to avenge Mrs. Haversham, and to make it as painful as possible for these bastards. It was the Tenth Avenue way. It was the American way that justice had to be served. Uncle Jimmy looked at his wife and swallowed hard. He had seen this look in her eyes before only once before in her eyes after she finished off the two miscreants in the apartment upstairs from theirs.

"Not if I don't get to them first, Anna." Uncle Jimmy said that very quietly, but Rose, and I heard it.

General Merriwhether had to think for a minute as what should take priority. Mrs. Haversham's computer was full of bullet holes, the telephone booth was wrecked, but miraculously, the red telephone on her desk remained untouched. When he picked up the telephone, the Langley CIA duty operator answered:

"Central Intelligence Agency Operator 4, how can I help you?"

"This is General Merriwhether, USEWOW. I need to speak immediately to the duty officer!"

"General Merriwhether, everything that comes to this telephone exchange is a national emergency. That being said, "Is this a collect call? If it is, The Central Intelligence Agency is no longer authorized or required by Congress to accept local, interstate, or international collect calls. Now is this a collect call?"

"No, it's not, operator. Please, this is a matter of life and death! Operator…"

"All calls to the CIA Langley Headquarters to this exchange are matters of life and death. Now, whom do you wish to speak to?"

General Merriwhether calmed down and realized that nothing untoward had happened yet to the White House or anybody because the CIA telephone operator was following her routine protocol. "Operator 4, this is General Merriwhether, USEWOW commanding officer. I need to speak to the Duty Officer, please."

"General Merriwhether, please spell it for me." The operator remained monotoned in a polite but obviously bored fashion. She was no doubt just waiting until change of shift.

"Spell Merriwhether or USEWOW?"

"Either one. You can start with USEWOW."

"U—S—E—W—O—W."

"Oh, its spelled just like it sounds. That means you must be General Merriwhether. It's an honor. Everyone at the CIA have heard of the top secret work you've been doing. Now how can I help you?"

"There's a terrorist threat against the White House. The threat is imminent! It's…"

"General Merriwhether, to direct your call further, do you know if it is a domestic terrorist threat or an international terrorist threat?"

"I can't say. But people have already been killed and the White House may have been breached."

"Well, I cannot direct your call any further until I know whether this is a domestic or international terrorist threat. I have to put you on hold. There's another call coming in."

General Merriweather's call was interrupted, and he was now listening to Guy Lombardo's 'Aud Lang Syne' from his last live New Year's Eve broadcast. In seconds, the operator returned.

"I'll be going off duty, but my supervisor instructed me to put you through to the duty officer. Thank you and good night." A click on the phone was followed by the CIA night duty officer.

"Night duty officer, how can I help you?"

"I am General Merriwhether of USEWOW. I must report a credible threat against the President of the United States and the entire White House – a poison gas attack. Zyklon B. And this may be happening now!"

"General Merriwhether, thank you for your concern. 'If you see something, say something.' Now is this a foreign or domestic threat?"

General Merriwhether tried to remember that this very junior officer was just trying to do his job. "Son, it's both domestic and international."

"Well, General, it's very unlikely it is both. But since you called the CIA, we will consider it international. Now, what is the nature of the threat?"

"A poison gas – Zyklon B gas - cyanide gas attack against the White House."

"Well, General if it's our White House – you do mean the White House in Washington, DC. I just want to make sure I have your message as accurate as possible." The General, just for a moment was speechless. "General, are you there?"

"Yes, I'm still here. Yes, the White House in Washington, DC. 1600 Pennsylvania Avenue."

"Thank you, sir. Thank you for the address. I've put your

report in the computer, and a terrorist threat at that address is a domestic threat. Don't hang up while I connect you to the FBI regional office. And General, thank you for your service." The CIA put General Merriwhether on hold. This time it was Sousa marches that played while he waited.

"FBI. We serve the nation. We are your FBI. Now sir, how can I help you?"

"It's a poison gas attack against the White House and The President of the United States. Zyklon B. It will kill every-body in the White House in minutes if we don't do something. We need to evacuate the White House. Get everybody gas masks, and search the grounds, immediately."

The FBI duty threat intake officer sighed and said, "I need your name, sir. And tell me where you are calling from."

"I am General Merriwhether. I am calling from the USE-WOW tunnel system below the White House. Someone has planted canisters of Zyklon B cyanide gas pellets in the tunnels below the White House. The President is in grave danger as is everyone else in the White House. We need help, NOW!"

"General, number one, thank you for your service. Now, this is the White House on Pennsylvania Avenue, and the president you speak of is POTUS, the President of the United States?"

"That's it. Someone has breached USEWOW…"

"Please say again."

"USEWOW. USEWOW. In the tunnels below the White House."

"General, please spell that for me."

"U…S…E…W…O…W,"

"I'm checking. No. No General, there is no USEWOW listed. But, if this is about a threat to POTUS, then it's not the FBI you need. I'll put you in touch with the Secret Service Night Threat OFFICER – The SSNTO, as we call him. Please hold."

General Merriwhether went through the entire story with the SSNTO. The conversation stalled until General Merri-whether told the agent it was the white supremacist's wing of

Black Lives Matter. The man on the other end of the telephone told him to evacuate as many people as he could, and he would take care of the rest.

Anna was standing next beside General Merriwhether in front of Mrs. Haversham's desk. "General, we should call Israel and Rachel. They need to know to evacuate everyone in the tailor shop, the dry cleaners, the laundry, the janitorial staff. We need to evacuate everyone." Aunt Anna was angry enough to take charge.

Uncle Jimmy was quietly examining the booted lower limbs, fragments of hair, clothing, shell casings, brain splatter on the walls, and anything else that he considered evidence. We all underestimated the expertise Uncle Jimmy had investigating a crime scene.

As I watched him, Aunt Anna whispered, "Your Uncle Jimmy knows his way around a murder scene. He's covered up enough of them. He'll figure this out before anyone, and…" Aunt Anna paused, then said, "and your uncle will correct the wrong committed here, unless I get to them first!"

"Well, Archy, you have nothing to say. Everyone is doing their part. Everyone is contributing. You need to take charge. Archy, take charge. This is embarrassing. All this bloodshed, and you haven't fired a shot." Well, Rose had a point. I made a note to shoot at the first target that was at least plausibly appropriate.

"Rose, I have a plan to turn the tide." I was emphatic but I had no plan. The only thing I could think of is to get the hell out of here before we're gassed to death.

In seconds, Rachel and Israel came through the USE-WOW door, tracking blood from the doorway into the lobby. That wasn't like them, to track through a crime scene. Mossad agents are never careless about evidence.

"General, they're all dead. The laundry room crew, the dry cleaners. Everybody in that wing, died where they stood. I don't understand."

"Israel, Rachel, they whoever they are, threatened to release Zyklon B gas. Some must have leaked. We need to leave, and we have to get our four translators out at the same time."

"General, I'll start calling maintenance and janitorial services to clear out. Rose, Archy, you two with Uncle Jimmy and Aunt Anna get the four translators out of here. Bring them down here, then we'll turn them loose. As long as they hang on to the four hands, we can track them."   Israel had been talking to Mossad, and they had no idea what this was about. And if Mossad didn't know, our intelligence services certainly didn't know, especially since they didn't even know USEWOW existed.

*　*　*　*　*

CHAPTER FIFTEEN

*"And Iudith was left alone in the tent, and Olofernes
lying alone vpon his bed, for hee was filled with wine.
... Then she came to the pillar of the bed, which was at
Olofernes head, and tooke downe his fauchion from thence,
And approached to his bed, and tooke hold of the haire of
his head, and said, Strengthen mee, O Lord God of Israel,
this day And she smote twise upon his necke with all her
might, and she tooke away his head from him, And tumbled
his body downe from the bed, and pulled downe the canopy
from the pillars, and anon after she went forth, and gaue
Olofernes his head to her maide. And she put it in her bag
of meate, so they twaine went together according to their
custom vnto prayer, ...So she tooke the head out of the
bag, and shewed it, and said vnto them, Behold the head of
Olofernes, the chiefe captaine of the armie of Assur, and
behold the canopy wherein he did lie in his drunkennesse,
and the Lord hath smitten him by the hand of a woman.*
[1611 King James Version, Holy Bible, Judith 13:2,6-10,15]*

Of the four of us, I'm the only one you should be listening to. I at least know I'm not President Xi of the Peoples
Republic of China. It appears General Merriwhether, who is a
real general, by the way, sent the tailor and his wife to fetch us
to bring us to wherever we're going to be freed. It's either that
or a more convenient place for execution. I learned in China
it's much easier to have the corpses walk to their disposal sites
than have to carry them, drag them, and then have to execute
everyone who carried the bodies and cleaned up the blood and
guts trail.   And I've seen the local secret police
commanders then personally execute the executioners not to
leave any witnesses. This was all in the middle of one of my
English lessons. Apparently, the secret police had a burning

desire to learn English and advance in the organization. That's why I survived – because they wanted to sound like the Americans on American television. And then be able to interrogate American prisoners effectively without torture – or at least a minimum of torture.

Now though, the burning question is, after we're freed, nobody has told us where to go. And I don't know that whoever demanded our release will know we were set free and know not to release the poison gas. That is, unless they have an inside man. Or they don't have an inside man and plan to release the Zyklon B anyway. And the third possibility is they don't have an inside man, are not going to release the poison gas, and had some other reason to do this. A reason like just to screw with the Americans. Or there was a reason, and whomever knew the motives and started this mission is gone, and so is the reasoning behind it. Just the aimless mission is left. That's the way it is in China, with so many people, so big a bureaucracy, those at the upper levels constantly being liquidated and replaced. Those at the lowest level afraid to mention anything for fear of being cancelled after their mission is cancelled.

In the United States, the people at the highest levels are immediately replaced when those in charge are either indicted or become lobbyists. And in the United States, with all the tumult in their personal lives, only the politicians' wives' divorce lawyers that prosper. Divorce is unheard of in the Peoples Republic. Old wives just disappear, new wives appear and just pick up where the last one left off. There are so many people, nobody notices. That's what President Xi told me and the rest of his subordinates when he introduced his new wife who looked and dressed just like his old wife. In fact, not to arouse suspicion, she dressed in his old wife's clothes. After that, President Xi personally thinned the ranks of his subordinates who might gossip. And to the best of my knowledge no one gossiped, and no one was promoted or demoted.

Is this all a dream? A bad dream that I will never see

my family again on this earth, or a good dream that I have the chance to start over in America. I will miss my wife and children, but there's no good ending for me where my family and I are reunited. But you learn that in The Peoples Republic of China, the cheapest commodity is human life, and especially the life of relatives. I have so many relatives. There are so many relatives in China, they are countless.   President Xi killed hundreds of thousands of his own citizens who were all somebody's relatives just to screw with President Trump and get him out of office. President Xi managed to ruin the U.S. economy and kill more Americans than any war since World War Two with his China virus. He had the good fortune to get Trump out of office by having his advisors teach the Democrats how democracy should really work, ruin the world economy, and allow China and Amazon to prosper like never before.

President Xi loved China and was happy to help the Democratic Party achieve what China had achieved more than a half century ago – one party rule. Now it would be easier to deal with America. So many American legislators, big tech, big sports, were already in pocket. When Xi drank too much, he would brag about it and how stupid the American people were to keep electing these people to Congress. He could sit back and do nothing but smile at American democracy. Xi told all of us that the American people were their own worst enemy.

Every time I accompanied any of the Chinese Communist officials I had to translate for, I planned in my mind how I would defect. Especially when we came to United Nations in New York. New York is the most wonderous city in the world. Even though the idiots in charge think they can turn it into a socialist paradise by letting violent criminals out of jail as soon as they are arrested. In our socialist paradise, these criminals are never jailed. Justice is dispensed economically and with finality as soon the guilty offender is apprehended. And they're all guilty as soon as their arrested. And justice is had by all, immediately.

But in New York, the people keep voting these idiots back

again and again because the people who vote think they can get something for nothing. In China, in the beginning, everyone wanted something for nothing until their neighbors who wouldn't do as they were told, were sealed in their apartments by the men in trench coats and wide-brimmed fedoras.

The complaints of the smelling rotten bodies that had starved to death brought the police, who opened the red and yellow Guojia Anquan Bu seal, cut the welded steel door, and carried out the swollen unfortunates, in full view of the neighbors. Sometimes television and print reporters recorded the event an either reported it as a murder suicide of guilty enemies of the state or accidentally being locked inside by a hard of hearing landlord who thought the apartment was unoccupied, ignoring the screams and pounding at the door.

The neighbors usually knew enough not to mention anything least they be the next ones accidentally locked in, permanently. In Beijing, we had nice neighbors who complained one too many times before being labeled enemies of the state and accidentally locked in their apartment. My family was next door. We could hear them screaming, pounding on the walls adjacent to our apartment and pounding on their door. It was more than a week before all the commotion stopped. It was another week before the smell of rotting flesh seeped into our apartment and out onto the common terrace. No one alerted the police for another week.

What the police pulled out was the bloated body of the wife and the partially eaten body of her husband. And they didn't have any pets. All the neighbors saw this, but no one said anything to anyone. No one knew who would turn them in, just for some advantage or reduce their own chance to be the state's next target for justifiable 'correction'.

As cold as it is, I even thought - fleetingly thought of defecting to Canada. But I had second thoughts. Between socialized medicine, their own welfare socialist state, and bad weather, I changed my mind. As bland and beneficent as any socialist system tries to be, the socialists can turn vicious and vindictive at any time. Such is the lesson of history.

I was really hoping to defect to Florida - no state income tax, great fishing, great food, beautiful weather, beautiful beaches, women in bikinis and rich widows. A lot of rich widows. I can make more than one of them happy with my Chinese moves. And in the Peoples Republic of China, there's a shortage of women, so you have to bring your 'A' game each and every time. Every man's motto is 'We aim to please.', and they all mean that literally. That's actually my generation. Now there's a shortage of young women, and the shoe is on the other foot for young men.

And being a kept man in Florida is a good life with the wonderful weather, good fishing, early bird specials and senior discounts. As long as she and I eat out of the same bowel and she takes the first bite, I know I would be safe. What more could a single man want. Being a kept man is unheard of in China. The whole population in China is 'kept' by the Chinese Communist Party. And the CCP is President Xi.

But my family and everyone else's families were always held hostage whenever they traveled overseas. I and everyone boarding international flights, except flights to North Korea, was always reminded by the Guojia Anquan Bu agent at BCIA, defection was an immediate death sentence for families.

All the agents wore a trench coat, no matter how warm it was, wide brim fedora pulled low over the eyes and an airport security badge around their necks marked, 'GUOJIA AGENT'. They used to hand out small, framed pictures of the entire family posed in front of a wall full of bullet holes - for us to put at our bedside in our hotels. But as a cost cutting measure, and the fact that the slave labor manufacturing the frames had to be executed for attempting an escape, now you only get the photo in a plane cardboard folder frame. And the Guojia have become lazy. It's the same photo all the time. My son and daughter have grown so much since it was taken. I was hoping to get a new photo for our family album.

I'm sure the Guojia knows I was kidnapped. And I'm sure

they know about the other translators. Hopefully, my family is still alive. Better in one of the prison slave labor camps and still alive than dead. Alive means there is still hope. If I'm found and returned to China, I will be debriefed and executed for possibly betraying the state. Having the opportunity to betray the state means death. Even if I didn't, the only way to be sure is to execute me. And if I admit I said anything, then my executioner won't even feel bad of possibly killing an innocent man. My family will then be executed. If they're not too far away, they will bring them to me for a last goodbye, for me to witness their execution just before mine.

There seems to be a CCP pattern here. The only way to be sure of anything is to execute whoever and wherever any doubt exists. Save legal fees, crowded courts, although some lower officials seem to need show trials to justify their actions.

Now, I'm sure they're being held at Number 14 Dong Chang'an Jie. As long as the Guojia can't find me. When that jail becomes crowded, they will be moved progressively to detention centers further away from Beijing. Eventually, they'll end up in one of the slave labor camps in the north. If they're lucky, they'll get indoor jobs making 'I' phones or Apple Macs twenty hours a day. With all the people in China, especially with the same name, the Guojia gets lazy and the first sign of confusion in their task as to who to execute, someone would notice if all the Wongs, Chin's or whatever had to be shot. It would overwhelm the system. The Guojia, like bureaucracies around the world, pass off all ambiguous orders the next lower rank, until the cleaning lady in the basement of Guoanbu Headquarters at the Xiyuan compound gets the final order, that then goes in the trash. And that's the way all bureaucracies work.

The only exception was the Stassi – the world's gold standard for all secret police. They kept track of everyone, individually in East Germany. And they did it all with index cards. The Stassi always knew who to execute and all their executions were with railroad timetable accuracy. All their execution sites were where the body disposal took place. And no firing squads leaving a lot of witness. A single executioner with his antique Luger with one bullet to the back of the head. In that way the prisoner fell neatly forward into the burial trench.

I've been told this by some of the Guojia commanders just before they were executed. Their last words were, that if they were able to achieve for China what the Stassi did for East Germany, they wouldn't be where they were. That particular commander was about to give me a message for his family, when his loyal subordinate entered the cell, pulled out his Lu Zi and shot him in the center of his forehead, midsentence. That is the commander was midsentence when his subordinate pushed me aside, pressed the barrel of 7.62x17mm 64 Shi Shou Qiang Type 64 automatic pressed between the commander's eyes and pulled the trigger all in one motion. He was obviously much practiced in the maneuver.

"If you don't want to have to clean up his brains, blood and hair on that wall, I suggest you leave immediately."

I couldn't help asking him, "He was your commander for years. Don't you have any regret or remorse?"

"I am the new commander. I was just promoted to his position with a new office and a pay raise. What do you think? I hate touchy-feely translators. I don't even know why we had to have you down here." Then he smiled. "I am the new commander. And more opportunity for advancement. Not bad for one day's work."

I stood and was about to leave when he grabbed my arm. "Here, take this as a souvenir of the occasion. It is custom to give away your pistol to the witness of your first kill as a commander. Just like giving a little boy the homerun baseball after you hit it. And this was my homerun. I did it smoothly without getting a drop of blood on my uniform." He smiled. "Commander, thank you. I will cherish it." I knew he wanted something. No one in Communist China gives you a 'gift' without wanting something in return. Especially when it's a personal sidearm. "Anything I can do for you?" He wasn't the kind of man you could deny any request.

"I need to learn English if I am to advance. That's why I brought you here. I don't want to end up like my commander in a dead-end job. You will teach me quickly or ..."

"Commander, I'm at your disposal." Maybe a poor choice of words.

"My deputy will contact you, soon. No one is to know of our arrangement. If I am seen as too ambitious, I can end up in this cell, and with you, too." He looked at the blood splatter on my clothes. He had none on his. He knew exactly where to stand. "Get changed. You can't go back to your office like that. Everyone will know where you've been."

He turned to leave the cell, then stopped, turned around and said, "My assistant is sworn to secrecy. He will take you to where you will give me the lessons. Once we're all together, I want you to shoot him in the back of the head. We can't have him alive with the temptation to talk. Just make sure I'm not standing directly in front of him. There's a round in the chamber. Just pull the trigger. That'll be later today. And just so you know, if you don't, I will shoot the both of you. And if you try anything, I will shoot you or let my deputy shoot you. Then I will shoot him and go through the trouble of appointing another deputy, which is pretty easy. Finding another English translator to teach me English will take a day or two. As I said, this has to be our secret." Another very warm smile and a pat on my shoulder, and the new commander was gone. I feel we made a real connection, and he would be an able and enthusiastic student.

If I'm not executed immediately after returning to China or after debriefing, I would probably have a comfortable position if that commander were still the commander. I did what the commander told me to do when we all met for his first and only English lesson from me. I could tell he liked me, but the commander was not a sentimental man. I knew that, but I'm hoping he is keeping up his studies. Every teacher wants his pupils to do well.

Thinking about it, considering everything, pursuing my

career in China might not be as wise and as tempting as you may think. I know for me, once I am free, I am getting as far away from these three maniacs as I can. At least I'm leaving here with a good suit with two pairs of pants. With my English, my knowledge of Mandarin, Standard Chinese, Hanyu, Jin Chinese, Wu Chinese, I could get a job in any PF Chang's Chinese Restaurant Chain or even local Chinese restaurants. As long as I don't show up as a translator anyplace, they'll never find me. One change I would make to any menu is to change the name of General Tso's chicken and shrimp to Zuo Zong-tang's fried chicken or fried shrimp or the Qing-Zuo chicken or shrimp. That would be more historically correct. Maybe even add that to the menu as a new item. If I have them add more oregano and creole spice to the breading, it could become a new dish on its own. I could start my own chain of Chinese fast-food restaurants. I could become the father of a vast empire of Chinese Restaurant franchises. Maybe even bring it back to China. Chinese food is exceedingly popular in China. With the billions of potential customers there, I could become the richest man in the world. That settles it, when I'm out of here, I heading to Florida where everyone loves Chinese food and there's no state income tax.

As translator for President Xi, I was with him when he met with world leaders at several conferences that included the Ayatollah, President Kim, and President Putin. I suspect these translators were at these conferences but are too crazy to remember.

Why would the American's want us to begin with? And why would anyone want our release? Besides, as soon as anyone knows I'm released, I will be marked for death by my country. And as soon as my kill is confirmed, my entire family will be executed, if they can be found in the maze of Chinese slave labor camps.

The other three are just delusional. They think that once they're free, they will be welcomed as heroes back in their capitals – the undisputed absolute leaders of their country. I know they're planning the many executions that will follow their return. I'm sure the real President Kim and the real Ayatollah have already executed their translators' entire families except the wives and children. They're kept as hostages until their translator husband or father is captured, interrogated, and executed, or dies 'accidentally' during transit. And then they'll be all goners. I suspect Kim has already carried out the executions, but the Ayatollah will keep the wife or wives and children alive just to execute them in front of their father. Public stoning will no doubt be the method of choice for all of them in Iran. Stoning is time consuming, and as traditional as beheading. Iran is a very traditional society, and my guess either choice will suffice, although stoning is more entertaining.

Our three would-be dictators don't realize they even have families in detention centers awaiting execution as soon as they are found and liquidated. That's actually part of the 'Dictators, Despots, and Tyrants Operating Manual, Guidelines and Best Practices', edited by Pol Pot. That manual is available to all dictators, assistant despots, and tyrant managers online on Kindle, or through Amazon Books, and Barnes and Noble. It's interesting that they also sell it in a boxed set with Mein Kampf, and Mao's Little Red Book. President Xi gave me the boxed set as a birthday gift. (I have the audio books, all narrated by Charles Manson some years before his death.) Originally it was a Harlequin Publication with a series planned for the Hallmark Channel. But the head of Harlequin and the president of Hallmark, both met with unfortunate accidents. Both companies had Chinese senior vice presidents heading the Peoples Republic of China's divisions. Interestingly, the vice presidents had the same name and had visited America before the two men died of food poisoning. No doubt a coincidence as so many Chinese have the same names and so many associated with Chinese businessmen die of food poisoning. The world is so full of coincidences, especially in China or involving Communist China with as many people as coincidences.

I know one thing; I'm certainly not going to stick around these three madmen. To save my life and my family's lives as bad as they may be in the slave labor camps, I need to disappear into the United States of America. And I'm not waiting around for the people who freed all of us. With a new suit, no identity, no family to weigh me down, and a stranger to everyone I meet away from here, I have the world at my feet. And if I can travel fast enough south, I can have at least Florida at my feet.

Now, though, I'm leading the procession. I'm followed by the Ayatollah, and the 'Dear One', Kim pushing the shirtless President Putin still glued to his desk chair. The old tailor and his older wife both have their guns drawn, are both behind us, walking side by side. The angle is such that the tailor has a clear shot at the Ayatollah and me, killing us with one bullet each. His wife could kill Kim and Putin with a single well-placed bullet. The way she is holding the barrel of her Colt, the bullet will go through Kim's mid back, through his heart, into the back of Putin's high back desk chair and into the back of Putin's head. I doubt the .45 ACP will travel any further than the interior of Putin's skull with the loss of velocity after going through Kim and the chair. By that time, I'm sure the tailor would have finished Kim and I off with two shots to the mid chest. If he is Mossad trained, he will walk up to both of us and put bullets into our heads to be absolutely sure we won't survive. I suspect that both of them are not afraid to die from the Zyklon B, as long as they kill all of us first.

I may be only a translator, but over the years, I've learned to read people pretty will. Especially people who want something from your leader. They're all very cautious because it may be more dangerous that the leader knows your name. Whether he says yes or no, you are at risk of being liquidated. If you've ever been critical of the leader, you would have to be crazy to ask for an audience to make any request. The first thing the leader's second-in-command does before your appointment is to check everything you ever said about the leader, the leader's allies, and the leader's internal and external foes. If you said anything negative about the leader, or anything good about one of the leader's enemies, you bought yourself a one-way ticket to a sleep-away vocational learning center somewhere in the north of the country, if you were among the lucky ones. If you said anything bad about the leader's opponent that becomes the leader's friend, or worse, replaces the leader, you end up in the same place or worse. Remember, it's not just you, it's your wife, children, parents, grandparents, grandchildren, and anyone else that may have been a friend, or even admit knowing you.

World leaders tend to be more forthcoming, even with all their diplo-speak. They're at least not afraid of being personally executed, except maybe by their own people. When you're an English translator in the Peoples Republic of China, those who need an English translator and get one, are powerful people but neither the most powerful nor are always the most expendable members of the Chinese Communist Party. These middle-management demi-tyrants are more expendable and most often terminated – permanently terminated – more by ambitious assistants. And the assistants are more often permanently 'transferred' than the janitors are transferred to another floor to clean.

And janitors, cleaning ladies and the like, never lose their jobs. They know more about what's going on than anyone anywhere. And that goes for every janitor and every cleaning lady in every capital, every organization, every top security agency, every military in the world. In fact, I personally know that many of the janitors are still talking about Mao Zedong. One janitor on my floor worked for Chiang Kai-shek. He told me that Madame Chiang ran the show and was to first to warn her husband about Mao. And apparently, she didn't have anything nice to say about Nixon, Kissinger, or Ho Chi Minh.

And like in any large organization, it's the lower ranks who do the work and are more difficult to replace. On the other hand, there's so many people in China, life is cheap, and anybody is interchangeable with another person. If the replacement person is too slow doing the job, nobody will notice. And you can always get two people for less than half the salary each. That enriches the state, and the workers are glad they have enough for a meal and weren't sent to a forced labor camp. But then the immediate supervisor has to explain his inefficiency in needing to bother with the constant shuffling. Any change anyplace always results in an inefficiency. But everything is so overstaffed, these things aren't usually noticed until there are so many new people, nobody knows anybody. And there's no retirement. You die at your job on duty. You're there until you drop in place. That's how you demonstrate loyalty to the Party.

The higher you go, especially in the Chinese Communist Party where you have to ruin people or wait for them to die and then ruin or kill your competitors to be promoted, the more expendable you become. And in today's China, the only golden parachute is the empty parachute bag you wear as you're pushed out of your airplane.

Those who use an English translator but who speak English and understand the language well, are the ones pulling the strings. They're just using the translator to keep the people they're dealing with at arm's length from knowing their true intentions. And both the near powerful and the powerful are subject to assassination, usually by one another. As a translator in Communist China, you wear your Kevlar to bed and learn how to duck.

"'Dear One', President Putin, Ayatollah – don't make any sudden moves. We are about to be released and we don't need any bloodshed, especially if it's your blood. It won't be my blood because I don't plan to take part in anything you three might be planning. I want you to know and our escorts to know, also." I stepped back and smiled at Putin, the 'Dear One', and the Ayatollah. I turned around and smiled and shrugged my shoulders at the tailor and his wife. I was hoping to get a reassuring smile back. They just stood there grim faced with their handguns, the tailor's pointed toward me and the Ayatollah, and his wife's pointed at Kim who was pushing Putin in his desk chair. Judging from their Yiddish accent, either they were from New York, or Mossad, or both. Either way, they knew their way around firearms.

"President Xi, we must get to the United Nations to unmask these false idols." The Ayatollah raised both arms above his head, at the same time the tailer's wife cocked the hammer of her automatic and took careful aim at the Ayatollah's head.

"Ayatollah, all I need is an excuse. In fact, Ayatollah, I don't even need an excuse." The woman didn't speak loudly. Her words were clear even with her accent and weren't hesitant. She had her finger inside the trigger guard, and we all waited for the gun to go off, except for the Ayatollah. He believed no woman would dare be so audacious as to speak directly to him let alone seriously threaten him. And a woman shooting the Ayatollah, beyond the realm of possibility – absolutely unheard of.

"Woman, you dare speak directly to the Ayatollah – the holiest of holly men. Have you no sense, woman of what is right and holy? I have honored you by speaking to you directly and will be considerate enough to beat you in private. Learn, now! A woman to even..."

I had to interrupt before he gets us all killed. As soon as one shot is fired, everyone tries to run and duck. Nobody will get more than two steps. And even if you stand perfectly still, everyone with a gun starts shooting and everyone without a gun gets killed who would have been killed anyway. And I mean the four of us. In formal prearranged assassinations in China, the translators are warned ahead of time don't make a sudden move when the shooting starts, that's the only way to be safe. You may not be told who the target is, but if they're warning you, you know you are probably not in immediate danger, unless you are directly in front of or behind the intended target. Accidents happen in the best planned assassination.

But if they warned you, you're probably safe unless you're the actual target and they're lulling you into a false sense of security. That's what you hope – that you're not the target. And I've been asked on more than one occasion I've been told, or with a hand motion to move a step to the left or right, before the three kill shots are fired. Two to the chest, and one to the head while standing over the body. And then there are the witnesses that may or may not leave the scene.

It's the blood splatter that can make you feel faint and at the same time freeze you in your place. You never really get used to it. Occasionally a translator has been wounded. Two died, one killed by a stray bullet that went through the target's chest, and the other had a heart attack. But that's so rare.

Even Kim wasn't stupid enough to pick a fight with an angry woman with a loaded pistol. And we thought Kim was the dumbest one here. "Just to let you know, Mr. Tailor and Mrs. Tailor, if we're all not released alive, they will release the gas and we'll all die." I know how to defuse a tense moment. On second thought, I'm not sure that was the right thing to say, either.

"Then we'll shoot all of you here and now and be out of here. Well take our chances outrunning the gas, plus have the immense satisfaction of…"

"Do you think you can kill all of us before one of us gets to you?" Putin was used to challenging people. He was, or thought he was the strong man of all Russia. "A tailor and a seamstress – do you think you are any match for a former KGB colonel? Especially a KGB colonel who is President of the Russian Federation? I didn't get to this position from being a great politician!" He still thinks he's Vladimir Putin, President of the Russian Federation, and not just some English translator who was in the wrong place at the wrong time. "I have moves that will outmaneuver your bullets. The KGB taught us these things in KGB school and you'll never know what happened." Now it's a tie. Our Putin makes Kim and the Ayatollah look better by the minute. Actually, it would be no great loss if the tailor and his wife shot the three of them. The problem is that they'll shoot me too.

Listening to the three translators, I don't know what kind of valuable intelligence they could possibly get from these idiots. And if they think that these jokers think like the dictators, they think they are, then the Americans should be at the same time feel assured that they're dealing with idiots and be frightened to death that these idiots can launch nuclear weapons. Now I'm frightened for the world. If the Americans see what I see, they will conclude they should make a preemptive nuclear strike. I need to talk with the commanding officer, General Merriwhether before we're released, and he issues any kind of report.

"President Putin, your glued to your chair. You're the last one we'll worry about and probably the last one we shoot. First two shots to the kneecaps, then two to the belly. You won't die right away. Your gut contents will pour into your abdomen and you will feel like you're burning from the inside out. We won't have to finish you off until the other three are dead if you survive that long." The tailor was more matter of fact than threatening. "Rachel, I am getting so tired of all this. Do you need a break, dear?"

"You see the way he talks to this woman. And the woman is his wife. To talk like that in public to a woman, especially a woman who is one of your wives, and I hope you have many. You disgrace yourself. Hopefully, your other wives are better and more respectful than this one. They should have been taught by their mothers that as women, they are subject to your every whim. You disgrace yourself, tailor. She shouldn't be addressed like that in public. No woman should be addressed in public unless to impart a necessary, a very necessary and simple commands that the inferior female brain can understand and had not anticipated. Where this becomes necessary, the woman should not be beaten in public. That should wait until you return to your home to do it properly. It is your husbandly duty to beat your wife. How else will she learn. And if she becomes a widow, she will be better prepared to serve her next man. Under the burqa, looks don't matter anyway. It's the way she is subservient that will attract another man." I think the Ayatollah was the king of Iranian marriage counselors.

"And, under any circumstances, no woman should ever need a break or ask for one. If her husband desires it, it should be done. It should be done without question and with eyes averted. And the woman should return to where her instructions were imparted for further orders. And make no mistake. Whatever a husband tells his wife, or suggests, is an order, to be obeyed immediately, completely, gladly. The wife should anticipate her husband's wishes and carry them out without a word being said. And she should always be ready for the next order. She may rest after he lays his head on his pillow and is asleep." The Ayatollah couldn't help himself. He is just asking for a bullet in the balls.

"Ayatollah, your wife prepares the meals with her sharpened kitchen knives. If she doesn't poison you, she'll cut your throat ear to ear holding your neck back by your beard. And you won't be able to say a word about it. And that's right from the Old Testament." Israel was a bit of a Biblical scholar. "Except in the Old Testament, Judith, after seducing and screwing the Assyrian General Holofernes, got him drunk, held his head up by his hair and cut off his head. But your beard would be easier to grab instead of rummaging through your greasy turban."

"Tailor, I have no worries. I never touch alcohol."

"Israel, let's get them upstairs, before…"

"I know Rachel. You can't change the Ayatollah, not with a gun to his head, and not when he's not even the Ayatollah."

"Don't forget your little sandwich bags."

* * *

…let us begin and create in idea a State;
and yet the true creator is necessity, which
is the mother of our invention.
[Plato (ne Aristotle) 428-348 B.C., Bk. II, 369c]

The Ayatollah and President Xi led followed by Kim pushing Putin in the desk chair. They all had their sandwich bags with the severed hands. By this time, all the bags were mostly stained with the old sticky blood that had already darkened like old ketchup left out of the refrigerator. Israel and Rachel, both with guns drawn didn't follow too closely, but were close enough to be able to get off four clean kill shots to the mid back through the mid thoracic spinal cord and heart.

Rachel already had her shot lined up. She accurately calculated that shooting Kim in the middle of his back with the .45 caliber Colt long barreled M1A1 would go straight through him, explode his heart, and hit the seated Putin in the back of the head. If the bullet went through Putin's head, she might also hit the Ayatollah in the mid back, but that would be a bonus. Of course, she was prepared to shoot Putin separately if the bullet changed direction when it hit Kim's spine. Unless it hit the Ayatollah in a critical blood vessel, it would probably not cause enough damage to kill him outright due to loss of velocity or if it fragmented into smaller pieces. But that still wouldn't be a bad outcome. At least the Ayatollah would suffer. That would leave only a single target for Israel, although she thought he might also fire on the Ayatollah before killing me - President Xi.

When they got to the elevator, Israel told them no talking. "Enter the elevator. Line up, side by side by the rear door. Hold your little lunch bag in your left hand and put your right hand behind your head.

"I am the Ayatollah. No one can stop me. You won't dare..." The Ayatollah turned around and lowered his arms when Rachel fired two rounds at him. One round hit the armrest of Putin's desk chair, tearing it off, and the other round took off the Ayatollah middle finger on his left hand. He mustn't have felt it initially. The noise of the gunshot stopped him. When he finally realized the wetness against his hand was his own blood, he screamed, grabbed the blood-pumping

stump of what was left of the finger and squeezed tightly trying to stop the bleeding.

"Rachel, the next shot goes to you. I need to operate the
elevator." Israel closed the vertical floor doors and closed the
brass scissors gate before pushing the operating handle away
from him and slowly then more quickly allowing the elevator
to ascend.

When we arrived, General Merriwhether met us. "You
are all free to go. Go." General Merriwhether was angry to let us
get away. None of us knew whether whoever demanded our release was going to honor their pledge not to release the Zyklon
B gas.

We didn't know that the threat was real until Israel said,
"My crew was killed by the Zyklon B. You four are as responsible as the people who planted the canisters."

"Your would-be rescuers went through the door to the
tunnels. No doubt they're waiting for you there. Why they
want you out of our hands, and what they plan to do with you,
I do not know. But as long as you are here, we're all-in danger
and so is the White House. Leave now through the tunnels.
Our instructions were to give you an hour. Those hands in the
paper bags will allow you to get through their booby traps.
Keep them with you. The people who are helping you get away
said they will disarm the Zyklon B devices once you and they
are out of the tunnels." General Merriwhether was grim.

No one said anything else. Jimmy was gritting his teeth,
Anna still held her hammer-cocked .45 caliber Colt with the
muzzle pointed toward the floor. Rose, our secretary/waitress
who turned out to be the colonel's wife was the most relaxed,
standing with her arms crossed.

The colonel stood at the door to our escape tunnel. He
had a blank look on his face and kept looking at Rose, the waitress for any direction. I'm sure he's been looking to his wife all
his life for direction. I told you I could read people.

*   *   *   *   *

CHAPTER SIXTEEN

"Let us learn our lessons. Never, never, never believe any war will be smooth and easy ... Always remember, however sure you are that you can easily win, that there would not be a war if the other man did not think he also had a chance."
[Winston Spencer Churchill, My Early Life]

"General, how much of a start do we give them?" I know Rose, Uncle Jimmy and Aunt Anna wanted to shoot the four of them, now. Israel and Rachel wanted to kill them all, painfully slowly, but their Mossad training taught them to play the long game and find out who planted the Zyklon B canisters. As far as Israel and Rachel were concerned, what they were taught by the Mossad was that as long as there was someone being held against their will, there was always someone else ready to set them free and make a profit or find a strategic advantage or both. And, as soon as you find out the who, you find out the why.

"Archie, just check Mrs. Haversham's desk for another laptop. As long as they have the hands, we can track them all. I'm sure that whoever wanted them released is also tracking the chips. And that's who we want." General Merriwhether was very calm. He must know who's behind this otherwise he wouldn't be speaking with such confidence. "It's just unfortunate I didn't realize who was behind this before all this happened. And I'm still not sure the why." But if the General knows the 'who', why doesn't he know the 'why'? And why does he know the 'who'? And knowing the 'who' without the 'why' seems impossible. I'll have to get Rachel to explain this all to me once we're alone.

"I'm not sure who you're talking about, but they're in

my gunsights. And I have friends on Tenth Avenue who owe me big time that will find them. And if I tell them, they'll find them, corner them and save these bastards for me to finish off." Uncle Jimmy was saying it with his seething voice. Uncle Jimmy rarely is angered, never upset by anything, and certainly never frightened. "My friends know I do my own dirty work – that is unless they also have a beef with them. And chances are, guys like this make enemies all over the place."

"Jimmy, not unless I get to them first. You would make things to quick and easy for them. Probably even painless." My Aunt wouldn't stand up to grocery clerks when they short-changed her at the supermarket. I never really saw this side of my Aunt. She turned out to be a real Tenth Avenue broad.

"And I'm no shrinking violet, either." I know Rose would do it all with her Colt .45, but slowly. No kill shot. Kneecaps, other extremities, then off centered belly shots to avoid major vessels. That would let their gut contents pour out and burn them inside out. Rose told me exactly what she had in mind for whoever they were. That's when she asked for a box of ammunition she could put in her purse. She assumed there would be more than one. Apparently, this was the WASP way, then claiming you didn't know the gun was loaded when it fired the six rounds without missing their target.

"While we're waiting, gather up any ammunition you can find. There are more weapons stashed in this lobby. And see if you can find any of those cloth shopping bags that everyone is forced to use since they won't give you any of the plastic bags." The General started with Mrs. Haversham's desk and found Aldi's cloth bags, and COSCO and BJ's bags. Now we knew where Mrs. Haversham shopped for her groceries and the fact that she bought a bag every time she went into the stores. The General also found six boxes of the .45 ACP Teflon-coated cartridges.

Uncle Jimmy broke open one of the locked stationary cabinets in the corner shadows. It was filled with copying paper, ink toner, scotch tape, staples, two stapling guns, paper clips, and boxes of ball point pens. The four M-16 fully auto-matic rifles and twelve spare loaded clips of ammunition were in one corner on a special gun rack. The cabinet was locked to keep people from taking home the copying paper and office supplies. Everyone here had their own weapons, but there was no other place to keep these rifles.

Uncle Jimmy took an M-16s. And so, did Israel. Aunt Anna grabbed two and gave one to Rose. Everyone searched for Kevlar body armor, but none was found.

"Time to go." General Merriwhether handed me Mrs. Haversham's laptop. "Archie, get the charger. We'll need it."

"We should take a ream of copying paper and some pens. You never know when you may need to make a copy of some-thing, and I don't have a pen." Uncle Jimmy was always think-ing ahead. "I have to remember where you keep your office sup-plies. There's something un-American having to buy your own office supplies when they are everywhere for the taking."

Now I had Mrs. Haversham's laptop, the charger and all the wires stuffed in my pocket on one side, a box of .45 ACP rounds in the other and Rose looking at me as if I were stupid. "You want to tell me something, Rose?"

"You look stupid." I can look at Rose and read her mind. "Grab a shopping bag. Put everything in your pockets in it and grab some extra boxes of ammunition. I don't want you look-ing stupid if you're wounded or killed. And don't get wounded or killed. Your other uniform is at the cleaners, and the clean-ers are all dead and the place is full of poison gas. You'll have nothing to wear or be buried in." Rose was always looking out for me. "Put these in the bag. When I need them, anticipate! If you count the rounds I fire, you'll know when I'll need the next magazine." Rose had three spare clips for her M-16. With her own Colt and the pistol's two spare clips in her purse, there was no room for anything else.

Before we started out, I found more boxes of .45 caliber ACP cartridges, but they weren't Teflon coated. Aunt Anna took one, put it in her purse and offered everyone a butterscotch candy. Uncle Jimmy took a box, and I took the last three. We all knew a .45 round out of a Colt M1A1 will still knock a man over even if it won't penetrate his body armor. It's curious that Israel and Rachel took none. I learned later that the Mossad teaches them never to trust someone else's ammunition.

Without another word, General Merriwhether went bursting through the door, his Colt drawn with hammer cocked. No one was in front, on the sides or behind the door that led to the tunnels. We knew to follow. Rose went first, gun drawn but without cocking the hammer, slinging her M-16. Israel and Rachel followed so quietly that you couldn't hear their footsteps on the gravel and debris on the ground. Uncle Jimmy had his gun drawn pointed at the ground and Aunt Anna, brought up the rear, looking backwards more than forwards to be sure we weren't being followed. She slung her M-16, but her Colt was in her hand with her thumb on the hammer and her shopping bag around her neck and shoulder so it wouldn't slip off.

There was a spotty trail of blood on the tracks and the walkways. We stopped several times to check the computer and knew the four translators were still together as one group. When we came to a large puddle of congealed blood, we could see the blood trail of at least two, possibly three people being dragged by their feet and one being dragged by his neck, with the marks of two boots that had gone through the blood puddle. Mrs. Haversham did a lot of damage before they finished her off.

It took an hour to reach the first vertical escape shaft. There was a puddle of clotted blood on the ground. Three gas masks and three black and blue tartan tam o'shanter caps, all covered in blood, all with bullet holes creasing the tops lay at the foot of the shaft. It was three slightly high head shots from Mrs. Haversham's Colt. These three may have survived, but her bullets tore up the tops of their scalps if not part of their boney skulls. We know that they haul away their wounded and dead, even though they left someone's lower leg behind.

The shaft cables were blood stained, but the dripping had stopped and some of the blood had already darkened to brown. When we looked up the shaft, we could see the outline of the pully system, the dumbwaiter a quarter way up, and a small stream of daylight through the tunnel dust. But daylight was fading.

The General said nothing for a moment as he looked us each of us individually in the eye. It was a bit odd if he was doing it for dramatic effect. This looks like something they taught him to do with troops you were sending on a dangerous mission. Well, we were already here. He finally spoke. "If I were them, I would be waiting for us with guns drawn. My guess is they have the plans for the tunnels, and they have a team of snipers at each exit. We can only assume they're monitoring our communications."

Israel looked at Rachel. "We're obliged to go after them. The rest of you aren't. Rachel and I will go up the shaft. You find another way. You should be able to track them with the laptop." Rachel nodded agreement.

"I'm with Israel and Rachel." Uncle Jimmy was going up the shaft. He tried to sound calm but wasn't. His voice had a bloody vengeful rumble I had never heard before.

"And I'm with you, Jimmy. We all have scores to settle." Aunt Anna threw the long loop of her shopping bag full of boxes of ammunition around her shoulders freeing one hand to hang on to the dumbwaiter cable and the other to draw her Colt.

General Merriwhether walked in front of all of us and blocked our way to the escape shaft, the ladders, and the dumbwaiter. "You know that this is Rex Seplechre's doing. Our Special Counselor will be smart enough to have someone at each of the escape shafts topside entrances to kill anyone who sticks up their heads. As soon as they hear the pulleys of the dumbwaiter, they'll shoot straight down into the shaft. That's what they expect us to do." General Merriwhether motioned to us to proceed in the tunnel and proceed as quietly as possible. We all thought better of our initial impulse and followed the General's instructions.

"We could never be sure if he left some of his troops behind to ambush us along the way. We can still track the translators who are probably in Seplechre's company. Our only choice is to go north to Fort Meade. That's two hours away by our golf carts."

"And we can get help there." Uncle Jimmy wanted reinforcements to deal with whatever uniformed force Seplechre had, even though he planned to finish Seplechre and the translators off himself. Aunt Anna said nothing, but I knew she would prefer to go up the shaft and shoot it out with whoever was topside, just to relieve some of her stress.

"We have bullets that will penetrate their body armor." She said nothing else. I knew Rose felt the same, except getting help to deal with Seplechre's armed force. She would kill them herself.

"Ladies and gentlemen, we get to Fort Meade and get proper transportation. As long as they have their severed hands and we have the computer, we know where they are and can follow them. Don't kill anyone until we figure out the why behind their mission." General Merriwhether made a lot of sense. "I am the senior officer and the commanding officer of USEWOW. I know that Israel and Rachel are also Mossad, but I'm sure they understand my reasoning." General Merriwhether turned to Uncle Jimmy and Aunt Anna. He put his hand on Uncle Jimmy's shoulder and took Aunt Anna's hand with his free hand. "You need us and the computer to find them. And there will be enough of them for you to get your revenge. My revenge will be watching the rest of you do what has to be done. I promise you all that."

With that, we walked north along the tunnel toward Fort Meade. We found two golf carts together, both with blood covered seats, but no bodies nearby. We wiped off the seats as best we could and proceeded north. Rose and I were in the driving one golf cart with Uncle Jimmy and Aunt Anna in the rear seats facing backward, with guns drawn. I drove, while Rose put her Colt back into her purse and held her M-16 safety off and at the ready. The General drove the other golf cart, with Israel in the front seat with an M-16 and Rachel facing backwards with one of the other M-16s.

The four translators' chips paused at a rest stop on Route 95 in Delaware. One chip temporarily disappeared, then reappeared some distance from the others and began heading south on Route 95. We could see, three of the translators, if it were the translators with the severed hands and chips began moving north again on 95.

"We can't lose any of them. We need another computer. Archy, when we get to Fort Meade, find a laptop, and put the satellite tracing program on it. You and Rose head south and follow the single chip. The rest of us will head north. My bet is three of the translators are going to the UN to confront the people who they believe are impersonating them." The General stared at Rose. He knew I would follow orders, but Rose had a mind of her own.

"General Merriwhether, as soon as Archy and I find whoever it is that went south, we'll kill him and fly north to New York. We'll rendezvous at the UN. We all know that's where they're heading. I don't know why Seplechre did this, but he is the only logical target. And if we kill him, what does it matter why. We could just kill whoever takes his place. In fact, we should kill anyone who is standing next to him!" Rose was smiling, almost laughing. She gets that way when she's overtired or misses a meal. Then I know I really have to watch my step.

"I have a message from the Secret Service. The Hazmat people have searched the White House, USEWOW and only a small portion of the tunnels. They keep finding Zyklon B canisters but without fuses or detonating devices. These are the original World War Two Nazi canisters. They look like they may have been kept at Edgewood Arsenal as museum pieces. Their pitted and ready to fall apart. What happen at USEWOW was the canisters just leaked on their own. Everyone at the White House and around the compound has been evacuated. That is, except for the press briefing room. No one wanted to accuse anyone of hiding anything from the news media, so if there was a poison gas leak, they would be the first to know." Uncle Jimmy smiled before General Merriwhether. As bad as things were, ...

"Enough. General Merriwhether, can't we just send the FBI after all these guys? That'll be a lot faster, even though I may not get a chance to shoot them dead." Rose had the obvious answer and Aunt Anna nodded in agreement. Uncle Jimmy said nothing. He was generally averse to calling any component of law enforcement unless he already had some sort of 'mutually beneficial relationship' with them, usually on an individual basis. And that's the way it is on Tenth Avenue.

In the two and a half hours it took us to get to Fort Meade, Mrs. Haversham's laptop battery ran out and by the time it charged, we lost the one chipped hand that was going south. The other three chipped hands were approaching the Lincoln Tunnel and about to enter Manhattan.

*   *   *   *   *

CHAPTER SEVENTEEN

"You Can't Cheat An Honest Man"
*[From the Title of the W.C. Fields, Edgar Bergen,
Charlie McCarthy 1939 Comedy]*

You wouldn't believe the luck I just had. I walk in to get a rest-stop hot dog off the roller heater. These hot dogs are legendary in China. Everyone whispers about them. When we travel, we dream of them. But diplomats never stop at parkway rest stops. We're flown in, limousine to fine restaurants, back to the embassies. We never stop at a fast-food parkway rest stop with the roller-heated hot dogs, sausages, chili dogs, where you pick out a plastic sealed bun and put on your own mustard and onions. America is such a wonderful country. All I've wanted is a rest stop roller heated hot dog. And I've never had one.

And now I'm here. At a genuine American highway rest stop. They tell me the hot dogs and sausages have been on the roller heaters for days, maybe weeks, and taste just as good as the first day out of the package. They smell so delicious and look so good. There were whispers these American foods back in China when I was growing up. But then with the cultural revolution, Mao disappeared those who spoke of bringing these delicacies to China, and from then until now, roller-heater hot dogs are only whispered about in the shadows.

This is truly the miracle of American chemical engineering. That and the eternal Slim-Jim. They are manufactured with no expiration date, and I am told they can be found in any gas station in America, on a rack covered in dust. But they are still great.

Anyway, I put the hotdog in a preheated bun they kept below the roller counter, waited until there was a big line at the cashier and tried to sneak out.

"Sir, you have to pay for that. Sir, over here." I went to the counter, with the hotdog in one hand, struggling with my paper bag with the severed hand in the other. Fortunately, the hand never smelled, but was drying, and becoming wrinkled – on its way to being mummified. By this time, all the blood from the hand had clotted and dried, and the blood stains on the bag were brown. It really looked like a sandwich bag stained with gravy. "And you have to pay for the sandwich, too." The young girl smiled. She had dealt with these kind of customers before. She smiled, and if the customer smiled back, she knew he would pay. She would challenge them only the one time, but she certainly wasn't getting paid enough by Loves chain to put up a fight.

"Madame, I beg your pardon, but if I can just return to my automobile to get my wallet."

"Sir, just leave your hot dog and sandwich here on the counter, and when you come back, I'll see to it you don't have to wait in line." She couldn't be nicer. People in China were never like that. The people in China are much more like New Yorkers or Parisians.

When I put the hot dog in the bun with the fried onions, no mustard – I wanted the onions but wasn't willing to chance mustard stains on such a fine suit – and I put the bag with the hand on the counter, the credit card reader began to click. I moved the hand, and it clicked again.

"Oh, you must be one of those government people with the charge chips. That must be so convenient. Give me a moment, and I'll give you your receipt. Be sure to keep it, so you hand it in with your expenses." As the receipt printed, she said, "Would you like a candy bar? It's for my son's baseball team. I can put it right on your government chip."

"Of course, my good woman. In fact, give me two." At two dollars a candy bar, I could imagine the profit margin was considerable. In China, it's usually the secret police and the DMV clerks who push the charity candy bars, and they don't even bother with the baseball team story.

"Thank you. You're very generous. You'd be surprised how many government people come through here. The wave their hands, some put their cats and puppies past the credit card machine to pay. Even though we don't allow pets inside, I sell a lot more candy bars by looking the other way."

"Miss, if I wanted to call for transportation, could you do it for me?" She had a telephone behind the counter. "I would even buy more candy bars."

"It would be much easier for you to get a ride share. Use your cell phone."

"But I don't have my cell phone with me. It's at home." Of course, home is Beijing.

"Then go over to aisle three, pick out a disposable cell phone. The good ones come with earphones and a charger. If you want a case, they're there, too. Bring them back to me, I'll activate it, put it on your charge, and you can even buy more candy."

"And the ride share? Can I use my 'chip'?"

"All the ride shares accept the government chip. It's better than any credit card. There's no complaining about the charge and losing the fair."

And that's what I did. I called an Uber. A very sketchy black guy with a menacing beard pulled up in front of the Love's doorway blocking the first row of gas pumps. As I got in, four of those soldier's that had 'rescued me', at least I think they had rescued me burst through the door of the store and were beginning to search the convenience store.

My Uber driver, at least he said he was my Uber driver asked for my destination.

"I put that in when I activated the app online."

"Well, sometimes I'm confused with an Uber."

"The cardboard sign in your window say 'Uber'.

But there was no time to spare. People behind him were

blowing their horns trying to get gas, and I could see the soldiers stop momentarily and look outside.

"Where to?"

When I told him to take me to Florida, he looked at me.

"Big state, mister. It'll cost a lot of money. Gas and tolls are extra."

"As long as I have the receipts." I don't know why I said that.

"Let's get out of here, fast." He pulled away from the front of Love's and stopped.

"I need your charge card first then I need a destination. Just so you know, just to the Florida border is going to be over four hundred dollars plus gas, plus tolls, but that includes the tip. And please I need a good review."

"It's a government chip charge. I have it in my sandwich bag. It's not convenient to pull it out and pass it to you."

"No problem." He took the charge card reader off its dashboard holder and held it back between the front seat headrests. The card reader started clicking as soon as I held the bag near it.

When he looked around, he smiled. The government chip was like gold. He couldn't be happier. He immediately sped out of the parking lot, speeding way over the speed limit south on route 95.

"By the way, my name is Gabriel. There's water in the cooler next to you. Please help yourself. When you need to stop, just let me know. But I will need a destination."

I couldn't see the man's face, but he had his cell phone in one hand and was about to make a call.

"Who are you calling?"

"I have to call my wife to let her know I won't be home until morning." Then he spoke into the phone. "Call Darlene."

The phone spoke back. "There is no 'Arlene' in your phone book."

"Darlene – call Darlene."

"Calling Darlene." I could hear the phone on the other

end of the call ringing. "Yes dear, I know, you're going to be late." Whatever Darlene told Gabriel my driver, she was annoyed. And Gabriel was obviously annoyed that she was annoyed. "Darlene, it's a fair all the way to Florida – and on one of those government chips. "Sweetheart, I got a fair out of the Delaware rest stop. All the way to Florida." Darlene said something, then Gabriel said, "It's a government chip fair – as good as gold. And I don't know where in Florida. There's no giving back to the money once the chip pays." Darlene said something else. "Darlene, the tip alone will pay for a week's groceries." She must have whispered 'I love you.' He said, "I love you too. I call when we get to the Florida line and let you know where we're going. And I'll be careful. I have 'my friend' with me anyway." The way he told that to Darlene, I must look sketchy to him, too.

I could hear her very loud and clear say, "Are you sure this is on the up and up? You always need to be reminded you're on parole. And I'm upset you brought 'your friend'." She was not just angry but concerned for her man. And the way Gabriel talked to her, she was a force to be reckoned with. The last thing she said to him wasn't another 'I love you.' What she clearly said was, "If you have to use it, make sure you wipe it off before you get rid of it."

Gabriel knew I overheard what his wife said. "She's a good woman. She stuck with me when I was in the clink."

"Tell Darlene, there will be a very generous gratuity in it for you." I had planned several stops and would need some assistance. "Gabriel, when you stop for gas, we'll put it on the chip, and you can still charge me." In Beijing, that's what Party officials do all the time. Double billing is a way of life in China. And even with that, everything is so cheap if a Party member doesn't run up sufficient expenses, his boss figures he's not doing his job and should be replaced. But you have to have the receipts to get reimbursed, prove you are doing your job, and prevent being terminated from the Party. And being terminated meant just that. Peaceful promotion meant someone at the very top died, and everyone moves up one rung in the ladder of Communist success in an orderly progression. That the circle of Communist Chinese life. It's when someone in the middle ranks is replaced that the knives (actually loaded pistols) come out.

When we got to the next rest stop, we pulled up, filled the gas tank from the self-service with the chip, and I went into the convenience store and bought coffees, potato chips, and two hotdogs for me and Gabriel.

"Gabriel, end the fair here. Let's pay up, give you your tip and start a new fair. Make the new destination, the Georgia-Florida state line, and the Florida welcome center. We should have enough gas to get us there." I passed the hot dog and the coffee up to him and put two bags of barbecue potato chips on the front seat next to him. "The cold water back here. That's a nice touch."

"Thank you. I was getting hungry. You know the tip is included in the fair." Gabriel started driving as soon as I got in the car. He took one hand off the wheel and grabbed the hot dog. "The cooler with the bottled water make's everyone believe I'm a real Uber. It's so easy to hijack their fares. And there are some real dangerous guys out there, even the real Uber drivers".

"You're very welcome. I didn't know it, but you deserve it." I had to ask him, "Do you pay taxes?"

"Actually no. All the driving is off the books. But my wife pays taxes on her salary. No taxes on her tips. We list her on the tax return as 'saleswoman' and not waitress."

"Gabriel, consider the extra tip as tax refund for your wife. However, we end up, you and your wife are a deserving couple and I'm glad to do it. Not everyone will take me to Florida. I intend to be very generous to you and to your Darlene. Do you have any children?"

"Two, both of them in elementary school. But the schools are poor, and the teachers stink. We both went and complained, but they're union teachers and there is nothing can be done. And no matter who you vote for, I can't vote but my wife can, all the politicians are in the teacher's union pocket."

"I guess in some ways, America is like the one party Communist Chinese Party rule."

"I don't know what you're talking about. We have two parties, but nothing changes. My children are stuck in these piss poor schools with piss poor teachers because we're stuck in our district. And the Catholic schools are too expensive. My wife works as a waitress during the lunch rush at the diner, then the dinner hour after I get home." Gabriel finished his hot dog and was sipping his coffee as we got back on Route 95 south.

"Gabriel, give me the aluminum foil from the hot dog. And from now on, I want you to save any aluminum wrappings from any sandwiches you get."

Gabriel passed the aluminum foil back to me. He adjusted his rear-view mirror to watch me wrap the hand. I was trying to prevent anyone from tracking us. Gabriel laughed. "If that's what you wanted to do, I have a role of aluminum foil under the right front seat. Just reach for it and wrap your chip to your hearts content. Do you know how many chip fairs I get, and how many people want to wrap the chips to make them untraceable?"

"Gabriel, you see a lot of these chips?"

"Yes sir. And as soon as I suggested the aluminum foil to hide the chips electronically, the better my tips. And I needed the wide aluminum foil rolls for everyone who wanted to wrap their dogs and cats."

"Once we get to Florida, we'll fill up again. Then we'll close this trip and start another. I guess you don't mind pets?"

"As long as they fit with you in the back seat." Gabriel couldn't be happier with the money he was making.

"Let me give you our itinerary. First stop, PETCO or PetSmart for dog food, leashes, collars, and doggy supplies – can food, kibble, doggy beds and whatever. Gabriel, do you have a pet?"

"A rescue springer spaniel. I love dogs. I'm just not a cat person."

"Gabriel, then you do the shopping for me. I want everything I will need for two puppies. You can use the chip, just don't take it out of the paper bag. And buy a toy and some stuff for your puppy."

"Do you know, I don't even know your name."

"I'm Mr. Xi Xi Jinping."

"Mr. Jinping, it's truly a pleasure. Love your suit."

"It came with two pairs of pants."

"You can't find that anymore. I can't even afford a suit with one pair of pants. When I turn up at a job interview, the suit they sent me out of prison with, doesn't fit and it practically says 'felon' on the back. I couldn't get a job. Our family was hurting, at least until I borrowed this car from my aunt and began working ride shares. But we're still behind in the rent. Your fair was a godsend." Obviously, Gabriel was happy with the arrangement. "You love dogs?"

"I always wanted a puppy. I brought home a puppy once when I was a newlywed. My wife was from the countryside and lived all her life on a farm. My first day of work after our one-day honeymoon, I came home to find my wife cooked my puppy for dinner. Baked my little furry baby surrounded by potatoes, carrots, onions with an apple in its mouth. I asked her what had she done? Gabriel, her answer was a typical Chinese newlyweds answer – "Well, you didn't leave me enough money for a baby pig, and a wild dog from the street would be too hard to catch. We need to start out our marriage with a clear understanding of our responsibilities. Catching dogs for dinner is the man's job. That's what my mother taught me, and she certainly taught that to my father. She set the example by cooking his pet dog. Except he was old and had to be barbecued."

China is a rough place. I was a translator for the local Guongu captain. I translated as he unofficially extracted funds from English speaking foreigners. He explained to me what he did was perfectly legal. They had committed offences against the Peoples Republic of China, and to conserve resources, he levied the fines. And since the fines paid his salary, he took his salary in advance of any bookkeeping and documentation he planned to complete as soon as time permitted. And I never asked for anything in return.

The morning after my wife served me my puppy, I came in and broke down in tears. When the Guongu captain heard the story, he too had a tear in his eye. He had a dog for many years. And he loved that dog more than he loved his wife. I went about my translating duties. We had many westerners pass through our Beijing substation. We had a fifteen-minute lunch break before a grueling afternoon. I was grateful when the captain sent me home early.   "You'll have a surprise waiting for you there."

When I walked through the door, I was greeted with the happy yelping and the happy pee of a new puppy. The dog was a beautiful Labrador retriever-German shepherd mix. Obviously chosen because he would have been too big for the roasting pan, small Chinese apartment ovens, and too tough to eat. And behind the new puppy was a new wife, more beautiful than the first. She bowed, took my overcoat and jacket, and immediately handed me a hot towel for my hands. She led me to our dining room table, set with the best flat ware, cloth napkins and lit candles.   "Your friend, the captain, wanted our first night as husband and wife to be very special. And I so want it to be special for you. He sent us the dinner for me to prepare for you." In the center was a roasted piglet, surround by potatoes and vegetable with an apple in its mouth. And somehow, she knew my favorite dessert was crème brulee. We had a happy marriage for many years, and two wonderful children. But I was a translator, and once I went missing, I'm sure they were picked up by our secret police and are being held hostage until I'm returned."

"Mr. Jinping, do you keep in touch with your friend? Maybe he can help your family."

"I did, Gabriel, on a regular basis. That is until he was executed for not sharing with whomever he should have shared. Sharing, turns out to be very important to the Chinese Communist Party." Talking about my family shadows my soul.

"Mr. Jinping, I didn't mean to make you sad." Gabriel is a more sensitive man than I thought.

"Gabriel, I have an idea. Can your wife get off from work and can you pull your children out of school?"

"Mr. Jinping, my wife doesn't like to miss work, and we both believe that as bad as the school is, it's the most important thing for the children. Whether they need it or not, every bit of homework is done with my wife's supervision. My wife and I painstakingly taught our children how to read. By the time I get home, she is just finishing the last check of the assigned homework. I start on the next reading lesson after our dinner that we all eat together.

My children read a page each out of a history book the library was giving away to clear its shelves. When I asked the lady behind the desk why these books, she told me, 'To make way for books that are more politically correct. Especially for people like you. We want people to read and have correct thoughts.'"

"That's just like home for me." You would think Gabriel's librarian was a reincarnation of Mao.

"Page after page, we are all learning American history from a guy named de Tocqueville. I don't know why library would give away a book like this. But it was free, and I didn't have to steal it to bring home to my children.

My wife believes anything they hand in must be perfect. And dinner is usually late. She tells me no dinner until all the homework is done perfectly. When I get home, whatever's not done and double checked, I help her complete it with the children. And she never starts cooking until it is all done." Gabriel was an easy man to talk to.

"You help me set up what I need to set up, you can work with me during the day and have your family with you in the evening. We can give them a little vacation, say at Disney World."

"It sounds like a pipe dream. It's a far cry from charging a cab ride and a couple of hot dogs and a cup of coffee to a Disney Vacation. And I can't afford the hotel. I can't afford to fly them down here. And what about my dog?" Just thinking about it exasperated Gabriel. It's something he wanted to do for his family, but even if he got into Disney World free, the rest of the expenses would be an entire year's salary for both him and his wife. I have to convince him I'm serious. At the same time, it will be a good test as to how far we can go with the chips.

"Gabriel, work with me. We can give it a try. Have your wife start withdrawing the money from your ride-share earnings. Unfortunately, all that income including the tips are reported to the IRS. But these chips are part of a top-secret project that nobody knows about. And anybody who knows about them can't discuss it with anybody. And if you have a chip that works like ours is working, why would you say anything anyway. And nobody is going to be looking for it and nobody is keeping track of the money being spent. What we are spending is not even an accounting rounding error for the government, let alone the Pentagon. Don't worry, Gabriel. I have a plan."

"If you say so, Mr. Jinping. I just worry about overreach when we have a good thing already."

"Gabriel, call your wife and find out when the next school break is. It's probably spring break or Easter vacation. They may get a lot of days for the Jewish holidays that we can string together."

"Mr. Jinping, I'm glad to help. You only need to pay me for driving you around."

"You will be doing much more than driving. And it will all be legal, almost, and will make life better for you, me, and your children. I see Catholic school for your children, in Florida. You and your wife will both work for me. And if I'm successful, I may even be rich enough to bribe enough people in China to free my wife and children."

*   *   *   *   *

CHAPTER EIGHTEEN

**Never attribute to malice that which is
adequately explained by stupidity.**
[Hanlon's razor – Robert J. Hanlon]

Rose and I lost the trace of the last chip hours ago when the chip crossed into Florida. If they were using the chip at all, somehow, they were shielding its transmission to the satellites or knew when the satellites weren't in position to receive a signal. There were only two circumpolar satellites assigned to following the chips, and they could easily slip through that surveillance, even though they could watch half of the earth's surface during each orbit. But not all at once. Apparently, the entire state of Florida is enough out of satellite orbital synch for us to lose them.   There is a third satellite, but that's in stationary orbit over Washington, DC. That only showed us the Secret Service moving the bodies of all the dead Seplechre left behind after his assault on the tunnels and the accidental release of the Zyklon B. The question is, do they have more of the canisters, and does Seplechre know that their deteriorating and could start leaking cyanide gas anytime?

I called General Merriwhether who made a quick calculation. "Archy, until we get additional satellites assigned to the chip frequencies, the Florida chip is lost. We need satellites orbiting closer to the equator – in great circles above and below the equator to cover Florida. Until then, we'll only be able to find them by scanning all the charges made at all the counter credit card scanners in the State of Florida – one at a time." The General told us to get a military flight into New Jersey's McGuire Air Force Base. He'll have an Army helicopter meet us at McGuire to take us to the Downtown Manhattan Heliport near Wall Street and Pier Six.

General Merriwhether with everyone in the gardener's truck picked us up and we drove up the East River Drive to the U.N. "Archy, we have to hope they keep using their chips. The micro batteries in the chip run low fairly quickly. They depend upon proximity charging from the counter credit card readers. When you get back to Fort Meade, find the satellites we need and program them for the chip frequency. If anyone asks any questions, just tell them you're doing it for me. I still carry a lot of weight at the NSA."

Rose took away my cell phone and ended the call. "You mention General Merriwhether at the NSA, you will either be arrested and shot, or just shot on sight." As I said before, Rose wasn't fond of General Merriwhether.

Seplechre must have shielded the chips as soon as he picked up the four translators from the tunnels. But we knew where they were going. They were already under the White House; the most powerful center of all the world's power centers. They managed to neutralize the entire White House and the President of the United States with the Zyklon B canisters, at least temporarily. We know, they would do it again. And Seplechre was smart enough to figure out how it could be done. The only difference between Seplechre and his deputy, Andrew Wolsstein, is Wolsstein would release the gas just to watch people suffer, then indict whoever survived for not inhaling enough of the cyanide to prevent the incident. That's what he did in essence to the accounting firm he put out of business and the twenty-thousand employees he put out of work.

The translators, Kim, Putin, and the Ayatollah, wanted to confront and probably kill the leaders they thought were impersonating them. And my thinking was Seplechre wanted to get everybody to the next most important world power center for whatever move he was going to make.

"We know, Seplechre worships power, his own power. He has a stranglehold over this country as the untouchable special prosecutor. He has his own army, and now he wants world power." Rose figured it out, at least before I did. I was afraid to say it, even if I thought of it first. In case I was wrong, Rose would kill me. And there was no way I could run this by her first.

"We have to take a guess as to where they're headed. And I'm betting it's the UN". I had to say something. I knew where they were going and believed in what I said. And it was a pretty good guess. I told this to Uncle Jimmy and Rose told me to shut up. If I were wrong, I'll look even more stupid for my "...dumb simplistic bad analysis...", and Rose would look stupid for marrying me, again. I mean she only married me once. I would just make her look stupid another time by me looking stupid again, another time, again. Rose hates it when I'm wrong, even when I turn out to be right in the end, I was still wrong, first. Rose always reminds me I'm never correct and I'm never allowed to be wrong, especially in her presence.

"I'm not going to guess." Uncle Jimmy put a call into Josey, the operator at Foreign Freight Sales and told her who and what to look out for. She called the railroad switchboard operators at Grand Central Station, and they called railroad switchboard operators across the country. Those operators told the conductors, who told the train crews. The brakemen told the flagmen who told the gandydancers. In less than the two hours before we even reached the Lincoln Tunnel, there was a nationwide net of railroad men (and women, too) looking for, the three translators, one glued to a desk chair, and Seplechre and his uniformed special prosecutor paramilitary force. And whatever Uncle Jimmy told them, they were all angry. There was something about all railroad men (and women) being 'Tenth Avenue' at heart. And just like on Tenth Avenue, they carried a grudge forever. Uncle Jimmy had to be pretty mad at Seplechre for having killed Mrs. Haversham to unleash all the railroad men in the country on him.

"Once we find them, we'll figure out how to stop them." That's what generals said to inspire the troops when they don't have any idea what to do, especially when they're outgunned and outnumbered. I think that's what General Custer said at the Little Bighorn.

Aunt Anna said, "We'll just cut off the head of the snake, and..."

"I'll manage the three translators, very quietly." Rachel added. "And Israel will cover me."

"I'm just sorry I didn't bring my one good kitchen knife. I may have to shoot them but having a beheading with bleeding from the stump of their neck – I could use the picture for my cell phone wallpaper. And maybe for my Facebook account, if I ever get a Facebook account."

"Aunt Anna, we'll find carving knives for both of us." My aunt smiled at Rose and she smiled back. It's so nice when your wife makes a close connection with your relatives, especially your favorite aunt. "And I want the Ayatollah's head."

"I know. He's just another enemy of Israel and all the Jews around the world. We've seen that before. And that's why the Mossad established the Metsada and Kidon. And that's why Israel and I joined." Rachel smiled at Israel and before Israel could say anything, Uncle Jimmy interrupted. "But Anna, if you really want his head, he's yours. And I'll can use your cell phone to take your picture."

"And we're bringing the two of you the World's Center of antisemitism – The United Nations." Israel just patted Uncle Jimmy on the back.

"We know. All of Israel knows. It's just the American Jews vos hobn keyn gedank os di UN umzin iz kheyding. Starting from the 'rekht fun tsuriker', so they can tseshtern Israel."

Aunt Anna didn't care where they were. "I'm still going to kill them for what they did to Mrs. Haversham." For Anna, even a Tenth Avenue rival for Uncle Jimmy was still Tenth Avenue kin and must be avenged. And Uncle Jimmy made her a blood relative.

Seplechre and his men beat us to the United Nations by three hours. That was the report from Uncle Jimmy's railroad underground. They reported there were at least eight dead uniformed soldiers from Seplechre's men in shallow graves near the tunnel entrances. I guess if Uncle Jimmy's railroad army found them there, Seplechre knew where the tunnel entrances were. Not the secret we thought it was. All but one were shot in the head. It was just one that appeared blue in the lips.

"Archy, it sounds like a good guess. We can't use the military or any police organization to move against Seplechre and his people. They have complete immunity and have full legal standing, even international standing. Everything they do, all their power and authority is 'Extra-Constitutional'. There's nothing to stop them." General Merriwhether summarized our predicament, I guess hoping someone would make a workable suggestion.

"General Merriwhether, we have my army – the Railroad Army. And I heard a rumor, they're all armed to the teeth. But that's just between us, and there's no telling how true that is."

"And your Railroad Army is willing to fight Seplechre and his men?"

"General, fighting them is a strong term. No railroad man is looking for a fight. Of course, the women tend to be more blood thirsty. No. I don't think there would be a fight."

"Uncle Jimmy..."

"General Merriwhether, do you know how immense the American railroad grid is? Do you know how many tank cars, hopper cars, coal cars, ore cars, freight cars there are?"

"And how many are there, Uncle Jimmy?" I knew Uncle Jimmy knew the answer. But I had to ask just to give him the opportunity to show off. Since I was a kid, he loved when I did that when we were with the family.

"Archy, don't be stupid. You're acting stupid again."

"Rose, I really want to know."

"Archy, there is almost a million and a half freight cars, countless refrigerator-freezer cars we can have at our disposal any place any time. There are thirty-two thousand engines all run by an army of over two hundred thousand railroad men. And they're the toughest, loyalist Americans outside of our military." Uncle Jimmy was always proud to be a railroad man.

And the way Aunt Anna was smiling at him, I knew she was proud of him and proud to be married to a railroad man.

"It's immense, the millions of miles of track, railroad yards, sidings - many more than I could count. I'm not sure what you're getting at."

"There are uncounted abandoned sidings that don't even appear on the official railroad track maps. We can lose whatever we want lost, forever. And nobody will remember who or what put any of these freight cars, or better refrigerator cars where, when or how."

"And Uncle Jimmy, if they're found, then what?"

"The freight car, you'll only need one, or maybe one refrigerator car. Seal the car with a hog ring, mark it with the government signs, 'Toxic Waste – Do not Open. Property of the Environmental Protection Agency.' There are sidings all over the country with these cars that haven't been moved or touched for years. You can tell how long they've been where they are by how high the grass has grown in between the railroad ties."

That's when Aunt Anna, frustrated with her husband dragging out the conversation with General Merriwhether, said, "Jimmy will just make Seplechre, his soldiers, the translators all of them disappear forever. That is unless you want them found, just to set an example for anyone else." For the moment, it seems Aunt Anna ended the conversations.

The only thing we could find at Fort Meade was this NSA gardeners' old Ford pickup truck with a crew cab. They left two power mowers, rakes and one leaf blower in the back. On both the right and left front doors was stenciled in military block letters – 'NSA'. On both rear doors was the warning, 'FOR TOP SECRET USE ONLY'. Israel was in the back seat with his wife and Rose. I was between Uncle Jimmy who was driving and General Merriwhether riding shotgun with Aunt Anna on sharing General Merriwhether's left thigh and my right thigh. I had to straddle the stick shift. And Uncle Jimmy had to drive. He was the only one who remembered how to drive a stick shift. And all his life, Uncle Jimmy rode the clutch.

The railroad people pinpointed all of Seplechre's caravan in less than a half an hour after our first call. The chips reappeared on the satellite tracking system at the front gate to the U.N. compound in New York ninety minutes after that. Now we know that the chips will work at the U.N. security check points. General Merriwhether followed the fourth translator heading south on route 95, intermittently disappearing and reappearing at highway rest stops. At the Florida border, that single chip was totally gone. It never reappeared. Not to get gas, not for snacks, not for a hotel or motel room. Nothing. As it turned out, the satellites were in the wrong position. We're sure they were still using the chips and no doubt taking care not to be detected. Finding that last chip, and President Xi will have to be a mission for another day.

Now, why is Seplechre and his SPAF soldiers with the translators invading the U.N. There is a reason, a nefarious reason, but what it is, I can't fathom.

At the gates of the U.N. compound, the security guards were about to approach the truck when General Merriwhether got out, waved his right wrist in front of the sensor, and the gates opened. The two security guards retreated to their posts, saluted, and waved us through. Only the guard opposite Uncle Jimmy approached the truck and told him to park in the visitor's lot that says 'Visitor's Lot – Chipped Guests of the United Nations'. Apparently, the lot closer to the gate but further from the UN entrance was marked, 'Visitor's Lot – Unchipped Guests of the UN. Temporary Photo Security Badges Required Beyond This Point – Obtain your Photo ID at the Front Desk before you Park or proceed Beyond this Point'.

Uncle Jimmy took a corner parking space near the parking lot entrance. It was a handicap space, nice and wide. A big wide sign in forty-two languages said- "Handicap Parking By Permit Only – Violators Will be Towed – Except if you have diplomatic immunity." It was an electronic sign that changed colors and languages with each flash. The sign was actually the

294

size of a highway billboard. Nobody else in the handicap spaces had handicap tags, and it didn't seem like anyone was checking. They all had a hanging tag indicating what nation's legation they belonged to.

As long as we weren't towed, we'd be alright. In the truck's glove compartment was the Fort Meade government parking placard that we hung from the rear-view mirror. It read, "US Government Business – TOP SECRET – NSA – DO NOT ENTER THIS VEHICLE or LOOK IN WINDOWS." In smaller print – "In doing so you may be subject to up to five years in prison or a $10,000 fine or 100 hours of community service."

"General, should we worry about being towed?" Rose grabbed me by the arm before I could finish my sentence, but that didn't stop me from saying it.

"Archy, who cares if we're towed. It's not our truck." Rose was right. Nobody cared.

"Archy, our government truck is now on international soil. Technically, we can't drive it out of here without a new treaty with the UN that specifically gives us temporary permission to drive a US military vehicle onto UN territory and then permits us to leave in that truck. In fact, if I remember my International Law class at the Army War College, we need two treaties. Unless we get a treaty specifically for this truck, with or without the lawnmowers. The treaties have to be approved by the UN General Assembly, the Security Council, voted on and approved by two thirds of the US Senate and signed by the President of the United States. And all before they close the parking lot until tomorrow morning. And that's if we're not towed. If we're towed, we've violated international law, and everything has got to go to the International Criminal Court in the Hague." General Merriwhether seemed satisfied with himself that he was able to explain the complexities of how international diplomacy and the United Nations has screwed America again. It's the commanding officer's obligation to explain the tactical situation in enough detail so the troops may understand what a mess they're in.

"General, if it goes to the Hague, the truck is lost." This is the first we've heard from Israel. "Once we're done with our mission, we can abandon the truck and take a cab and rent a car from Avis or Hertz and get us back to Fort Meade. We can use our chips, charge the government, and not get stuck with a compact. We can get maybe a three bench SUV. Let the UN keep the truck."

"My husband is right. The United States Senate never ratified the International Criminal Court Treaty, Israel never recognized the Court, and neither did China, India, Iraq, Libya, Qatar, and Yemen. We can't even argue the case. If we want the truck back, we'll have to go to the US Senate, ask the President of the United States to sign the treaty and then fly to the Hague to argue the case. And this is a secondhand truck that doesn't even belong to anyone here."

"So that means they can't impound the truck. But it does that mean they can still tow it?" Uncle Jimmy had a point.

"But does towing mean impounding once it's disconnected from the tow truck?" Rachel was still concerned about the truck's status in front of the International Court of Justice.

"But I signed for the truck. Even if we abandon the truck, not only do I have to pay for the truck, but I will have to pay for the daily parking fees. And if the Senate doesn't approve the treaty with the UN and the President doesn't sign it, I'll be paying the parking fees forever. I can't take them to a US court because they have diplomatic immunity plus the UN is not part of US territory. And I can't take them to the International Criminal Court because we have no treaty. Rose, my sweet, my darling, what am I going to do?" All I could think of is a lifetime of paying parking fees to the UN. It was worse than alimony. At least alimony ends when the ex-wife dies, you die, or the ex-wife gets married, and then you die. Then it's too late. But the parking fees are forever. The fact that I began to sob over the parking debacle didn't help me with Rose.

"I would borrow Rachel's little friend and put you out of your misery, but I love you too much plus I enjoy watching you suffer. Then I'll get stuck with the parking fees. If we get divorced, I will be free and clear of the parking fees, get half your stuff and all your money." I know Rose was trying to be comforting about not shooting me. "We'll figure something out." Rose smiled. I don't know if she had a plan to help me or if there was no plan. But at least I know a bullet to the back of my head was off the table as far as my wife was concerned. At least until the parking fees are settled.

"But if they tow the truck, that must mean it's impounded." Sometimes I think we're on the cusp of an international parking incident. And it's these littlest things that can lead to war. I still worried about getting the truck back. I signed for it from the NSA motor pool. It never looks good to lose a major piece of equipment you signed for unless you and it was involved in combat.

And then it's better if it were blown up beyond repair rather than captured by the enemy. Rose told me that. That was her rule for any piece of Army equipment I was responsible for, and that included me. It would be unfair of me to be captured by anybody. If that happened, she said, there would be no insurance and she couldn't move on. I was to be sure that, wherever I was, they found my lifeless body in a minimally identifiable form.

"And their tow impound lot is over there." Aunt Anna pointed to a third parking lot, with cars being claimed and driven out after the exchange of unmarked envelopes. "Don't worry about the truck. A little bribe will get us in and out of here. Remember this is the UN. It's just like the New York City government – inefficient and slow moving until lubrication is applied."

"For God's sake, Archy. If you're that worried about the truck, then move it out of the handicap space." Rose has been short tempered the entire trip. She's like that when she misses a meal or people attempt to shoot her. She doesn't get this upset when people shoot at me.

"Rose, I can't drive stick shift. And I have a right to

be worried about the truck. I signed for it. As an officer, everything I sign for it is my responsibility. My solemn oath represented by my signature is my promise to safeguard the military property in my purview and return it in the same condition I found it, combat aside."

Rose put on her softest, sweetest voice. "Archy, love of my life who I can't live without for a moment. This is parking, not combat, dear. Move the fuckn' truck before I shoot you in the balls!" And she did say it very softly and sweetly, and with her southern drawl.

"I'll move the truck. Archy can't drive a stick shift." Uncle Jimmy just put out his hands and General Merriwhether tossed him the keys. He walked to the truck, started it, ground the gears loudly in reverse because he was annoyed at all of us for not liking the parking space he chose, and re-parked in one space over in a non-handicap parking space.

By the time we finished with the parking situation, it was already late afternoon, and most people were leaving the UN for the day. Early cocktails followed by late cocktails, later dinner then drunken stupor until the next morning. After sitting through a General Assembly meeting, everyone needed to drink, especially the translators. They were really the only ones paying attention to every word uttered.

As we approached the lobby, the crowd became thicker. We waited to go through the revolving door.

"General, they must have metal detectors at the entrance. What do we do with our weapons?" We weren't going to get away with this. Somebody in security must be concerned about an assassination attempt, with all these diplomats.

"Archy, don't worry. The chips signal the metal detectors that we have a security clearance. It works wherever there's a security check point, including the airports. It's the same company that did USEWOW and the entire US government. The metal detectors see our weapons, but automatically the chips give us a security clearance. Plus, we can charge anything we want at the gift shop." It sounds like something my father sold to the government.

At least twenty paces in front of the door was a marble and stone counter that ran at least thirty feet with a large plain dark marble wall behind it. On the front of the counter was carved the United Nations' logo highlighted with gold-leaf paint. The lobby was at least fifty feet high with the UN emblem in gold-colored brass hanging twenty feet off the ground from the ceiling from thin silver steel wires directly over the counter. It swayed with every breeze, looking like it was going to fall any second. On the wall behind the counter, there was a top row of framed pictures of the ten past Secretary-Generals of the United Nations, with the present Secretary-General, Rogelio Cuterres in the center. The lower row of frames were the no smoking signs in six different languages in each frame with a cigarette in a round red circle with a line through it at the bottom. Below the universal no smoking symbol was the statement. "Smoking may result in fine, imprisonment at the United Nations or both."

There was nobody at the desk. We waited and were about to go to the right corridor where the biggest crowd was coming from when a man in a movie usher's uniform popped up from behind the counter. Over his left jacket pocket, he wore the gold UN emblem, had gold braid rope through both jacket epaulets, and a jaunty blue beret with the UN insignia. He started reading from a preprinted card in front of him.

"Welcome to the United Nations Headquarters. We offer guided tours with recordings – when you rent our official United Nations vintage cassette tape recorder and earphones. You may keep your cassette tape as a souvenir. You may want to purchase one of our used official United Nations surplus cassette players, batteries are included, to enjoy your guided tour tape in the comfort of your own home. If you have a very old car, you can listen to the tapes in your car while commuting to and from wherever you commute to and from to or from.

Live guided tours, live guided tours with recording, recordings without the tours, and photo ops in the General Assembly and Security Council with cardboard cutouts of the representatives of the member nations are available, both framed and unframed. With the Grand All-Inclusive Tour, you will get a complimentary framed photograph of you behind the General Assembly podium with the world leader of your choice standing above and behind you. You get to choose three different world leaders with each photograph purchased. These will be suitable for Christmas cards, greeting cards, Valentine's Day cards, birthday cards, anniversary cards, sympathy card, preprinted thank you cards, all with a gold embossed United Nations logo. There are samples of deluxe and superdeluxe cards. They can be ordered and purchased in boxes of one hundred through our souvenir store when you pick up your complimentary framed photograph. All items at the UNGiftShop.com may be ordered on-line at any time."

The man behind the desk, put down the card. "I already know at least one of you is a chipped guest, and we can charge any or all our offers to the US government. The United States Government actually pays for everything at the United Nations anyway. But we still charge for everything again. Double billing. It's a United Nations' tradition." He smiled. "We can still sign you up for a tour. The last Grand All-Inclusive Tour starts momentarily as soon as I finish here. I will be your tour guide, and tipping is not only permitted, but encouraged. Even if you don't take a tour, I will accept gratuities, which are expected. At the United Nations, we're here to save the world. When you're saving the world, you're not reticent about anything, especially tipping. And every tip I collect helps me save the world."

"We're looking for a group that came through. Soldiers in uniform, three out of place individuals. One who looked like President Kim of North Korea, President Putin, and the Ayatollah of Iran. They all looked like each of those leaders. And the President Putin look alike is shirtless and glued to his desk chair."

"Let me check." The man behind the desk looked down,

obviously at a computer monitor. "This may take some time."

General Merriwhether was becoming annoyed. "One man was glued to a desk chair." You can't tell us if they came through here?"

That's what Uncle Jimmy stepped up. "Do you have a chip reader?"

"Of course." Now the man smiled at Uncle Jimmy, who seemed to understand how to do international business at the U.N." The man pulled out his credit card chip reader attached to its extension cord and computer line. Apparently, they hadn't converted to the newer Wi-Fi connected readers. "General Merriwhether, put your wrist here." The General did just that. The little machine clicked. Uncle Jimmy turned the machine around. "I need my glasses. Help us out and punch in your gratuity for me." The man punched in a one-hundred-dollar tip. "Thanks."

"No, thank you sir. Thank you for helping me help save the world." The man behind the desk was all smiles. "I'm sure things will go quickly from here. Now, how may I assist all of you?"

"All right. Did they come through here. Uniformed men, all armed, President Putin glued to his desk chair, ..."

"First, sir. We need to settle the parking fees."

"I understand. I run parking lots. But the fees are usually calculated when we pick up our vehicles."

"We are all trying to save the world. There is a lot of detail work. We try to be efficient. That makes more time to save the world." The man's smile was beginning to annoy all of us.

"And what are the damages, sir?" It was Uncle Jimmy asking the questions. He had a string of itinerant parking lots he opened as New York City temporarily rented empty lots. He took every lot he could get and closed them when the city ended the temporary lease. He knew how parking lots worked and he exactly knew the parking lot scam the UN was running.

"Well, the fee is sixty dollars for all day up to four PM. You arrived at three-thirty. So that is sixty dollars, times two.

You occupied two spaces. Then there is a premium dinner fee, sixty dollars for from four PM to eight PM. After eight PM, the fee is for overnight parking until eight AM. That is one hundred and twenty dollars, for any part or all of that time. And it's a new fee for every time you leave and enter. And don't forget that the fee is for each space you occupied at any time you were in the parking lot."

"That's highway robbery. And I run parking lots." Uncle Jimmy almost got shot for less.

"This is the U.N. That's the U.N. way." He smiled again, pulled out the credit card chip reader and pushed it toward General Merriwhether. "Tips are not included. But an adequate gratuity will encourage our attendants to watch your vehicle closely enough, so the wrong person doesn't drive away with it. A less than adequate gratuity, they watch your vehicle, but won't stop anyone from damaging your vehicle or steeling your wheels and battery." He paused and looked at everyone in the group. "Any one of you may put your wrist chip here, and I can help you enter the adequate gratuity I know you'll want to give – not to me, but our parking attendants."

"What parking attendants? There are no parking attendants." Rose was infuriated, first at the man's audacity at trying to take advantage of is, and second at his condescension.

"I see this is the U.N. way." Uncle Jimmy smiled and turned to me and Rose. "I can make the whole U.N. disappear into the railroad boxcars."

Rose pushed the General away from the counter. The man leaned across the desk, his face inches from Rose. "Yes sweetheart, how can I make your day much more pleasurable?"

Rose slammed her purse on the desk. In one motion, she pulled .45 Colt out of her purse at the same time cocking the hammer and with her left hand grabbed the man's tie by its Windsor knot and slammed his face onto the marble counter hard enough for his nose to bleed. Blood was coming from his mouth where Rose at least loosened some front teeth – as it turned out, both uppers and lowers.

"You must be a real pleasure for all the women you have. Maybe I can be one of them." Then Rose pulled his head up and slammed it down again into the counter. This time he spit out three teeth but couldn't say anything because Rose had tightened her hand around his windpipe. What stopped him from struggling was the barrel of her Colt she pushed into his mouth knocking out all of his front teeth that he had to swallow, because he didn't spit them out."

"I'm going to let you breath." By this time, his lips were blue, but he was still conscious. Rose was smart enough to know not to let him become unconscious. That would just waste time.

"I'm proud of you, niece. I've never seen such a smooth move. You have to show that to

Aunt Anna. She would have just shot him in the balls and then question him. And gunfire attracts so much unwanted attention."

"Thank you, Uncle Jimmy." Rose was smiling, but the man she was choking was completely cyanotic with his eyes closed. Rose had to support his entire weight by his necktie. Rose let him go and let him slump to the floor behind the counter. There was no movement for a whole minute. Then the man on the floor gasped.

We all rushed behind the counter. General Merriwhether checked the visitor's logbook. Uncle Jimmy and Aunt Anna started back playing all the video from the lobby cameras. Rose and I checked the video from the cameras covering both banks of elevators. Israel and Rachel stood watch at each end of the counter making sure no one would approach us from behind.

People were still streaming from both corridors with the banks of elevators. Most looked straight ahead, some turned their heads to see what the commotion was, but never slowed their pace. Finally, two armed security guards approached the front of the desk. We were all behind the desk. One guard looked over the counter and saw the partially conscious man begin to vomit and begin to struggle to get up.

"We know what it's all about. The parking. No matter what you do to him, he'll never give you a refund. He double charges everyone if you pull partially out of your space just to straighten your car out then pull back in." This guard smiled. "He's done that to all the security guards, all the diplomats, and even the Secretary-General of the United Nations. Nobody gets away with the parking fees. And everyone is afraid to challenge him. All I have to say, for everyone at the United Nations and everyone around the world who ever came to the United Nations, THANK YOU!"

The other guard turned his back to us, obviously disgusted by the situation, leaned up against the counter. "This is the second time this week. They don't pay us enough to be the parking police." He turned around, very seriously said, "Maybe I can help you? And I can't do anything about the parking fees. He'll still charge you when he wakes up. But I can probably help you with anything else."

General Merriwhether walked to the front of the counter to speak to the two security guards. "We are looking for a group of men. We don't know how many men in uniform, a man dressed like a sleezy lawyer, ..."

"Sir, the sleezy lawyer could be anyone of a thousand people at the UN. The sleezy diplomats dress like lawyers, and so many of them are lawyers." The obviously senior security guard smiled, and the other guard nodded in agreement.

"There are three men with them. They look like and think they are world leaders. They're delusional. One thinks he's Kim of North Korea, one thinks he's President Putin, bald and he's glued shirtless in his desk chair, and one thinks he's the Ayatollah of Iran." General Merriwhether knew we were all getting close to finding the enemy. For a brief second, he realized we were outnumbered and outgunned.

"You look so worried. You've come to the right place. This building has hundreds of delusional people who think they're their countries' leaders. Who do you think goes to the General Assembly meetings. You would have to be both crazy and stupid to attend. Sometimes I have to do security duty there. And even the delusional crazies in the gallery are listening to soccer games through their earphones."

Rose was getting inpatient. She kicked the man she choked in the teeth and then came around to the front of the counter. "Well, did you see these guys? The crowd with the bald man with no shirt glued to his desk chair?"

"Honey, this is the opening of the United Nations General Assembly. Do you know how many bald-headed shirtless people go through here thinking their Putin."

"George, there was only one glued to his desk chair. We sent him directly to the General Assembly Hall with the rest of them. There's a pool betting on who will shoot whom." The second guard pulled out the grid that looked like the March Madness college basketball betting pool.

"So, they all went to the General Assembly Auditorium?" Rose was using her sweetest voice, even though she left her Colt's hammer cocked as she put it back in her purse. She left her left hand in the purse with the Colt, she later said, "Just to keep my Colt company.".

"Apparently, your Putin, Ayatollah and President Kim, that's who he said he was, all went to the General Assembly Hall. Kim was pushing Putin. The General Assembly is in session late today. And it wasn't worth the bother to do anything out here. They're the problem for security assigned to the General Assembly. We handle all the people who complain about the parking fees. That's really our job." The security guard leaned over the front of the counter and looked down at the man on the ground beginning to open his eyes. "I guess we got here a little too late. And I feel terrible." The guard smiled. "I'm sure George feels terrible about all this, too."

"I do. But there are no refunds no matter how many teeth you knock out of his head." George turned to his partner.

"And if you shoot him, you'll never get your car back. We can't arrest you for killing him. There is no treaty with the United States over extradition from this international territory, but we can impound your car. Then you have to fly to the Netherlands to litigate. And in the end, you'll still pay the parking fees, fines, and legal fees. Your lawyers here. Lawyers at the Hague and all the lawyers' agents. You know all agents get their vig.

Uncle Jimmy was a native New Yorker but had never been to the United Nations. "And who is at the General Assembly?"

"Some actual ambassadors, but mostly delusional ex-translators who think they are their countries leaders. And nobody seems to mind. They say the first time they come to New York it's fun. After that, to come to the General Assembly every year, try to stay awake through all the speeches, especially with the music selections they have in the translation earphones - they're simply happy to have somebody impersonate them. It's no fun coming to the UN and you're always risking assassination or running afoul of the parking people.

And then the diplomats don't even get to stay at a good hotel. They have to stay at their embassies. And in New York, they're not even the embassies, they're the counselor ligations. And none of them are as nice as their embassies in Washington. And they all complain that none of them are as nice as the Plaza, the Ritz, the Roosevelt, or the Pennsylvania Hotel. Substandard food and no in-room movies. Most of the ligations have cut back and only have basic cable tv. That's all there is for them after being bored all day and eating UN cafeteria food."

"Officer, they tell you all this?"

"We hear this every day. With hundreds of national representatives, we get cornered at least twice a day. And where the only ones they can complain to. We're their 'therapy' guards." The two security officers looked at each other. "We really have to get back to our rounds. Good luck finding who you're looking for. As far as the parking, it is what it is."

"And they tell you two all this?" Uncle Jimmy couldn't believe it. He was going to have to get their names. They have enough valuable information that he could monetize for him and them, too.

"Who else are they going to talk to. They can't talk to their ambassadors. They can't talk to their staff. Any complaints like that, they could be out of a job. Either voted out, jailed or assassinated, depending on the country and its constitution, I guess. That's what a couple of these world leaders told us. We all talk while they're waiting for their cars out front."

By this time everyone was in front of the desk. General Merriwhether took charge. "And where did everyone else go?"

"George and I escorted them all to the Secretary-General's office, his private offices on the top floor of this building."

"And you just let them up there?" Uncle Jimmy was incredulous.

"There was a lot of them, they all had guns, and they asked politely." George said that like it was obvious what was the correct thing to do.

Uncle Jimmy asked Aunt Anna to get their contact information, and remind him that their information would be invaluable, but not to hire them as security guards. Uncle Jimmy asked if he got their names of the people who went to the d's office.

"I didn't ask, and they didn't offer any introductions. As I said they were polite, and they all had guns. It didn't look like they wanted us to look too close at them. And the by-word for UN Security is 'Always Courteous, Always Helpful, Always Employed'."

With those last discouraging words, the two security officers headed for the revolving lobby door for their rounds at the parking lots.

* * * * *

CHAPTER NINETEEN

"Lay the proud ursurper low! Tyrant fall in every
foe! Liberty's in every blow! Forward! let us do, or die!
[Robert Burns, 'Robert Bruce's March to Bannockburn']

I'm a poor defenseless woman. But all our men do is analyze, talk to themselves, analyze again, then discuss with each other what could go wrong before they even think of what could go right. At least I can talk to Rachel. She is a wonderful, devoted wife, an accomplished seamstress that could support herself in her woman's trade. She took the time to learn a man's profession. She became an expertly trained assassin in her own right. I see her retiring from the Mossad and becoming an independent contractor – just a part time job, nothing too stressful. Shorten dresses or gowns, take in and let out the men's pants or jackets, and the occasional assassination with or without body disposal. Israel would have to help her with body disposal. That's a two-person job under any circumstances, unless you want the body found. Just enough work to keep her in BINGO money in her twilight years. And from what Israel told me, she makes it look easy – both the dressmaking and assassinations. Israel said he always respected Rachel's expertise, judgement, and professionalism and allows her to make her own decisions.

If it were up to Archy, he would make his own decisions and make decisions for me. And we would still be back at Fort Meade. I would be forever a second lieutenant's wife. And he would be the oldest second lieutenant in the Army. Now what kind of life is that.

Sometimes Archy needs just a little guidance, a gentle push. And its softly limiting his options and my use of subtle suggestions makes him believe he's making his own decisions.

I guide him to the correct path in life – the path I've been leading him on since we both met at NYU. And there were times I had to lead him with a ring through his nose. – I love him, but he gets more like my prize bull every day. When he's no longer useful, he becomes a tough steak.

Like now, standing in front of the impressive United Nations' Information Desk, with the man, still on the ground behind it coughing and choking on his own blood, spitting up teeth. Poor man. Now at this juncture, you would think Archy would take charge. But he always waits for me. We shouldn't tarry. But the men are all huddled together in some top-level meeting, with no room for any of us 'girls' in the inner circle.

They can go on talking forever. And they complain about us. They're casual enough to be discussing their favorite sports teams. Generals are the worst in getting things going. They wait for their staff officers to make a decision to choose from. And the rest of the men, if their wives are nearby, they expect the women to make the decision and then do all the work. Men just like to sit back, 'supervise' from a distance, and then take the credit for a job well done. And if it doesn't go exactly as planned, it's 'us girls' fault.

Come to think of it, the Federal Government operates the same way. Now with the new 'woke' generation of feminism, it's so much easier to blame the women for everything that is going wrong. And things are always going wrong in the permanent Federal bureaucracy. In the old days, everybody blamed the elected officials, and then voted them out of office. The people we elect, whatever they think they're deciding, they're not making the decisions. There're just the fall guys for when things go wrong. Come to think about it, it's Adam, Eve, and the apple all over again. Eve got the blame, but people are still eating apples.

Let me inquire as to where to go next, since no one else is doing shit! I always must remind myself to be demure, ladylike, and speak softly and respectfully to men, all men, especially if one of them is my husband or I'm in my husband's presence.

And that is if I'm allowed to speak at all. At least our men allow us to speak, ever so briefly, in public. The Ayatollah won't allow women to speak at all. If I blow the Ayatollah's brains out in front of everyone here, that will go a long way to correct this sexual inequality. I have to make a mental note to put that on my agenda. That is if Rachel doesn't get to him first. The problem is if Rachel does it, all the men are sexist enough to think it wasn't her idea. She was only carrying out orders from Mossad. If I do it, it makes a statement and strikes a blow for all women.

"Shit face, where did they all go?" His speech is being garbled by the vomit and blood. Let me try to help him by putting my heel on his throat. "Now, where did they go?" He's speaking but I still can't hear him. This is when I had hoped Archy would at least bend down and try to hear what he was saying. Do you think Archy would even ask this man a question? No. He's still waiting for me.

Archy is always waiting for me to do anything. And when he does decide on his own and acts on it, it's always the wrong thing to do. Even when it's the right thing in the end, it's the wrong thing at the time, and he embarrasses us both. You would think, after all these years, he would learn what to do on his own.

And when he is right, and that's wrong, he's always wrong first. I have to ask Aunt Anna and Rachel if their men are the same way. Maybe they can tell me if all men are like that. My gut says it's genetically determined – God placed it in the male gene. Starting with Adam. I think I told you about Adam. He took the apple after being told by God not to, and blamed Eve. Nobody recorded whether Eve yelled at Adam, but I bet she did as soon as they got thrown out of the Garden of Eden. I'm sure, if this guy doesn't wake up or dies, Archy, and all the men will blame me.

"Rose, let me kick the shit out of him."

"Aunt Anna, he just regained consciousness. He probably would barely feel it." I knew if Aunt Anna did that, this guy would just end up unconscious again. Then we'll have to start all over.

Let me get him closer to my ear. I'll just grab the end of his tie that's not covered in bloody green and yellow vomit. Archy is watching me with one eye and holding a conversation with Uncle Jimmy and General Merriwhether. Archy, Uncle Jimmy and the General are just watching me struggle. Let me ask this ass, that is if he can hear me before he slips into a permanent coma. "Kind sir, where did you say they went?"

Aunt Anna had her .45 Colt in her hand, put the muzzle up to his left eye and commanded him to "Speak!" like you would tell a dog to bark. But he was barely awake and probably didn't realize that the Anna's Colt was about to be cocked and ready to fire the round in the chamber through his left eyeball. I could say for certain, the angle she was holding it at, the projectile would go through the eye, eye socket, and just crease the bottom of the cranial vault, if I remember my anatomy correctly. At least, in the short run, he would survive the bullet wound. We could probably take bets on that. But even if he survived for enough time to answer, he probably couldn't. Anna didn't realize it, but this move would be totally unproductive.

He was beginning to move his arms. He was obviously coming out of his coma, so now seemed a better time to repeat the threats we made before. They would no doubt be more effective if he could hear it through his mental fog and physical pain. They actually taught that at my girls' finishing school. That was part of the 'picking the right husband' seminars.

I leaned closer to his mouth with my ear. I can hear him whispering, "Upstairs, the Penthouse. ..." Then he coughed, vomited, spit up more blood and teeth, and could barely whisper, "No smoking, please!" before he completely passed out.

"Rose, would you want me to finish him off quietly. I have my .22 revolver, and I can use that water bottle behind the desk as a silencer. I didn't know if you minded leaving any witnesses."

"Rachel, that's very sweet of you to worry about me. But with no treaty with the International Criminal Court, and the security guards more concerned with parking, we can leave him back there until change-of-shift." Rachel is a very sweet woman. A professional woman who was still motherly. She had the talent to make prom dresses, wedding gowns, evening, and ball gowns, and assassinate people, all endeavors efficiently and expertly accomplished with little to do. And she never brags or tries to take credit for every little thing she does. Not like most men!

The men were still standing around, trying to decide whether to go to the right corridor or left corridor. Against the far wall was a large arrow and brass letters "Secretary-General".

"Read the sign. That's where we're going. I'm sure the Secretary-General of the United Nations has the penthouse suit on the thirty-ninth floor. If he doesn't, whoever is up there is more important and that's where Seplechre is heading."

With men, you have to spell everything out for them. They can't figure out anything on their own. They may try, but if a woman is present, they abdicate any decision-making responsibility. And then take all the credit.

Just think of the Bible. Adam had to wait for Eve to offer him the apple. And the idiot took it after being told by God not to. Leave it to men to follow the wrong advice. And that was the big one. Of course, Abraham was going to follow through with a bad idea of cutting Isaac's throat. Men listen to bad ideas, and don't listen to good ones. God had to send an angel to stop it. God has to be a man to come up with such a bad idea. And Abraham knew it was a bad idea and was going to do it, anyway. Men are all the same.

Down the right corridor to the bank of elevators, the wall had NO SMOKING signs, framed in brass, with the UN logo at the top and bottom in four languages a sign. We pressed the up button. When the elevators opened, we could only see the faint outline of the passengers through the thick clouds of tobacco smoke. All the women had cigarettes dangling from their lips. Every man had either a cigarette or cigar, and a handful of men were smoking their pipes.

The ashtrays to the sides of the elevator doors were filled with cigar and cigarette butts as was the floor around them was littered with the butts, many still glowing, that missed their target.

We stopped at three other floors on our way up for people who pushed both the up and down buttons. Each elevator foyer was cloudy with smoke, and everyone who got on to go up to go down was either smoking a cigarette or cigar, including the women. And three women, ugly fat women, were smoking joints. My mother told me smoking doesn't make you look sexy; it makes you look stupid and ages you prematurely. Plus, you smell objectionable and only another smoker will tolerate the smell. And nobody wants somebody who is not thinking straight unless they just want to screw them.

We walked down the hall and every door was marked 'Office of the Secretary-General' followed by a number. The door at the very end of the corridor, was solid wood without an opaque glass and no lettering indicating who or what was inside.

"This must be it."

"Are you sure, Archy?" Archy said nothing, he just drew his Colt. Uncle Jimmy had his out of his shoulder holster, Aunt Anna had her Colt out and Israel and Rachel stood behind us, guns drawn covering our rear.

"Archy, stand aside. This is my command. Come what may, I'm going through the door first." General Merriwhether drew his Colt and slowly turned the doorknob. The knob turned freely. The door was unlocked. General pulled the door open. It turned out to be the janitor's closet.

"General Merriwhether, Archy, Rose, everybody. Put your guns on the floor in front of you and put your hands up very slowly." This sounded funny with Rachel's Yiddish accent.

"She's not kidding. They got the drop on us. We're completely outgunned." Even with their guns drawn and ready to fire, there were too many of Seplechre's SPAF soldiers for them to come out of a fire fight alive.

Archy put his gun down. Then General Merriwhether. Jimmy and Aunt Anna followed. I still had the Colt in my hand when I heard someone cock the hammer on their weapon. I stopped in my tracks and put the gun on the floor.

"You wouldn't shoot a poor defenseless woman?" I thought the southern drawl might soften them, but I heard more hammers being cocked.

"That's good. Now all of you, turn around." It was Seplechre and his SPAF – Special Prosecutors Armed Forces. Ten men with fully automatic M-16s and Glocks had their weapons shouldered and pointed at us.   Glocks didn't have hammers. Someone in the crowd had Colt automatics. Behind the soldiers was another man in a three-piece suit. It was a beautiful suit, fitting perfectly with matching vest. It was an Israel Beilin suit. No one else could fit anybody in a suit the way Israel did.

"You, in the back. I made that suit for you, with two pair of pants. You've lost some weight. The suit looks good, but it needs to be taken in. Come by the shop. All alterations are free for as long as you own the suit." Israel recognized the suit and remembered it was Andrew Wolsstein. He had a Colt .45 automatic in one hand and a single action Colt Peacemaker in the other. By reputation, Wolsstein made Seplechre look like Mother Theresa's mother.

"Thank you. If you survive, I'll come by and you can take my suit in. And while I'm there, I'll order a summer lightweight khaki." Wolsstein held his Colt automatic pointed directly at Israel. Israel was the least perturbed, but Rachel was furious that anyone would threaten her love.

"Mr. Wolsstein, gentlemen don't wear khaki suits or khaki anything except military uniforms. I don't even carry bolts of khaki cloth for suits. Think of something else." Israel and Wolsstein were both smiling at each other. Rachel was not amused.

*   *   *   *   *

CHAPTER TWENTY

"All's well that ends well; still the finis is the crown.
[Shakespeare]

"What's all the commotion out here?" An older man, his necktie untied, his shirt tails out of his pants, and his suit jacket and vest both unbuttoned, stepped from behind one of the doors the furthest from us. An older woman, but not too old, followed him. She had more than adequate hips in a grey tight business jacket that flared at the waist, and matching skirt that fell above her strong thighs, big ass but surprisingly shapely calves. Her stiletto patten leather heels improved her shapeliness. When I was a little girl, my mother always told me heels always improved a woman's front and back presentation, and did wonders for her calves, even with varicose veins.

This woman, with her hair mussed and falling on her shoulders had a youthful look, even though the wrinkles in her face and neck gave away her age. She moved next to the older man and whispered something in his ear. He pulled up his zipper. He had a cigarette dangling from his lower lip and she had her long black cigarette holder with a sterling silver band clenched between her teeth. I didn't immediately recognize Ms. Therese Defarge from the Justice Department until she spoke to the SPAF captain.

I had to think a minute. I had seen this man before. Of course, it was the present Secretary-General, Rogelio Antonio Cuterres. He didn't really look like his picture in the lobby. He had obviously gained some weight and in his lobby portrait, he had his hair combed over his bald spot. Or his bald spot got bigger since they took the picture. Either way, that was who he was.

"Mr. Secretary-General, please return to your office. Mr. Wolsstein and I will be in momentarily to discuss the matters at hand. Ms. Defarge, you too, please wait with the Secretary-General. Be ready to take notes for us. That's why you said you should come along. To make sure this was all done correctly and recorded for history. And today, I will make history."

"No. That's what you said, Rex." She turned to the Secretary-General and said loudly enough for all of us to hear, but in a come-hither voice, "Rogelio, I'll be in when I'm done out here. They all become annoying one time or another. We'll have to put them in their places." Ms. Defarge pulled her shoulder length grey and blonde hair together in a bunch and tried to get it into her original signature bun. The Secretary-General took a yellow and red large plastic barrette from his jacket pocket and handed it to Ms. Defarge.

"Here, Tessie. I didn't think you would need it this soon. This will make it easier for you." Ms. Defarge gathered up her hair in a ponytail away from her ears and clipped the hair with the barrette to one side of her face.

"Rogelio, we can finish up at your Sutton Place residence. Your office here just isn't as comfortable as I remember it. And I know how comfortable your living room couch is. It's more fun on there than in your bedroom."

"Tessie, my wife. She'll be home. And she really prefers the bedroom when we have company."

"We can make it a threesome, again. Ask her to send out for dinner for us, so she's not cooking all afternoon and then too tired for later. Chinese food would be my choice, but I could go for anything she wants." She smiled at the Secretary-General and pinched his cheek. "Nothing too heavy. We can't have her fall asleep like the last time. It's bad enough you always fall asleep when you're done. But that's expected in a man. Amelia and I can still be enjoying ourselves until the wee hours or until you wake up for your final nightcap. And no wine this time until we're all done."

Ms. DeFarge, took her half-smoked cigarette from her

cigarette holder, let it fall to the floor and crushed it out before it burnt the rug. The Secretary-General did the same with his. He pulled a soft pack of twenty from his jacket pocket, offered another cigarette to Ms. DeFarge, took one himself, and lit them both with a gold lighter he pulled from his jacket pocket. We could all see, when he reached for the lighter, his double action Barretta's leather shoulder holster with the gun butt strapped in with a brass clip. The Secretary-General was sure to make it clearly visible for all of us to see.

"Now I have an evening to look forward to." The Secretary-General walked up to the front of the crowd. "You two, …" He pointed directly to Seplechre and Wolsstein. "…we will all meet in my conference room." He turned to Ms. Defarge. "Tessie, who are these other people? Do we need them or should we just throw them out." Then he turned to us. "And if you leave quietly, I can validate your parking and give you a discount at the souvenir shop." The Secretary-General put on his warmest diplomat's smile and soft tone of voice. The same voice he used to negotiate disarmament treaties, stop wars, or explain to his wife who else he was sleeping with – all in the cause of world peace.

"In the first place, I'm the only one who can validate parking. Rogelio, we need them inside. I've been listening to Seplechre, Wolsstein, and this pain in the ass General and colonel and his wife, all of them back at the Justice Department. Between the General and our Special Prosecutor friends, everything is liable to be screwed up for all of us." Ms. Defarge appears to be the one really in charge. "SPAF – take up your positions and keep this hallway clear and allow no one off the elevators or into the Secretary-General's office suite. No one."

"Ms. Defarge, I don't know who you think you are, but I'm in charge of the Special Prosecutor's office. I command SPAF. As Special Prosecutor, I have a stranglehold on the President of the United States, every member of Congress, and the entire unelected United States Government. And with the United States funding the United Nations, I now will rule the

United Nations. Ruling the United Nations means I can rule the world, finally."

Seplechre was staring into the ceiling as if receiving a message from the heavens. "As the most special of the Special Prosecutors, I have a stranglehold on America. Today I will dictate to the United Nations General Assembly with all the world leaders present for their opening session, their last opening session of the General Assembly, how I'm going to centralize my rule of the entire world. And the General Assembly opening session will be the closing session for all their governments. By the end of the day, I will have a stranglehold on the world. All for the good of the earth, for the good of mankind, for the good of the environment, for the good of the oceans, for the good of the icecaps, and most importantly for the greater glory of the Seplechre Dynasty."

"And you two don't know it, but I have a stranglehold on you. Seplechre, Wolsstein, get your asses into the conference room. I want everybody in the conference room." Ms. Defarge didn't yell but her voice was firm with the absolute resolve to accomplish her own mission. She took one last drag on her cigarette, let it fall to the floor. The Secretary-General offered her a third cigarette which she put in her cigarette holder without removing it from between her teeth. The Secretary-General let her light it with the end of his lit cigarette before he replaced his with another for himself. She paused and then remembered to crush out the embers of her cigarette and the Secretary-General's cigarette with the soul of her stiletto shoes. "I love your gift, Rogelio."

"It was one of two Franklin Roosevelt's cigarette holders. It makes you look sexier if that is at all possible. It was a gift from President Obama." The Secretary-General patted Ms. DeFarge on the ass. He was an international sexist, and she enjoyed it. You could tell by Ms. DeFarge's girlish laughter through her smoker's cough.

I could see General Merriwhether, Uncle Jimmy, my husband and Israel forget they were being held at gunpoint. They all smiled, slowly dropping their hands. As Ms. Defarge twisted her leg like a dancer crushing out the cigarette butts, they turned and watched her do this and realized how shapely her calves and ass were. Aunt Anna, and Rachel just looked at me, frowned and shook their heads at their men's stupidity.

"Even the threat of imminent death doesn't let them stop being sexist pigs." Rachel nodded in agreement with Aunt Anna. All I know is, when she's right, she's right.

"Ladies, women do rule the world. Men just don't know it."

The Secretary-General, retied his tie, buttoned his vest and jacket, even though his shirt tails were still hanging outside his pants, and was the first through the door into his office suite. He held the door for Ms. DeFarge before he lit up another cigarette with the last cigarette he was smoking.

Before he was completely through the door, Israel said, "Mr. Secretary-General. You're wearing one of my suits, too. I always have my tape measure and tailor's chalk with me. Before I leave, I can see if it needs alteration. I can come to you, pick up the suit, make the alterations and come back for a refitting. For an important person like yourself, we make a special effort. I can see your Beretta is new and doesn't allow your jacket to hang the way it should."

"New York is a dangerous place with the new bail laws – or lack of bail laws. It's as bad as any third world country. At least I have diplomatic immunity and can carry without any fear and shoot without any regret. One of the few perks of working for the UN."

"Mr. Secretary-General, you should have come to the shop as soon as you needed a refitting. And maybe pick out some new fabric for several new suits. We relocated to the White House. You could make a day of it with you and your wife, the President and the first lady. Rachel and I could do fittings for you the President and your wives. Then I'm sure he would invite you for a state dinner. Bring your formal wear or we could let you use whatever we have on the rack. I'm sure we have your size." Israel never passed up an opportunity for more business for his shop, whatever the occasion or circumstances. Even being held at gunpoint. That's being a good businessman.

"Yes, this is a Beilin suit. And with two pair of pants. We can even do the fitting before you leave today. I have a change of clothing so you can take the suit with you. When you come back, bring some samples so I may order one or two more suit. And all with two pair of pants. Right?"

"All my suits come with two pair of pants. Mr. Secretary-General, they'll be made to perfection. It'll make you look like an athletic twenty-year-old, and always with two pair of pants. Here, or at my shop. Or both." Israel was always happy to get return customers. That was especially true of diplomats who never worry about the cost of their cloths, and in particular if they are armed. A well fitted suit with two pair of pants would bring in more business from the diplomatic community, especially if the Secretary-General is seen on television. And at least Israel and Rachel would be less likely to be shot to death.

"Mr. Beilin, I miss your Williamsburg shop. Many of the diplomats do. If you don't mind, I'll tell them when you are returning. I'm sure they'll want their measurements taken for additional suits. Also bring a sample of the pinstripe bolts for formal morning suits. Every UN representative needs a morning suit for formal embassy receptions."

"For you, I can come to the U.N. or to your Sutton Place home. Whichever is more convenient. For the other diplomats, we can meet anyplace they desire – the UN, their consulates, at their 'libhabers heym'." Apparently, all the UN representatives had 'libhabers'.

"Maybe you can bring your wife. I'm sure my wife would want a new formal gown."

Rachel put her hands down and stepped forward. "Mr. Secretary-General, I can certainly come to your home and take your wife's measurements. But a woman likes to pick gowns they see on the rack. That's half of the enjoyment, seeing yourself in the mirror in a new frock. I'm sure Mr. Seplechre understands that. I know he enjoys looking at himself in the mirror."

That's when everyone laughed except the SPAF men. They just smiled. "A woman needs a selection they can choose from. They need to try them on. I can custom make all forms of formal wear in your wife's exact measurements. Then she could choose any or all of them. There are so many styles – mermaid, Cinderella princess, backless, simple elegant black fitted with a slit up the side to show off as much leg or thigh as she would desire – or you would want. And then all the extras with ruffles, taffeta, beading, sequins, pearls, with or without modesty pieces, depending on the occasion and what other women are present. I would need a moving van to bring a proper selection."

Rachel looked at her husband, and then General Merriwhether. "Our shop is actually near the White House. She could helicopter down to Washington. In fact, right to the White House lawn. Mr. Secretary-General, you can be a guest of the President, while your wife shops with me. I could have everything ready in her exact size to try on in a few days."

General Merriwhether put his hands to his sides. "I could arrange for that. We could make it a real occasion. Even arrange for a state dinner. We can have state dinners for every fitting. This President believes in internationalism. I'm sure he would love it, and he won't remember one state dinner from the next." General Merriwhether paused. "At least once they're sure there's no more of Mr. Seplechre's Zyklon B."

That's when everyone turned to stare at Seplechre.

"We need to shoot these intruders, here and now. They're too dangerous and they know too much." Seplechre motioned to the SPAF officers. The SPAF officers stood motionless in the military at ease position.

The SPAF officer with captain's bars on his collars came to attention, saluted, and asked, "What are your orders, Ma'am?"

"Captain, what do you mean, 'Ma'am? Who do you think you're talking to?" Seplechre was astounded by the turn of events. He knew, or rather he thought he had the absolute power over the office of the Special Prosecutor and all that it commanded, including all of the SPAF.

All the officers stood stone faced. Only Wolsstein had a smile on his face. Wolsstein was in on it.

"Rex, you had a good thing going for you. You had a job for life, and you were being paid for being on a permanent vacation. My God, you're the Special Prosecutor. Nobody really expects you to do anything. Now, what do you think you're doing?" Ms. DeFarge was too sure of herself to be asking questions she already knew the answer to.

"Tessie, why don't we take this to my conference room before somebody gets shot out here and ruins my rugs. You can never match this paint exactly to cover the blood splatter. And the rug, it took weeks to get a rug to compliment the lobby rug in my offices. It was on backorder from Amazon. And when they come to the UN, because it's an international delivery, there's an extra fee. And none of this is Amazon Prime. It even tells you online, any blood stains or bullet holes make the item nonreturnable."

"I'm tired of standing here, and my butt hurts." Ms. DeFarge scratched her ass, then pulled down her skirt to straighten it out."

"I know dear. Your hemorrhoids. I have your pillow inside." Rogelio was very solicitous of Ms. DeFarge, as if she were more than a lover, but a second wife. She turned toward the door she came out of, waited for Rogelio to open it, then walked in. Rogelio followed.

The SPAF captain drew his sidearm, kept it pointed at the floor and then motioned us to follow the Secretary-General. By this time, we had dropped our hands. I went to pick up my Colt off the floor, when the captain just said, "Don't. We'll pick them up latter and return them to whomever survives." The captain was polite and matter of fact about returning everybody's firearms – everyone who lives through whatever was happening. That's secret police etiquette you don't learn on the fly.

Rogelio very proudly told us, "I just had my personal conference room redone, and the woodwork is all hand carved. The same people who did the New York Central Board Room at Grand Central Station did my conference room and is redoing the entire office suite. We call it the 'Refugee Recovery and Rescue Conference Room', thanks to the United States Congress. As we find refugees outside of UN headquarters, they come up here for interviewing and processing. As part of the UN Refugee Relief Initiative Package for the Disadvantaged, Advantaged and those refugees in-between disadvantaged and advantaged, we give them a twenty percent discount on their parking. And that's a big deal. Most of them are from Long Island." The Secretary-General was proud of his UN and all it was doing for humanity, the less fortunate, especially those who couldn't find a parking space anywhere in the city.

"Rogelio, I give them the discounted parking. And that's only because you're so cute, I let you get away with taking the credit for that." I never saw this side of Ms. DeFarge before.

"Before anything else, I want them all shot! All dead and lying on the floor! Now!" Seplechre first turned red with rage, then his lips began to turn blue from him involuntarily holding his breath. When none of the SPAF officers did anything but look straight ahead, Seplechre reached into his jacket obviously for the pistol he carried in his shoulder holster – his great grandfather's, PaPa's, Nagant.

Seplechre moved his hand slowly and deliberately, not knowing Ms. Defarge already had her antique Luger in her hand. She raised it and pointed it at Seplechre much faster than he could pull out his own pistol.

"Please, Tessie. Don't shoot him here. This part of the office has just been repainted and it takes forever to get the blood out of the rug, and even longer to replace it." Rogelio was always concerned with appearances and abhorred the inconvenience of redoing anything. He was upset enough when his wife made him redo his kitchen at Sutton Place, even though the US Government paid for it twice. The UN paid for the kitchen once and was again reimbursed by the US Treasury when he submitted the receipts. And then the contractors billed the US Treasury directly, got paid and declared bankruptcy before anyone wanted any of the money back.

"All right, Rogelio. Let's take this into your other offices." Ms. DeFarge motioned to the SPAF officers and they stepped aside from one of the office doors. "Rogelio, you find us a conference room."

Rogelio led Seplechre, Wolsstein and all of us through the outer offices and to another conference room, the newly appointed Secretary-General's conference room. We opened the door, there was the smell of walnut and mahogany mixed with deep musty leather of the chairs and cigarette and cigar smoke. Cuban cigars.

Ms. DeFarge looked in. In each corner of the room and directly overhead were video cameras and microphones. "All the recording is sound, and motion triggered and is stored in the 'cloud', whatever the 'cloud' is. It sounds religious."

"It is religious, Rogelio." Ms. DeFarge smiled. "But this won't do."

"Tessie, this is the only conference room I would present to you. Anything else would be an insult." Rogelio said all this while holding Ms. Defarge's left hand. She was still holding her antique Luger in her right hand and awkwardly shouldering her leather bag.

"There are so many rooms here. There must be another." Ms. DeFarge, her smile, and dimple had the Secretary-General charmed. She knew how to be firm, insistent even, without being a pushy female. She took her Franklin Roosevelt cigarette holder out of her mouth and flicked the ashes. Rogelio again told her it made her look sexier. And he meant it.

"Rogelio, your mind is wandering."

"Tessie, this way." The Secretary-General led us down the long corridor passed office doors, closets, and more office doors. At the end of the corridor, a single door facing the long hall was marked, 'Conference Room Two'. "By the time we redo this room, we'll have to start all over at the top of the hall."

This time, Ms. Defarge was the first through the door. The room smelled of stale sour cigarette smoke, not the sweet smell of good cigars and fresh cigarettes. The room was poorly lit, but the walls and ceiling were freshly painted. You could see where holes had been patched by the sunken spackle that had been hastily applied. The floor was an old cheap linoleum that you would find in a tenement, but there was evidence that it was once covered with wall-to-wall carpeting. Under the linoleum was a cold concrete slab from the original construction.

"Seplechre, you sit to my right. Wolsstein, you sit over here." Ms. DeFarge pointed to the chair directly to her left. The conference table was an old scratched deep walnut table. It had the stained circles of coffee cups, alcoholic beverages, and some cigarette burns from glowing ashes that missed the ashtrays that once were there. It was hard to tell with the poor lighting, but it appeared that some chips and holes in the tabletop were repaired with cheap wood cement, but no one bothered to stain it the same walnut color as the table. I checked the ceiling for cameras and microphones. This room was so old, it still had a plasterboard, or maybe even a plaster lathe and a cracked plaster ceiling. The ceiling had even more holes in it that were also recently but poorly repaired but not painted over.

General Merriwhether took a seat to the right of the Secretary-General at the far end of the table. General Merriwhether offered the Secretary-General his hand, and the man gave it a welcoming shake. After General Merriwhether sat, Israel and Rachel took the two chairs to the Secretary-General's left.

Archy didn't wait for me but pulled out the chair next to Seplechre. "Archy, I want to sit next to Rachel."

"I don't mind at all." Archy took an extra stupid pill this morning. You would think he would know enough not to sit near an angry woman holding a Luger, especially a woman with a chip on her shoulder like Ms. DeFarge.

"Archy. Come here, pull out my chair like a dutiful husband. Be sure I'm seated comfortably and sit next to me, like a dutiful husband fulfilling his duty, as a husband should."

Archy slammed the chair he had pulled out next to Seplechre, was obviously annoyed, took a deep breath to say something, looked at me with his mouth open, …

"Well?"

"Nothing dear." Arch sat next to me and just stared straight ahead afraid to make eye contact with anyone. "I just wanted to be sure I could hear what they were saying." Archy took two stupid pills this morning.

"Rogelio, you have a good thing going with the UN. You get to live in New York, all expenses paid. I comp all your parking. And the US pays for everything, right?"

"Tessie, truer words were never uttered by a woman as beautiful, charming and sexy as you." The Secretary-General was all smiles, but for some reason he took the seat at the furthest end of the conference table facing Ms. DeFarge. "And the beauty of it is the US Treasury many times pays for things twice. And then they apologize for the contractors.

It's just so hard to get contractors to get anything done. Would you believe it, this was once Pol Pot's conference room. Two contractors later, one day they come fill a hole, plaster a crack, then they never come back. You call, there was a delay because of supplies, union difficulties, permits. And you don't need permits at the UN because we are on international territory. I told the contractors that and then they explained they still had to have a permit from somebody for anything else to proceed. And they had to get paid to get the permit they didn't need. That's not the permit they didn't need and couldn't get because the UN doesn't give out permits on international soil. As soon as I mentioned international soil, they wanted an environmental impact statement and a soil analysis. At the UN, there's no soil. Everything is paved with concrete and blacktop. And then they go bankrupt. Then you start again with another contractor. And it all stops again when they can't get a permit. At the UN, we all thank God the US pays for the same thing no matter how many times they're charged for it."

"Rogelio, the UN isn't unhappy with the world situation?"

"Of course not. If we weren't unhappy, we wouldn't be happy. And if we were happy with the world, we'd be out of work. Now my only problem is Xi Jinping. We have so many crazy translators who think the leader of the Peoples Republic of China, we can't keep them straight. And we can't keep them alive. Xi's used his Chinese virus hurt the US and get Trump out of office. In the meantime, he killed so many and ruined the world economy, that every representative at the UN is out to kill him. He hasn't set foot out of China in over a year. I don't know how many Xi body doubles corpses the UN has disposed of."

"And the Chinese Communist Party is protecting him?" General Merriwhether knew many old friends who were killed by the Chinese virus and wasn't just asking the question for academic reasons.

Ms. DeFarge looked straight at eye. "More powerful than the Chinese Communist Party. More powerful than all the members of the UN Security Council. More powerful than all the nuclear nations in the world. He's being protected by Amazon. Xi got even with Trump and the US and Amazon made a killing with the lockdowns around the world."

"You don't hear any of this." General Merriwhether didn't handle this news well. On the one hand he was happy that someone was trying to kill Xi. But being protected by Amazon. Now he knew why no one was successful. "I have to believe no one has done it because they were not trying hard enough."

"General Merriwhether, we ship out the bodies of the dead Xi impersonators in diplomatic crates, and a man named 'Uncle Jimmy' has them loaded on a freight car and lost forever."

Uncle Jimmy and Aunt Anna were still standing but took seats next to Archy. "I'm proud to have been of service to the Community of Nations."

"Don't tell me, you're Uncle Jimmy!"

"In the flesh, Mr. Secretary-General. If someone actually kills the real Xi, let me know so we're sure the body is found."

"Enough of this chit-chat. So, Rex, you want to take over the world." Ms. DeFarge reached into her bag and pulled out another of her pillows she planned to sit on. It was a white cream with 'MOTHER' embroidered in the center. She half stood out of her chair and slipped it under her bottom.

"I have a stranglehold on the United States of America. If I control America, I control the UN. Everybody here has to realize that once I control the UN, I'll control the world. You will all obey me. Nothing can stop me."

"And Mr. Wolsstein, what say you?"

"Ms. DeFarge. As far as I'm concerned, we have a good thing going."

"You do have a good thing with the Special Prosecutor's Office. And Rogelio has a good thing going with the United Nations. With Seplechre running the world, peace is liable to break out the UN will be out of business. As far as controlling the world, that's in my hands. Seplechre, you say if you control America, you control the UN. Well, that may be true. And you say if you control America and the UN, you control the world. There you have a misconception.

What controls the world is the person who controls all the parking. Cars, trucks, boats, airplanes, armies, navies are all dependent on parking. And I will control all the world's parking."

I saw Uncle Jimmy and Aunt Anna put their fingers in their ears.

"Tessie, I love you because you are a goal oriented strong women."

While the Secretary-General spoke, with his hands going to cover his ears, Ms. DeFarge raised her butt, pulled out her pillow and put it against Seplechre's face and fired three rounds from the antique Luger, blowing the top of his skull with the brain contents and blood spattered on the ceiling and the wall behind his chair. He fell face forward into the pillow onto the table in front of him. Blood pumped for a full minute running across the table onto Wolsstein's lap. Ms. DeFarge immediately stood, not to let the stream of blood heading in her direction stain her clothing.

"Rachel, you told me you used these pillows as silencers. The pillow didn't silence anything." Ms. DeFarge put her Luger back in her bag and just left the pillow on the table in front of Seplechre's body.

"Ms. DeFarge, it works with a little .22 caliber, not a Luger." Rachel pulled her small .22 caliber automatic from her purse. It was so small it fit in the palm of her hand. "It's quiet and does the job with a single head shot."

Ms. Defarge nodded to Rachel. Then to Wolsstein: "Mr. Wolsstein, you're in charge of the Special Prosecutor's Office as of today. You have a good thing going. Don't fuck it up." Then she looked to General Merriwhether. "General, maybe you can join the Secretary-General and I at his Sutton Place residence for dinner and a night cap."

"Thank you, Ms. DeFarge. And thank you, Mr. Secretary-General. But I have to get back to the White House. It's a mess with the poison gas. Too many people have died already, and the President and the White House are completely disrupted. And I'm going to get the blame. I have to go back and fix it."

Ms. DeFarge turned back to Wolsstein. "Do you see your old boss. Do you want to end up like this? The first thing you're going to do is make sure the Zyklon B is all gone. Clean up all the bodies, and…After that, make sure you lay off my friends."

"Ms. DeFarge, if I can be of any assistance getting rid of these bodies…"

"Not this time, Uncle Jimmy. They died honorably in the service of their country. They deserve a formal funeral." She turned to Wolsstein, "See to it!"

"Tessie, you must be exhausted."

"Rogelio, and I'm hungry, too."

The Secretary-General a normally gregarious person, was even more hospitable. "How about something different. Instead of a stogy restaurant, we have a new food court in the basement of this building. 'Xi and Gabriel's International Foods'. It just opened." Ms. DeFarge got up, took the smoking cigarette butt from her cigarette holder, and put it out in the bottom half of Seplechre's skull that was still attached to his body. The pooling blood in the hollow bottom half of the skull put out any smoldering embers. The Secretary-General walked over to Ms. DeFarge, went to hold her hand and did the same thing with his cigarette butt.

"That sound excellent. As far as the mess here, if you pack up Mr. Seplechre in a diplomatic transport trunk and leave him out by the sidewalk, I'll have my railroad friends pick him up and he'll never be seen again."

"Thank you so much, Jimmy." Ms. DeFarge, not to be outdone, said, "And I'll comp everyone's parking."

"Israel, can you get my suit cleaned?"

"Mr. Wolsstein, I'm happy to. I can even take measurements, refit your suit, and you can change into Mr. Seplechre's suit until I'm done. When I come back, I'll have samples for the Secretary-General to pick from. You can choose something for a new suit for yourself. And always with two pair of pants. But never khaki.

*   *   *   *   *

Acknowledgement

It was may father who taught me how to read and with my mother, enabled me to succeed in life. It was my father and my (Uncle) Mario Puzo who encouraged me to attempt writing fiction.

My eternal thanks to my lifelong friend and colleague Louis J. Lombardi, MD, whose encourargement and counsel aided me throughout my career and helped me to complete this book.

ABOUT THE AUTHOR

Dennis J. Cleri, M. D.

Dr. Cleri has spent a lifetime dealing with infectious diseases, and spent years dealing with the AIDS epidemic. He is a graduate of Brooklyn Technical High School, New York University, and the Jefferson Medical College of Philadelphia. He is a retired infectious diseases specialist. He has co-authored over 100 scientific articles, reviews, textbook chapters, abstracts, co-edited a textbook, and wrote a short textbook on airborne infections. He was a reviewer for the Journal of Clinical Microbiology and a book reviewer for the New York State Journal of Medicine. His proudest day was his commissioning as a second lieutenant in the US Army Field Artillery. He seved as his active-duty as director of the emergency room at Kimbrough Army Hospital, Fort Meade, Maryland. And he considers that Army Hospital the finest and best run medical facility in his almost fifty years as a physician.

Made in the USA
Middletown, DE
01 November 2023

41635570R00195